OPERATION: SNARE DRUM!

USS BULL SHARK NAVAL THRILLER SERIES
BOOK ONE

SCOTT W. COOK

D1711617

SPINDRIFT PRESS

A USS *Bull Shark* Naval Thriller

By:

Scott W. Cook

Copyright © 2021 by Scott W. Cook and Spindrift Press.
All rights reserved.

Book cover and formatting provided by Trisha Fuentes

No part of this book may be reproduced in any form or by any electronic or mechanical means, including information storage and retrieval systems, without written permission from the author, except for the use of brief quotations in a book review.

PREFACE

At the end of World War I, a League of Nations was formed in an attempt to stabilize the fractured European political theater as well as to create an organization to tie together the participating nations and help to maintain a lasting peace. The Treaty of Versailles was also created in an attempt to stifle another German uprising and to keep the German Empire from reforming. The treaty limited Germany's military buildup as well as disallowing any territorial expansion by the bankrupt country.

By the mid-1930s, however, Adolph Hitler and the Nazi Party had assumed absolute control over Germany and withdrew from the League of Nations. The Nazis simply ignored the Treaty of Versailles as they began a massive military buildup. Simultaneously, Japan was also rapidly and aggressively expanding its own Empire in the Pacific and in Asia.

With Japan's invasion of China joined by Germany's invasion of Poland, the fuse was lit. On September 1, 1939, the Nazis marched into Poland, and Britain issued an ultimatum: withdraw or else. This ultimatum was ignored, and on September 3, 1939, Britain and France declared war on Germany and were joined by Australia, South Africa and Canada, among others.

The United States, as in the previous war, attempted to maintain a neutral status. However, this neutrality didn't stop them from sending supplies and even war materiel to the beleaguered British Isles. Additionally, America imposed trade embargos on Japan, attempting to limit their expansion and their much-needed Pacific supply lines of oil and other goods. After more than a year of this, the Axis powers had enough, and on December 7, 1941, the Imperial Japanese Navy launched a massive attack on the U.S. Naval Base at Pearl Harbor. This officially unprovoked attack led the United States to declare war on Japan, and a week later, Nazi Germany declared war on the United States, and the world's largest conflict blossomed into a full global conflagration.

This book and those that follow is the story of a single American fleet submarine and her crew. A tale told from the personal perspective of those men, and women, of what is aptly known as the Greatest Generation. People who banded together, not always unanimously, to rise up to defeat a powerful enemy. This tale is meant to humanize and make digestible a massive history-altering event. To show what things were like for everyday Americans in and out of the service. Their trials, their fears, their triumphs and all of the personalities, warts and all, that went into a fascinating and compelling tapestry.

This book is a work of fiction. Most of the names are made up. However, as this is a piece of historical fiction, many true names and places are used, although used fictitiously. Admiral Richard Edwards, ComSubLant, Reinhard Hardegen and Captain Willingham of the *Tautog* are just a few examples. Even Lieutenant Charles Taylor, whom you'll meet toward the end of the book, is a real officer used fictitiously. Lt. Taylor is probably best known as the commander of the ill-fated flight 19 – an Avenger training mission out of Fort Lauderdale in 1945. All five of the planes vanished and began the still ongoing legend of the Bermuda Triangle.

Additionally, I, your humble tale weaver, have taken some liberties with exact times and dates. For instance, the sinking of the Nazi U-boat U-85, which in this story was performed by the *Bull Shark* a few days early. In truth, the U-85 was fired upon and depth charged on April 14, 1942, by the American destroyer USS *Roper*. Chuck Taylor's flight of Avenger dive bombers uses this famous plane a few months before its official release… and our hero ship herself is a bit out of time… a little dramatic license to season the pot.

Finally, this book and those that follow are dedicated with great respect to the men and women, both military and civilian, who helped to win World War 2. Their dedication and sacrifice paved the way for a better world. In particular, I'm honored to recognize the fifty-two American submarines and the more than 3,500 officers and men who never returned. They remain on eternal patrol; their bravery and sacrifice will stand for all time.

No words of mine can adequately honor these men, yet I humbly hope that this tale at least brings them to life through stories that entertain, inform and celebrate them.

PROLOGUE
PEARL HARBOR

DECEMBER 7, 1941 - 0737 LOCAL TIME

It was easy for those who were there to look back on what was about to happen and make bold claims. To suggest that on that bright and mostly clear Sunday morning that there was a special feeling in the air… or to say that they just knew something was wrong or that they sensed something momentous was about to happen.

This was, of course, only natural. People *needed* to look back and latch onto something like that. Some sort of trigger or intuition that a history-altering event was about to occur. It helped give some closure and helped others to try and make sense of something so senseless.

The hard reality, though, was that nobody knew. Nobody suspected, even in spite of the warnings that the Axis powers had long since had enough of the United States' form of neutrality. It would be fair to say that many people, both civilians and the thousands of Navy, Marine Corps and Army personnel on base that day assumed that a war was oncoming. Yet no one foresaw the way in which it would come and how quickly and brutally all their lives would be forever changed.

Lieutenant Arthur Turner certainly didn't know. To him, this was just another Sunday in the beautiful paradise of Hawaii. He was looking forward to a relaxing day with his family that would start with church, a breakfast with Captain Willingham, a barbeque at the Turner's house and a friendly softball game between the *Narwhal's* and the *Tautog's*. The outcome of which would give the winning crew bragging rights and the losing crew the job of hosting next Sunday's crew and family picnic.

As Turner neared the end of pier two, where the *Tambor*-class submarine *Tautog* was berthed, he tried not to think too much about the imminent war. By now, it was common knowledge that the Japanese were planning an attack somewhere in the Pacific. Negotiations had broken down, and the scuttlebutt from the upper echelons was that the Emperor and Yamamoto had their sights set on the Philippines.

As XO, it was Turner's job to get and keep the *Tautog* ready for action. To make sure that the boat had its entire complement of twenty-four Mark 14 torpedoes… which she did. To see that the three-inch stainless steel deck gun had sufficient ammunition and propellant… which it had. To keep the Bofors 40mm cannon, known affectionately as the Pom-Pom… and the smaller Oerlikon 20mm cannon ready with a full load of ammo as well… which they did.

That was hardly the end of his list, of course. A three-hundred-foot submarine and her crew of fifty-four men and half a dozen officers needed a staggering amount of supplies and in dizzying varieties to keep them alive and even comfortable on a standard seventy-five-day patrol. Food, drink, office supplies, toilet paper, razor blades, medical equipment, galley staples, small arms… and this didn't even include what the men brought aboard as personal belongings. Not that they had a whole lot of space to store it in, of course.

Then there were spare parts, auxiliary gear and the fuel. It always amazed Turner how much diesel oil a ship so small… small in comparison to the big wagons in Battleship Row anyway… could greedily consume. It just didn't seem conceivable that a three-hundred and seven-foot-long, twenty-seven-foot-wide and fourteen-foot-tall tube could take on almost a hundred-*thousand* gallons of the stuff.

All that, and the complexity of a machine that could dive below the surface of the sea and stay down for as long as two days at a bare minimum speed. It could be mind-boggling to really ponder it. Yet it was also a tremendous source of pride for the enlisted and the officers of the *Tautog*, as it was for all submariners. They were a special breed of sailor, and they knew it.

"Sir!" a voice called from the end of the pier.

Turner saw Lieutenant JG. Joseph Dutch, *Tautog's* sonar officer, striding toward him with a tall and burly enlisted man at his side. Both men wore smiles on their faces, and it took Turner nearly until the two men were within handshake range before he recognized the sailor.

"Buck?" Turner inquired as his own grin began to spread. "Well, blow me down! That isn't Paul 'Buck' Rogers by God!?"

Rogers was about Turner's height, a little over six feet and about the same age as well, making him around thirty-two. Although Turner was a lean muscular man, Rogers was built like a linebacker. He extended his hand, and the two men shook vigorously.

"Hell, I haven't seen you since we were both in Panama," Turner observed. "Finally made Chief, I see. How are ya', Buck?"

"Prime, sir, prime," Rogers replied, shaking Turner's hand. "How about yourself? How's Joan and the young'ns?"

"All well," Turner replied. "Little Arty is in first grade, and Dotty's in Kindergarten. They're picking me up to head to church in a few. What about you? Any lady manage to get a solution on you yet?"

Rogers chuckled, "Not me. Too many delicious choices at the buffet."

Dutch laughed, "Same old Buck. I ran into him just a few minutes ago and figured I'd show him the boat."

Joe Dutch was a small, wiry man a few years younger than the other men. He was gifted with a good nature that was reinforced by earnest brown eyes. His close-cropped black hair framed a face that was handsome if a bit boyish. Those that knew him well, however, knew Dutch to be a very competent officer with a pair of ears virtually unmatched in all the submarine service.

"You on a boat now?" Turner asked Rogers as the two other men about-faced to walk him to the end of the pier.

"Hell no," Rogers groused, pulling a cigarette out of a pack in his khaki blouse and lighting it. He offered one to Turner and Dutch. Turner took one, but Dutch shook his head no. "I'm on the *Downes*. It just ain't the same."

Turner grinned, "Still, you're probably getting some ASW experience. Working on a tin can lets you see things from the other side of the scope, as it were."

Rogers snorted derisively, "The wrong fuckin' side, excuse me, sir."

Both officers laughed, and Turner clapped Rogers on his broad shoulder, "Well, you're welcome aboard any boat I'm on for what it's worth, Buck."

The three men simultaneously stopped in their tracks and stood rigid for a long moment as a long, low echo began to howl over the base. It took them several seconds to realize what they were hearing and several more to get a handle on their disbelief.

"This a drill? For Chrissakes, it's not even zero-eight..." Dutch asked as they stood and listened to the air raid horns bellowing across the harbor. They also realized that the horns were blending in with a number of ships' horns as well.

"Gotta be," Rogers said. "Ain't no way—"

A voice that itself sounded as incredulous as it did panicked filtered over the public address speakers situated all across the base. Even with the echo and the distortion of the speaker system, there was no mistaking the deadly earnest of the announcement.

"*Air raid! Air raid, Pearl Harbor!*"

"My God..." Turner breathed, trying to get his mind around what was happening.

Had the bigwigs been wrong? Had the Japanese decided to attack *Pearl Harbor* of all places and not the Philippines? That just couldn't be...

"Hear that?" Dutch asked, his eyes wide and his face pale.

"Gotta be a *drill*..." Rogers muttered in earnest hope.

Rogers and Turner waited for a long moment. All they could hear was the repeated mournful wail of the sirens. And then it came.

Growing slowly at first but steadily taking on definition, a low buzzing sound began to assert itself over the sirens. It only took seconds before the buzzing grew into a mechanical roar so enormous that the sirens could barely be heard beneath it.

"Jesus!" Rogers shouted and pointed to the southwest.

The men watched as a horde of locusts seemed to fill the sky. Hundreds of them. Small black shapes that grew in size and became airplanes. Torpedo planes, dive bombers and fighters roared in over the base so low that their combined engine noise seemed to fill the world with a mechanical throbbing buzz that left the three men stunned by abject horror.

"Come on!" Turner shouted over the din as he forced his dazed mind to work. "Let's move!"

He grabbed the other two men and shoved them back toward the other end of the pier. They seemed to snap out of it too, and the three of them began to sprint for the submarine, which suddenly seemed a dozen miles away.

The sirens had stopped by then, and the screaming, shouting and the terrible sound of weapons fire began. Machine guns rattled across the sky, and the whistling of bombs being released made Turner want to puke.

This was happening… it was really happening…

Aboard the *Tautog*, what sailors hadn't already left for church or to enjoy their day off began pouring out of the open loading hatches fore and aft and crowding onto the cigarette deck around the conning tower. They were shouting and waving their hands frantically, like marionettes being jerked about by some maniacal puppeteer.

As Turner raced up the brow to the submarine's deck, he was met by a wide-eyed sailor, "Sir! Sir! The Japs—"

"I know, dammit!" Turner shouted and shoved the boy out of his way. "Where the hell is everybody?"

He was asking about the officers, even though he knew full well that there were none. He'd volunteered to stand a harbor watch the previous night along with the handful of sailors still aboard. The captain and the other officers and chiefs had gone home for the night.

"Dutch!" Turner grabbed the sonar officer by his arm. "Get down into the conning tower and sound the general alarm. Call for battle stations gun action! See if we can't get these assholes to screw their heads on tight!"

"Aye-aye!" Dutch said as he practically dove down the hatchway behind the bridge.

Turner looked to Rogers. He was going to order the chief to start assembling men to man the deck weapons, but Rogers was already doing that. He'd gathered several men and shoved them at the Pom-Pom and was headed aft, shouting at more men to station themselves at the 20mm Oerlikon.

"Where the hell are your fifties?" Rogers roared. "A couple of you pukes get below and get me as many fifty cals as you got on this barge and as much belt ammo as you can carry! Move it, *Goddammit!*"

"Good old Buck..." Turner mumbled as the ship's general alarm began to blare and Dutch's voice began to call out for men to get to battle stations.

Between Rogers and the alarm, the frantic sailors seemed to get ahold of themselves and started assembling around the weapons. A team was even getting the three-inch ready. Normally, this weapon was used only against other surface targets as it was very difficult to hit an aircraft with a single shell. However, with the sky so full of planes, Turner figured why not?

They may or may not hit something, but it would make the men feel as if they were fighting back and help to keep the panic down.

And they needed that. *He* needed that. Explosions now roared into hideous, demonic life, and Turner was horrified to see blooms of orange fire and black smoke rising from Battleship Row. It looked as if several of the big wagons had been hit already and were burning out of control.

Then he saw multiple plumes of smoke rising over Hickam Field, and his stomach nearly turned itself inside out. He and Joan and the kids had been about to head over to the chapel there... and now Hickam...

"Open fire!" Turner shouted. "Take out as many of them fuckin' Nips as you can get your sights on!"

Terry Jacobs, a gunner's mate, shoved a fifty-caliber machine gun up through the bridge hatch. Turner grabbed him and hauled the man up, the extra weight of the two belts of ammo slung over his shoulders, making the XO strain. Jacobs grinned and bolted aft, sliding the machine gun's stud into a special socket on a reinforced cigarette deck stanchion and locked in a belt of ammunition.

Nearby, the big *Narwhal* was getting her topside weapons into action as well. Although the two submarines and the others moored at the base had little to offer in the way of resistance to an armada of aircraft, they might just throw up enough anti-aircraft fire to make an approach on the sub base difficult for the enemy.

Tautog's machine guns started to rattle out, finally giving something back against the onslaught that had already wrought so much devastation. How long had it been? Fifteen, maybe twenty minutes?

Already Ford Island had taken hits and multiple ships were burning in their slips. Magazines were exploding and munitions were cooking off… God help them all.

The locusts seemed to have moved off, headed out to sea and probably arcing back to the huge carrier group that must be somewhere off Oahu. Men around him began to cheer, but Turner didn't join them. Somehow, he knew this wasn't the end. It couldn't be. No way the Japanese would come four-thousand miles just for a single sortie. Although plenty of damage had been done, it wasn't crippling by any means. And that had to be their objective. A sneak attack to cripple the Pacific fleet so that the Japanese could do whatever it was they planned to do with limited opposition.

Already ships were beginning to get underway. Even some of the battleships that had been hit were pulling out, fires and all. One of them, Turner thought maybe the *Oklahoma,* was beginning to roll… rolling… all the way over… and the *Arizona,* Admiral Kidd's flagship, had been hit multiple times. She was already sinking, huge gouts of flame soaring hundreds of feet high from where a bomb had penetrated down to one of her magazines and exploded.

He couldn't tell ship from ship now. The tears that filled his eyes blurred his vision and the horror that filled his mind gave the scene before him a sluggish, surreal nightmare quality. How many ships? How many men?

Was it a nightmare…?

The roar of another wave of Japanese planes disabused him of that notion. Another horde of locusts to descend upon them and devour them all… God, how can there be so many…

"Where are our fucking planes?" someone shouted. "Why aren't we *fighting* these bastards?"

Turner suddenly realized he was getting hoarse from shouting orders. He'd been ordering men to fire, reload, pick targets… he hadn't even realized it for several minutes. How could that be?

As the second wave flew over, his men on the AA guns and those on the *Narwhal* next door began firing into them, setting up walls of flack in an attempt to at least give the enemy something to think about.

A horde of Nakajima Kate torpedo bombers, escorted by Mitsubishi Zeros above them and Aichi dive bombers above the Zeroes, swarmed almost right over the submarine base without seeming to take any notice of them. Clearly, like the first wave, these dozens… no hundreds… of planes weren't interested in anything in the southeast lock. They wanted the battleships, the cruisers and the destroyers. Well, the submariners weren't about to let them pass unmolested.

Cheering rose as more than one aircraft flew straight into the lead curtain above them, their delicate aluminum wings and fuselages ripped open and their fuel beginning to burn.

Men roared in defiance, hurling curses into the sky along with bullets. Although it was gratifying to see some of the Japs explode or spin out of the sky to smash into the harbor, Turner knew that it was little more than a fart in a windstorm. A few planes out of what…? Three hundred? Four hundred? It wouldn't make any difference. Although the entire base was getting mobilized now and even a few American planes had gotten into the air, it wasn't near enough to stop the attack.

It ended only when the Japs ran out of bombs and torpedoes. Only when their fuel began to get low, and they had to head back to their carriers. It ended not because the United States Navy, Army, Marine Corps and Army Air Corps had mounted a successful defense and beaten them off… no, it ended only because the Japs simply had nothing left to throw at the base.

The mechanical roar of hundreds of piston-driven aircraft began to dwindle and fade, leaving behind not quiet… no, certainly not *quiet*… but a hollowness that felt strange—a sense of emptiness in the souls of the men who remained.

But there *was* sound, to be sure.

Sirens wailed, fires roared, motors revved… and men screamed in agony and in despair. Screams of *thousands* of men… some dying in the oily water, some burning alive on devastated ships… some just voicing a horror that no words could frame.

In less than two hours, the lives of everyone at Pearl, everyone in America and everyone on Earth's lives had changed forever.

Turner glanced dazedly at his watch. It wasn't even ten in the morning yet… still breakfast time…

"Sir…" Rogers was shaking Turner by the shoulder.

Turner looked into the Chief's face and saw what must be in his own. Despair and anger, "Yeah, Chief?"

"You think they're coming back?" Rogers asked dully.

Turner stared up into the bright sunny sky as if somehow the answer to the question would be written there. As if the heavens would send down some kind of answer or explanation for the past few hours. He finally looked back at Rogers and shrugged.

"I don't know, Buck… I don't think so," Turner said, trying in vain to pull himself together. "That had to be damned near four hundred planes… would take half a dozen Jap flat tops to mount a force that size. If I had to guess, they'll head back, and the Jap fleet will hightail it out of here before we can get mounted up and go look for them. If there's anything to be grateful for today… and I can't even imagine using that word right now… but it would be that our carriers were at sea."

Rogers scoffed, "Grateful… so we stay at stations, then?"

"For now," Turner said glumly. "Our section of the base wasn't hit. And you saw… our boys did get a couple of Nips…"

That tiny victory was small consolation to either man, or to any of the men on the submarine's deck. All they had to do was look around the large harbor and see the devastation wrought in cold blood to remind themselves of how pitiful knocking down a handful of airplanes really was.

And as the Navy men stood on the deck and stared around them with fear, sadness and rage brewing in all of their hearts, none wanted consolation. Nobody was thinking about comfort or their missed breakfast or Sunday picnics.

No, just about everyone at Pearl Harbor who still breathed on that infamous Sunday morning wanted only one thing. One thing that might give them solace and might start to close a gaping wound in their souls.

They wanted *revenge*.

1

MARSHALL ISLANDS

MID-PACIFIC

JANUARY 13, 1942

This was not what Arthur Turner had hoped for.

The *Tautog's* XO stood on the submarine's small bridge with the quartermaster of the watch and gazed out over a placid sea and the last red glow of a tropical sunset and was miserable. Eighteen days on the ship's first official war patrol… eight days of it in transit from Pearl… and they hadn't even sniffed a single goddamned Jap.

Yes, he knew damned well that this was a reconnaissance mission and that ComSubPac didn't expect many Japanese vessels in the area… yet. But for the love… the Japs had held the Marshall Islands since The Great War… so where were they?

Tautog had paid particular attention to Kwajalein, the main atoll and capital in the chain. If the Japanese were going to be anywhere, it'd be there. Nothing. Then they patrolled Rongelap, Bat, Wotho and Bikini. Still nothing. Day after day of mostly beautiful weather, calm seas and the only surface contacts were Marshall Islanders in outrigger canoes and small fishing boats.

If it went on much longer, Turner was certain he'd go stark raving mad.

"Beautiful evening, eh sir?" The quartermaster of the watch, a young man in his mid-twenties named Stimson asked casually as both men scanned the horizon with their naked eyes.

"Yeah, Stimps... real peaceful."

The petty officer eyed the XO sidelong and arched an eyebrow. Naval discipline had always differentiated and maintained a tangible gap between the enlisted and the officers. A tradition that had been passed down for thousands of years. Even in the modern American Navy, this held true, although it wasn't quite as rigid as what might have been found in the Royal Navy of the Napoleonic era. Even this rigid discipline and clear distinction between the common sailor and his gentleman officer was never as harsh as history made it out to be.

When it came to the Silent Service, however, the line between enlisted and officer became so blurred as to nearly be invisible. Partly this came from the fact that when you crammed sixty or seventy men into a three-hundred-foot-long, sixteen-foot-wide cigar tube (counting only the pressure hull and not the ballast tanks) and forced them to live and work together for months at a time... you either grew close and developed a strong sense of comradery... or you killed one another.

Another reason for the unique sense of family aboard a fleet submarine was the high degree of cross-training. A submarine, once it left the safety of the harbor, was really on her own. Communication was limited. The ship carried enough food for the duration, made its own water and carried enough spare parts to fix just about any problem. It had to. Because should the vessel suffer damage or a breakdown that immobilized her, help was very unlikely.

Submariners had to rely on each other and on their boats to an unprecedented degree. Men had their specialties, but they also trained in everyone else's. The captain and the officers could do any job aboard... from working on a diesel motor to loading a torpedo to tracking down an electrical issue. Conversely, every man on board from the Chief of the Boat, or COB as he was known, to the lowliest seaman apprentice could man the periscope, take the helm or do most non-hyper technical jobs like operating the torpedo data computer or the sound gear.

It was, therefore, not a breach of regs or tradition for an enlisted man to chat amiably with the high and mighty first officer while they stood a watch together. It was welcomed, in fact.

Turner treated Stimson to a ghost of a wry grin, "Sorry, Stimps… pretty sad when a man can't enjoy a tropical sunset, ain't it? It's just…. It's just that it's been thirty-seven goddamned days… Thirty-*seven!*"

Stimson drew in a deep breath and let it out slowly, raising his binoculars to his eyes. It was a little silly, as both men knew, since they had no less than three lookouts up in the periscope sheers who could see several miles further over the horizon than either man on the bridge could. Yet, it was a good habit to keep.

"I know what you mean, sir," Stimson finally replied. "I had a buddy on the *Shaw*. When that destroyer's bow went to pieces… he was on the focs'l."

Turner gave the man's narrow shoulder a pat, "I'm sorry, Stimps… I didn't know that."

The younger man shrugged, "It's war, XO. But yeah, I get it. I want to lay into those slant-eyed sons of bitches bad as anyone."

Turner sighed, "We'll get our chance, Stimps… not this friggin' cruise, apparently… but we will."

Stimson chuckled, "Yes sir."

The upper limb of Sol slipped below the enflamed edge of the world and, as it always did in the tropics, darkness rapidly overtook the submarine from the east. The Kwajalein Atoll was virtually invisible, its many islands inside the reef too low to be seen from the bridge at their present distance. It could be felt though. The scent of green and growing things floated on the light northeast trade wind that ruffled through the light fabric of the men's shirts. The wave patterns were different, too. It was a subtle thing, especially in a sea that wasn't running more than two feet. Yet seasoned sailors could detect the altered flow of the waves due to the interference of land nearby.

"Bridge…" one of the lookouts called down uncertainly. "I think… I think I've got a surface contact, bearing seventy-degrees horizon."

Turner exchanged a quick glance with Stimson and turned to call up to the men in the lookout perch, "You *think*, Barnes? I'm not interested in what you think, son. I'm interested in what you *know*. Now make a proper damned report in the proper form and with proper information, hear me?"

The executive officer's tone was firm but not angry. This was still new to most of the men, and he understood how to balance a rebuke so that it could be a lesson rather than just a dressing down. There were a couple of muted chuckles and snickers from the other two lookouts before Seaman Second Class Arnie Barnes cleared his throat, "Sir... definite surface contact bearing starboard zero-seven-zero degrees horizon. Not quite hull up and small. Don't know who's it is, though, sir."

Turner grinned at Stimson and bent down to speak into the bridge transmitter, "Control, bridge... lookouts report possible surface contact bearing zero-seven-zero degrees. Not quite hull up. Getting anything, Dutch?"

There was a pause before Joe Dutch's voice came from the tinny bridge speaker, "*Affirmative, bridge. Faint sonar contact on that bearing... headed approximately west at seven knots.*"

"Confirm with the sugar dog," Turner ordered.

A pause, "*Radar range is two-zero, triple-zero yards, XO.*"

"Better alert the captain," Turner said, itching to give the order to intercept but knowing it wasn't his place.

"He's already been alerted, Arty," came a deep voice from the hatch behind the bridge. Lieutenant Commander Joseph Willingham stepped out onto the deck and moved to the starboard side of the cigarette deck near the bridge.

Willingham was a man of medium height and build, with tough-looking features accentuated by his Marine Corps style haircut. His face, although average-looking, was more often than not seen with a friendly look or a smile on it, which it held now.

"Think it's a Jap?" the captain inquired.

"I sure as hell hope so," Turner offered.

"Well, let's go over and have a look-see," Willingham suggested. "Intelligence says that there isn't much enemy activity here yet, but they've got to have *something* operating. Officer of the watch, alert control to get the plotting party assigned and have helm execute at two-thirds. Confirm vessel position with a radar sweep."

Turner spoke into the two-way bridge radio again, "Control, bridge. Start a plot on unknown vessel. Hit them with the sugar dog."

There wasn't even a second of hesitation, *Bridge, control. Vessel bears six-eight degrees relative, two-seven degrees true. Plotting party posted.*

"Acknowledged, control. Secure the radar," Turner replied. He then spoke to Stimson. "Make your course two-seven degrees, all ahead two-thirds."

"Helmsman, bridge," Stimson spoke into the speaker now. "Come right to course zero-two-seven. All ahead two-thirds."

Willingham smiled at the cleanly repetitious efficiency of his watch standers. To the uninitiated to the ways of the sea, this continuous repeating of orders to men who clearly overheard it the first time would seem rather silly. Certainly Joe Dutch had heard the captain tell Turner what he wanted and then heard Turner tell the quartermaster. Yet this constant reiteration ensured that no mistakes were made and also preserved the chain of command.

Although Willingham was the captain and had ultimate control, it was the duty of the watch officer to give operational orders. Even with the captain standing right there, for example, the lookouts were supposed to report to Turner, and Turner would make his report to the captain. Further, once the officer of the deck had a maneuvering order, it must pass to the helmsman via the quartermaster. When submerged, of course, things were a bit different. Yet this madness most certainly had a method.

The ship turned to her right, and all the men on the deck felt the surge of power as the electric motors increased their output and the vessel accelerated from her lazy six knots to a modest twelve. There was no need to rush, and by the time the other ship caught sight of the low-profile submarine, if it even did, it would be full dark.

"Bridge, control," Dutch reported. *"Course is zero-two-seven, speed twelve knots."*

Stimson repeated this to Turner, who grinned and said, "Very well."

The breeze freshened in their faces as the submarine's forward progress almost directly into the wind combined with the ten knots of the trade. All three men on the bridge and cigarette deck shivered slightly in spite of the January tropical temperature of seventy-two degrees.

"Sir, would you care to take the deck?" Turner asked his captain.

Willingham smiled, "No... I think I'll let you handle this one, Arty. Let's see what you're really made of."

"Aye-aye, sir," Turner said, feeling quite pleased. The likelihood was that this single ship was Japanese. It could be a small merchant vessel or even a minelayer out to seed the large pass through the reef on this side of the atoll. It should be an easy target and an easy kill.

"Control, bridge... open all outer doors," Turner ordered the transmitter. "Set depth on all weapons to ten feet, repeat, ten feet."

The order was acknowledged, and several moments later Turner received confirmation that both torpedo rooms were ready.

"Anything new up there, Barnes?" Turner called to his lookouts.

"Vessel hull up now," Barnes reported. "Looks like a small cargo ship or minelayer."

Turner rubbed his hands together and glanced over at his captain, who had lit a cigarette, "Skipper, should we stay on top or go down for the attack?"

"What do you think, Arty?" Willingham asked casually. "You know what the book says about night surface attacks. Not that I give a damn, though. Even if the Japs can detect our radar, it won't help them in this case."

Turner frowned, "I'm not so sure about these fish, sir. We both know that Mark 6 exploder is a boondoggle. Hate to get caught with our pants down should the damn thing fail to explode."

"Concur," Willingham said with a grin.

"Clear the bridge," Turner ordered.

The three lookouts scrambled down the periscope sheers and down the hatch. Next went Stimson, followed by the captain. Finally, Turner went down the hatch, releasing the holding latch as he did. The hatch was dogged, and Turner took his place in the conning tower near the periscopes. Willingham lounged nearby, watching.

Turner gave the appropriate orders and the boat slid silently below the surface. At sixty-five feet, Turner raised the search scope and pressed his face to the rubber-coated eyepiece.

"Target bears dead ahead," Dutch said from his position at the sonar station. "Range is decreasing. Target seems to be reducing speed and making a starboard turn."

Turner's scope was low in the water, barely above the surface. Yet even at a little more than two miles in the darkness, he could see the shape of a surface ship in the distance. She was running without lights. From the look of her, Turner agreed that the vessel was probably a minelayer. She had a low freeboard and an even lower fantail structure from which the mines were probably deployed.

"Any sign she's spotted us?" Turner inquired.

"Not so as I can tell," Dutch reported. "Still moving at three knots and making a very wide turn. Maybe starting her mine seeding."

"When do you want to shoot, sir?" Lieutenant Ben Shives asked from the TDC. Shives was the ship's gunnery and torpedo officer and charged with the operation of the torpedo data computer. It was Shives' job to make sure that all torpedoes were supplied with the appropriate gyro settings. This complex set of calculations was constantly performed by the mechanical computer and electronically sent to each torpedo. Servos in the tubes would continually update each weapons' individual gyroscope settings so that the torpedo would go where it was supposed to when fired.

Before the advent of this mechanical marvel, the only thing a submarine captain had was raw mathematics, his paper target plot, which they still used, and a simple device known as an IsWas. The IsWas was a circular slide rule with several layers that could be adjusted to produce an angle that was then used to feed the gyro settings on the torpedoes. Even now, with the TDC and its direct tie-in to the torpedo rooms, the target-bearing trackers up on deck, radar and/or sonar and the ship's own dead reckoning tracer, the gunnery officer still double checked himself with the IsWas.

"Let's not screw around here," Turner said. "I want to get into a thousand yards. Helm, ahead full. Down scope, up attack scope. Diving officer, take me up to forty-five feet."

Turner snapped the handles of the heavier search periscope up, and as the larger scope lowered into its well, the slimmer attack scope rose. He snapped these handles down and peered through at his target.

"Best guess... range now appears to be... two-zero-five-zero yards," Dutch announced. "Target is settling on course... three-two-five."

"Helm, come left and steady up on course three-two-five," Turner ordered. "Radar, verify range, please."

The radar operator activated the SD system, whose powerhead was now out of the water due to Turner's decreased depth. He turned and reported very similar numbers to Dutch's own.

"Damned good guess, Joe. Diving officer, bring us back to periscope depth," Turner ordered.

Out of the corner of his eye, he saw Willingham nod. Turner had to swivel his body and the scope in order to keep the target in view now. With an overtake speed of roughly five knots, it would take a little more than four minutes to get to the thousand-yard range he'd specified.

The minutes seemed to creep past. Turner never took his eyes off the target, which was now very clear in his scope. There was good moonlight now, and the ship's gray hull shown dully against the blackness of sky and ocean.

"Bearing on target... mark!" Turner stated.

"Zero-one-five!" Stimson said, reading the bearing from the bearing ring that surrounded the periscope.

Turner now adjusted the stadimeter control below his right handle. This device worked by measuring angles from the target vessel's masthead and then determining range. It was problematic, as without an accurate masthead height for a vessel in the recognition book, or if the enemy vessel raised or lowered the masthead, the range setting would be off. Some deviation was acceptable, and Turner made his best guess.

"Range to target... one-two-zero-zero yards," he announced, and Shives plugged that into the TDC. "Angle on the bow... two-zero-zero- port."

"You can shoot, XO!" Shives announced excitedly. "We've got a solution."

Turner waited until the stadimeter gave him a reading of one-thousand yards, "Okay, BeauOrd says our fish are ingenious, so we'll try with the one… fire one!"

The ship shuddered as the thirty-three-hundred-pound, twenty-one-inch wide and twenty-foot-long Mark 14 torpedo was shoved out of the submarine with a hammer blow of compressed air and water. Dutch flipped a switch on his console and the high-pitched shriek of the torpedo's steam-powered engines filled the conning tower.

"Fish running hot, straight and normal!" Dutch announced. "Impact in forty-five seconds."

Turner stared through the attack scope, his stomach in knots. This was the first torpedo he'd fired in wartime and at a real honest to God target. He counted down the seconds as the fish closed the distance between itself and the minelayer, eating twenty-two yards of ocean with each passing second. The wait was interminable, and then…

…nothing! He'd missed!

"Goddammit!" Turner grumped and then smacked his fist on the side of the scope. "I missed! Motherfucker!"

"I do not concur," Willingham said. "Dutch, what do you say?"

Dutch shook his head, "Our fish passed right through my bearing, sir. Depth was set at ten feet…"

"Book says that ship draws *ten*," Willingham said. "The damned torpedo ran too deep and that shitty Mark 6 exploder didn't work! *Again!*"

That mollified Turner slightly, "Okay… maybe… phone talker, order both rooms to reset their depth to two feet."

From the bottom of the ladder down to the control room, the control room compartment talker repeated the order into his sound-powered gear. He then reported both rooms acknowledged and then that the depths were reset.

"Aspect change!" Dutch announced just as Turner watched the ship in his scope begin to turn and a definite foaming wave begin to form along her bow. "Screw revolution increase, too… shit! Active pinging!"

"Means she's got depth charges and not just mines," Willingham stated.

"Concur," Turner griped. "Would you like to take over the attack, Captain?"

"Nope," Willingham said with a grin. "Still on you, Arty. Don't kill us, though, huh?"

"She's turning right for us," Turner said. "She's got the bone in her teeth, too. Probably doing fifteen knots or more now. Ballsy little slope, ain't he?"

"Probably headed for our torpedo track," Shives observed. "Should we fire, XO?"

"Negative..." Turner said. "Down scope... Diving officer, make your depth one-zero-zero feet, hard dive! Phone talker, tell after room to stand ready."

The submarine angled forward as the stern planes were set on full up angle and the bow planes on full dive. Willingham chuckled.

"Gonna pass right under his keel and send two fish straight up his ass, eh, XO?"

"Aye-aye, sir!" Turner said. "Phone talker! All compartments, rig for depth charge attack! Seal all watertight doors! Stop ventilation! Smartly, goddammit!"

"Sir, my depth is one-zero-zero feet!" the diving officer called up into the conning tower.

"All stop!" Turner ordered. "Dutch?"

"He's almost on top of us," Dutch said, holding his earphones. "Pinging like a son of a bitch..."

Everyone on the submarine could hear it. The twin screws of the two-hundred-foot minelayer churned so loudly it seemed as if the propeller blades must start gouging the conning tower. In truth, there was fifty or sixty feet of water in between, but that wasn't much. So close was it, in fact, that the submarine was being slightly buffeted by the prop wash, despite its larger length and depth.

Turner's plan was simple. If the minelayer started dropping depth charges, then they'd most likely be set lower than one hundred feet. The ship would assume that the submarine would dive deep. Also, when the ship passed over the diving *Tautog*, she might lose the sonar signal in her own prop noise. They'd be picked up again, but by then, it'd be too late.

"Splashes," Dutch said. "They're dropping depth charges… Christ, almost right on top of us…"

"Give me your best range estimate, Dutch," Turner ordered quietly. "Hang on…"

Seconds went by, and then four resounding *booms* rocked the ship from below. Gear rattled in its mounts, bits of cork insulation fluttered down from the overhead and several lightbulbs in the conning tower shattered. The charges had gone off several hundred feet below, so the effect was thankfully minimal.

"Range now approximately four hundred to six-hundred yards," Dutch announced.

"Fire seven!" Turner exclaimed. He counted down from six and then: "Fire eight! Close all outer doors. Helm, make turns for three knots, full left rudder. Diving officer, make your depth three-hundred feet, repeat three-zero-zero feet, smartly!"

The submarine began to move, nosing down and leaning into her port turn like an airplane banking into an attack.

"Sir… torpedo impacts!" Dutch announced and then cursed. "No detonation! Both fish failed to explode, sir!"

"Fuck!" Turner roared and then got himself under control. "Understood, sonar… what's our buddy doing?"

Dutch chuckled, "Continuing on course. I think he's lost his appetite for the game, sir. Probably felt them two fish smack his bottom and feels he got off lucky. Now turning… I think he's headed off to the east, northeast."

"Back through the reef," Willingham stated and sighed. "We were damned lucky."

Turner sighed and wiped the mild sheen of sweat from his face, "That's not how I'd put it, sir."

The captain clapped his first officer on the shoulder, "Arty, you did great. A finely executed attack and a damned fine adaptation. Not your fault those fish are defective."

"Wish somebody would tell that to the Bureau of Ordnance," Turner cranked.

"Officer of the watch, order all compartments opened and the men can stand easy at battle stations," Willingham stated. "Let's stay wet for another half hour, and if our friend up top doesn't come back, we'll surface and continue with our recon. Cooks can serve coffee at station until we rise. Smoking lamp is lit. Art, I'd like to meet with you in the wardroom when your watch is up and go over this. Put together an after-action report and see if we can't get somebody at Pearl to listen."

With that, the captain went down the ladder and the *Tautog* continued on her way, not much worse for the encounter.

Although nothing had been gained in terms of sinking enemy shipping, Turner did realize that several important things had happened for the submarine's crew. They'd fired their weapons for real, and they'd even been through a depth charge attack. Mild though it was, it still showed them that they could do it. It was one small step into turning the crew into a well-oiled fighting machine.

2

MARE ISLAND NAVAL SHIPYARD

SAN FRANCISCO

FEBRUARY 18, 1942

Lieutenant Arthur Turner was more than a little surprised upon his arrival at Mare Island. After pulling *Tautog* into one of the submarine repair houses at Mare Island and getting the ship secured, he exited the enclosed hangar and found his wife Joan and their two small kids waiting outside the secure work area.

Suddenly, the cacophony of air drills, welding machinery, clanging, shouting, and the diesel and ozone smells of a shipyard vanished at the sight of his little family. Turner's face split into a huge grin and he had to brace himself as Joan and the kids piled into him.

"Hey!" Turner exclaimed, trying to hug everyone at once. "What in the world are you guys doing here?"

Joan was a slender woman. Even after two kids, her body was slim and her proportions enticing. Her sky-blue eyes danced like the sun in her curly blonde hair and were both outshined by her brilliant grin.

"We were shipped over from Pearl a week ago," Joan explained, pulling back a little and giving her husband some air. "I was told you'd be needing us for a while. Kind of hush-hush… you know the Navy."

Turner chuckled and bent down to give a little closer attention to his children. Arthur Turner Jr. had jet-black hair, his father's strong jaw and his mother's eyes. Dorothy "Dotty" Turner was the spitting image of her mother, the two girls even wearing almost identical heavy wool skirts, sweaters and light jackets against Northern California's winter air.

"I got to go up to the bridge," Arty Jr. said proudly. "On the way over from Pearl, Pop."

"You did?" Turner asked excitedly. "What'd you come across in?"

"A nice passenger ship," Joan said. "Every luxury. Gave us a suite on the top deck."

"We had a swimming pool!" Dotty cut in. "*Inside* the boat, daddy!"

Turner laughed and hugged his kids before standing up, "Did the brass tell you *why* you guys were shipped over? What about the house?"

"Somebody from the general staff filled me in," Joan said as they began walking away from the dockyard. "He just said that you'd be putting in here and would be stateside for a couple of months or so. Thought we'd like to come and stay with you for the duration. I was sort of concerned about Arty's school... but the Navy has provisions for that, I'm told. Tutors and so forth for... oh, what did they call it... T... TA..."

"TAD," Turner replied with a shrug. "Temporarily assigned duty. I didn't think we were gonna be here that long. What I heard was the boat was getting a few tweaks is all. Some things they can't do at Pearl right now, and then we'd be headed right back out there."

"Well, for now, they put the three of us up in a very nice little house at the BOQ," Joan explained as she directed Turner to a small car parked in the Navy lot. "As for the house on Oahu, they'll probably rent it out."

"Sir!" A young second class yeoman came to attention a few steps away. He'd been escorting them but at a discreet distance astern.

"As you were, thank you yeoman," Turner said with a smile. "Mrs. Turner appreciates your escort."

"My pleasure, sir... ma'am," The sailor said as his boyish face split into a grin. "If you'll just let me know where you'll be, ma'am, we'll have Mr. Turner's gear packed and sent along ASAP. Unless you'd rather do that yourself, sir."

"My gear?" Turner asked in confusion.

"Yes sir," The yeoman announced as if this were the most natural thing in the world. "Orders from admin, sir."

Turner thought about asking the man just what the hell he was talking about but held off. The nineteen-year-old sailor wouldn't have a damned clue. He only shrugged and said that he'd appreciate his gear being sent ashore. Joan told the young man their address and he trotted back into the yard.

"Why do I feel like I'm the last one to know what the heck is going on?" Turner asked as he climbed into the passenger seat. "Do you, honey?"

Joan frowned slightly, "Not exactly… but something's up. We've been invited to dine with Admiral Peale, he's the base commander, and his wife this evening. I've met them both. He's very personable, and his wife's a doll. But as to *why*… I don't know for sure."

"Maybe it's a secret mission, Pop," Arty chimed in from the back seat. His six-year-old enthusiasm irrepressible and infectious. Dotty giggled and Turner laughed.

"Well, it certainly isn't to get a medal," he said with a head shake. "Not after that foul-up in the Marshall's. I fired three fish at a little Jap minelayer, and they were all duds."

"That's not the way I heard it," Joan said as she steered the car toward the other end of the island. "Mary Perkins says she has it on good authority that you did *very* well and that those torpedoes missed because of that defective exploder mechanism… and you know she has the… ear… of Captain Rhodes at staff."

Turner was continually amazed at how much scuttlebutt his wife picked up through the grapevine of the officer's wives club. Not only did she seem to know everything that went on… a lot more than he did… but she knew how to weed through and judge what was proper intelligence and what was simple gossip.

"I wouldn't presume to question your sources of intel, Joanie," Turner said with a wry smile.

"That's wise, sailor," Joan said. "Not if you want to experience an *authentic* submariner's homecoming."

Turner felt a little butterfly in his belly and a tightening in his groin. His wife was still deliciously sexy for a woman of thirty who'd had two kids. On top of that, she was tender, adoring and possessed a hunger for their marriage bed that often kept him up nights while aboard his submarine.

He grinned broadly at her, "And what if I did question you?"

She laughed, "Oh, you'd still be welcome. I haven't seen you in two months…"

Apparently, the BOQ was further away than Turner thought. They passed a dizzying array of warehouses, admin buildings, a power plant and even a foundry. Joan guided the small sedan over the bridges and into the city of Vallejo. She quickly drove into a small neighborhood near the waterfront and pulled into the driveway of a three-bedroom house with white siding and pale-yellow shutters.

After chatting together for a while, Joan got the children packed off to the next-door neighbor, a plump and friendly woman in her mid-thirties. Apparently, her husband was a full commander and worked as a Naval architect at the shipyard, and the couple had a boy and girl about the same age as the Turner children.

"What time is the big dinner?" Turner asked as Joan re-entered the house. "It's only five now. A little early, isn't it?"

Joan narrowed her eyes, and her soft smile made his hairline tingle. She came close, took hold of his hands and slid them under the hem of her sweater. Turner's hands slid over the baby-soft skin of her belly and was pleased to note that she had not worn a bra beneath her sweater and light jacket. Her full round breasts filled his hands and her nipples hardened almost instantly at the touch of his warm skin.

She sighed happily, "Not until seven… I figured we needed a little appetizer before the main course, love…"

Joan drove them to a large and very exclusive-looking restaurant along the waterfront. As Turner got out and came around to open her door, he swore his legs were wobbling ever so slightly.

Joan was dressed in navy blue, trimmed in white and gold, and her heels gave her the impression of great height, although she still was half a head shorter than her six-foot-one husband.

"You look beautiful," he said, gazing at her diamond earrings sparkling in the light from the parking lot. "I think you've weakened my knees, woman."

She smiled and took his hand, "Just wait, sailor. That was only the preliminary attack. The kids are staying with the Weathers' tonight... be prepared for a full-on beach assault."

"Yes ma'am," he said, saluting her.

They were both still chuckling when they entered the restaurant and approached the hostess stand.

"Oh, Commander and Mrs. Turner," The young lady said cheerfully without having been told who they were. "Please follow me. The admiral and his guests are waiting for you."

"Wow," Turner muttered.

"Stick with me, kid," Joan whispered with a little giggle, "and you'll go places."

"You mean besides heaven?" he whispered back.

"Stop that," she chided but squeezed his hand firmly.

The hostess led the Turners through a curtained archway and into a small parlor-like room in the corner of the restaurant. The two outward-facing walls were dominated by large windows that overlooked San Francisco Bay. The lights of the cities and towns around sparkled on the nighttime water before them.

The room featured a set of sofas and padded chairs near the windows, a large fireplace that was aglow with an admirable blaze and a six-person table set with fine linen, pearlescent flatware, gleaming utensils and fine crystal that caught the firelight that danced along the curving surfaces.

"My God..." Turner mumbled to his wife as they entered. "Hope we're not picking up this check..."

She surreptitiously elbowed her husband just as the three people already in the room stood from where they'd been sipping drinks on the comfortable lounging furniture.

There was a medium-tall, burly man dressed in a Navy uniform with a rear admiral's stripe on his sleeves and a fairly impressive fruit salad on his breast. His hair was salt and pepper, and he looked to be in his early fifties. His face was wide and his smile friendly. Beside him, a stylishly dressed, short and sturdy woman with raven hair that shined in the firelight smiled as well. Her body, although strongly built, was blessed with deep curves and a bosom that put Mae West to shame, Turner thought. The last of the three was a tall, lean man of about forty with auburn hair and a thin mustache.

"Oh…" Turner said, looking down at his civilian suit. "I didn't know this was a uniform dinner, sir…"

"Nonsense, lad!" Admiral Peale all but roared good-naturedly as he stuck out his hand. "This is an informal occasion. Admiral Millard Peale, at your service, Mr. Turner. And it's a very great pleasure to see you again, Joan. Thank you both for coming on such short notice. I know your boat just got in, Lieutenant."

"Oh, not at all, sir," Turner shook the beefy hand with equal vigor. "Delighted to be asked."

"Betty, this is Arthur Turner, and you already know Joan here," the Admiral introduced.

"A great pleasure, Mr. Turner," Betty Peale said in a mellifluous southern accent. "I've had the pleasure of spending a little time with your lovely wife and your charming children. It's so good to put a face with the name."

"Thank you, ma'am," Turner said, clasping her hand gently. "Please call me Arthur, or just Art if you like."

Her pretty face glowed with pleasure, and she led Joan over to sit on one of the sofas and poured her something in a tumbler.

"Turner, this is Mr. Web Clayton," the Admiral introduced the civilian. "He made a special trip out here from D.C. just to meet you. Web, here he is. The man who engaged the entire Goddamned… er…"—Peale glanced sheepishly at his wife who only shook her head and grinned—"the whole blasted Japanese attack force at Pearl. Then fired three torpedoes at a Jap ship a few weeks later."

"Pleasure to meet you, Mr. Turner," Clayton said, offering his own hand to be shaken. The grip was firm but lacked the over-exuberant zeal of the Admiral's. "A damned fine exhibition if you ask me."

Turner flushed slightly, "As for Pearl… we just reacted, almost unthinkingly. And as for the minelayer… well… none of my shots did a thing. Not so proud of that, I'm afraid."

"Nonsense, Commander," Peale boomed. "Mr. Clayton and I agree that wasn't your fault. Those damned jackasses at BeauOrd need to pull their heads out of their… to get them on straight, I mean."

Suddenly something Peale had said seemed to register with Turner. As it did, he recalled that the hostess had said it too. They'd both referred to him as *Commander*…

Apparently, the burly Admiral read his mind because he laughed heartily, "No, son, I'm not getting senile! We'll make it official in the morning, but I might as well spill the beans now since your good lady is here and all… you've been promoted. Congratulations, Lieutenant Commander Turner."

Joan let out a muffled but enthusiastic whoop of delight. Turner's face split into a huge grin, "Why… uhm… thank you, sir. I'm honored."

Peale beamed, "That's not all, but maybe I'd better let Web here fill in the blanks. Come and drop your hook here and let me get you some torpedo juice."

The three men sat in individual easy chairs after the Admiral poured Turner a stiff brandy. After getting settled, Turner decided to take the lead.

"Is there something going on besides me getting a half stripe, Admiral?" he asked and then turned his gaze to Clayton. "Something to do with a man coming all the way across the country from Washington, by chance?"

"There is," Peale said more seriously. "Would you like to field this, Webster?"

Clayton sipped from his snifter and leaned forward to address Turner. The women grew quiet and attentive, "You're familiar with Admiral Ernest King?"

Turner nodded, "Of course. He's the Navy C in C. Why?"

Clayton sighed, "How about Vizeadmiral Karl Dönitz?"

Again Turner nodded, "Head of Germany's U-boats… the Kriegsmarine."

"Exactly," Clayton said. "Well, old Admiral Donut has sent a number of Type IX U-boats across the pond, and they've been attacking merchant shipping from as far south as Florida up to Maine since the first week of the war. It's being called 'Operation: Drumbeat.' The Brits have been making suggestions about how to defend ourselves, but old hard-nose King can't stand the British and isn't listening. We've already lost several *dozen* ships within sight of the shore, for God's sake."

"Christ..." Turner breathed. "And I take it we just don't have enough assets on that coast to deal with this? What about convoying?"

Peale barked out a derisive laugh, and Clayton scoffed, "What indeed... there's more, Commander, which we'll talk about more in private. However, the long and short of it is this... we need a man in the Atlantic. An aggressive man who's proven himself under fire. A man who isn't afraid to take the bull by the horns. We're going to give that man command of a new experimental class of submarine. One that's already being built at Groton as we speak. And that man, Captain Turner, is you."

"Me?" Turner asked in shock. He met Joan's eyes and they shone with pride.

"You," Peale said. "You're due, Art. We need capable and aggressive sub drivers now more than ever. You're getting a new boat and you'll even get to take a few old friends with you. Not that this is my decision, but since we're on my base and I happen to know Web here..."

"I've heard that *Tautog*'s sonar man has a sharp pair of ears and is a good all-around submariner," Clayton stated. "I'll send him along if you'd like. There's a seasoned man whom I'm told you also know... Paul Rogers... who'll be gun-decked and sent on from Pearl if you want him for your chief of the boat. Name's Rogers. He's been working to refit his destroyer but has expressed an interest to rejoin the Silent Service. I can get him on a flight tonight, if you're all right with the choice."

"Happy to have them both," Turner said, feeling more than a little dazed. "Will Dutch be my XO?"

Clayton shook his head, "There's another young man already overseeing the construction. He's already slated for the boat's XO slot.

The captain was badly injured in a car accident a week ago, but this young guy has high scores and is senior to Dutch. You'll like him. Smart and capable."

"Some night, huh, honey?" Joan remarked with a smile.

Turner beamed, "So what's so special about this boat, Mr. Clayton?"

"Call me Web," the civilian said. "She's part of a new class. *Balao*-class. Not that different than your current boat, with a few improvements. The whole class isn't even slated to come into service until later this year. The *Bull Shark,* that's your new boat, is only the number two boat. *Balao* will still be the official class leader, but we think we can get *Bull Shark* off the ways as you Navy boys say, within a few weeks."

"So she's experimental?" Joan asked, just the slightest tinge of doubt in her tone.

"Not anything outlandish," Clayton reassured her and Turner. "Based on the *Gato*-class but with some improvements. Hell, the next class after this one is already on the boards. However… the *Bull Shark* is being built with higher strength and thicker steel. Nearly doubling her test depth. In truth, tests show she's got a probable crush depth of over nine hundred, but I hear the official test depth rating will be four hundred. Anyway, she'll have both air and surface search radar, two five-inch guns, a couple of big AA cannons, improved sound gear… the works. Interested?"

"Most certainly, Mr..…. Web," Turner said. "What's my mission exactly?"

Clayton cast a quick glance at the women, "We'll talk more about that on the flight. We leave tomorrow noon for New London."

Both Turner and Joan met each other's gaze, and the sense of loss was visible. Clayton smiled thinly, "Not to worry. Ms. Joan here and the kids will be taking the train out to Connecticut day after tomorrow. They'll stay with you there while you oversee the completion of the boat and while you're stationed at New London sub base. If all goes well, we'll have you clean up this mess and have you back at Pearl before the next school year begins. We figured that you'd enjoy having your family around for a few months, though."

"I would, Web," Turner said, watching as Joan pulled a handkerchief from her purse and began dabbing at her eyes. He was grateful for her outward expression of emotion; otherwise, he might have teared up himself.

"Now that that's settled," Peale said cheerfully, "what say we call for some provisions?"

"Mil!" Betty chastised her husband. "You're forgetting."

Peale made a pained face and then chuckled, "Right you are, sweetheart! Mrs. Turner, you probably know by now that there's a little ceremony when a man is promoted. Although we're not ready to pin the oak leaves on yet, but I think a celebratory kiss is in order."

Joan jumped up and wrapped her arms around Turner's neck and kissed him deeply, holding him tight and biting his lower lip gently before pulling back and saying: "Congratulations… Captain."

Turner grinned and felt himself flush with pleasure and no small amount of desire, "Thank you, Mrs. Captain."

"Well now!" Betty Peale said and laughed. "I think it's time to get this celebration underway!"

3

ATLANTIC OCEAN - 31°33" N, 75°21" W

200 MILES EAST OF CAPE HATTERAS, NC

1300 ZULU

The SS *Mortimer P. Blanch* plowed slowly through an easy swell headed south by southwest at a leisurely five knots. Her matte-black hull did not gleam in the morning sun, as it was intended not to do. Her white gunwale trim and deckhouse did stand out against the blue of the sea, however. Although somewhat hard to differentiate beyond a few miles, thanks to the royal-blue paint that had been used to coat her dorsal surfaces, it was possible to spot the ship from far off if one knew what one was searching for.

The pilot of the AR196 floatplane did spot the vessel from nearly five miles out. However, he did have direction from the cargo ship herself, and he did, in fact, have his, his co-pilot and his observer's eyes peeled specifically to spot the ship and the strangely camouflaged upper surface paint scheme. A paint scheme that blended well with the surrounding ocean if it was observed from above.

There was a swell running, perhaps six or eight feet in height, but it was a long and rolling swell that would prove to be no problem for the German-built floatplane. As the pilot guided his bird down in the direction of the waves, he eased his trim, throttled back and slid the plane onto the sparkling blue waters with practiced ease. He then carefully motored the airplane alongside the freighter and waited for the riggers to attach the hoisting gear that would lift the reconnaissance plane out of the water and deposit it safely amidships on the large flat main deck.

It was an odd sight, a German seaplane floating next to an American-built vessel. Yet they were both the best in their classes and eminently practical and well-suited to their duties.

The thick cables were lowered over the side with two riggers clinging to them. The men's feet touched delicately on the Arado's upper wings, and they quickly attached the hooks to the hardened hoisting eyes on the aircraft's fuselage and wings. One of the men shouted upward and the airplane, its crew and the riggers were lifted five stories into the air, swung inboard and gently deposited on a specially cleared area of the main cargo-handling deck. The riggers leapt down, attached tie-down straps to the airplane's floats and then unhooked the lifting cables so they could be stowed properly.

The pilot exited the aircraft, gave the tie downs a cursory examination, was satisfied that they'd been laid on properly, and led his two men into the deckhouse and on into the well-appointed officer's mess. Coffee had already been laid out at a table, and three men waited there. One was the mess steward, ready to take their breakfast order. One man was the ship's captain, and the other an apparent civilian advisor. For although the merchant ship appeared to be just that, she was, in fact, a military vessel and crewed by personnel from the Navy. In spite of her blocky, somewhat unappealing construction, the *Blanch* was equipped with the latest in radar, sonar and radio gear. She carried fuel, supplies and munitions to augment other military vessels operating within her sphere of influence. Her role was that of a Q-ship. A vessel designed for intelligence gathering and to act as a command-and-control ship for active military units.

And she was, it must be made perfectly clear, not an American Q-ship. Although she'd been built in Baltimore three years earlier, her allegiance had changed dramatically since then. The ship was a prize of war, although technically, no war had existed at the time of her capture. Her name had been changed, but still American, and she was now one of the most advanced and effective Q-ships in the Kriegsmarine… the Nazi Navy.

"Welcome back, Herr Michner, the *Blanch's* captain, Curt Diedrich said. Diedrich was a fortyish man of heavy build, medium height, and a hard but handsome face dominated by a broad clefted chin. "I trust your patrol was productive this morning?"

"Indeed it was, sir," Lieutenant Brenner Michner replied. "Hans has a complete list of the shipping we tracked and appropriate data."

"Excellent, Lieutenant," the other man, Klaus Brechman, stated. Brechman was a tall, thin and angular man. His severe appearance was not helped by his almost permanent glower, his harsh voice and his brusque manner. Brechman was a man sent to do a job for the Reich, and that was his only concern. Others' personal feelings meant nothing to him. "Please hand me your report. I shall review it and ask questions when and if necessary."

"Please sit down, men," Diedrich implored, waving them into empty seats on the opposite side of the table. "You must be famished after almost five hours in the air. Have some coffee and order breakfast."

Michner and his men placed their order and the steward vanished into the officer's galley. As the three flyers sipped their hot coffee, Michner watched the civilian and the four-stripe captain pressing themselves close together so that they could review Hans' notes. It was an odd sight to Michner, the *Kapitan zur See* and the somewhat mysterious Brechman cozying up to one another.

In truth, there was little mystery surrounding Brechman. He was a spymaster for the *Schutzstaffel*… Heinrich Himmler's own SS. Although he didn't wear any official uniform, Brechman's manner and his duties aboard the Q-ship made his association obvious. It wasn't that the man attempted to delude anyone about his affiliation, it was simply that, just like all good intelligence agents, he didn't speak openly of it.

Not that Michner gave much of a damn about the SS officer. He was already an *Oberleutenant* or Senior Lieutenant at the age of twenty-eight and held the observer and sea battle badge from the

Luftwaffe as well as a meritorious service clasp from the Kriegsmarine. Michner had seen action several times in Europe, both over land and at sea. He was no stranger to either danger or secrecy.

His crew, however, were both about as green as green could be. Hans Volmer, his observer, had only recently been promoted to Oberfähnrich zur See, a sub-lieutenant only fresh out of the Academy. Gunther Schultz, his co-pilot, was only slightly older and had himself only just graduated and earned the same rank as Volmer. Both men were intelligent and had so far proved themselves competent and levelheaded. These were both admirable traits for the type of work they were doing.

"They are *still* not convoying their vessels," Brechman noted with evident disgust in his tone. "This is madness! We know for certain that the Limeys have warned the Americans time and time again. I have personally overheard a telephone conversation where their naval commander and chief Earnest King was specifically advised to do so."

Diedrich only shrugged and chuckled softly, "Thus making our job all the easier, Herr Brechman. With both Type IX and Type VII boats operating along the American eastern seaboard and our *Milchkuh* submarines to refuel them... not to mention *our own* supplies... this campaign has already gone and should continue to go splendidly. We hit Yankee trade hard right off their beaches and then our wolf packs decimate them in the North Atlantic. This should be a very *short* war, no?"

Michner had to agree with the captain. He'd seen it himself. Lone freighters traveling along the coast in broad daylight. Ship's running fully lit at night, and the coastal cities with their lights burning brightly. All of the U-boat commanders in the field report seeing vessels clearly silhouetted against the beaches and their lights. Even more so, the big cities cast bright glows in the sky, and this only exacerbated the problem... for the American sailors, at least.

Brechman sighed, "Perhaps, Kapitan... perhaps. The Americans have no real experience with this kind of warfare. They haven't lived and grown up in Europe, where war has been a way of life almost incessantly since before the days of the Roman Empire... yet they are not fools. They will learn... and they have many advantages. The industrial might of the United States is not to be believed. Remember, Herr Captain, that this country is larger than all of Europe combined, save Russia. They're blessed with every possible natural resource imaginable and need to import virtually nothing. On the other hand, they can export virtually everything."

Diedrich grunted and lit a cigarette, "All true... yet they must get all of this materiel across the sea... and it is *we* who now control the sea, Herr Brechman. The way the mighty Royal Navy once did in the days of Napoleon."

Brechman permitted himself a short laugh, "Indeed... yet remember, my dear Diedrich... the United States fought a war with Britain then, and the *roast beefs* found their Yankee cousins an intractable and highly dangerous enemy. Remember the Great War, for that matter. Yes, we will defeat them and strangle their trade to Britain... yet we must not underestimate them."

"And that is why we are out here, is it not, Herr Brechman?" Michner spoke up between bites of ham and eggs.

The severe gaze of the SS man settled on Michner and nodded ever so slightly, "It is, youngster. Even more because the American Navy has no idea that we're out here."

"Indeed not," Diedrich added. "They don't even know the full extent of our operational sphere. How many submarines we're running and where. From the Gulf of Mexico up to Maine and even down in the Caribbean."

"Thus far," Brechman continued, "our U-boat commanders have struck out randomly and have contained themselves. These first few months have been to probe the American defenses and for us to learn how prepared they are."

"From all we've seen, sir," Hans spoke up for the first time, "they don't seem to be taking any precautions against us... or even seem to care."

Diedrich grinned, and Brechman shrugged ever so slightly, "That so, young man?"

"Yes sir," Hans continued more confidently now that he hadn't received a rebuke. "They don't even fly air cover most of the time, at least not away from their bases. We've never once been challenged, even when skimming the shoreline. Of course, on the few occasions we've ever been contacted directly, Lieutenant Michner can speak in a flawless southern-American accent, and we've never had a bit of trouble."

This was partly due to several factors, Michner knew. Yes, he'd trained himself on how to speak English and do so in the peculiar drawling tones of those who lived in the southern parts of America. Also, their aircraft was painted much like the ship that carried it. The royal-blue upper surface color made the plane very hard to spot from above, allowing the crew to skim the wave tops below both radar and normal fighter patrol flight levels. Third, the plane was painted with a standard American-style identification on the tail with a combination of numbers and letters. Finally, painted on either side of the fuselage was a large smiling dolphin. Anyone seeing the floatplane from the beach or near a harbor would assume it to be some tourist flight or private aircraft and suspect nothing.

"You have given us quite a few targets, men," Diedrich said. "Several of these freighters are traveling directly into the paths of one of our boats. By sunset or soon after, there will be more wreckage littering the Outer Banks of the… North Carolina. Get some rest, gentlemen. Tonight, I want you to sortie back to your patrol area and observe the kills."

Michner was never as comfortable with night missions as he was with morning ones. On pre-dawn flights, he and his crew would end their mission in daylight. However, in these early evening sorties, they left the ship in daylight and had to come back in darkness.

Somehow, this left the young pilot with a vague sense of unease. Because of the distances involved and the length of the missions, the plane rarely landed with more than fifteen or twenty minutes of fuel remaining.

It meant that on night missions, the three men in their small aircraft had to fly two hundred miles out to sea in darkness. There was a sense then of the true vastness of the ocean, and it seemed to underscore how lonely and fragile they and their little airplane really were. And they had to find their ship in all of that vastness.

On those nights, especially when there was little or no moon, five hundred feet of length didn't seem nearly large enough. A ship by itself operating in unfriendly waters. Suppose the Americans had found her? Suppose some British vessel coming from Bermuda stumbled across the *Blanch* and figured out what she really was and sunk her. It would mean that Michner and his two young crewmates would be flying into a darkness that would claim them forever.

Michner watched as the last sliver of sun slid below the ocean, the finger of golden light that connect it to his ship suddenly vanishing. Although flying directly into the setting sun made things a little difficult, the German pilot was sorry to see it go.

"We are nearing our waypoint, Brenner," Schultz, the co-pilot and navigator, reported. He held his chart unfolded across his lap and was tracing a line with a pencil. "Recommend we slow to minimum airspeed and come to a heading of … zero-three-zero."

Michner smiled. Schultz was a good navigator. He could already see the coast of North Carolina in the distance. Technically it would be Cape Hatteras and the other islands, but it was land all the same. Solid Earth and this eased Michner's unspoken apprehensions nearly to nothing.

He throttled back, reducing the aircraft's speed from nearly maximum, about a hundred and eighty knots, down to eighty. This was fifteen knots over her stall speed. A comfortable margin and it would also allow Hans to make more accurate and detailed observations.

Almost immediately, Michner spotted lights on the horizon. Their first target for the evening was right where it was supposed to be. A large freighter they'd spotted off the Cape Fear River that dawn. She'd traveled the hundred miles Hans had estimated it would go during the day. The ship would be in Virginia waters very soon. And it was also running straight into the razor-sharp teeth of a man-made shark known as U-123, a Type IX Submarine commanded by Reinhard

Hardegen. Even Michner, a Navy flyer, knew of Hardegen's reputation. The man was bold, highly skilled and ruthless.

Again, the young pilot felt his nervousness increase. Why was that? It certainly wasn't fear for themselves. Even after two months of this operation, the Americans simply weren't responding in any definitive way. No air cover, no escorts, or at least none to speak of. Even now, with twilight still visible off his port wing, Michner could see the lights of the North Carolina coast. And the freighter they were now approaching was glowing like a carnival in the oncoming darkness.

If not personal fear…, was it fear for his crew? No, that made no sense either. If he wasn't in danger, then Hans and Gunther weren't either. So why was he so keyed up?

The freighter, its name unknown, was growing larger very quickly. Moving at eleven knots, the ship was getting a mile closer every minute, thanks to the aircraft's seventy-knot overtake rate. She was a large vessel, perhaps larger than the Q-ship Michner served on. A freighter of perhaps ten or twelve thousand tons fully loaded. There were possibly thirty or forty men aboard… and passengers?

And they were all about to die.

Suddenly, Michner knew what was bothering him. What had been bothering him for weeks now. Tonight was the first time he'd actually *observe* a U-boat operation. The first time he'd watch from the safety of the air as the most dangerous predator in the sea made a kill.

The ship had no chance, and the people aboard would probably not survive. If the ship could launch life rafts, perhaps. The vessel wasn't more than a dozen miles from the coast, after all. Yet the U-boats, and Hardegen in particular, were efficient. They fired spreads of torpedoes. Several for a target the size of the American vessel below. That meant that there was a good possibility that at least one would strike the ship's boilers… and if that happened, the resulting explosions would blast the ship into chunks, and no one could survive that.

"I'm beginning a clockwise orbit, Hans," Michner reported calmly, none of his inner misgivings finding outward expression. "I'll keep the vessel to starboard. I expect an attack any time now, so keep vigilant."

An unnecessary suggestion. Hans knew his duty and did it well.

Michner turned to the west and then banked the aircraft to starboard, putting it into a slow turn that would circle the slow-moving ship five-thousand feet below.

"Can you get us lower, Bren?" Hans asked. "It's getting dark, and I'd like to get a closer look."

"Little danger of even being spotted now," Gunther put in, anxious to watch himself.

Michner nodded and descended to fifteen hundred feet. The big cargo ship was off their starboard beam now, looking large at the lower altitude and glowing with running and steaming lights as well as illumination for the deck. It was almost too much light. Michner worried that it would affect his night vision.

They had red-tinted goggles aboard for just that situation, yet they would make spotting unlit objects that much harder. It was still dusk, and some ambient light remained, so night-blindness from the white lights of the ship was not yet a problem.

"Submarine!" Hans shouted excitedly. "Three o'clock, perhaps two miles seaward of the freighter!"

Instantly the tension in the aircraft mounted. Hans had his clipboard ready, and Gunther pulled a small eight-millimeter motion-picture camera from under his seat and uncapped the lens. He then swung his window open, filling the cabin with a light breeze. It was neither a windstorm nor extremely loud, the design of the aircraft allowing for this type of observation at lower speeds without much discomfort. It meant, though, that now sound would be added to the sensory experience they were all about to witness.

Michner continued his slow wide arc, the bow of the freighter now pointed directly at the plane from two miles away. He could clearly see the long narrow shape of the submarine running on the surface straight for the freighter. Even in the dying light, her foaming wake was still visible, stretching out behind the low and deadly shape.

"My God!" Hans breathed, scribbling furiously. "How do they not see—"

From below, an alarm began to blare. Some lookout on the freighter had finally spotted the onrushing U-boat. It was too little, too late, however.

"Torpedoes in the water!" Hans all but shrieked. "I can see their bubbles! Get us closer, Bren!"

Brenner tightened his turn and made sure to keep the scene in view for his two observers. The freighter seemed to be turning, yet this was just an illusion brought on by the float plane's own movement. Michner himself could now see the three bubble trails rapidly closing the distance to the large starboard side of the big freighter.

Then it came.

The first impact took the form of a geyser of water along the ship's starboard bow. The column of water rose a hundred feet in the air and was eerily lit by orange light from the explosion. It wasn't until the second torpedo hit amidships that the thunderous fuh-*boom* of the first impact reached the aircraft. The second hit was less spectacular, raising a red-lit bulge along the ship's side. Now the freighter was turning, her helmsman having thrown the wheel hard to port. Yet it was a useless act of desperation.

Even if the first two torpedoes didn't sink the ship, and that was possible by sealing watertight compartments on a ship over five hundred feet long, the attacking U-boat had more ammunition and could even use its deck gun. With no escort and no defense, the freighter was doomed no matter what happened.

That was all moot, however. As the three men watched, Hans and Gunther whooping in exultation at the two hits, the third torpedo struck, and this time the impact was beyond spectacular. A bright white-orange flash, a monstrous tongue of flame that reached far up into the night sky and a thunderous boom whose shockwave rattled the small airplane.

"My God!" Michner breathed in amazement and horror.

The fireball expanded and even in the darkness, the light from the fire and explosion clearly illuminated the tons of debris hurtling into the sky. Bits of metal, pipes, globs of burning fuel and bodies soared hundreds of feet into the air. The ship suddenly broke apart, its bow and stern separating, tilting and rolling in a horrifying display of physics.

"She broke in two..." Hans said, his elation long forgotten.

Gunther continued to film, holding the camera in a death grip and unable to turn away from the carnage below. What was left of the stern fell onto its side and then plunged downward and out of sight with shocking swiftness. The bow, the larger of the two halves, tilted slowly skyward, pointing upward and starting to slide down with almost agonizing slowness. As if the great ship was resigned to dying with some dignity.

Michner descended much lower to a hundred feet over the sea and began to circle the wreckage in a tight arc that tilted the aircraft so far over that Gunther and Hans were looking almost straight down at the scene.

A huge oil slick coated the surface of the sea, dotted with debris. As the pilot circled, they saw the U-boat closing in. Men on the bridge and on deck waved at the airplane.

"Any sign of survivors?" Michner asked Hans.

There was a long pause. Very long. Michner had completed a full circle before his observer finally answered in a sepulchral whisper: "None Lieutenant… no survivors."

Yes, their beloved Deutschland was at war with America. Yes, the three young men were officers, and it was their duty to fight their fatherland's enemies. To win glory for the homeland and for the Reich they served.

Yet what they'd just witnessed didn't feel like glory. Those people weren't soldiers or American Navy sailors. They were civilians delivering bolts of fabric, auto parts, canned beans, toilet paper or who knew what to some distant New England port or other. They were, by the rules of war, legitimate targets… but they didn't *feel* like enemies to Brenner Michner.

He didn't feel like a hero. He suddenly felt hollow and depressed. He felt dirty.

"Course to our next… our next target, Gunther?" Michner asked flatly.

Gunther put his camera away, having seen more than enough and consulted his charts. He cleared his throat, "Come to course zero-two-zero. Suggest increasing speed to one-hundred and twenty knots. That should put us off the southern Virginia portion of Chesapeake Bay in an hour or so. We have one more observation to make before returning to the ship."

Michner climbed back to five thousand feet and increased his speed. The three men would say nothing over the next hour. There was little to say. Each man was alone with his thoughts, and that suited Brenner Michner just fine.

4

NEW LONDON SUBMARINE BASE, NEW LONDON, CT

FEBRUARY 19, 1942

0430 ZULU

I t had been a long flight and Turner felt drained. Although the specially equipped C-47 had been comfortable, with plush seats, bunks and even a small galley, it had still taken over twelve hours of flying to cross the country. All Turner wanted was to climb into a rack and get some shut-eye, but that was apparently not to be just yet.

The only thing Webster Clayton would talk about on the long flight regarding *why* Turner was on this flight was that Admiral Dick Edwards, ComSubLant, would fill him in when they arrived. He did mention that the new boat, soon to be christened the USS *Bull Shark,* SS-333, was nearing completion, that officers and crew were already assigned, and that Turner would attend, if possible, an abbreviated version of PCO, or Prospective Commanding Officer School. He did have a few revelations that Turner, Dutch and Rogers were very interested to hear about.

The four men were sitting sipping coffee around a small collapsible table in the aircraft's passenger compartment when Clayton dropped a bomb on them.

"The Mark 14 torpedo is defective," the government man came right out and stated as he lit a cigarette.

The three Navy men exchanged looks, and Turner frowned at Clayton, "What do you mean, exactly?"

"We've been receiving reports about this torpedo since before the war," Clayton explained. "But the old, gun-club Admirals and the Bureau of Ordnance refuse to acknowledge the problems. You didn't miss, Art. Your torpedoes were defective."

"That's what I've been tryin' to tell you for weeks now," Dutch put in.

"Can you be more specific, Mr. Clayton?" Paul Rogers asked. "As the chief of the boat, it's my job to make sure everything runs smoothly."

Clayton sighed and leaned back in his chair, "First off, the torpedo runs too deep. They were tested with dummy warheads, of course. Well, the dummy warheads make the fish more buoyant than when they've got nearly seven hundred pounds of torpex in the warhead. They tend to dive under their targets."

Turner scowled but said nothing. He saw Dutch and Rogers nod in understanding.

"Second," Clayton went on, "the torpedoes can prematurely detonate. This seems to happen on a longer run when the fish takes a while to angle onto a target. Further, there's the contact exploder that often fails to ignite the initiating charge that detonates the main charge."

"Jesus Christ…" Rogers breathed.

"Why in the hell is BeauOrd sending these shitty fish to sea with us, then?" Dutch asked in horror. "How the hell do we win a war if our own damned weapons don't work?"

Clayton scoffed, "Exactly. They also sometimes veer off course into a circular run. However, there's a major problem with the 14 that, when corrected, mostly fixes the others. The Mark 6 magnetic influencer exploder mechanism *doesn't work.*"

The submariners knew all about the Mark 6 exploder. It was a version of something both the Germans and the British had developed and, in theory, was brilliant. A next-generation weapon that could be a war winner… if it functioned.

The idea was simple. As a steel-hulled ship traveled through saltwater, it generated a magnetic field. The Mark 14's depth would be set to run under the keel of the target ship, and it would home in on the magnetic field once close. Upon reaching the target, the warhead would detonate directly under the ship's keel.

Since water didn't compress to any measurable degree, the entire force of the explosion was driven straight up and into the ship, blasting it open and breaking the ship's back. Theoretically, only a single torpedo would be needed to sink something even as large as a battleship.

"The problem is that the Mark 6 simply doesn't function as designed," Clayton stated. "At least nine out of ten times. My people believe that one major problem is that the system doesn't account for the Earth's own magnetic field... it can't tell the difference. So we've developed a workaround. The magnetic exploder is disabled and the torpedo simply relies on its contact exploder. Our secret tests reveal that if you do this and set the depth much shallower than you otherwise would, the torpedo works most of the time. You still get a few duds, and there's still a small chance for a circular run... but otherwise, it's a good weapon."

"Okay," Turner stated, grabbing a cigarette from Clayton's pack on the table. "Good to know... but as I understand things... any skipper or officer or leading crewman who tampers with the Mark 6 is liable to a general court."

Dutch and Rogers both groaned.

Clayton lit another smoke and sighed, "Unfortunately true... but it won't be for you. You and your boat will be given... special dispensation. A part of the mission we want you for, admittedly a secondary goal, is to prove that the modified Mark 14 works. To force it down the old, gun-club boys' throats. We need to arm our submarine captains in the Pacific with a weapon that works, because right now the submarine is about to become our most powerful and effective weapon against the Imperial Japanese Navy."

Turner could see that, "Very good, Web. I'm glad to hear it."

That had been about the extent of what Clayton would tell them. When they arrived in Connecticut, Dutch and Rogers were assigned accommodations in the BOQ and BEQ, respectively. Turner was rushed into a car, driven over to admin and hustled into a large and comfortable office decorated in nautical brass and teak. A medium-height and burly man in his mid-fifties met Turner and Clayton as they walked in. Rear Admiral Richard Edwards, Commander Atlantic Submarine Fleet, wore only working khakis. His close-cropped salt and pepper hair matched an iron-gray mustache that framed an open smile.

"Captain Turner, welcome and congratulations," Edwards said. "Please have a seat. I trust Web here has briefed you?"

"Not quite, sir," Clayton replied. "I've talked to Turner and his men about the 14, but not the mission or the boat. I thought it would be better coming from you."

Edwards shook their hands and planted himself behind his desk again, "Christ, Web, it's nearly zero five-hundred. Captain Turner must be wiped out... well, I'll try to be brief, Captain. We'll have plenty of time to jaw while your boat is being fitted out and between classes at PCO school."

"Yes sir," Turner replied, as if he had any other option.

"Let's talk about your new boat first," Edwards said, sliding several photos across the desk. "She's based on the *Tambor* and the new *Gato*-classes. Same size, but a little heavier and with a few important modifications. For one, she's got a more streamlined conning tower. She's equipped with both SD air search and the SJ surface search radar system. New and improved hydrophones and sound gear, too. She's equipped with a snorkel system that lets you run diesels from periscope depth. She's got a five and a quarter deck gun, a Bofors quad cannon and the dual 20mm Oerlikon that you're probably used to. Typical cigarette deck stations for fifty cals and the like. However, it's what's below decks and the structure of the boat itself that's really interesting. New higher strength and thicker steel gives her a test depth of about four-fifty. Your particular boat will be fitted out with General Motors diesels and General Electric motors. Very powerful and very reliable. Your TDC is also top-notch."

"As I understand it, sir," Turner said, "this class of boat isn't even supposed to come into service for another six or seven months."

"Correct," Edwards said. "*Balao* is the official class ship. But yours, the *Bull Shark,* is going out… under the radar, you might say. Literally and figuratively. You'll be doing a lot on the mission I have for you, Captain. Not the least of which is testing the new boat and proving those goddamned Mark 14s are shit unless we rig 'em. We clear?"

"Yes sir."

Edwards drew a deep sip from a large white coffee mug, "Your boat is scheduled for sea trials by mid-March. As with all new captains, you're going to spend every available minute over at Groton learning her systems and overseeing the final construction. You're also going to spend every *other* minute in the attack trainer here at New London. Somewhere in that impossible schedule you'll spend time with your wife and kids and socialize with your officers and me."

"Looking forward to it, sir," Turner replied with a wry grin playing on his lips.

Edwards chuckled, "It's gonna be a ball breaker, son… but I think you can handle it. After you take *Bull Shark* out on a short shakedown, I'm sending you on a hunt. Web?"

"What do you know about the war against the Nazis?" Clayton asked.

Turner shrugged, "Not a whole lot… other than what you told me about Operation Drumbeat… my focus has been in the Pacific theater since the Japs bombed Pearl. I know the Nazis declared war on us not long after that, though. I know that German U-boats are, and have been, taking a toll on shipping headed for Great Britain."

"Well, Hitler and his dogs have expanded their scope," Edwards all but growled. "Those Kraut sons of bitches have come over here and are sinking *our* ships and right under our goddamned noses!"

Turner felt himself pale. The very thought was disturbing. America hadn't fought any kind of military operation in home waters since the War of 1812. Yet now, both Japan and Germany had attacked American shipping in American waters. He cleared his throat to ask a question, but the Admiral beat him to the punch.

"No, Captain… we aren't doing shit about it," Edwards stated angrily. "Admiral King isn't listening to the British. We're not organizing convoys, observing coastal blackouts or flying air cover. We've got a dozen DDs sitting in New York harbor doing *nothing!*"

"My God…" Turner breathed.

"Our intel is scant as of yet," Clayton put in. "We suspect at least half a dozen U-boats operating between Maine and Florida, and rumors have it that they're headed into the Gulf of Mexico, too."

Turner frowned, "Sir… I'm no expert on German U-boats, but most of them don't have sufficient range to come all the way over here, run a campaign and then go back."

"The Type IX does," Edwards said. "At least enough fuel and food to drive across the Atlantic and make a couple of cruises up and down the coast before going back. However, they don't have many of those and rely more heavily on the Type VIIs."

"Which does *not* have the range to do the job," Clayton said. "Which means that there are a couple of Milchkuh's… what the Germans call milk cows… operating over here and keeping the Type VIIs fueled."

"But that's not all," Edwards gently prompted.

Clayton sighed, "We've gotten bits and pieces of intelligence from merchant ships, aircraft and even one of our S boats that there's something else out there. This is a big operation, and it requires some organization on station."

"A command-and-control ship?" Turner asked.

"Got it in one," Edwards grinned.

"Precisely," Clayton stated. "We believe that there's something offshore, probably within a couple of hundred miles of our coast. A vessel that's directing and coordinating and possibly carrying extra ordnance, supplies and fuel as well."

"Probably within two hundred miles," Edwards observed. "Far enough out that we wouldn't notice and close enough in that they could send in aerial recon flights using a floatplane."

"Any idea of what kind of ship?" Turner asked.

Both men frowned and shook their heads. Edwards opined: "My guess would be a merchant vessel made to look like a friendly. If we did come across them, they could claim to be one of ours or an ally. A military ship would stand out too much. You know what a Q-ship is, Commander?"

"A non-combatant vessel used to gather intel or support covert military operations, I believe," Turner replied.

"Exactly," Edwards said. "Your job, Captain… is to find that son of a bitch and send him to the bottom."

"Cut off the head and the snake dies," Clayton added. "Or at least becomes far less venomous. We're calling it Operation Snare Drum… bit of a play on words, but why not? Good enough for Dönitz, it's good enough for us."

"You're also tasked to sink as many U-boats as you can," Edwards stated.

"The trick for you, Art, is going to be to not just *find* this Q-ship, but to make certain it is what we suspect it is," Clayton pointed out. "Wouldn't do to send a friend down to meet old Davy Jones now, would it?"

Edwards chuffed, "Don't worry about details now. We'll have time to go over this more thoroughly. Let me give you a quick rundown on your officers and leading crew."

Turner sipped his own coffee and leaned in. He was both excited and nervous about this. These two men were laying a heavy responsibility on him. He was getting an untested boat, an unknown crew… for the most part… and seeking a vague target. He only hoped he was up to the task.

"We're gonna show your weapons officer, COB and leading Petties in both rooms how to modify the fish," Edwards started. "Because of BeauOrd rules and regs, you're going to need to modify the exploders *after* leaving dock. Should you come in with any…"

"We put them back?" Turner asked. "What about the special dispensation?"

"That's in play," Edwards said. "No, don't return the fish to original specs. I *want* you to come back with modified fish to show how they can be altered and how effective they are. Hell, I'd love it if you shot all twenty-four at live targets and came back with none, naturally. But whatever you bring back, you leave rigged. Those gun-club jackasses are going to have to face facts sooner or later. You're covered, so don't worry about a court-martial."

"Aye-aye," Turner said with more confidence than he felt.

"Now, you've already got your comm officer," Edwards stated. "He's a good man, and I think you should keep him there even though he deserves a better post. Your new XO is a young guy, very capable but a little on the uncertain side. Elmer Williams is his name. You'll like him, and I think he'll like you. He knows his stuff, but he needs you to help him develop his grit. There's Lieutenant Frank Nichols, your engineering officer. Kind of quiet. He's a Navy reservist, but he knows his stuff. He's got a lot of promise. Masters in electrical and mechanical engineering from MIT. His assistant is an ensign named Andrew Post. He's quiet too, probably more than a little green but a sharp and personable fella. Finally, your torpedo and gunnery officer is a solid hunk of a man named Pat Jarvis. Served on S boats in the Med and a destroyer in the Atlantic. Let's see… you've already got your chief of the boat… your chief electrician, machinist and yeoman are all solid men. Fifteen to twenty years in the submarines. Now, you're leading petty officers in the rooms… Walter Murphy in the after room and Walter Sparks in the forward. Sparks is senior. They call him Sparky partly to differentiate the two Walters and partly because Sparks is a big loudmouth. He's very competent, and his bark is worse than his bite. You'll get to know all of this over the next few weeks."

"Aye-aye, sir."

"Well, I know you two gents are tired," Edwards said, stretching and cracking his back. "Why don't you get some shut-eye?"

"Sounds like good advice for you too, Admiral," Clayton said as the three men rose.

Edwards waved that off, "No rest for the wicked, Web. We'll talk again soon, Captain. Welcome to the Fleet."

5

ELECTRIC BOAT SUBMARINE YARD – GROTON, CT

MARCH 6, 1942

"Come on you guys! You gotta drag your heads outta your asses and onto this goddamned boat! These fuckin' fish ain't gonna *walk* down this loadin' hatch! Any of you greasy sons of bitches so much as scratches one of these Mark 14s, and I'll *personally* make sure the Old Man docks your pay! And that's *after* a swift kick in the ass from me!"

Joan Turner snickered uncontrollably. It was only partially at the uncensored words being shouted in a heavy Alabama drawl by a huge man standing on the *Bull Shark's* forward deck. Mostly though, it was the beet red blush on both her husband's and Paul Roger's faces. The idea that a genteel lady like herself was witness to such foul talk was simply *scandalous.*

"Oh, you think this is funny, huh?" Turner asked his wife with a crooked smile showing.

"You two boys," Joan said, reaching out and patting the two men between whom she stood. "I'm a sailor's wife. You think this is the first time I've heard a man swear? Hell, you should hear how we wives and sweethearts talk when you boys are out playing with your big toy."

Paul Rogers laughed, "You're one in a million, Joanie. So what do you think of our new toy?"

"She's a beaut, Buck," Joan replied.

In truth, the submarine was a study in chaos and looked rather hideous with hoses and cables running to and from her deck and along it. There were welding arcs shooting great showers of sparks into the winter air, the clang of hammers, the whir of industrial drills and the shouts, curses and laughter of men practically tripping over each other to get the boat ready for sea.

Beneath the industrial harshness, however, the lines of the new submarine were clean and proud. At three hundred and eleven feet long and twenty-seven feet across at her widest point, the ship was long and lean. Her pressure hull was sixteen feet in diameter, and a long, slightly sloping wooden deck was mounted to her topside. Amidships, the angular conning tower rose, surrounded by an elevated deck, known as the cigarette deck. At the forward end of this platform was the small bridge. Mounted abaft the bridge were the periscope sheers, the radio mast, the SD and SJ radar masts and the snorkel.

Perhaps the most dominant features on the upper deck were the five and a quarter-inch stainless steel deck gun mounted forward of the conning tower along with the 40mm Bofors quad-barrel cannon, known colloquially as the Pom-Pom and the Oerlikon twin-barreled 20mm cannon. The Pom-Pom was mounted on a semi-raised blister forward and below the bridge and aft of the deck gun. The smaller anti-aircraft weapon was mounted and accessed at the after end of the cigarette deck. All in all, a formidable armament for a submarine.

Her main weapons, though, were the six forward and four aft torpedo tubes. Both of these rooms had loading hatches which were currently open. Cranes were even then lowering a torpedo into both hatches, and it was the petty officer in charge of the forward room, Walter "Sparky" Sparks, who was bawling his gang out as a torpedo eased down into the compartment below.

"Beautiful?" Turner asked. "She will be once the mess is cleaned up and she gets her paint job."

"Well, she is," Joan insisted. "A sort of… savage beauty, though. Like a lioness crouched in the high grass watching a herd of water buffalo meander by. Waiting to cut one from the group and take it down."

Rogers chuckled, "Pretty apt, Joan."

"I see you're showing off our new boat, Skipper," Joe Dutch commented as he strolled up to the edge of the dry dock where the three stood watching the show slightly below them.

"Hi Joe," Joan said. "Has May arrived yet?"

"I'm actually due to pick her up at the train station," Dutch replied. "Just gonna ask the captain for permission to retrieve Mrs. Dutch."

Turner chuckled and patted him on the shoulder, "Just can't wait, huh, Joe?"

The younger man beamed, "We've only been married six months, Art… you know how it is…"

Joan again snickered as Dutch's face took on a red hue. She reached out and put an arm around his waist and squeezed, "Good for you, Joey. She's a lucky gal."

"Thanks, Joanie," Dutch replied. "If she feels half as lucky as me, then we're in tip-top shape. You met the new officers and chiefs yet, sir?"

"Nothing more than a hi and a handshake," Turner admitted. "But Joanie found a great seafood place here in town and has reserved a room. All the officers and wives are dining together at nineteen hundred tonight. Give us a chance to get to know Nichols, Jarvis, Post and our new XO, Elmer Williams. It's only been a few days since we've gotten here, and it's been practically round the clock for everybody. I don't even know any of the chiefs except for Buck here."

"I've met them all," Rogers said.

As chief of the boat, or COB, it was his job to coordinate the entire crew and oversee them. COB was a unique position found only on submarines. More than an enlisted man and not quite an officer, the COB was a vital link between the officers and the men. Although on a submarine, this line of demarcation was so blurred at times it was practically invisible. Yet when it came to sensitive matters among the men, or a minor disciplinary action, the COB would usually handle things quietly and effectively. He was the man that everybody, officers and enlisted alike, turned to with their problems. Albeit different *sorts* of problems.

"What're they like, Buck?" Joan asked.

Rogers shrugged, "Harry Brannigan, he's our chief electrician in charge of the maneuvering room, is a quiet guy. Pushing forty and really knows his business. Then there's Mike Duncan, chief machinist, knows diesel engines in and out. Got special training at GM just for ours, in fact. Could take them apart and put em' back together again, and they'd get a hundred more rpm. He's pretty young to wear the chief's hat, though. About Mr. Dutch's age. Kind of tall and wiry but strong as an ape. He's been an engine snipe since he was eighteen and knows the job. He takes care of his engines and his men. A bit like Sparky there. A lot of bark but a mild bite. Chief yeoman is a guy named Clancy Weiss. Haven't met him yet. Jewish fella… hope that won't be a problem."

"Not for me," Turner said with a shrug. "Never served with a person of the Jewish faith before but doesn't make any difference to me. It better not to the men, either. We're at war now, and the Navy, and a submarine in particular, has no room for bigotry."

Joan smiled at her husband.

"Agreed, sir," Rogers said. "And since we've got no less than three black cooks coming aboard, plus six Hispanic crewmen, a couple of kids with German last names and a Navaho Indian no less, we'll be a melting pot."

That was no surprise. America herself was a melting pot, so it made sense that her Navy would also be. Of course… there were no Japanese-Americans serving. That was one line that wasn't being crossed since Pearl Harbor. Already there was talk of segregating any Japanese living in the United States, either immigrants or who were born there, into detention camps for the course of the war. It was a terrible thing to contemplate, yet the feeling of outrage after the surprise attack at Pearl was still a fresh and very raw wound.

Contrarily, however, as with all wars, there were those who opposed America's fight with either Germany or Japan. War protestors were calling it Roosevelt's War. Turner found it more than a little ironic.

The United States was savagely attacked without warning from a nation that had not declared war. Well, said the detractors, we were impeding their trade and strangling their oil supply. The Nazis had invaded Poland and were already in a death match with Britain. They'd rounded up millions of Jews and had them in forced labor and concentration camps. Rumors were already spreading about the gas chambers.

Well, said the detractors, that was Europe's problem. Nobody told America to stick its nose in where it wasn't wanted. The true irony was that in neither Japan nor Germany would any vocal dissention be allowed. Should a citizen speak out against his or her country's actions, they could be fined, jailed or even put up against a wall and shot for daring to express an opinion that didn't perfectly jive with Hitler's or Hirohito's.

In Turner's view, that was one of many reasons that America would win this war. That America had right on her side. Because her military utilized the nation's diversity. Although the country had a long way to go when it came to how whites viewed other ethnicities, things were changing, and the war was accelerating that change.

In a nation where most southern states still practiced open racism… where a black man or woman wouldn't dare drink from a "white" water fountain or sit at the counter in a diner next to whites or even deign to ride in the front of a bus… black sailors were treated more as equals.

The U.S. Navy no longer practiced segregation. It wasn't Shangri-La by any means, of course. Black sailors and soldiers still did most of the jobs that nobody else wanted. Cooks, janitors and dangerous munitions manufacturing and loading. Yet, the Navy had taken the lead when it came to treating black men the way they should be treated.

Many black sailors fought to enter the submarine service because there they were truly treated as equals. Even more than that, black men in the submarine service received the same intensive training as the white sailors. All of *Bull Shark's* black cooks were also trained in electrical, mechanical and auxiliary systems. They would be trained on radio operations, sonar gear as well as helm and diving plane systems. They would be taught how to handle torpedoes and the deck guns. At any stage of an operation, either of the black cooks or the black baker might have to steer the ship or fire a gun or take over a torpedo room. And the black sailors on a new boat were among the first to earn their silver dolphins, a mark of eminent distinction that told all the world that they were fully sub qualified.

It was this cross-training and nonstop policy of education that made submariners the most highly skilled warriors in the Fleet and created such a strong brotherhood and sense of family. That closeness was what would help the United States play catch up in this global war and allow them to defeat two powerful enemies fighting them on two gigantic fronts.

Suddenly Joan shivered and hugged herself. She reached out and took Turner's hand, "My God... this is really happening, isn't it? I mean, we're really at war with the entire world..."

Dutch excused himself so that he could meet his new wife's train and Rogers drifted off to go over to the boat and monitor the activity a little more closely.

Turner pulled Joan up close against his side, "Well... we're at war across the world, but not with all of it."

Joan sighed, "I know... it's just the *scale*, Art. Thirty years ago, we had the Great War. The war to end all wars. Now they're calling it World War One. Know what that means? That this is World War *Two!* Sometimes it's hard for me to comprehend. And then you shove off on a war patrol like you did in December... and it's suddenly very real."

Turner sighed, "I know, honey... but it's not like I've never shipped out before."

"During peacetime," Joan pointed out, although not with rancor. "There was no real sense of danger. But for Christ's sake, Art... your first wartime patrol on *Tautog* and you were depth-charged. I know you said it was just a couple... but..."

"It's war, baby," he said softly, kissing the top of her head. "It's big and scary, and who knows what's going to happen... but we're in it now. Maybe this one is just a continuation of the first one. At least for Germany. I don't know. I don't have a handle on the broad geopolitical situation. I'm just a bubblehead who likes driving submarines. I'm just a guy who wants to do his part."

"I know… and I'm very proud of you," Joan said quietly. "Art… are you scared?"

Turner drew in a deep breath. He wondered how much he should admit to her. Was it his job to hide his feelings and be strong so as not to burden her and increase her fears? Or should he be honest and share the burden with her?

"I am," he admitted. "There are a lot of unknowns. Two intractable enemies who want to destroy us… but I'm also angry, Joan. I'm angry at the Japanese for what they did. Yeah, I know their excuses. But you talk, you deal… you don't sneak up on unsuspecting people and bomb the shit out of them. You don't fire on women and children going to *church*, for Christ's sake… Hirohito and Tojo want an empire and we got in their way. They wanted a fight and I intend to give them one. As for Germany… same thing. Hitler wants to conquer the world, for God's sake… he says his people are the *master race* and that their rightful place is to rule over us all. And I believe the rumors… they're abusing and murdering Jewish people, Joanie… they must be stopped."

"And you want at 'em," she said with a half-smile playing at her lips. "You're not just scared and mad… you're excited, too."

He nodded, "I guess I am. I finally get to put my training to use. I'm a little worried for me… but mostly what scares me is leaving you and Arty and Dotty alone. Every second I'm out there, I'm fighting for you guys. Not just to keep you safe, but to make sure that I get to come home to you."

"Good," she whispered. "You keep that in mind, Arthur Turner. I don't have the time or the patience to break in a new husband. I've finally gotten you trained after nine years."

He laughed, "Yes ma'am."

———

"Griggs!" Sparky Sparks shouted to a skinny second class torpedoman standing by the forward torpedo loading hatch. "What the hell are you doin'?"

Griggs, barely twenty and on his first assignment to a submarine, jumped visibly, "Uhm... nothin', Sparky."

"Exactly," Sparky drawled quieter but no less menacing. "Get your skinny ass down that hatch and help stow that last fish. We got eleven more we gotta put away before supper, and it ain't gonna happen with you standin' around scratching your nuts."

"Pretty hard on these boys, huh, Sparky?" Buck Rogers asked as he sauntered up beside the burly torpedoman.

Rogers was six feet tall and broad in the shoulders with a well-muscled frame. Even as large as he was, though, he didn't quite match Walter Sparks in size. An inch or so shorter than Rogers, Sparks was a good thirty pounds heavier and had biceps as large as some men's thighs. He'd been a shrimper out of Mobile before joining the Navy after high school and was not only a good seaman, but he understood how to lead men. Sparks knew how to walk the line between scary and caring in a way that Paul Rogers had never seen before.

Sparks grinned and winked at Rogers, "Hell, Buck, you gotta ride these kids every damned minute. Good for 'em. They think I'm a hard-ass now, just wait until we go to battle stations."

"They don't have to love ya, but they will fear ya, huh Sparky?" Rogers teased. He'd only known the other man for a few weeks, but already they were becoming fast friends.

"Shit no, COB," Sparks drawled and then laughed. "They're gonna do *both* fore I'm done."

"How you getting along with Murph?" Rogers asked.

Sparks shrugged, "Good guy. We've served together before. Different styles. In my book, he's way too soft on the boys... but he runs a good room, and they get the job done. I ain't criticizing."

"Glad to hear it."

Sparks looked over the boat's starboard side to where the Turners were standing tightly against one another and watching the proceedings aboard the ship.

"Now you tell me about this Old Man," Sparks said quietly. "Way I hear it, he ain't even gone through PCO School. Was the XO on a boat outta Pearl and got gun decked onto this boat and now we gotta do a Chinese fire drill to get her floated. What're we in for, Buck?"

"I've known him since he was an ensign," Rogers said. "We served together on a destroyer and on the S48, an old S boat. He's a cool cucumber, Art Turner. Keeps his head, knows his business and has an easy-going way about him. He's quick to praise and slow to bitch. He runs things tight, and so long as you follow the rules and do your best, he's a good man to serve under. You fuck up too much, though, and he'll plant his foot up your ass."

Sparks nodded thoughtfully, even approvingly, "Okay… but can he *fight*, Buck? I heard his only war patrol he fired three fish at a Jap mine layer and missed with all of 'em."

Rogers chuffed, "You haven't gotten the word yet, then?"

Sparks narrowed his eyes, "What word?"

Rogers chuckled, "The 14 is defective. Mostly the Mark 6 exploder is. BeauOrd has a big hard-on for these fish, Sparky, but some of the big wigs believe the rumors and the practical results. We got orders from Big Dick himself to disconnect the magnetic feature and use the contact exploder only. *That's* why Art Turner missed, not because he can't shoot."

"Jesus Christ…" Sparky muttered. "And the fuckin' Navy is sending us out to fight Japs and Krauts with these fucked up pickles?"

Rogers laughed, but this time it was sardonic, "You know the Navy, Sparky. There's two ways to do things… the right way and the Navy way. Fortunately for us, though, Admiral Edwards has seen the light. We're going out with this new fancy boat for a special mission of some sort, and he wants to make sure we get the job done. You, me and Murph are gonna receive special training on the fish."

Sparks looked incredulous, "You shittin' me, Chief? Break BeauOrd regs and commit a court-martial offense?"

"You heard me say Big Dick gave the word, right, Sparky?" Rogers asked. "The Old Man will take total responsibility."

Sparks cast a quick glance at where the Turners had been standing. They'd moved off arm in arm. He shrugged his shoulders, "Well, hell, Buck… I'm workin' Navy. I go where the officers tell me to and do what they tell me to do… only better."

Rogers clapped him on the shoulder, "That's the spirit, Sparky.

Now, after the shift is over, you, Murph, Harry, Mike and me are gonna head outta these gates and pound a few back, whaddya say?"

"Sounds good, Buck," Sparks grinned. "If you're willing to pitch in and lend a hand loading out."

"Happy too, Sparky," Rogers said. "By the way... what do you hear about our other officers?"

"Between you and me?"

"Of course."

Sparky sighed, "Nichols is a feather merchant, but what I've seen and heard so far... he's solid. Smart as a whip and even-keeled. Ensign Post, he was gonna be the comm officer until Mr. Dutch showed up, he's second engine and commissary. Good kid... a little high-strung, I think. Though he does seem kinda... green. Jarvis... don't know him from Adam."

Rogers didn't miss the omission of the XO. He waited.

"Here comes another'n, boys!" Sparks bellowed down the hatch. "Hope you got an empty rack! Well, Buck..."

Rogers frowned as the two men watched the twenty-foot-long, thirty-three-hundred-pound Mark 14 torpedo swing out over the railing of the dry-dock and ease down toward the loading hatch. It was unusual for a boat to load weapons in Groton right in the shipyard. That was usually done once the boat was moored over in New London. But the Admiral wanted as much multi-tasked as possible, which meant twelve- and fourteen-hour days for the ratings.

"Walter," Rogers said earnestly, looking Sparks in the eye, "if there's something screwy about Lieutenant Williams... I need to know. Hell, the *skipper* needs to know."

Sparks bit his lip. For all his griping and grumbling and bitching about the officers, he respected the Navy and the chain of command. It galled him to speak ill of a man, especially one he didn't really know well.

Finally he resigned himself, "He's a good man, let's get that straight. Friendly, sharp and is more than willing to strip down to his skivvy shirt and pitch in with the hard work. Ain't a day goes by that he's not crawling around in the bilges learning valves and connections and shit. But he seems... unsure of himself. Guy I know was with the

S60, Williams's last boat, where he served as torpedo officer. He knows the job, and he knows everybody else's job too, Buck… but my buddy said he had a tendency to hesitate. Like he didn't trust his own judgement. Took way too long to plot an attack… and that was in training, for Christ's sake. What's he gonna do in a real fight? It's just… there are a lot of unknowns with this boat, Buck. All new everything. New crew, new officers, new skipper. Ain't a single one except Nichols and Post who have been here all the way."

Rogers drew in a deep breath and started to unbutton his winter blue shirt, "That's the Old Man's problem. He knows his business, but he also knows when to listen to the guys that know better. He says you drop your insignia at the gangplank, and you don't earn your dolphins until the department heads say you do… meaning us, Sparky. He's a good head, Captain Turner. If Williams needs a little seasoning, the skipper will see he gets it. And he'll see that we take him under *our* wings, too. Trust me."

Sparks grinned, "Okay, COB. I'm puttin' myself in your hands. Now let's get below and light a fire under these greenie butts."

6

Mama Flannigan's Seafood had been a staple in New London since the First World War. Located on the Thames River not far from where it emptied into the Atlantic and Long Island Sound, the restaurant featured a huge outdoor deck for summer dining and lots of large bay windows for the inside diners to enjoy the view, to watch submarines and other vessels coming in and out of the base. They could also look across the river and view the Electric Boat facility. Now dominating the view was the huge new steel truss bridge that was being built over the river and was supposed to open in less than a year.

In one corner of the restaurant, a small private dining room was opened, and a large rectangular table that bulged slightly on its long axis was set for ten guests. The room looked north and east and gave a wonderful view of the military facilities, the bridges and the wide Thames that sparkled with lights and the reflected moon. A fireplace crackled cheerfully along one wall, and along the shorter wall with the archway into the room, someone had set up an impromptu bar complete with a variety of liquors and a large ice bucket.

A small chandelier hung over the table, and its dozens of lights gleamed off the fine china and refracted beautifully on the stemware.

"This is *lovely*, Joan!" May Dutch emoted as she and her husband entered the room.

Hands were shaken and hugs exchanged. Turner grinned knowingly at his friend, "How was your trip, May?"

"Oh, just fine, Arty," May bubbled. She was a very pretty brunette with a slim petite form and a ready smile. "It's nice to get off the darned thing, though. I can't wait to sleep in a real bed tonight."

"Where's everybody?" Dutch asked.

"They'll be along," Joan said. "It's still a little before seven. Probably waiting on their girls, you know, Joey."

"How many other ladies are coming tonight, honey?" Turner asked his wife, the officer in charge of the event.

Joan grinned, "Well, I know Mr. Nichols is married… young Mr. Post has a sweetheart… Mr. Williams isn't accompanied… and I haven't been able to find out about Mr. Jarvis. So it's just four ladies against six men."

"We're outgunned, sir!" Dutch joked.

Just then, Frank Nichols and his young wife were shown in by the hostess. Nichols was a shortish man in his late twenties whose gold-rimmed cheaters seemed odd on a face that was chiseled and handsome. His wife was a somewhat shy girl about his size. A little on the plump side but pleasantly shaped. Her pretty and open face was set off by thick auburn hair and enormous green eyes. Introductions were made, and soon the Nichols' both held cocktails and wore bright smiles.

Next came Andrew Post and his date. Post was an athletic, medium-height man of twenty-three with short, curly blonde hair and boyish good looks. His date was as tall as he was, making her about five-foot-eight or so. She was blonde, pretty and buxom, and possessed an outgoing personality and charm that made her instantly popular.

The next guest to arrive was Patrick Jarvis. As Joan had indicated, he was alone, which was a surprise to the four women. Jarvis spoke with a strong Rhode Island accent. He was about thirty years old, six-foot-two, broad in the shoulders, lean in the waist and muscular. His jet-black hair was cut military-fashion, and his blue eyes peered out of a very handsome face. Jarvis' bright smile was an instant charmer to the four women and gave him an open and gregarious air. This was confirmed by his hearty introductions, friendliness and charming but respectful attention to the ladies.

Finally, Elmer Williams hurried in, rubbing his hands together and blowing on them. The late winter night had taken a cold turn and the temperature outside was no higher than thirty degrees.

"Our executive officer at last!" Turner said, coming forward and clasping Williams' hand.

"I hope I'm not late, sir," Williams said in a half-apology.

"Right on time, Mr. Williams," Joan said, stepping forward and taking his hand in both of hers. "It's a pleasure to finally meet you."

Williams was Turner's age and about Post's height but with a broader build approaching, but not quite reaching, plumpness. His wavy brown hair framed a round and handsome face that was open, honest and friendly. Final introductions were made, and everyone sat at the table to enjoy their cocktails and a thick lobster bisque brought in by the wait staff.

"How's everyone getting along with this rush to take our boat to sea?" Turner asked from the head of the table.

"I've been so busy with the boat, I haven't had much time for PXO School," Williams admitted. "It's amazing how fast the work is being done."

"Helps when the crew is loading ordnance and provisions while the final work is being done," Jarvis put in. "Kind of unusual… but then again, we're at war now and what's more unusual than that."

"Yeah, except for the old guard sub skippers and the higher-ups," Dutch added, "nobody really knows how a war should be run."

"On-the-job training, huh?" Post asked cheerfully and his date giggled.

"What I'd like to know," Nichols put in, "is how come Mr. Dutch here is our comm officer rather than Andy? Your seniority should put you in *my* place, shouldn't it?"

"Well," Dutch said, "I'm still fourth officer, so don't you boys forget it." "Besides, I hear a lot better than I tinker."

This got a polite laugh from everyone.

"Truth is," Turner stated, "Joe here has ears like a damned bat. I haven't met anybody I'd rather have on sonar. No offense to anybody else here… I don't know your skillsets well enough to compare yet."

Williams smiled, "Well, Skipper, you know how it is on a boat… we'll all get a chance to do the other guy's job soon enough. Isn't that right, Mr. Jarvis?"

"Goddamn well-told… oh, sorry ladies," Jarvis smiled sheepishly.

"Oh, hell, boys," April, Post's date put in, "we're none of us delicate flowers, here. From what I've learned about Joan, that's true. And me and May and June Nichols all know each other well. Don't hold back on our account, handsome."

That got another laugh from the table, and Turner was pleased. April would make a good officer's wife when and if she and Post got hitched. Jarvis bowed to her at the shoulders.

"Hey, it just hit me," Joan said. "We've got the whole spring season right here at this table! April, May and June!"

The laughter was more uproarious now. The talk flowed freely as the soup was removed and a salad and then appetizers were brought in. Dinner wound on until its inevitable ending around ten p.m.

At that point, the couples began to break away. Joe and May were anxious to get settled in, Post and April were beginning to make moon eyes at one another, and Frank Nichols and June were both beginning to yawn. The two bachelor officers said their goodbyes and left together, both having an early morning of it.

As Turner drove himself and Joan back to their quarters on the base, Joan slid across the bench seat and snuggled up to her husband for the chilly ten-minute ride. She sighed happily.

"Have a good evening, love?" he asked.

"Very nice."

"Me too. Thanks for setting that up."

"I like your officers," Joan said. "And the Spring Girls are terrific. Need to find somebody for that Jarvis, though. Elmer, too. I think he could use a woman's touch."

Turner half shrugged, "Well, from what I hear, Pat doesn't need any help in the lady department… although he doesn't' seem like a womanizer."

"I didn't get that impression either," Joan said. "But Elmer…"

She hesitated, unsure of how much to say. As usual, Joan had already plugged into the military wives' grapevine, and as usual, she knew more about the private lives of everyone around her husband than he did.

"Something on your mind, honey?" Turner prodded gently. "If you think it's important... I don't want to pry into my guys' lives... but like it or not, a submariner's private life affects the whole boat."

She nodded against his shoulder, "Well... it's just that Elmer *did* have a girl up until a couple of weeks ago. Guess his being busy at PXO School and all the extra work of getting the boat ready to sail... she broke it off. She said she felt neglected and didn't want to marry a man who was already married to his job."

Turner frowned, "Damn... they were engaged?"

Joan sighed, "Seems so. I don't know her, so I won't judge... from a woman's perspective, I can understand it. We all love a man in uniform, but we want that uniform hanging in our closets more often than not. Now with the war and everything... still... there *is* a war on...."

Turner squeezed her as he stopped at the guard gate to clear them through, "It's a young war yet, Joan. Your average American hasn't felt the sting of what it can be like. Give it a year, and if we're still fighting on two fronts, people will get it. There's going to be rationing, a lot of men volunteering... more being drafted... hell, a lot of American housewives and single girls are going to probably start doing 'men's work.' This war is going to change a lot of lives. You think Elmer is okay? How'd he take it?"

"Hard," Joan empathized. "Luckily, he's so busy he doesn't have much time to eat himself up... but I could see it in his face tonight at dinner. He's lonely and heartbroken. Just something to take note of is all."

"Poor guy," Turner stated as he parked. "Well, *Bull Shark* will be ready for sea trials in about a week. Maybe some sea air will do him good."

Joan suddenly shivered, "A week..."

"Not to worry, honey," Turner said as he got out and opened her door for her. "It'll be a quick couple of days to shake her down. Test the engines, fire a couple of dummy fish, run the electronics through their paces and the like. Probably less than a week cruising Long Island, Block Island and Nantucket Sound. Then back to the dock to fix what's wrong. Even when we go out for real, our station is New London, so I think the patrols won't be long."

"Still…" Joan said slyly, "it means I'd better take advantage of you while you're home, Captain Sir…"

Pat Jarvis and Elmer Williams didn't go right home after the introduction supper. Although it was true that they both would be up and on deck by zero-five-hundred, the two men had some drinking to do. Elmer Williams had hardly been able to scrape five minutes together to lament the loss of his fiancé, Margaret. Jarvis, being the son of a fisherman and a fisherman himself, not to mention always ready to perpetuate the hard-drinking Irish stereotype, had promised that he'd take Williams out for a good old-fashioned sorrow drowning.

The two men were in many ways as different as night and day. Where Williams was somewhat reserved, quiet and a little on the reticent side, Patrick Jarvis was boisterous, confident and quick-witted. Yet the two men were roughly the same age, the same rank, with Williams only beating Jarvis in seniority by a few months. They were both dedicated Navy men, loved the submarines and knew their business.

For Williams' part, he was drawn to Jarvis' strength and kindliness. Even if he did feel the other Lieutenant could be a bit *too* boisterous at times. For Jarvis' part, he was drawn to Williams' quiet Midwestern manner and felt a sort of big-brotherly feeling for Elmer, even though the two men were the same age.

After leaving Mama Flannigan's, therefore, the two bachelor sailors found themselves at Lucky's, a local dive not far from the base in New London. Predominantly a military hang-out, Lucky's was frequented by officers and enlisted alike with no barriers or restrictions on rank. The place was sort of a typical juke joint, with regular live music, a lot of single townie girls looking to hitch themselves to a man in uniform, plenty of pool tables, dart boards and a perpetual cloud of cigarette and cigar smoke.

Pat and Elmer sat at the far end of the long bar. They had a good view of the sultry-voiced and very sexy torcher singing up on the small stage. After a moment or two, a broad woman with heavy but pleasant features ambled up to them, slinging a bar rag over her shoulder, "Evenin' sailors. What'll you have?"

"Some good Irish," Jarvis said with a charming smile. "My pal here is celebrating."

Williams blushed.

"Oh yeah? Whatcha celebrating, handsome?" The bartender inquired.

"I'm... I'm not really," Elmer protested weakly. "My fiancé and I broke up a couple of weeks back."

"Oh, I'm sorry honey," The bartender, whose name tag said Betty replied kindly. "So your buddy here figures he'll drown your sorrows in some nasty old mick shit, huh?"

Jarvis snorted and clapped his hands together, "Kinda harsh, Betty. Nothin' beats a good Irish whiskey... or an Irishman drinkin' it!"

Betty chuffed, "I know you, Pat Jarvis... you think way too much of yourself."

"You know you wanna come across," Jarvis said in a pretty good Humphrey Bogart.

Betty laughed, "You couldn't handle it, squid boy."

"Jesus, Pat," Elmer said with a shake of his head as Betty moved off to get their drinks.

"She's a good egg," Jarvis said. "We tease each other all the time. Believe it or not, she went to school with my older sister. Known that broad most of my life."

"Not really a whiskey drinker," Elmer said.

Jarvis patted him on the shoulder, "So much to learn, young Williams. You're in the Navy now, son. Need to break you out of that Norman Rockwell, Indiana upbringing of yours. In the Navy, you drink hard, and you fight hard... and you love hard whenever you get the chance."

Elmer chuffed bitterly, "Tried that and it didn't turn out so well."

Pat sighed, "Yeah, I know, pal. But there's somethin' you need to remember… it's her loss. And I know it's hard to hear now, Elm, but you're better off this happened now. Madge couldn't handle a submariner's life. Better that you both learned that before you tied the knot. It's not easy on the lady you leave ashore."

Betty placed two low ball glasses filled with a semi-clear liquid and ice before the two men. She also set down two pints of Schlitz as well, "Enjoy, boys."

"All the more so as I stare at the back of ya' walkin' away, Betty," Pat said, hoisting his whiskey in salute.

Betty grinned and moved back down the bar, her ample but not displeasing backside swaying prominently as she did so.

"I guess you're right, Pat," Elmer said, taking a rather large sip from the smaller of his two glasses and coughing and wheezing a bit. "Christ!"

"Take it easy on that torpedo juice! You sip that stuff, Elm, don't pound it back. Give your pallet a chance to ease in, for Christ's sake! Ha-ha-ha! You know what you need?"

"Oh hell…" Elmer groaned good-naturedly.

"You need a fresh boarding action to… clear your pallet," Pat suggested. "I think that's mission number two tonight."

"Take it easy, Pat… one thing at a time."

"We'll see, m'lad, we'll see… hey, there's an open table, let's go over and shoot a little pool, whatdya say?"

Elmer agreed and the men moved their drinks over to a small side table next to the end of the first of the eight tables. Pat slid a dime into the coin catcher and the balls were released, "You wanna rack or break?"

"Break," Elmer said. "Figure anybody knows about handling balls, it's you, Patty."

Jarvis laughed uproariously, "That's the spirit… say, don't look now, Elmtree… but I think one of the local ladies might be giving you the old beady eye."

Elmer flushed beet red. This was one of those times when Jarvis' excess of personality began to reach Elmer's limits. It was as if he were of two minds. His reserved nature cringing and wanting to slip away…

and yet another part of him knew that this was exactly what he needed. He suspected that Jarvis, for all his easy-going and jovial nature, was far smarter about people than he let on. That the big, handsome man who seemed to fear nothing and never ran out of self-possession understood just how to play his new friend's psyche in order to help him heal. Elmer felt simultaneously mildly annoyed and grateful.

At least until he turned to see the woman Pat had indicated and nearly choked on the sip of whiskey he was taking. A pretty blonde slip of a girl had just placed her purse down on a table not ten feet away and was staring at him. He stared back and cursed the heat that steadily rose into his cheeks.

"Madge...?" he breathed.

Pat heard and looked at Elmer and then at the woman and scowled, managing to direct it down at the rack, "Oh *hell*..."

"Elmer?" Margaret asked. "What're you doing here?"

"Uhm... what're you doing here?" Elmer replied awkwardly.

"Just out for a drink," Madge said. "It's... it's nice to see you. Would you like to join me?"

"I..." Elmer didn't quite know what to say. Here was another person who produced mixed feelings in him.

"Well, well, well!" came a loud and somewhat inebriated sounding voice from the direction of the bar. "If it ain't wishy-washy Williams!"

Elmer's feelings were no longer mixed as he caught sight of the shortish stocky man moving toward them with two beers in his hands. He had no trouble identifying with the anger that suddenly rose up in him. Especially when he saw that the man in question set the two drinks down at the table where Margaret stood.

"Hey, Pendergast!" the new man bawled across the barroom. "Look who's here tonight! It's the luckiest son of a bitch in the submarine Navy!"

"I see you still haven't learned to keep your trap shut, Begley," Williams said sternly. Both he and Pat saw another man, this one about six feet tall and muscular, heading toward them from the bar as well with a short thickly built brunette in tow.

"Yeah, that's right, Elmer," Begley said. "And I'm still cleaning up after your messes, too. Fixing things you screwed up, ain't that right, Maggie?"

Maggie flushed, "Tom… don't."

"Well, raise my scope!" Pendergast announced as he approached with his date. "It's like old times, huh, Tommy? Me, you and Elmer here. Maybe you boys will let us play doubles on the table, huh? Be a nice *long* game, ladies. On account of old Elmer here takes his sweet time before he ever makes a move, ain't that right, Williams?"

"You're out of line, Mister," Pat snapped, stepping forward.

Pendergast scoffed, "We ain't on duty, pal, and this don't concern you."

"Oh boy… guess we're going to the brig tonight…" Jarvis muttered to himself, although not with any apprehension. Louder he said, "You know these two clowns, Elmer?"

"Sure he knows us," Begley said, gulping an inch out of his beer. "Served together on S60 out of Coco Solo, huh, Elmer? He was torpedo officer; I was chief engineer and Burt here was comm. Then wouldn't you know it, old Elmer here gets his step and sent to PXO School before either of us. Guess some guys get all the breaks no matter how bad they *fuck* up, right Elmer?"

"I see you still haven't learned any manners, Tom," Williams said tightly. "Not even with ladies present."

Pendergast's date's eyes were bright and excited. She didn't seem at all scandalized by the vulgarity. Margaret, at least, had grace enough to look abashed.

"Stop it, Tom," she admonished. "Let's not get unpleasant and ruin the night."

"Such a sweetie," Begley said, grabbing Margaret's hand and kissing it. "Not the kind of girl a man wants to let get away… oh, sorry, Elmer. Guess that might sound kind of insulting, huh?"

"I suggest you men take a walk," Jarvis said angrily. "I don't give a damn who you are or what your problem is. You're both a little drunk and letting your big mouths run away with you. Now beat it if you know what's good for ya'."

"Listen to this asshole," Pendergast blurted. "Fuckin' tough Yankee, huh?"

"Be happy to show ya'," Jarvis announced.

"Why don't you do as he says," Elmer said evenly. He looked at Margaret. "So this is what you want instead? A loud-mouthed loser."

"Who you callin' loser, shithead!" Begley snapped, shoving the table aside. "It weren't for you, I'd be in fuckin' PXO School now. You blew that exercise and cost us the war game and you're number two on some new boat? You torpedoed our careers, Williams, and there's some reckoning you owe us."

"You remember it however you want," Elmer shot back. "And you're right, Tom... I do owe you something. And if you and your idiot friend don't shove off, I'm gonna give it to you."

Begley's face went crimson and he swung for the fences. It was a typical punch from a man who didn't know what he was doing. A big haymaker right that was meant to knock a man's block off.

While Elmer Williams was a mild-mannered Indiana boy, he wasn't timid. He'd done some boxing in high school and college and he'd seen Begley's punch coming a mile away. Even as Margaret screamed, Elmer side-stepped and drove a hard straight left into Begley's eye, followed it with a right cross and a left hook into the man's neck and gut that sent him toppling backward, knocking over the table and the drinks set on it.

At the same time, Pendergast rushed at Pat. The big sailor grinned broadly, reveling in the action and welcoming pendergast's assault. He slipped a wild and unbalanced left from Pendergast, knocked away a short right and then drove his own right cross straight into the man's jaw. It snapped Pendergast's head back, opening him up for a series of short punches to his body. Jarvis' body blows hadn't traveled more than eight or nine inches, but they drove the air from Pendergast's lungs and drove the man to his knees and to the deck, where he curled up in a fetal position and tried to catch his breath.

Lucky's was not unused to such activities, not with a steady stream of sailors and Marines in the place each night. As such, Lucky's employed four bouncers, all of whom were big and brawny. They usually stopped any shenanigans before the shore patrol needed to be called.

By the time three of them arrived, the fight was over. Pat and

Elmer stood over the other two officers, who were on the floor nursing their various wounds and looking around dazedly. The brunette who'd accompanied Pendergast was eyeing Jarvis with an expression that could only be described as hungry. Margaret, on the other hand, was gathering her handbag and seemed to be in a huff.

"What happened?" one of the bouncers asked.

"Mild difference of opinion," Jarvis stated. "We think we're a couple of swell gents and these two jackasses did not agree."

"Guess you showed them," another bouncer said with a wry grin.

"Sorry about this," Elmer said in embarrassment. "Please tell the manager that we'll be happy to pay for any damages."

"You didn't have to hit him, Elmer," Margaret huffed.

"What're you kidding me?" the third bouncer asked in disbelief. "Honey, I saw and heard the whole thing. Your boyfriend there took a swing at this guy. Not to mention badgered the crap outta him. In my book, he got what he deserved."

"Had it comin', frankly," the first bouncer said. "Guy's a big mouth. Always has been."

"It was just an excuse to get even," Margaret said. "Because I chose Tom over *you*, Elmer."

Elmer stared at her in shock, "Madge…"

"Don't ever speak to me again!" Margaret said and stalked away.

"Wow… what a little…" the second bouncer began but caught himself.

After settling up with the bar for the broken table, Pat and Elmer left. As they stepped out into the cold night, Jarvis put a hand on his friend's shoulder.

"Nice moves," he said. "Sorry about Madge."

Elmer scoffed, "Guess you were right, Pat. Guess I'm better off."

"So what's the deal with those two turkeys anyway?"

"I don't wanna talk about it now."

Pat nodded, "Okay. For what it's worth, Elm… she traded down. You can do better."

Elmer drew in a breath and let it out slowly, "Still doesn't make it hurt less."

"I know, pal, I know... you'll feel better when you get a moving deck under your feet again."

The morning of March 13 was overcast but mild for a southern New England late winter day. The temperature had risen to the mid-forties and would get over fifty by the afternoon. A taste of the spring just around the corner.

The men, the officers and the spectators who had gathered to float *Bull Shark* out of her berth in dry dock number three all wore jackets and hats of some type. The sailors wore their dress blues and white covers, the officers wore their dress blues, which included coats and ties and billed caps. The civilians wore all manner of semi-formal clothing. Joan Turner and the Spring Girls, as they were now being called, wore heavy dresses with long overcoats, gloves and broad-brimmed hats.

Arthur Turner stood on the bridge with Elmer Williams at his side, and the other officers lined up on the cigarette deck to face the crowd. All seventy of the boat's sailors, with a few notable exceptions, lined the deck fore and aft and faced the crowd as well.

The exceptions were the line-handling party stationed at four points along the ship's port side. Their job would be to cast off the lines when ordered. Chief of the boat, Paul "Buck" Rogers, stood by near the periscope sheers to hoist the Stars and Stripes at the appropriate time. The other chiefs, Brannigan, Duncan and Weiss stood near the men at attention, their chief's hats, new for several of them, bright against the dull gray sky.

"*Stand by for flooding!*" came a disembodied voice over the yard's public address system. "*Commencing flooding in dock three. Line handlers, stand by to take in slack!*"

Several sets of electric motors began to hum, and from equidistant points along the dock's length, thick streams of icy Thames River water began to pour forth. Their half dozen flows, each as thick as a man's body, began to slowly fill the five-hundred-foot long, seventy-foot wide concrete hole and wouldn't stop until the level was equal to that of the river just behind the huge steel doors at the far end. It wouldn't stop until there was thirty feet of depth in the dock, giving sixteen feet of clearance below the new submarine's keel.

Everyone stood in silence as the roar of the water slowly climbed above the supports beneath the ship and then up her sides. There was a subtle shiver under Turner's feet as he felt the buoyancies equalize and the sixteen-hundred-ton submarine begin to float off the cradle from whence she'd been born.

"Vessel is afloat!" called Nichols, the engineering officer and diving officer.

A cheer rose up among the crew and the several hundred wives, sweethearts, friends, dock workers, sailors and officers watching. It wasn't over yet, of course. There was a lot to check on and test. It was a good start, though.

"Permission to go below and check hull integrity," Nichols asked Turner.

"Granted, Frank."

"Brannigan! Duncan! Float party, report to float test stations!" Nichols called out.

He, Post, the two chiefs and sixteen men separated themselves from the crew and went down the various deck hatches. Two men would be stationed in each compartment to visually inspect all through-hull fittings, manual vent and valve systems for the ballast and trim tanks, as well as other minor potential flooding issues. The officers and chiefs would make sure that the control systems that operated the planes and rudder, as well as the stuffing boxes where the two drive shafts exited the boat, were holding.

On the edge of the dock, eight men, two to a cleat, were slowly taking in slack on the portside mooring lines. Another party of eight men was doing the same on the other side of the dock. They would make certain that the boat stayed in the same relative position in the dock as the water level rose. As he watched, the long wide dock gangway began to level off from its angled-down position to the *Bull Shark's* main deck. It was more than halfway there, only tilting at a fifteen degree down angle now.

"*Bridge, Control*," Frank Nichols' voice called out from the tinny bridge speaker. "*So far, so good. Screw shafts dry, rudder and plane mechanisms dry. Stand by for compartment reports.*"

"Very well," Turner acknowledged, sounding a bit officious in his own mind, but he couldn't help himself.

"*Bridge, forward torpedo appears tight,*" came the first report from the leak party. The rest followed in quick succession. "*Forward battery tight... Control room tight... After battery tight... Forward engine tight... After engine tight... Maneuvering tight... After torpedo tight.*"

Turner and Williams exchanged broad smiles.

"*Bridge, Control,*" Nichols announced again. "*All compartments show green. No leaks detected.*"

"Very well, Enj," Turner replied. "Stand by to go off of shore power. We'll run on batteries only for the move."

"Skipper?" called Admiral Richard Edwards from the railing on the edge of the dry dock, which was now at the same level as the boat's bridge.

"We've got a sealed boat, sir!" Turner called over. "COB, hoist the colors!"

Edwards grinned and lifted a radio handset to his lips. His strong voice suddenly boomed out over the P.A., "*Now here this! As Commander Submarines Atlantic, it is my very great privilege to announce to one and all that the newest* Gato-class *diesel-electric submarine, the* USS Bull Shark, SS 333, *is ready to be commissioned. She'll be moved over to New London for final fitting out and I invite you all to attend the official christening and launch ceremony this afternoon at sixteen hundred hours! That's four p.m. to you civilians! Congratulations to the crew and to the folks here at Electric Boat for a very fine job well done!*"

The announcement that the new boat was a *Gato*-class rather than the second in the experimental and not even ready to commission *Balao*-class was a subtle security protocol. In truth, the *Balao* herself, which wasn't even being built at EB but at the Portsmouth Naval Yard in Kittery, Maine, wasn't due to be officially laid down for three months. It was an unusual circumstance, but that's how things went sometimes.

The exigencies of the service and all that.

Raucous applause rose along with cheers, whistles and catcalls. Turner felt that if his smile grew any wider, it'd split his face. The sound of the pump machinery stopped and the huge doors ahead of the submarine began to swing slowly open, clearing the way to the Thames.

The move across the river was accomplished seamlessly. Turner conned the boat out into the channel and across to her berth at the submarine base. Under her General Electric motors, powered by the two massive one-hundred twenty-six cell Sargo batteries. So large were these batteries that each one had its own compartment, one forward and one aft of the control room. They lived beneath the compartment's deck and could be accessed, like all the sub-deck machinery, by taking up access panels in the deck itself.

The ship slid into her New London berth, and linemen stood by to toss heaving lines to the mooring crew on the boat's deck. Rogers stood amidships to supervise.

"Now boys," he said in an easy-going tone that by now the men had learned to pay close attention to. "Don't try and catch those monkey fists when they're thrown. There's a lead core inside and you'll snap your fingers like kindling. Let 'em hit the deck, and then haul in on the bite and put it on your cleats. The shore party will tighten up. Got me?"

The four men acknowledged, and Turner had to cough quietly into his fist to hide his smile. This was the way it would be done from here on in. Submarines on active duty didn't carry certain vital pieces of equipment. They didn't store mooring lines in their lockers on deck because if a depth charge blew a locker open and freed the line, it could foul a propeller blade or a plane. Further, no anchor and chain were carried because of the noise they'd make when rattling about during an attack. The stanchions and lifelines that normally encircled the deck were also removed for the same reasons.

"All secure!" Rogers called out.

The boat was hauled alongside the pier, power and phone lines were connected and the gangway extended. Now there would be a last-minute scramble to load provisions, examine how the equipment had worked on the short trip and perform more electrical, mechanical and buoyancy system tests. If all went well, the ship would depart the next day on her sea trial.

Things moved at lightning speed, or at least they seemed to for Turner. The christening ceremony was a big hit, with Joan Turner herself swinging the champagne bottle. Afterward, the men and officers were given the night off to relax and enjoy themselves before they shipped out for real. There were a lot of laughs, almost as many tears and a great deal of passion expressed. There would be, as there usually was under such circumstances, one or two send-off babies quickened on that night. War was an exercise in death, and it tended to elicit an equal fervor for an exercise in life.

7

FIVE MILES SOUTH, SOUTHWEST OF BLOCK ISLAND

MARCH 8, 1942

1100 ZULU

False dawn was just beginning to show in the periscope's eyepiece as KorvettanKapitän Reinhard Hardegen slowly turned the device through an entire circuit. His submarine, U-123 was in standby mode, all diesels shut down and running only on batteries. The electric motors were also not operational. The U-boat simply hung in the water at periscope depth, a silent and patient predator awaiting the approach of prey.

In the two weeks since he'd sunk the American freighter off Cape Hatteras, Hardegen and his crew had been slowly prowling up the American coast to the northern tip of Maine and back down along the coast of New England. They'd entered Chesapeake Bay along the way, but Hardegen had chosen not to fire on any of the shipping there. The Norfolk Navy base was close, and although the United States' response to his and his brother U-boat captains had been laughable, there was such a thing as being too bold by half.

An American airplane had tried for them not long before, although to no effect. Sooner or later, the seasoned submariner knew the United States Navy would pull itself together and begin taking more definitive action. In the meantime, it was his job to wreak as much havoc as he could. New York, the southern New England coast and Massachusetts

Bay had proven to be, and would continue to be, prime hunting ground.

"Very faint contact on sonar!" the sound man piped up. "Appears... northwest approximately thirty-thousand meters. Slow screws... possible merchantman, Kapitan!"

The boat was facing in that general direction, pointed between Block Island and Long Island. However, at thirty kilometers, the ships wouldn't be visible at periscope depth. The head of the scope was barely a meter out of the water. Hardegen would either have to surface or use a high periscope sighting, which would still be ineffective that far away... or he could close on the target and see for himself.

"What is the battery status, Einsvo?" he asked, still gazing through his rubberized eyepiece.

His first officer, *erster vacht offizer,* or Einsvo for short, was a lean and angular young man of thirty whose black eyes rarely revealed anything he was thinking. In his hard voice he said: "Ninety-percent charge, Kapitan."

"Very good..." Hardegen stated. "Pilot, engage the electric motors... come right to course three-four-zero. All ahead two-thirds. Mr. Verschmidt, please stay glued to that contact. Update me on anything you hear."

"Yes sir," the young sonar officer, Yohan Verschmidt, replied. "The signal is very weak at this distance, but I should be able to get you a more accurate bearing and possibly heading as we draw near."

Hardegen stepped away from the scope, "Down periscope. Diving officer, make your depth fifty meters."

"Mr. Williams," Arthur Turner said from his place on the bridge beside his XO. "Take her out, if you will."

Williams cast a furtive glance at his captain before clearing his throat, "Take her out, aye. Line handlers, standby! Control, bridge, bring all diesels online. Captain, all shore power, water and phone lines have been disconnected."

Turner nodded as the four powerful General Motors, sixteen-valve engines rumbled to life, coughing smoke into the air from their exhausts. The ship vibrated beneath him in a way that it hadn't on the trip over from Groton. That ride had been smoother on only the electric motors. Now, however, five thousand plus horsepower was chomping at the bit, and the whole ship seemed to vibrate with anticipation.

Behind them, the duty signalman hoisted the colors, and the ship's horn howled, announcing her intention to get underway. Everyone above and below decks and on the pier tensed in anticipation.

On the pier spectators cheered, and the Navy band began to play *Stars and Stripes Forever.* Turner could see Joan and the other officer's ladies huddled together against the dawn cold. They waved handkerchiefs and he replied by lifting his cover and waving back.

"Cast off four, three and two!" Williams shouted to the men on deck, who instantly released the ship from three of her four mooring lines which had already been singled up. "Control, bridge… port back one-third, starboard ahead one-third."

The stern of the ship began to slowly swing away from the dock. Williams ordered the number one line cast off and then all back slow. The long thin shape of the *Bull Shark* eased herself slowly from her berth and backed into the Thames River as the band struck up *Anchor's Away.* Once the bow was well clear, Williams ordered full right rudder and starboard shaft stop. The submarine swung around until she was perpendicular to the dock.

"Control, bridge… all ahead one-third… rudder amidships!" Williams ordered excitedly. "Captain, vessel is clear and underway."

"Very well," Turner said and then grinned like a kid in a candy store. He rubbed his gloved hands together. "Well done, Elmer. Secure the shove off party and set the standard seagoing watch. Captain has the deck."

The line handlers were dismissed, but they all elected to stay on deck and observe as the ship made her way down the Thames and out into Long Island Sound. There were a few other idlers topside as well. Those men who weren't assigned to the maneuvering or engine rooms. The three lookouts were already posted in the periscope sheers, and everyone was watching as the ship drew near the bridge that would soon be connected to I-95.

"Left standard rudder," Turner spoke to the bridge transmitter. The submarine slid out into the main channel. "Rudder amidships… stay sharp, helm. There's a bit of a tidal eddy as we go under the span."

It was hardly felt as the *Bull Shark* steamed beneath the bridge at six knots. The river was wide at this point, and before long, the Thames opened out into the Atlantic and the submarine began to feel the effects of long rollers crossing the sound.

"Let's clear the topsides," Turner said. Then into the speaker, "Control, bridge, what's Enj say about opening her up?"

"*Nichols here, sir,*" the engineer's voice filtered up through the tinny waterproof speaker. "*Recommend standard breaking in procedures. These engines haven't been run with a true load on them yet. Recommend we stay at one-third for another hour, then we can run at two-thirds for an hour and then we can try standard ahead and then a flank bell.*"

"Very well, we'll do it your way, Enj," Turner said. "Helmsman, maintain one-third, come left standard, steady up on course one-five-zero. We'll head out into the Atlantic proper just southwest of Block. ETA?"

"*Bridge, control… three hours at this speed, sir,*" Buck Rogers reported from the control room.

"Very well," Turner said once again, enjoying it immensely, "continue normal watch rotation."

"That's me, sir," Williams said.

Turner clapped him on the shoulder, "Sorry, XO. A chilly morning to have to stand a watch."

Williams shrugged and smiled, "Looks to be a beautiful day, though. Sun's almost up and hardly a cloud in the sky. XO has the deck."

Turner patted him on the shoulder and dropped down the hatch into the conning tower. There was a marked difference in temperatures, even with the bridge hatch open.

One of the great advantages that the big fleet boats had over their older S and R boat predecessors was the installation of air conditioning. The system could also generate heat, of course, yet heat was rarely a problem in a boat with massive diesels running. Even with the big engines shut down, the electric motors which actually turned the screws put out quite a bit of heat themselves.

It was part of the concerted effort the Navy made to create an environment as comfortable as possible for its submariners. These men were subject to very great dangers and had to live very closely in a three-hundred-foot cigar tube. So every effort had been made to make the fleet boats tolerable, if not luxurious.

In addition to air conditioning, the boats had two evaporators that made several hundred gallons of fresh water each day. Most of it went to the two giant and very hungry batteries; the remainder was used to top off the ship's freshwater tanks and used for cooking, cleaning and washing. Although the boat did have showers for both the enlisted and officers, they were generally still rationed to two or three showers a week per man.

Aside from that, the boats offered a high quality of food, with three square meals per day and a midnight snack prepared by the ship's cooks and baker. There was even an ice cream machine in the crew's mess. Although the officers ate the same food as the enlisted crew, they generally ate in the wardroom. The officer's steward also had a small prep galley along with the officer's pantry where he could prepare special items.

Turner entered the tiny wardroom and accepted a cup of coffee from Eddie Carlson, the officer's cook and steward, "Thanks, Eddie. Colder than a witch's tit out there this morning."

"Guess that's why you left Mr. Williams on deck to mind the store then, huh, Skipper?" Carlson asked with a wink.

"Rank hath its privileges," Turner said, blowing across the mouth of the cup and taking a tentative sip. "Oh yeah... anything good for breakfast, Eddie?"

Carlson grinned and set a plate of sweet rolls and bacon in front of the captain, complete with an already peeled banana, "Nothing too fancy with getting underway and all. Bakers got some pastries and such ready during the middle watch, and I've whipped up some bacon and that fresh fruit."

"Goes down gratefully, Eddie," Turner said, digging into the bacon.

Pat Jarvis slid the green curtain aside that acted as a door to the small room and entered, followed by Joe Dutch. Carlson set coffee and plates before each man as they slid behind the table that was bolted to the deck.

"Figured we'd grab a quick bite while the XO and engineers were at it," Jarvis said, sipping his coffee. "Oh, that's great coffee, Eddie."

"Here, here," Dutch put in.

"Man likes to see his work appreciated," Carlson remarked pleasantly.

"If you're half as good a gunner as you are a cook," Turner added, "we'll be invincible. How's our girl doing so far, gents?"

"Running like a top," Jarvis began. "Frank and Andy are bouncing between the engine rooms and maneuvering with Brannigan and Duncan. So far, everything is 4-O."

"Sound gear is working beautifully," Dutch said. "I got Chet Rivers on it now."

Turner frowned, "Christ... I feel like I'm so far behind the eight ball on this whole thing... a captain should know every inch of his boat and every man in his crew when he puts to sea... and I feel like I'm at about twenty-five percent, and that's being generous. Which one is Rivers?"

"That carroty-haired kid from Florida," Dutch said. "He plays the piano and has a good ear."

Turner nodded and made a mental note of that information and the name. He'd go aft and memorize the young man's face after breakfast as well. He'd always had a good memory for names and faces.

"What's your take on weapons, Pat?" Turner asked.

Jarvis swallowed a bite of roll and wiped his mouth, "Great shape. Couldn't ask for two better guys in the rooms. Ammo lockers are full... got four fifty-cal, an assortment of small arms and stuff. In my humble but accurate opinion, Skipper, we're ready for a fight... anxious for one, frankly."

Turner nodded gravely, but there was a gleam in his eyes, "Amen to that."

"So when are we supposed to meet the target ship?" Dutch asked.

"Should be later today," Turner said. "She's steaming along the coast out of New York. Probably gonna head south of Block Island, I'd guess. What do you think, weapons officer?"

Pat Jarvis smiled, "Yeah, he'll pass south of Block. He could go into the sound, though. Plenty of deep water between the island and Narragansett. I grew up there and did a lot of sailing out here."

"That explains that accent, then," Dutch teased. "Thought you were from Boston. Maybe Harvard Yard."

He pronounced it "Havid Yad" in a harsh, somewhat nasal tone. Jarvis frowned and flicked his ear.

"I don't sound anything like that, Joe," Jarvis quipped. "Rhode Islanders have a much softer accent. Closer to New York. We pahk ah cahs... yuge difference."

The three men laughed. After polishing off their breakfast, they prepared to rise and relieve the other men so they could get theirs when a young motor mac named Mike Watley, rapped his knuckles on the frame outside the curtain.

"Come," Turner said.

The young man, not yet twenty, slid the curtain aside, "Mr. Nichols respects sir, and he has a complete report for you in control."

Turner did remember this lad's name, "Thanks, Watley. Run aft and tell him, Post and the COB to meet me in control."

"Aye-aye, sir!" the kid snapped off and vanished.

"Eddie, would you have plates ready for Nichols, Post and the XO?" Turner asked. "We'll relieve them."

"Already started, sir," Carlson replied.

All the officers except Williams met at the main gyro table in the control room. Williams had the bridge intercom open so he could monitor as well. The quartermaster of the watch, a petty officer named Ralph "Hotrod" Hernandez, was just pricking the chart laid out on the table when the five officers and the chief met.

"You've got the word for me, Frank?" Turner asked.

"We're in great shape," Nichols said. "All diesels running like a top. Auxiliary generator kicking along smoothly and both electric motors purring like kittens."

"All two-hundred and fifty-two cells of both batteries taking and holding a full charge," he reported, consulting a small spiral notebook he slipped from his khaki uniform shirt pocket. "Evaps both online, although at reduced output since we've got full tanks."

"Only real troubles we have," Rogers added, "is me and Harry noticed the stuffing boxes on both shafts are dripping a little."

"Hmm… they were fine in the drydock yesterday… Nothing serious, I hope, Buck?" Turner inquired.

Rogers grinned, "Nah… dripping about twice a minute. Depth tests will really show it, though. It's not a problem. Harry says he can tighten the stuffing up with just a few minutes on all stop. Otherwise, we're good. Standard breaking in on new shafts, Harry says. Duncan reports no oil or fuel leaks. Again, though, we're running on top. Taking her down will be the real test."

"Very well," Turner said. "Let's you boys get some chow first. Pat and Joe will relieve you gents. I'll go topside and let Elmer get his breakfast. We still need to run the diesels for a while anyway. We'll do that and then try out a test dive."

"Oh, she'll dive," Post said proudly.

Turner treated the young engineer to a stern look, "That so, Ensign? I've no doubt… but the real test is getting her back up again."

"Oh, didn't think of that, huh?" Jarvis teased, levelling his own stern gaze on Post.

"Uhm… well, sirs, I…" Post stammered, going red in the face.

"These kids they turn out now," Dutch said sadly. "They just don't teach them *everything*, do they?"

"Hell," Nichols added, folding his arms across his chest. "I'm just a *reservist* and even *I* know you gotta surface eventually."

Post opened his mouth, closed it and opened it again. Finally, he snapped to attention and said: "Well aware of that, *sir!*"

The older officers and Rogers broke into laughter and took turns patting Post on the shoulders and back, Turner shook his head.

"At ease, Andy, at ease," the captain said kindly. "Just a little ribbing. Part of your sub qual is being gaslighted once in a while. All right, gents, let's get to work. Who knows, might find our quarry before we find out if Andy can get us back on top again."

As if on cue, Rivers called out from the sonar gear located in the conning tower, "Sir! I'm picking up what sounds like a slow single screw... very faint... bearing something like... one-one-zero... range maybe forty-thousand yards. Almost can't hear it at all at that range, though."

"Keep your ears on it, Chet," Dutch ordered, calling up through the hatchway. "See if you can get a heading over time."

"Shall we start a plot, sir?" Jarvis asked eagerly.

Turner grinned at him, "Can't wait, huh, Pat? Yeah, make a note on the chart and then again at ten-minute intervals. Hopefully Rivers will be able to determine a track and speed. Plenty of time, though. We'll proceed as is for the time being."

After mounting to the bridge and sending Williams down for chow, Turner took a turn around the main deck of his new boat. The sun was well up over the eastern horizon now and the cobalt-blue sky above was decorated with fluffy, white cumulus clouds sailing placidly along. The ocean around him was clear of anything that could be seen from the deck. It was a deep shade of royal blue, only broken by the flash of glittering sunlight that reached out from the *Bull Shark's* port bow to the horizon. The air was cold and crisp, yet not as biting as it had been before sunrise.

Turner mounted the cigarette deck and took his soon-to-be customary position on the small bridge. He glanced up and behind him at the three lookouts crowded into the lookout perch on the periscope sheers and was pleased to see all three young men with their binoculars dutifully trained on their sectors.

"*Bridge, control,*" Dutch called through the tinny bridge intercom unit. "*Rivers has some good data on that unknown. Range now thirty-four thousand yards, heading approximately zero-seven-zero. Looks like she is indeed running on a course south of Block Island.*"

"Excellent," Turner replied, bending down to ensure his voice was heard over the ten-knot breeze. "Give me a full sweep with the sugar jig. See if we can't confirm sonar's readings and get an independent fix."

The SJ surface-search radar began to spin above the lookouts' heads. Referred to colloquially as the "sugar jig," just as the SD air-search radar was known as the "sugar dog," was a powerful addition to the boat's equipment. It was specially designed for surface scans and far more effective at locating and pinpointing surface targets than the air radar unit.

"*Sweep complete, Bridge,*" Jarvis reported now. "*Target is large surface vessel, confirm sonar's heading and speed appears eleven knots. Estimated size four-hundred feet. Assess merchantman and our test ship.*"

Turner grinned, "Very well. Secure the radar. Dutch, have radio send the pre-set engage signal. Let's see if this is our buddy."

A moment or two went by before Joe Dutch's voice spoke from the speaker, "*Confirm, Bridge. Vessel is* SS *Chester Clyde, dry cargo freighter contracted to the Navy. Lieutenant Archie Poole commanding. He sends his compliments and advises ready to engage in test fire... he also adds please be sure we're only firing dummies.*"

Turner heard the laughter from the conning tower through the open hatch and from the speaker. He chuckled as well, "Very good, Control. Give me an intercept course, please."

"*Course to cross her bow is one-six-five true,*" Williams suddenly reported. As XO, he was also the navigator and was now taking charge of the plotting party. "*Plotting party assigned. Recommend maintaining speed and diving upon lookout visual confirm.*"

"Concur," Turner replied. "Hope you had a good breakfast, XO. We'll submerge to periscope depth. Advise all compartments that they have…"

Turner did a rough calculation in his head. He figured the new course of the *Bull Shark* even as she made a slight adjustment to starboard, and the distance traveled at his vessel's ten knots and the target's eleven. They were both converging on either side of an acute triangle that would meet some dozen or so miles ahead.

"…thirty-five minutes for final pre-dive checklists," Turner said.

Twenty miles away and only three miles off the starboard quarter of the lumbering merchant vessel, Reinhard Hardegen smiled as he peered through his periscope at the bulky mass of his target. He'd just received word that the radio antenna, which was extended just above the water as well, had intercepted the exchange between the freighter and what was evidently an American submarine. His sound man indicated that in addition to the single screwed freighter, he thought he heard faint twin screws only detectable because of their different pitch.

"Take us down to periscope depth," Hardegen told his diving officer. "Lower the radio mast. Open outer doors on all forward tubes. Standby to shoot on my orders. This will be an interesting problem."

The boat slanted slightly down from forty feet to sixty, having been only shallow enough for her radio mast to peek above the waves and listen. As the captain stepped back from the scope and sipped a cup of coffee, his torpedo officer, a seasoned man several years older than Hardegen, stepped closer.

"Are you going after the submarine or the freighter, sir?" he asked quietly.

"The ship, of course," Hardegen replied. "That is a new submarine on sea trial. If we play this just right, Ernst, our friend Herr Brechman will be *most* pleased."

8

"What is your plan, Herr Kapitan?" Heiman Richter, the executive officer, asked quietly.

"We're going to move in on the freighter," Hardegen stated. "My guess, Einsvo, is that this submarine is on a sea trial. She will probably fire exercise torpedoes at the freighter."

Richter met his captain's eye and a ghost of a smile flittered across his angular face, "And you intend to shoot simultaneously so that the Americans think their own eels sank the ship? That's very good!"

"I thought that might amuse you, Einsvo," Hardegen said, although with less obvious relish. He turned to his torpedo officer, Ernst Albrecht. "I want a constant solution on that ship. We're going to approach from an oblique angle, just as it appears our American counterpart is doing. I'm going to keep the freighter between us and them. I hope that anyone on that ship will be paying more attention to the submarine than looking out for true enemies. However, we're going to have to approach using sound only. When we're within a thousand meters or so, I'll raise the scope and take a fast bearing and range. Then you must be prepared to shoot the moment the other submarine does. Do you understand, Ernst?"

Albrecht was a portly man with a round and friendly face. That face now beamed with triumph as he said: "*Jawohl, mein Kapitan.* I am with you entirely."

"And you, Yohan?" Hardegen asked his young sonar officer.

The most junior of his officers, a tall, broad-shouldered man of twenty-four, nodded his head vigorously. He had the clunky headphones over his ears, with the right cup pulled back just behind the ear so he could also hear any orders given.

"I have the hydrophones trained on the American," Yohan stated. "His noise is very faint at this distance… but as we draw near, it slowly gets clearer. I can differentiate him from the freighter because the ship has but one propeller. I shall continually update Herr Richter."

"Good man," Hardegen said, patting the younger man on his heavy shoulder. "How long until our Yankee friend closes to optimum firing position, Yohan?"

Verschmidt listened for a moment and then glanced at Richter.

"Thirty minutes," Richter said as he examined his plot. "Do you concur, Verschmidt?"

Yohan nodded, "I do, sir."

"Excellent," Hardegen said. 'Pilot, increase speed. Make turns for eight knots."

"Bridge!" called one of the lookouts. "Visual contact! Surface vessel bearing zero-four-zero starboard horizon!"

"Okay, here we go," Turner said with a grin. "Control, Bridge… target is in sight, bearing zero-four-zero. Distance eight miles. I'll give you an exact read with the TBT when I have him in sight."

"*Bridge, Control,*" Williams replied. "*Sound and radar concur. Continuing track.*"

"Prepare to dive the ship," Turner announced. "Clear topsides."

The lookouts scrambled down from the periscope sheers and down the hatch. Turner hit the diving alarm three times before he followed. He pulled the lanyard and closed the hatch behind him. Hotrod Hernandez squeezed up beside Turner to spin the dogging wheel and secure the hatch.

"Hatch secure," Hernandez announced.

"Stop all engines," Turner ordered. "Standby to answer bells on batteries."

"Maneuvering answers all stop," the helmsman reported.

Nichols called up from the control room. "Captain, diesels shut down, we're on battery power."

"Very well. Rig out bow planes. All ahead two-thirds," Turner called. "Close main induction."

The large pipe that allowed air into and out of the boat and allowed the diesels to breathe as well as provide fresh air inside the pressure hull was sealed. Although with the addition of the snorkel, the *Bull Shark* could still run on diesel power even at periscope depth. However, like the periscope, the snorkel would leave a feather line wake on the surface and could be spotted in daylight or even at night with good lighting and phosphorescence.

"Main induction closed," Nichols reported. "Christmas tree is green. Good pressure in the hull, sir."

Down in the control room was the master diving board, or Christmas tree as it was known because of the many red and green lights. When all lights were green, the pressure hull was fully sealed and holding air. This was necessary for diving, or there could be a leak or a catastrophic hull breach at great depths.

"Open main vents," Turner ordered.

At the top of the main ballast tanks, vents were opened to allow the pressurized air to escape. These tanks were permanently open to the sea on their undersides. When the pressurized air was vented upward, this allowed seawater inside. Although this made the boat heavier by several hundred tons, it wasn't quite enough to sink her. A submarine is designed such that when her ballast tanks are flooded, she's as close to neutrally buoyant as possible. Of course, there are trim tanks, the safety tank and the negative tanks that can also be partially or fully flooded or blown out to adjust buoyancy to be either negative or positive.

However, neutral buoyancy, or even a slight positive buoyancy, is always desired at depth. This way, should power be lost, the submarine will either hover at depth or even rise slowly. To compensate for this and to actually maneuver the boat up and down in the water column, there are two sets of horizontal planes that allow the crew to "fly" the ship through the water.

The bow planes, normally stored folded against the hull when on the surface, are extended and then angled downward to dive. This forces the bow down. At the same time, the stern planes, which are located to either side of the rudder, are angled in the opposite direction. These planes control the boat's angle through the water. To dive, the planes are angled upward, which in turn forces the stern up. This has the effect of angling the propellers upward as well, which then drives the boat downward. Once at the desired depth, the bow planes are set at an angle that keeps the ship level and then the stern planes will be used to change depth, except in extreme maneuvers.

"Fifteen degree down bubble," Turner ordered. "Nice and smooth, gents. Flood negative."

A relatively small, centralized ballast tank, known as the negative tank, was often used to assist in surface dives. This tank would be fully or partially flooded, giving the submarine negative buoyancy to get her off the surface in order for her planes to achieve purchase. Once at the desired depth, the negative tank would be blown out to restore balance.

"Depth now forty-five feet," Nichols announced.

"Blow negative, close all vents," Turner ordered.

In order not to leave a bubble trail, the water in the negative tank is never blown completely out. When the tank reaches its desired level, any excess pressurized air is then pumped inside the hull.

"Periscope depth," Nichols called out.

"Level off," Turner said. "All ahead full. You ready to adjust your trim, Andy?"

As second engineer, it was Post's job to manage the submarine's trim and backstop the diving officer during battle. This was a complex job and required a considerable amount of effort to do it correctly.

It's been said that keeping a fleet submarine trimmed properly is not unlike trying to balance a yardstick on a razor blade. Careful pumping of water and air into the variable ballast tanks, monitoring the diesel oil tanks, and during battle, keeping track of torpedoes all goes into this critical dance.

When a torpedo is fired, the ship instantly loses thirty-three hundred pounds. This is somewhat compensated for by special ballast tanks beneath the torpedo rooms called water round torpedo or WRT. This tank is flooded at the time of a firing in order to help compensate for the sudden loss of weight. Of course, when firing multiple torpedoes, the ship will lose that much more weight and other tanks must come into play along with the planes. Granted, a ton and a half against the almost seventeen-hundred tons of the submarine on the surface, and half again that much below, is negligible, but fire half a dozen torpedoes in under forty seconds and this can dramatically affect the ship's trim. So much so that at periscope depth, submarines have been known to breach due to the sudden imbalance, and this could be disastrous under the right conditions.

"All set sir," Post said, consulting his spiral-bound notebook, "I've already made calculations for the two exercise fish we're about to fire. No problem, sir."

"Glad to hear it," Turner said. "Raise the attack scope, Hotrod."

Post handed the control box that operated both the search and slimmer attack periscopes to Hernandez and dropped down into the control room to take a position near the air manifold. Hotrod pushed the button for the attack scope, and it began to rise. Turner snapped the handles down and pressed his face to the rubber-coated viewing section.

"There she is, hull up in the scope now," Turner said. "Initial bearing... mark."

Hotrod looked at the bearing ring around the scope and said: "Zero-three-five."

Behind Turner, Jarvis cranked that into the torpedo data computer.

"How about those fish, Pat?" Turner asked as he gazed at his prey.

"Well, the live 14s have been modified," Jarvis reported, "but tubes one and two are ready to be loaded with dummies. They should run at the depth set. From what I was told, the 14s with real warheads are running deep because the heads are so much heavier than the dummy test fish."

"Yeah…" Turner muttered, "we'll need to keep that in mind in a real combat scenario. For now, though, we'll set the depth on both torpedoes to eight feet. Range to target is now… four-thousand yards. Down scope."

"What's your desired firing range, Skipper?" Williams called up the hatch.

"We'll shoot at a grand," Turner said. "Good view when the fish hit, and we can be sure of our aim, too."

"In that case… intercept time to shooting range is twenty-two minutes. She's making eleven knots to our nine, so we'll be somewhat astern of her when we fire."

"Very well," Turner said. "Frank, any chance of more speed?"

"We're already at a hundred percent," Nichols replied. "I'd prefer we weren't even running that hard yet… and I'd like to at least let the new motors break in a little more before we overload them."

That chafed Turner a little, "Wasn't any of this done at the yard?"

"To a degree, sir," Williams added his voice to Nichols, "but with the rush job and all…"

Turner sighed, "Fair enough… no criticism intended, Frank. Phone talker, advise forward room to load exercise shots into tubes one and two."

Up in the forward torpedo room, Walter Sparks stood between his tubes and glared at the torpedo gang. All the men that lived there, ten in all, were standing by. Three of his most junior torpedomen were ready on either side of the tubes with the loading gear. His two senior torpedomen were both standing by to observe the load and to ready the tubes. Sparky looked at Tommy Perkins, Sparks' assistant, who was standing near the after end of the compartment in front of the watertight door and next to the officer's head. He laid a hand on the shoulder of the young seaman who was acting as the room's phone talker and nodded to Sparky.

"Control room orders load two exercise fish into tubes one and two, Sparky," the phone talker announced excitedly.

"Take it easy, kid," Perkins said as he clicked a stopwatch around his neck. "It's just a test."

At the words of the phone talker, the quiet room burst into action. Men began to release the torpedo straps that held the twenty-foot long, thirty-three-hundred-pound Mark 14 torpedo to its skid as they hooked up the hoisting gear and the tailing tackle, or tagle, which was used to help shove the massive weapon into the breach of the torpedo tube.

"Let's go, boys!" Sparks bawled. "Get the lead outta your asses and get that goddamned fish aloft already! Move, move, move!"

Perkins had to bite his tongue in order to stifle a laugh. He knew that Sparky loved this work more than anything in the world. He often teased the big man about how he'd rather shove a fish into a tube than his own torpedo into a good-looking broad.

Sparky would laugh and say it was a damned close-run thing.

"Easy does it, tube one," Sparks coached as the weapon slid forward. "Just think about your old lady. Ease it in, now!"

"Jesus Christ..." Perkins heard Griggs half groan and half chuckle.

"Why come we didn't do this shit at the dock?" another man unwisely asked.

"Cuz we don't fight a war at the fuckin' dock, numb nuts, that's why!" Sparks hollered. "Now *heave* you bastards!"

Perkins did laugh this time.

"Belay tube one... belay tube two!" Sparks barked.

The two torpedoes were nearly home. Sparks unhooked the tackle and, with an impressive heave, pushed the two weapons the last few inches into the tubes until they gently touched up against the stopping bolts.

He then snatched the propeller guards off, backed off on the tail stops on both breech doors and closed them.

"Okay, Wilkes, Jonesy, you're up!" Sparks called. "Fish are home, breech door is closed, now what? You other men pay attention now."

Perry Wilkes, a brawny man in his late twenties from Idaho, stepped up to tube one, and Bob Jones, a big blonde kid from California almost as bulky as Sparks, stepped up to tube two.

"We tighten down on the tail stop," Wilkes said. "Then, since there's no rubber on it, we back it off again about a tenth of a turn."

"Why's that, Griggsy?" Sparky put one of the young greenies on the spot.

"Uhm… cuz… cuz you don't wanna jam up the stopping bolt?" Griggs replied uncertainly.

"You askin' or tellin', kid?" Sparks prompted firmly but with a twinkle in his merry eyes.

Griggs swallowed, "Tellin', Sparky."

"That's right," Sparks said. "Now what, Jonesy?"

"Since we already tested the flood and impulse systems," Jones said. "We flood the tube and set the gyro, depth and speed spindles."

This they did quickly and then set the ready fire levers. Sparks looked aft, "Phone talker, report tubes one and two loaded and ready to fire."

"Sixteen minutes," Perkins reported, consulting his stopwatch and making a note on a slip of paper.

Sparks glared around the room, "Slower'n dog shit… good procedures, but we're gonna have to work on time. Plenty of opportunity for that when we routine these fish and reload these tubes after we fire."

Sparks turned to the tubes and positioned his hands over the manual firing triggers for tubes one and two. Although the torpedoes would be fired from the conning tower electrically, the men in the torpedo room would also depress the manual triggers almost simultaneously as a backup in case the remote firing system failed.

A few minutes later, Turner turned to Pat Jarvis, "What's the generated bearing on our target now?"

"Zero-two-three," the weapons officer reported. "Should be close to firing range."

"Okay," Turner said, squatting before the attack scope. "I'll ride her up, grab the range and bearing and then back down again. Six seconds or less. Ready, Hotrod?"

Hernandez held the control box and grinned, "Ready, sir."

"Up scope!" Turner ordered.

As the attack periscope began to rise, he grabbed the control handles, snapped them down and let them carry him upright even as he gazed through the eyepiece and turned the scope just to the right of dead center. In his lens, the green of the sea foamed and cleared. "Stop scope! Okay... I've got her... bearing, mark!"

"Zero-two-one!" Hernandez said excitedly, and Jarvis cranked this data into the TDC.

"Range to target... one triple zero yards, repeat one-thousand yards... angle on the bow is two-two-five port! Down scope!"

Hernandez hit the button as Turner snapped the handles back into their upright position.

"Five seconds, Skipper!" Hotrod said with a grin. "*Muy bueno!*"

"Muy Bueno..." Turner muttered. "Boat load of wiseasses. You watch that shit, Hotrod."

"*Sí.*"

Everyone in the conning tower, including Turner, chuckled.

"We've got a solution, Captain," Jarvis said with barely contained zeal. "Shoot anytime."

"Fire one!" Turner ordered and then counted back from seven. "Fire two!"

Jarvis pulled the plungers for tubes one and four, "Tube one fired electrically... tube two... electric failed, but Sparky got her on manual."

"Both fish running hot straight and normal!" Dutch reported from the sonar station behind Turner.

"Run time?" Turner asked Jarvis even though he knew what it was.

At forty-six knots, the torpedoes covered about twenty-three yards per second. Which meant a running time to target, taking in a correction for the target's own movement, of about fifty seconds. Turner was pleased when Jarvis had that figure instantly.

"It's not like they don't know we're here," Turner said. "Surface the boat. Let's get everybody up here and in the con who is free to come up and watch the hits."

"No question now," Yohan Verschmidt reported. "American submarine closing to within a thousand meters of the freighter. The ship's own screw noise is making it harder to hear them, but she's out there."

"Now it's our time," Hardegen said. "Up periscope…"

He looked through the scope and gave final bearing, range and target course. The entire crew was silent, waiting tensely for the word to fire.

"Tubes one and two," Hardegen said. "Coverage is one degree… Yohan, the moment you hear—"

"They've fired!" Yohan shouted. "Hot transients! Torpedoes in the water!"

"Tube one… *los…!* Tube two, *los!*"

The ship shuddered as two fists of compressed air, six seconds apart, hammered the two torpedoes out of the tubes and toward the target. Knowing that the Americans on both the freighter and the submarine would be intent on watching the exercise, Hardegen did not lower his attack scope.

Instead, he gazed through the eyepiece and counted down in his head. His own boat was slightly further from the freighter's starboard quarter than the American boat was from the port, and of course, the live German torpedoes would strike the opposite side of the ship… yet the close proximity of the hits would no doubt make the Americans believe that the exercise torpedoes were in fact live war shots.

At least the confusion would last long enough for U-123 to get deep and head south, hopefully below a thermal layer so as to be undetected by even active sonar pinging.

Then, with only thirty seconds to go on the eels' run, Hardegen saw the submarine break the surface, water streaming from the limber holes in the upper deck. As he watched, several figures emerged onto the bridge and the cigarette deck. No doubt the officers and a few men sent up to watch the show. Hardegen laughed sardonically. They were certainly about to get their money's worth.

"Come right," he ordered softly. "Reduce speed to all ahead one-third and make your new heading due south, pilot. We are now going silent."

Hardegen spun the periscope to keep the target ship in view as his submarine turned away and slowed down. Then it happened…

A geyser of water infused with a bright orange flame erupted from the freighter's bow. Six seconds later, another sprouted amidships. Two great waterspouts shot fifty feet into the air and seemed to belch smoke and fire. The ship hadn't broken in two, but she would sink. There was no doubt of that.

Hardegen took no pleasure in the kill. While he felt a distinct sense of satisfaction from doing his duty and doing his job well, he also felt pity for the men aboard his targets. No matter what the nation or political ideology, there was a shared fraternity between men and women who went to sea.

They all faced the same perils and shared the same experiences. Anytime a fellow mariner was consigned to the deep, Hardegen felt for them. Yet it was war, and this was his duty.

9

"Jesus Christ!" Elmer Williams cried as two tremendous rolling booms seemed to hammer their way across the intervening sea.

Following this stunning set of sounds were the pillars of black smoke and flame that seemed to erupt from the freighter's bow and mid-section like infernal geysers. The half dozen men on the cigarette deck and bridge only stared in horrified silence at the totally unexpected destruction before them.

Turner gained at least partial control over his wits first, "What the *hell* happened? Did we fire live fish, Pat!?"

The torpedo officer's handsome face was pale with shock. For a long moment, he could only stare, his mouth slack. He turned slowly to Turner and shook his head no, "No sir... those exercise fish were clearly marked..."

"Control, bridge!" Turner barked. "Come right fifteen degrees! Get a rescue party up here on the double and pass the word for the pharmacist's mate... and tell Sparky to get his ass to the bridge on the goddamned *double*, you hear me?"

"*Wilco, skipper,*" Buck Rogers called out from the speaker. "*What's going on up there?*"

"The freighter has been hit with two torpedoes," Turner said.

"She's afire and starting to list! Get them on the radio if you can, Buck. Dutch, get below and contact that ship and tell them we're on the way and ask... ask what they know."

Almost as soon as Dutch disappeared through the hatch, Walter Sparks shot up through it, followed by half a dozen men with lines and throw rings. Sparks stepped up next to Turner and gaped at the freighter.

"Mr. Sparks..." Turner began.

Sparky's face was as pale as Jarvis' had been. As pale as Williams, Post and Nichols' were now. Probably as pale as his own.

"No sir!" Sparks clearly understood what was being asked. "Them fish were dummies. Clearly marked, and we even inspected 'em on the way out. Only thing they had were exercise poppers so we could see them make contact. No goddamned question on it, Captain."

Sparks seemed almost put out by the implication, but Turner didn't give a damn. *Somebody* had slammed two torpedoes into the ship they were now approaching, and he knew for certain his own ship had fired two fish.

"Sir..." Sparky said, half indignant and half pleading. The flinty look in the captain's eyes daunted the big man.

"Okay, Sparky," Turner said more gently, clapping the man on the shoulder. "I trust you. Take over the rescue party, will ya'?"

"Aye-aye," Sparks said, glancing at the now burning ship. "She's listin' to starboard, sir."

"Elmer, you stay with me," Turner ordered. "Pat, Frank, Andy, get below and man your stations. If we didn't hit that ship, then there's a goddamned submarine out there. I want him *found.*"

"Bridge, I've got Lieutenant Poole on line, patching him into the bridge transmitter," Dutch said.

There was a pause and then a crackling erupted from the bridge speaker. At first, Turner thought it was static but then realized that it was the sound of fires in the background.

"Bull Shark*! This is Archie Poole, do you read?"*

"I read you, Lieutenant. This is Captain Art Turner here. What's your situation? Can you tell me... did... did we..."

"Thank Christ you're here, sir! No, it wasn't your fish that did this. We saw them hit and pop off the water rounds. No… the live shots came from our starboard quarter. I don't know from who, though. Our gear is shot to hell."

Williams was behind Turner, conning the submarine and calling down helm and speed orders through the open hatch. *Bull Shark* ranged up fifty feet from the high side of the freighter, which was already heeled over noticeably. Men on the deck four stories above were rigging a large cargo net over the side.

"Lieutenant… how many souls aboard?" Turner asked tightly, dreading the answer.

A long pause, *"We had forty officers and men and… and ten passengers, sir. Everyone that's alive is up on deck now. I've got… twenty unaccounted for, including half a dozen civilian passengers, sir."*

God help us, Turner thought, "Understood, Lieutenant. Can I call you Archie?"

"Call me anything you want, Captain… as long as you call me over for lunch," Poole tried to joke.

Williams was guiding the submarine closer. The rescue party, led by Sparks, was reaching out with extendable boat hooks to draw the lower end of the netting over to the deck. Four more men began to secure it to cleats. The crew above tightened the net and men began to clamber down it with agonizing slowness. Four men were followed by four more and then four women.

"Stand by with the axes!" Sparky ordered.

By now, the freighter had settled deeper, and even though she was now listed over at least twenty degrees, her bottom paint wasn't yet showing. Time was short.

"I'm gonna need you to speed this up, Archie!" Turner hollered upward. He'd given up on the radio and just yelled up to Poole, who was standing thirty feet above overseeing the evacuation. His khaki uniform shirt and light jacket were obviously scorched.

"Dutch, any sign of who did this?" Turner called down the hatch. "Go active on sonar."

With all the excitement, Turner had forgotten about the mystery foe. Yet with the *Bull Shark* literally tied up, she was an easy target.

Either the other submarine, it couldn't be anything else, was even now bearing down on them, or it was rapidly leaving the area.

"Aren't we going to fire on the American boat?" Richter asked indignantly.

"Negative," Hardegen said as he lit a cigarette. "We have sunk the freighter, this is sufficient for now."

"Depth is now one-hundred and sixty meters," The chief at the ballast manifold control station reported.

"All ahead full," Hardegen ordered.

"Sir... they are a sitting duck, as the Americans say," Richter protested. "We could sink them easily."

Hardegen eyed his first officer over the glowing cherry of his Lucky Strike. He knew that Richter himself, a strict Nazi who blindly followed any of Hitler's doctrines, hated smoking. Further, he knew that it galled the Einsvo that Hardegen liked to smoke Western brands, especially the popular American Lucky Strike. The two men were as different as night and day in many ways, save their devotion to duty.

Richter was an avid supporter of the war and saw everyone that wasn't German as the enemy. By extension, then, they must all be destroyed without mercy. Hardegen didn't share this bleak and inhumane view.

"We will have our chance, Einsvo," Hardegen said finally. "But not within throwing distance of the largest submarine base on the coast. Not yet. I feel that we must leave them with a mystery as well as the knowledge that once again, the Reich has struck silently and with deadly consequences."

Richter frowned but didn't argue any further. Hardegen had already extended a courtesy by explaining himself and the first officer was too dedicated a sailor to question orders.

"Sir! Active pinging by American submarine!" Verschmidt reported from behind the two men. "Very powerful pings..."

Everyone in the zentral, the control room, listened to the eerie sound of the high-pitched pings echoing through the water. The U-boat was already a mile away now, and the distance was distorting the sound beams, lengthening them and giving them an even more ghostly and unnerving tone. They did steadily grow louder, but no closer. Then suddenly, the sound weakened, distorted and became inaudible.

"Depth now two hundred meters," the chief announced.

"I believe we may be below a salt layer," Yohan said quietly. "I don't believe they'll locate us."

"Even if they did," Hardegen stated confidently, "they couldn't catch us submerged. If they tried to chase us down on top, their sound systems would be degraded by their engine noises. A submarine is not a destroyer. Reduce speed to two-thirds. Steady on course one-hundred and eighty. Open compartment hatches, but quietly. Send a runner to tell the men to stand easy at their battle stations. When we're far enough away that Yohan says it doesn't matter, Einsvo, cancel battle stations and secure from silent running. What was the name of that submarine again?"

"The... *Bull Shark*," Ernst Albrecht said, having a little trouble with the English words.

Hardegen, who spoke perfect English, chuckled, "Such names they give. A bull shark, eh? The most vicious of the great sea predators. Excellent. We will meet again, *Bull Shark*."

Arthur Turner was beside himself that he had to turn back to port. He wanted to go after the U-boat that he knew must have torpedoed the *Chester Clyde*. It had to be a Nazi boat, there was just no other explanation. Any surface ship would have been detected, as would an aircraft.

But he couldn't just leave the rapidly sinking and burning ship with its human cargo fighting for life. Now he had forty people crammed into the boat that was already crowded with its seventy-five crew.

Most of them were crammed into the crew's mess. The cooks were providing them with coffee and sandwiches. The women had been given the officer's staterooms along with Turner's own tiny private cabin. It would only be a few hours until the *Bull Shark* reached New London again, but after what they'd been through, the captain wanted to give the ladies what little comforts he could offer them.

At the moment, he, Williams and Pat Jarvis sat at the wardroom table with Lieutenant Poole, who had been given a clean set of submarine dungarees, T-shirt and sandals. He sipped a mug of coffee, and Turner noticed that the young man's hands shook a little.

"You okay, Arch?" Jarvis asked kindly, patting the younger man on the shoulder.

Turner passed over a half-empty pack of Camels that Dutch had left on the table. Poole pulled one out and lit it, taking a long and grateful drag.

"Thanks," he said finally. "I needed that. Yeah, I'm fine... it's just... it's just I've never had a ship blown out from under me before."

Turner nodded, "I understand. Never happened to any of us, either. It's got to be a jarring experience. Is there anything you can tell us, Archie? Maybe something one of your crew or passengers saw? Something you might have picked up on radar or sonar that seemed odd?"

Poole frowned and shook his head, "Nothing, Captain. I wish I could... don't know how that Kraut snuck up on us like that."

"What makes you think it was a Nazi boat?" Pat asked.

Poole scoffed, "Who else could it be? Doubt the Japs are over here shooting at us. Everybody knows about the U-boats prowling around the coast since Christmas time... what I don't get is why nobody's *doing* anything about it!"

"I wouldn't say that," Turner reassured him.

Poole puffed and sipped, "Yeah, but you're out here on a sea trial before they ship you off to the Pacific. The Navy isn't doing a goddamned thing over here in the Atlantic... leastways not on our side... sir."

Jarvis frowned and cast a look in Turner's direction. The captain sighed and sipped his own coffee, "That'll change, Poole."

Pharmacist's mate Henry Hoffman rapped his knuckles perfunctorily on the frame to the wardroom, "Skipper?"

108

"Come on in, Hoffman," Turner said. "How is everyone?"

A submarine, even a big fleet boat, didn't carry a doctor. Instead, they carried a pharmacist's mate. An enlisted man who was essentially a glorified medical corpsman. Hoffman was a first-class petty officer with fifteen years in the service. Turner had only met him the day before, but the man seemed levelheaded and capable.

"Mostly minor scrapes and bruises," Hoffman said as he pushed aside the green baize curtain that acted as the wardroom door, accepting a cup of coffee from Carlson. "Thanks, Eddie... the only exception being the lady in your berth, Skipper. Pretty nasty bonk on the noggin. I've also stitched up a laceration on her left calf. Not too deep, but she did need half a dozen stitches."

"She going to be all right?" Jarvis asked.

"Oh, she'll be fine," Hoffman reassured them, reaching for one of Dutch's smokes. "May I?"

"Please," Turner smiled.

Once invited into the wardroom, enlisted or not, a man was welcome to make himself at home. Hoffman placed the cigarette in his mouth and Jarvis lit it for him. "She did ask to speak to the captain, though."

"Can she have visitors?" Turner asked.

Hoffman waved his cigarette in the air, "Sure, long as she's up to it. The knock on the head didn't create a fracture, though it's swollen pretty bad. I'm a little concerned about concussion, but once we put in I'll send her to the hospital for a double-check."

"Very well," Turner said, draining his cup. "I'll go look in on her now then, so she can get some rest."

Like most of what were laughably called "staterooms" on the *Bull Shark,* the captain's cabin was separated from the corridor only by a heavy green baize curtain. Turner knocked twice on the frame, and a soft female voice bade him come in.

The captain's cabin aboard a fleet submarine, even the larger ones like the new *Tambor, Gato,* or the not-even-released yet *Balao*-classes was large enough only for a bunk and a small desk with a chair. There was a small sink for handwashing and shaving along with a tiny hanging locker and chest of drawers, but that was the extent of a commander's luxury.

Lying on his bunk, wrapped in a blanket and with a hot cup of tea clutched in her hands, was a rather lovely woman of perhaps thirty-five. Her long golden hair was tied back, and a large cold compress had been placed on her forehead. From what Turner could see of her, the woman seemed tall with willowy limbs and a generous bosom. Her face was lovely with high cheekbones, full lips and large sky-blue eyes.

"Captain Turner?" she asked quietly but not timidly.

"Yes, ma'am," he said gently and slipped inside. "How are you feeling?"

She smiled thinly, "Like I've been torpedoed. Won't you sit down?"

Turner pulled out the chair and sat behind his desk.

"I know it's a bit pretentious of me to offer you a chair in your own quarters," she went on, still smiling.

"Not at all, ma'am," Turner replied with a smile of his own. "My casa is your casa for the duration."

Her smile grew, "Thank you... I'm Mildred Allman. Please call me Milly."

"A pleasure to meet you, Milly. I'm Art," Turner replied. "I'm sorry for the circumstances, though. My pharmacist's mate said you asked to see me?"

She sipped her tea and nodded, "Yes. I wanted to tell you that I believe we were torpedoed by a German submarine."

Turner nodded. There really couldn't be any other explanation, "We've assumed that as well. There just isn't any other reasonable option. But tell me... what makes you say so? Speculation?"

She shook her head, "I saw the periscope... or at least I *think* I did. My cabin was on the right... the *starboard* side of the ship, in the main hull. I knew that we were going to watch a new submarine test fire a couple of torpedoes, so I was coming up on deck to see the show. As I said, though, my cabin was on the opposite side of the ship, so I was coming up the righthand... oh, what do they call it... so many nautical terms to remember..."

"Companion?" Turner offered.

She grinned, "Yes, the companion. That's what the nice young

Skipper called it. So there I was, just stepping up on deck and looking around. I remember Archie saying that the submarine would be coming up on our port side. So I was sort of surprised when I saw what looked like a pencil sticking up out of the water. And it was leaving a thin line of foam behind it."

"A periscope," Turner said.

Milly nodded, "I suppose so. I only saw it for a few seconds before it seemed to disappear. At first, I thought I'd imagined it, and then I thought it must be you, playing a little joke by coming from the other side… I wish I'd been more on the ball and reported it right away… maybe…"

Turner reached out and took the hand she extended at the same time. He gave it a little pat, "Now don't blame yourself, Milly. You couldn't have known, and even if you'd sounded the alarm right away… there's nothing that could've been done. If you saw the periscope with your naked eye, and it was probably the attack scope, which isn't even two inches in diameter… then the boat was close and the captain was making his final observation. There was nothing that could be done."

She sighed, "I found the captain a minute later and was about to tell him what I saw when everybody, it seemed like most of the people aboard, on the port railing sent up a cheer. That's when you surfaced after firing *your* torpedoes. It was exciting until I realized that you were on the *other side* of the ship from where I thought I saw the periscope. I tried to shout a warning, but nobody heard… and then… oh God… then the world erupted into a *roar!* I've never heard anything as loud as those two booms. The whole ship shook like we were in an earthquake, and then alarms went off and people began to run around shouting… then the fires seemed to shoot up from the other side of the ship… they were so *hot*…"

"Take it easy, Milly," Turner soothed, coming to sit on the edge of his bunk and taking her hand. "It's all over now. Don't distress yourself."

Milly set her cup on the desk, sat up straight and pressed herself against Turner, who held her gently. She shivered for a moment or two and then lay back, "Thank you."

"Why were you aboard the freighter, Milly?" Turner asked casually. He hoped a little conversation would settle her.

Milly chuckled bitterly, "I'm in logistics. I handle all the shipping schedules for Northeastern Cargo, the company that owns... owned... the *Chester Clyde*. Or I did work for them... after today..."

"Oh, I'm sure they won't blame you," Turner stated matter-of-factly. "We're at war, and the Nazis have brought it to our beaches; that's the unfortunate truth of it."

"And the Navy doesn't seem to be doing a hell of a lot to protect our shipping," Milly said with undisguised bitterness. "I don't mean any personal criticism, Art... it's just..."

"I understand... If I may offer a small suggestion, though, Milly?"

She locked her large blue eyes on his, "Please."

Turner drew in a breath, "If you are still the logistics person for your company... make a suggestion that from now on, they start shipping cargo in convoys. Convoys with lookouts posted twenty-four-seven, okay?"

She chuckled, "Will do, Skipper. And I'll tell them Lieutenant Commander Arthur Turner, captain of the USS *Bull Shark,* said so."

Turner chuckled now, "Right... that oughta scare the pants right off 'em."

The laughter that followed was hearty and welcome for both of them.

10

After tying up in their slip at the New London Submarine Base and seeing to the passengers, Turner called Nichols, Post, Brannigan and Duncan into the wardroom along with Elmer Williams. He asked the men to prepare as thorough and as quick a report on that day's outing as best they could.

"I know it was hardly a proper shakedown," Turner sighed as the six men crammed in around the wardroom table, "but you gents probably have a few items on your punch lists. For one, I'd like to know why Sparky had to manually fire tube four."

"So far it's a pretty short list, Skipper," Duncan stated. "Those diesels are in tip-top shape

"We'll have to chase that one down," Post said. "Off the top of my head, I'd say a bad relay either in the conning tower or in the forward room."

Brannigan nodded, "My juice jerkers will start testing the whole fire control system, sir. As for maneuvering, the motors and the batteries, we're in good shape. Nothing unexpected yet. Then again, we ain't had much time to find the bugs."

Turner sighed, "Well, we will if I have my way. I want to get back out there ASAP. So you gentleman figure out what you need and start the process with SupReq. I've got a meeting with the Admiral, and then… we'll see. Get started, but don't burn the midnight oil, guys. It's been a rough day. Let the men have the night off and we'll get back at it tomorrow. I'd like to shoot for the day after tomorrow to pull out again. Think that's reasonable, XO?"

Williams shot a look at the two engineering officers and the two chiefs. All four men gave a curt nod and a thin smile. "I'll also make sure all divisions have their condition reports for admin, too."

"Good, then I won't keep you. Thank you, men," Turner said.

The four men stood and exited and were almost immediately replaced by Paul Rogers. He slid in behind the table and accepted a cup of coffee from Carlson.

"What's your read, COB?" Turner was asking Rogers in his capacity as chief of the boat to give his impression of the men's attitudes as well as performance.

"Hard to say now, sir," Rogers said. "Hell, we were only out for eight hours or so. I've spoken with Mike and Harry… and also with Sparky and Murph… nothing out of the ordinary to report. The problem is that we just didn't have enough time to put anything or anybody through the paces."

"It *was* only a couple of watches, COB," Williams pointed out with a wry grin.

"Yes sir," Rogers replied slowly. "But that's my point… I've known the skipper here a couple of years and I think he's askin' us if this boat and her crew are ready for real action and right now."

Williams' brows rose in disbelief, and then he looked at Turner and they slowly fell again, "That so, sir?"

Turner sighed, "Elmer… did they tell you much about why *Bull Shark* is being rushed into service?"

Williams frowned, "Just the usual line. War is on, things are heating up… we need more boats to spearhead offensive raids against the Jap fleet, that sort of thing. I've hardly had time to do more than eat and sleep the last month or so, what with PXO School and getting the boat rigged out. The yard over at Groton has been going twenty-four seven."

Turner sighed, "Buck already knows the scoop. He flew over with me from Mare Island, and even if he hadn't… the COB knows all, or does sooner than later."

Rogers grinned.

"It's like this, Elmer… the Nazis are running a U-boat campaign off our east coast, which you already know," Turner explained. "Apparently, there's some kind of command-and-control ship out there directing the operation and it's our job to locate her and send her to the bottom."

Williams nodded, "Yeah… that certainly puts it all into perspective."

"What happened today is just one more example of the need for *somebody* to get their asses out there and do something about it," Turner said, anger creeping into his voice. "And I want that to be us. Thoughts?"

"Most of these guys *are* greenies," Rogers said. "At least forty percent of the crew has never served or even gone to sea before today."

Turner nodded, "And your assessment of the officers?"

Rogers scowled, "Sir… it's not my place."

"Buck, I'm not asking you to criticize anybody," Turner added. "Not directly. Just your impressions from your unique position. Not holding your tootsies to a fire here."

"Well…" Rogers prevaricated. He sighed and then pushed on: " Mr. Nichols, although clearly competent, is a reservist. A feather merchant. We can certainly vouch for Mr. Dutch. That Mr. Jarvis seems like a good head, but we don't know him, or Mr. Post either."

"Or me," Williams admitted.

Rogers shrugged but said nothing.

"What you guys are saying is that we've got a new boat that was rushed off the ways, as it were, with new technology and a new crew," Turner said. "A group of officers that are mostly strangers and even a new captain. What we do have, thank God, are three well-seasoned chiefs and two guys leading the torpedo rooms who could make chief after a war patrol or two. Sixty percent of the crew was already in; that's something too. And I'll not judge Nichols just because he's a reservist. I've read his jacket and he's very qualified. Master's in both electrical and mechanical engineering from MIT, no less. I know we're jumping the gun a little… but dammit… the Japs and the Jerries sure as shit aren't giving us much of a choice. This war isn't even three months old and we're already *way* behind the eight ball."

The two men nodded in agreement.

"This isn't a perfect situation," Turner said, "but we're going to deal with it. Whatever comes up, I'm going to depend on the experienced men on this boat to help me deal with it. You two know as well as anyone that if it's gonna go wrong, it's gonna go wrong out there. So I suggest we keep our fingers on the pulse of the crew, work the ship and iron out any bugs with her and ourselves as we go. Root out the goldbrickers, the rack rangers and the sea lawyers… if any… and get them with the program fast. Any objection?"

Rogers smiled, "No sir. We'll keep her together."

Williams frowned and then shrugged, "It's as you say, Skipper."

"Good," Turner said with a weary sigh. "Now, I've got to go see Admiral Edwards… I think you should come too, Elmer… and then maybe I can spend a couple of hours with my wife and kids. Let's see what tomorrow brings. Thank you, COB. Hang with me a moment, would ya', XO?"

Rogers stood and vanished through the wardroom curtain. Williams frowned and looked a little concerned, "Sir?"

"At ease, Elmer," Turner said gently. "Now that it's just you and me and we've heard from Buck… what are your thoughts?"

"Thoughts, sir?"

"Yeah, thoughts… thoughts on the boat, the men… on what happened today. Just between us girls."

Williams sighed, "I think we were damned lucky, sir. This boat isn't ready for a fight."

Turner cocked an eyebrow at that, "From what I just heard and saw today, I'm surprised to hear you say that, Elmer."

"You asked my opinion, sir."

"I did… care to explain it?"

Williams pulled in a long breath and let it out slowly, "Every new boat needs a shakedown, sir. A week at least to really iron out the bugs. This is one of the most complex machines ever built… and this one was rushed. I'm not comfortable racing blindly into an unknown scenario with an untried boat and crew... sir."

"Elmer, relax," Turner said kindly. "And call me Art, for God's sake. Is this your official position?"

Williams hesitated, "Well... no sir, I'm not saying I won't follow orders or something... I just feel we need more time."

"Is that the opinion of Elmer or the XO?"

Williams looked slightly bewildered, "Isn't that the same thing, Art?"

Turner leaned back in his chair, "I don't know, Elmer. I think there's two dudes, Elmer and Art... couple of young guys who like sports, women and a good steak, if you see what I mean. Then there's Wiliams and Turner, the XO and CO of a warship. Two unique points of view finding expression inside one noggin. We're one thing on shore with wives, kids and sweethearts... and we're another at sea with eighty guys' lives riding on our decisions. Maybe the two are the same, maybe they blend eventually until they are... but I think both points of view are valuable."

"Pretty metaphysical," Williams said. "And honestly Art... I'm not sure about either Elmer or Williams. Both have a lot to learn, need a little work and both aren't quite sure of themselves right now."

It took guts to admit that, especially to a new captain you hardly knew. Williams' stock rose a point or two in Turner's mind. He smiled and said: "Join the club, pal. I know the thing with your fiancé hit you hard and I know being rushed into the XO slot maybe before you're quite ready may be equally or even more daunting... but my gut says you're up to dealing with both. And I think like me, like our guys and like our boat here... trial by fire may be just what you need."

Williams shrugged, "Maybe... but I'd still be happy with more shaking down."

Turner sighed, "Pragmatically, Elmer, I agree with you. Christ, a couple of weeks ago *I* was the XO of a boat... but the Nazis aren't waiting around. They've already sunk several *dozen* ships and the damned war is only three months old. Admiral Edwards feels we're the spearhead and since nobody else is doing anything... I agree. Whatever problems we may have with this boat, and frankly I see very few, we're going to have to work out on patrol. We can't afford to sit idle. That's *my* official position, XO."

"Aye-aye, sir," Williams said without conviction. "It's just…"

"It's a little too much like flying by the seat of our pants for you, eh, Elmer?"

"I'd agree with that, s… Art."

Turner drew in a deep breath, "Elmer… we're at war. As somebody somewhere said, war is hell. It ain't easy, it ain't safe and in spite of the occasional beer party or whore house on leave… it ain't fun."

Williams grinned, "Yes sir."

"Okay," Turner said. "I think we'll have time to tweak as we go. For now though, we've got an hour or so before the meeting. Get your report together and we'll brief the Admiral."

"Goddamn those Ratzi sons of bitches!" Edwards railed. "Shooting one of our ships right under our goddamned noses! The fucking *balls!*"

Turner and Williams simply sat at attention and waited for the Admiral to blow off his head of steam. He was pacing behind his desk, occasionally gesticulating toward his windows and occasionally beating a meaty fist into his palm. Finally he stopped, heaved a long sigh and dropped into his chair.

"Gentlemen," he said more evenly, "let me make something clear. I'm not blaming you for this. This attack was cleverly executed and well-timed."

"The Skipper did want to go after the other boat, sir," Williams offered.

"No… no, you did the right thing, Art," Edwards stated. "You couldn't just leave all those people out there… and what would be the point, anyway? The only way to sink another submarine is on the surface. You'll get your chance."

"Glad to hear it, sir," Turner said. "I've already got my engineers, chiefs and other officers working on the short punch list we put together yesterday. We should be ready for sea again day after tomorrow. Provided we can get two more fish to replace the dummies."

"Done," Edwards said. He looked at Williams and smiled thinly. "I'll bet your XO here would like more of a shakedown before going on active duty, though. I assume since you're here, Elmer, that Art told you about the Nazi C and C out there someplace?"

Williams nodded, "Yes sir… and considering what we saw today… I agree with the Skipper. We can shake the boat down while we hunt her down."

"Good man," Edwards said, leaning back and scowling. "This is *intolerable!* I can't understand why Admiral King doesn't *do* something about this! I'm ComSubLant, but what the hell does that mean? I don't really have a submarine fleet. Mostly the new construction and a couple of old S and R boats scattered along the coast. You're my big gun, Art. What we should have is a damned fleet of heavy tin cans and escort DDs out there escorting convoys! Every time I launch a boat, it goes right around and through the canal and into Robert English's hands. I understand why, but we've got a war in this ocean too, for Christ's sake!"

Turner empathized with the Admiral's frustrations. They were shared by many line officers. He also knew that he should not repeat anything being said in that room. Technically, Edwards was bordering on insubordination, at least concerning his remarks about Admiral King, the Navy's current commander in chief, Cominch.

"On top of that we're getting shit pickles from BeauOrd," Edwards ranted. "They won't even test them. Just keep sending them out to skippers and then blaming the skippers for misses. Jesus…"

"At least you had the wherewithal to take matters into your own hands, sir," Turner offered.

Edwards yanked a cigarette from a pack on his desk and lit it, "Yeah, at the risk of my own professional ass. If it wasn't for Web here, I might already be up for a general court."

Webster Clayton had been silent during the Admiral's tirade. He leaned forward in his chair and grinned, "It's early days yet, Dick. The Navy will learn. In the meantime, let's focus on what we can directly affect."

"I don't suppose you have any further information, Web?" Turner asked.

"Not as yet," Clayton responded. "Just random bits and pieces. One or two reports of submarines off the beach at night from Fort Lauderdale up to Cape Cod. Most are probably bunk. This has gone on long enough for the civilian population to know about it and see phantoms around every corner. You're still looking for a civilian merchant vessel carrying a floatplane. The only definitive report I've got is that a freighter was sunk last week off Cape Hatteras and reported a floatplane circling as part of her distress call. Again, I feel this means the control ship must be within two hundred or so miles of the coast."

"A lot of water for one boat to cover," Turner observed.

Clayton sighed, "True… and even if you come across a ship, you have to make certain she's really a German. God help us all should you sink an allied vessel by mistake."

"How the hell do we prove that?" Edwards pondered.

"We could board her," Turner suggested with a wry grin. "Take her as a prize."

Clayton laughed, "Captain, if you could do that, I'd personally put you in for the Medal of Honor."

"Maybe you'd like to come along, sir," Williams suggested to Clayton.

"Part of me does," Clayton said. "But other duties keep me here. I'm due in Washington at nine in the morning, in fact. For now, I'll say good luck and good hunting, Art."

With that, everyone stood. Edwards showed them all out, and the two submariners walked out of the admin building and into the cold March night.

"Maybe we should work double tides, sir," Williams offered.

"Not tonight, Elmer," Turner said. "It's already half-past six. Let the men and the other officers have a little downtime. We'll roll up our sleeves in the morning. See you then."

When the *Bull Shark's* captain arrived at his assigned house, he was mildly surprised to see Joan sitting in the living room and having coffee with Mildred Allman. He hung his pea jacket in the small hall closet, went into the parlor and kissed his wife.

"Welcome back, dear," Joan said.

"Nice to see you again, Milly," Turner said as Joan poured him a cup of coffee. "Should you be up and about?"

The woman had removed the compress on her forehead and covered the purplish bruise with her yellow bangs. She smiled, "The doctor doesn't think there's any danger of concussion. The leg is a bit tender, but not enough to prevent me from walking on it. I was on my way home… well, that's to say, to the nice cottage your Admiral Edwards let me have for a night or two before I take the train back to New York. I thought I'd stop by to say thank you again. It also gave me the pleasure of meeting your lovely wife. Turns out we've got a lot in common."

"Oh?" Turner asked.

"We both have family in North Carolina," Joan said. "Her sister lives on Wrightsville Beach."

Turner grinned, "How do you like that?"

Milly smiled, "Joan's mother lives in Wilmington too, she tells me. I wonder if they know each other."

"Could be," Turner said. "Wilmington is a pretty small town."

"Although mom has only been there about two years," Joan said. "We're from Michigan originally. Art and his people are from South Florida."

They chatted for a few minutes before Milly stood to excuse herself, "Well, thank you so much for the coffee, Joan. It was a real pleasure meeting you. I'll probably head back to New York tomorrow. I'd like to extend an offer to take you both to dinner if you can get away some Friday or Saturday night. It's only ninety minutes by train, and I'll even put you up in the company's reserved suite at the Waldorf. You can meet my fiancé and we'll make a night of it."

"Sounds delightful," Joan said. "If we can get a sitter for the kids. And if Art is in port, of course."

Milly shook Art's hand, "Oh? Going after that U-boat soon?"

Art grinned at her, "Something like that. Still need to shake down the new boat."

Milly chuckled sardonically, "I'm surprised to hear you're not headed out tomorrow to get the bastard. Wish I could see it... it's not every day a girl gets torpedoed, you know."

"You've certainly taken things in stride, Milly," Art said, getting to his feet. "Well, you drive carefully. Glad to know you're all right."

"Thank you again," Milly replied, taking Turner's hand. "Like I said, you two come down. Or I'll see you up here. I'm back and forth a lot."

Once their guest had departed, Joan called the kids down for supper. The Turners ate, listened to the radio and played *Sorry* until bedtime.

Later, Art and Joan lay in each other's arms, panting heavily after a very passionate bout of lovemaking. Joan had her head in the pocket of her husband's shoulder when she said, "She's very pretty."

"Who?"

"Milly, you dope," Joan teased. "Who do you think?"

He chuckled, "My mind is on another woman at the moment."

Joan smiled, "Well, I think hers might be on a certain dashing submarine captain."

"Well, hot damn!" Turner exclaimed and then scoffed, "Oh, come on. She's engaged to be married, lives in New York and... oh yeah... *I'm* already married."

Joan shrugged, "Call it woman's intuition if you want. But she didn't just drop by on her way back from the hospital to say thank you."

"Why not? Maybe she wanted to meet you, too."

"I'm sure she did," Joan responded. "To size up her competition."

"Joanie..." Turner chastised her gently. "Don't tell me you're jealous."

"You know I don't get jealous, dear," Joan said calmly. "It's not that I'm worried about you... it's just a sense I get from her."

Turner pondered that for a moment, "I'm not gonna mock woman's intuition. You've certainly proved it's a real thing... but I don't know... her being khaki-whacky for me?"

"Well... she's interested in you," Joan stated. "How far that goes, I don't know... but there's more there than grateful courtesy."

Turner sighed, "Well… anyway, it doesn't matter now. She's headed out of town and I'm headed out to sea. We'll probably never see her again if we don't take her up on that offer to come to the Big Apple."

"Who knows?" Joan asked. "I do like her, for all that. She's nice and she's sharp. Besides, I may run into her when I go down to visit mom in a couple of weeks."

"You're going to Wilmington in a couple of weeks?" he asked.

"I was thinking about it. You'll be at sea for a while and the kids have a break from school coming up. Why not? I mentioned that to Milly, and she said that maybe she could get away for a couple of days and visit her sister, and we could get together."

"Sounds like she's interested in you," Turner said with a chuckle.

Joan shrugged again and snuggled closer to his warm muscular body, "It's a small world, darling."

11

APPROXIMATELY 125 NAUTICAL MILES WEST, SOUTHWEST OF THE BERMUDA GROUP OF ISLANDS

MARCH 25, 1942

2230 ZULU

The Nazi Q-ship, SS *Mortimer P. Blanch,* was headed due south with only enough way on her for her rudder to bite. The late afternoon sun glittered pleasantly off a nearly glass-calm sea. The big freighter's long shadow stretched out many hundreds of feet from her port side and did a remarkable job of camouflaging the gray and black hull of the U-123, which kept station thirty yards off the freighter's beam.

The air was pleasantly warm, thanks to the influence of the Gulf Stream. Warm enough to allow the four men to feel comfortable in shirt sleeves as they sat around a table set up on a small open promenade deck just abaft the ship's bridge. Two of the men wore only white duty shirts, their submariner's leather jackets having been removed. One man, a civilian, wore his dress shirt open at the collar and had loosened his tie. Only the full captain still wore his uniform jacket.

"I would say things are going quite well," Klaus Brechman observed. "Kapitan Hardegen's sinking of the American freighter right under their noses was certainly a bold stroke."

"And has given us some valuable information," Curt Diedrich

added, puffing on a Cuban cigar. "We now know of a new submarine that has been launched. For what that's worth."

"In truth, Herr Kapitan," Hardegen opined, "this is nothing surprising. The Yankees are being forced into a major war in the Pacific by the Japanese. They need all the submarines they can build. It's rather ironic when you think of it."

"Ironic, sir?" Heiman Richter inquired.

"Yes, Einsvo," Hardegen said, taking Deidrich's cigar torch and lighting the cigar the captain had given him. "That the Americans are going to have to use their submarines in *exactly* the same way as we do. In order for them to effectively fight the Japanese while they rebuild their Pacific fleet, they'll have to adopt the tactics of the evil Kriegsmarine! I find that rather funny."

Diedrich chuckled, "Indeed, Reinhard. I wonder how long it will be before they start employing wolf packs, eh?"

"Regardless," Brechman said, attempting to get the briefing back on track, "every bit of information we acquire is helpful. We are, in a sense, all alone out here. Currently, we're too far from the mainland coast of the United States to perform air reconnaissance."

"Why are we meeting so far out?" Richter said. "And yet so close to Bermuda?"

"That is our concern, *Oberleutnant zur See*," Brechman said sharply.

Richter's face reddened slightly, but he held his tongue. It didn't do to antagonize an SS officer who could not only make things unpleasant for Richter but who could also do so for his family back home.

"Klaus," Diedrich said reasonably, "the U-123's first officer is only asking a reasonable question."

Brechman drew in a breath and let it out slowly, "Yes... yes, Herr Richter. It's only that in such operations, we must work under the rules of need to know. The less said the better. Or, as the crumpet suckers say... a nod is as good as a wink. However, as this directly affects your boat, I will explain."

Hardegen only puffed placidly on his cigar. It was quite good. Richter had overstepped slightly, but it was forgivable under the circumstances. Had Brechman not backed off, Hardegen would have had to step in and defend his executive officer.

He would have done so without trepidation. For one, he was more seasoned than Richter. He did not fear the SS. His family, what little of it there was left, was either well-placed in the Party or members of the SS themselves. Further, Hardegen's military record gave him considerable gravitas. He also understood the ways of tact. He would be able to back Brechman down without a direct confrontation... although the thought of one did amuse him slightly.

"Our spy network reports that the Americans are beginning to suspect that this ship is out here directing this operation," Brechman stated. "If that is so, then they will send a ship, most probably a submarine, out to find and sink *us*."

"So you've pulled back from the theater of operations to allow the tension to fizzle?" Hardegen asked.

"Temporarily," Diedrich stated. "We are at war and risk is part of our duty. Also, should we come into contact with an American vessel, we have men aboard who can speak to them in their own language and even dialect. Our chief pilot, in fact, can sound as if he were from the region we've been patrolling. It's so convincing that there are times when we're nearly fooled."

"If there is a submarine to be dispatched," Hardegen opined, "then I have a strange feeling I know the boat."

"The one at the scene when you sank that freighter the previous week? The..." Brechman consulted a notepad in front of him. "Ah... the *Bull Shark,* was it?"

Hardegen nodded, "The SS-333. We were listening to the radio exchange between the two vessels. The captain is a man named Arthur Turner. I don't suppose your intelligence network knows anything of him, Herr Brechman?"

"Very little," Brechman admitted. "Fortunately, it is remarkably easy to spy on the United States. Even after the Great War, many Germans immigrated there or went to seek higher education there. Their... *open door* policy makes them particularly vulnerable and weak. They allow niggers, spics and even *kykes* into important jobs and even into their military! I have it on good authority that there are a number of Zionists serving in the United States Navy… *pathetic…*"

"It will be their undoing, Herr Brechman," Richter agreed.

Hardegen only puffed languidly on his cigar. He neither made a comment nor allowed any expression to cross his face. He did not share the Party's views on racial purity. Although he did agree that white men were intellectually superior to their colored brethren, there was no real hatred there. Simply a feeling of superiority.

Neither could he find it in himself to loathe the Jews as the Führer wanted the country to do. Hardegen's own grandmother had been Jewish and a wonderfully warm and caring woman. Rumor had it that Hitler himself was part Jewish. And for a man who touted such vehement ideas on racial purity, he himself was hardly a fine specimen of Aryan beauty.

"What are your thoughts on the matter, Kapitan Hardegen?" Brechman needled, noting the submariner's lack of a response.

Hardegen flicked an ash over the stern railing and said: "I have no doubt that you are correct, Herr Brechman. There are many Germans living in the United States. No doubt they are part of your informational pipeline."

It wasn't a bald agreement with the man's previously expressed opinions on race and the SS officer knew it. However, he didn't push the issue. It was clear that Hardegen wasn't a man to be pushed or to lose his composure. Submarine captains were made of sterner stuff.

"Another reason we are here, gentlemen," Brechman continued, "is that I wish to recon and then attack the Royal Navy Yard or at least some of the shipping near here. As you may know, Bermuda is a jumping-off point for convoys from Canada to Britain."

"It's heavily defended," Hardegen stated, "as I understand it. We've never attacked Bermuda, not since we sent in the cruiser *Admiral Scheer*. Part of the reason is that it's too shallow. The only route inside the reef to the Great Basin is fairly narrow and well-guarded by both sea and air."

"Thus the recon flight," Brechman said pointedly. "Even a simple and ineffective attack will draw attention away from the coastal operations in the U.S. for a time."

"It might make the Americans believe that this command-and-control ship is over here rather than within flying distance of their coast?" Richter asked.

Brechman nodded.

"A game of cat and mouse," Hardegen said neutrally.

"With the American submarine, should they send one, as the mouse," Brechman said with a hard smile on his hard face. "Between our submarine fleet, this ship and our airplane, we should have no trouble locating and dealing with anything they send."

Hardegen wasn't so sure of that. He had a feeling that Turner would be coming for him. Hardegen had torpedoed a ship right in front of the American captain, and Hardegen knew how he himself would react to such a flagrant move. He'd take it personally.

Further, the *Bull Shark* was a brand-new submarine. Larger, faster and better armed than even his Type IX. Although the U-boat had an advantage below the surface in that she could dive deeper and was at least as fast if not faster than the newer *Tambor* and *Gato*-classes, he would not underestimate the *Bull Shark* and her ten torpedo tubes.

"When do you intend on sending this reconnaissance flight?" Hardegen asked.

"Very soon," Brechman stated. "Our chief pilot, Lieutenant Michner, is no doubt readying his plane at this very moment."

Hardegen rose, "I should like to accompany him."

Diedrich grinned, "He already has a co-pilot and an observer. Perhaps you can take the latter's place."

"Good," Hardegen said. "If I'm going to take my boat into this situation, which I assume is why we're here this evening, then I wouldn't mind a bird's eye view."

"Excellent!" Diedrich said. "I would not mind hearing the thoughts of a seasoned ship's captain on what you observe tonight myself. Herr Richter, please compile a list of anything you might need by way of replenishment. We can take care of that while your captain is taking his joy ride, eh? Good."

Hardegen found Brenner Michner inspecting his plane as the rigging crew was connecting the lifting gear. The young senior lieutenant noticed the submarine captain and came to attention.

"As you were, Lieutenant," Hardegen said casually, sticking out his hand. "I'm *Corvettenkapitan* Reinhard Hardegen. I'm told you're taking a little aerial tour this evening."

"Aye sir," Michner said, shaking the older man's hand warily. "We're to observe the Royal Navy Base and surrounding waters."

"And then my crew and I are no doubt going to have to go in there and do something foolish," Hardegen stated. "So I thought I'd accompany you on this flight."

"Of course, sir… but we usually only carry three."

"Understood," Hardegen replied. "A co-pilot and an observer. No more to keep the weight and fuel consumption down, no doubt."

"Yes sir."

"Then let's let the two other men have the night off. I've done some flying, believe it or not. I've even flown one of these. I'll act as co-pilot and observer. That'll keep the weight down by a further sixty or seventy kilos, yes?"

"Uhm… yes sir, it would, but…" Michner wasn't sure what to do in this situation. Hardegen outranked him and was already well-known in the Kriegsmarine. It would not do to contradict him.

"It's all right, Lieutenant," Hardegen said kindly. "I've already discussed it with Kapitan Diedrich *and* Herr Brechman."

That seemed to ease the pilot's mind some. He even smiled slightly, "Very well, sir. Then I recommend going to the head one last time. We're about to be launched."

Little more than an hour later, the Arado AR-196 was flying low and slow over the water. The sun had not yet slipped below the horizon, and Michner didn't want to approach the islands backlit by the glowing orb. They were still seventy kilometers from the archipelago, and at the plane's current seventy-five knots, just over stall speed, they wouldn't sight them for another twenty or twenty-five minutes yet.

"I saw the sinking of a freighter off Cape Hatteras a month ago," Michner suddenly said, breaking a silence that had mostly hung over the cabin since takeoff.

Hardegen had his hands on the yolk, getting used to the plane again after not having flown in for over a year. He glanced over at the younger man and raised an eyebrow, "That was U-123. Yes, I saw this plane after the attack. It troubles you, Lieutenant?"

Michner seemed to stiffen ever so slightly, "No sir... they are enemies of the Fatherland."

Hardegen chuckled softly, "Come off it, Michner. Your SS watchdog isn't around now. Be honest. It distressed you to see that ship blown apart and all those sailors killed."

Michner stared at the submarine captain for a long moment, trying to gauge what was in his mind by his expression. The pilot could see nothing. The submariner must be an excellent card player.

"I... yes sir, it did," Michner finally admitted.

"Good," Hardegen said not unkindly. "It should bother any man with a soul. Yes, they may be enemies of the Fatherland, but they're sailors, too. Just like us. Hell, some of them might have been of German descent. The man I suspect may be coming to hunt me down is named *Turner*. A good German name, that.... you're surprised?"

Michner had to admit that he was, "Yes sir, I am. I always thought submariners were made of ice."

Hardegen laughed, "No, we're made of steel. It's a very dangerous job and takes enormous fortitude. Some of us can do our duty and still pity our foes... some of us, like my first officer, seem to lack that empathy. It makes them good at their jobs... but in my opinion, not men I'd place in command. Yet that's not my decision to make. At any rate, Herr Michner, don't worry yourself because you feel bad about killing Americans or British. War is a political affair. It's hard to fight men who were once your friends and who, once the war is over, may be so again. It's a very difficult thing to manage."

Michner seemed to relax, "I'm very glad you shared that with me, sir. I've been having a bit of a war with my conscience ever since that night."

"That makes you a decent man," Hardegen said. "Just remember that when it's all said and done... you owe your loyalty to our beloved Deutschland. Your country. More than the Nazi Party, it's Germany that matters. So feel pity and remorse when you see an enemy ship go down... when your reports send my torpedoes into their sides... just don't let the sentiment overwhelm you. The more ships we sink and the more aggressive we are, the sooner we win this war, and the sooner peace will reign."

"The more we kill, the less we'll have to kill?" Michner asked.

Hardegen nodded, "As ludicrous as it sounds… it's true… I must say, Lieutenant, this bird handles very well, even at low altitude and low speed."

Michner felt more comfortable talking about his passion, and he felt a swell of gratitude for Hardegen. This was clearly an intelligent man who understood how to command souls as well as machines, "Oh, yes sir. She's got quite a range if handled right. I've personally flown nearly eleven hundred kilometers and landed with twenty minutes of reserve fuel."

Hardegen nodded, "Which is why the *Blanch* can hang three-hundred or more kilometers off the coast of America and still fly a recon of several hours. Impressive aircraft. Do my eyes deceive, or is that land ahead?"

The sun was gone now, and twilight was fast approaching. The band of deeper darkness growing in the east. On the horizon, several shapes dark against the navy-blue sea interrupted the sameness.

"Yes sir," Michner stated, placing his hands on his yolk. "I'll take over now if you don't mind. Climbing to seven-hundred meters, increasing to one-hundred and fifty knots."

The BMW radial engine roared as Michner opened the throttle and angled the aircraft to go higher. As they leveled off at twenty-one hundred feet, it appeared slightly brighter as they rose a little higher over the Earth's curvature.

"Why are we speeding up and climbing?" Hardegen asked. "Surely we'd be harder to spot on radar at one hundred meters or less."

Michner grinned, "True… but not impossible. Consider, sir, you're a British radar man and you see a slow-moving aircraft at low altitude heading toward the base. What would you think?"

Hardegen grinned as well, "That we were a couple of Huns up to no good."

Michner actually laughed, "Exactly. This way, we're just another flight coming across from Virginia or North Carolina."

"Won't they spot us and make radio contact?" Hardegen asked.

As if he'd conjured it, the radio crackled, and an English voice said: "*Unidentified aircraft headed east at two-one-five-zero feet, this is Royal Navy Air Station Boaz. Please identify self and intention.*"

Hardegen glanced over at Michner with a raised eyebrow. To his surprise, though, the pilot was in no way discommoded. He picked up the radio microphone and, in perfect English with an astonishingly accurate accent, replied: "Howdy, good buddy. Nice to know you're lookin' out. We're a private aircraft took off from Wilmington, North Carolina 'bout four hours back. Comin' over for a couple of days to unwind and enjoy your weather. Damn chilly back yonder. We're headed for the commercial seaplane dock on the main island. Over."

Hardegen chuckled, "Should I wonder if you're not an American spy?"

Michner laughed, "I get that a lot, sir. Comes in handy, as you'll see."

"*A Yank, eh? Have a decent flight?*" The air controller asked. "*Mind if I ask for your identification?*"

"Not at all, partner," Michner said, laying on the cowboy talk a bit thick, Hardegen thought. "Zebra two zero two one King Baker."

"*Very well, Z-2021-KB... you're course will take you very near the naval station, so be mindful. We've got three incoming flying boats. Recommend you stay at current altitude until you make contact with Bermuda approach.*"

"Will do," Michner replied cheerfully. "Thanks for the heads-up."

There was a pause, and then the British voice said casually, "*By the way... one of our pilots has you in sight. Says you look like a German floatplane he's familiar with.*"

Hardegen felt his stomach tighten. Again, though, Michner didn't seem to appear worried. Instead, he keyed the mic and laughed good-naturedly, "Hot damn, partner! Your fly boy got him some good eyes! This crate *is* German. My pappy bought her year before last. Them Krauts make a floatplane almost as well put together as Marlene Dietrich!"

The British controller roared with laughter, "*Righto! Can't argue with that, mate! I also very much doubt the Jerries would paint a bloody*" *dolphin on the side, eh? Well, welcome to the Islands, and mind how you go... cheers."*

"Preciate that," Michner said and signed off.

Hardegen laughed, "My God..."

"You're the observer now, sir," Michner said, angling to make a wide loop over the naval base and throttling down slightly. "Make sure to take good notes."

Hardegen did just that. Although the light had nearly faded, there was enough to see several ships in the Great Basin. He also took note of several small patrol craft outside the reef and the channel inside.

"I hope you've seen what you needed to, sir," Michner said. "We've got to head southerly or it's going to start looking suspicious."

Hardegen sighed, "I think so. A difficult prospect. I'll have to look at a chart, but it's very shallow around here, especially inside the reef. With multiple vessels, and I'm certain I saw two destroyers anchored... and the air station... an attack would be nearly impossible to survive, I should think."

"I wonder if that matters to Herr Brechman," Michner said sourly. He glanced over at Hardegen and frowned. "I beg your pardon, sir."

Hardegen sighed, "No need, Lieutenant. I understand. It'll be my and my crew's asses he risks next. He seems to me to be one of those men we spoke of earlier... dedicated to his duty but with no feeling for anything or anyone. Be wary of men like that... to the Brechmans of the world it matters little if you're a Jew or a blue-eyed member of the *master race.* You're simply a tool for him to achieve his ends."

"Yes sir," Michner said evenly.

They turned south and began to descend. At one hundred meters, Michner pressed the throttle to the firewall and slowly banked them to the southeast, where he'd keep them on course until they sunk the land and then would head back for the ship. They'd burn a lot of fuel at that speed and altitude, but it was necessary to slip away from the prying electronic eyes of the Allies.

12

6 MILES EAST, SOUTHEAST OF VIRGINIA BEACH, VA

APRIL 6, 1942

1030 ZULU

Unlike their U.S. submarine counterparts in the Pacific, and unlike their U-boat adversaries in the Atlantic, the USS *Bull Shark,* SS-333 did not run on the surface at night to recharge and run submerged during the day. They were not, after all, trying to hide from anti-submarine warships and aircraft. On the contrary, the submarine was herself as much an anti-submarine weapon as she was a surface ship killer.

With this somewhat backward schedule, Elmer Williams, the ship's primary navigator, had the opportunity to take both solar and lunar observations. With an accurate sextant and a hyper-accurate chronometer set to Greenwich Mean Time, the first officer could plot the ship's position north of the equator as well as exactly how far west she was from Greenwich, England, and do so day and night.

By running during daylight on her diesels, the boat could cover large areas of ocean very rapidly, going as far as two hundred miles without pushing things. During the long night hours of early spring, the boat would submerge to forty feet and cruise at a modest four knots for the duration of darkness.

Although she could run much faster thanks to her snorkel, the boat's skipper wanted to remain silent and listen, both with his advanced sonar gear as well as at a shallow enough depth to raise his radio and radar masts so as to intercept communications and to spot surface vessels. It was the best of all worlds in terms of her crew's circadian rhythms. Men could actually go to sleep at night without the clatter of the big diesels for the most part.

Of course, this wasn't a permanent situation, as the watch rotation ensured that everyone on board worked every shift in an ever-rotating cycle. If anyone went without sleep on a regular basis, it would be her captain. His officers would do so also, if he allowed it. However, Arthur Turner wanted to maintain a high level of readiness, and that meant that all the men aboard ate and slept well. He pushed himself, but that was his prerogative as the captain.

For several weeks now, the *Bull Shark* had been prowling down the coast of the United States. Her course was an erratic zig-zag that took her to within sight of coastal lights at night and out to, and well past the continental shelf, depending on where the continental slope began. This meant that the submarine would travel as far as three hundred miles from the shore at times, and at others track a course something between that and the beach.

On this particular morning, the boat was maintaining minimum headway close enough to the shore that the lights of Virginia Beach could be seen through the periscope. Hours before, word had come through on an encrypted radio transmission that three freighters had left Wilmington, North Carolina and had exited the Cape Fear River at twenty-hundred the previous night. The small convoy, the idea of the shipping firm and not due to any Navy influence, should have covered the one-hundred and thirty miles or so and would be passing by the boat any time.

The freighters were carrying textiles and refrigerated goods. And one had been converted into a troop transport with more than a thousand souls aboard. A prime target for a Nazi U-boat. Turner could only hope that the small convoy hadn't been waylaid during the night.

At forty feet, the submarine could use her eyes, both human and electronic, to scan the ocean around them and still remained submerged. However, in both cases, the range wasn't very far. Although the head of the periscope was twenty-eight feet above the water, this meant that the visual range was no more than eight or nine miles. The SD air search radar could scan for a considerable distance, but the SJ surface search radar also had a limited range due to it being much closer to the surface than the head of the periscope. *Bull Shark's* ears, on the other hand, were listening intently both above and below the surface.

So far there had been no radio contact. This was no surprise as any convoying ships would be maintaining radio silence. They'd use signal guns to communicate or short-range walkie-talkies if necessary.

Joe Dutch and Chet Rivers, the boat's two best sonar operators, were huddled together down in the control room. They were slowly scanning the surrounding ocean, the boat's JK sound heads, both the QC and QB, suspended below the keel from the forward torpedo room. The JP sound head, mounted topside, was secured since the deck was only fifteen feet or so below the surface.

The advantage of the lower heads was that they could also send sonar pulses should the need arise. Also, with two heads trained and sweeping through two different arcs, the submarine's hearing was improved.

"Nothing, Skipper," Dutch reported glumly.

He and Rivers had the sound gear outputting to the loudspeaker so they could both listen and watch the magic eye display together. Turner, who would normally be in the conning tower searching with the periscope, was standing at the gyro table examining the chart. Elmer Williams was on periscope watch in the conning tower along with Pat Jarvis and Andy Post. Nichols was in the control room with Turner. Petty Officer Richie "Mug" Vigliano was stationed on the helm. Buck Rogers, as COB, was stationed at the ballast manifold controls. Motor machinist Mike Watley was sitting at the stern planes and Electrician first-class Sherman "Tank" Broderick at the bow planes. It was quiet in the control center, save for the occasional click and whirr of machinery, the sound of the ventilation and a small creak or pop from a chair being adjusted in.

When the ship's cook, a tall and wiry black man named Henry Martin, stepped in through the after hatch accompanied by the smell of fresh coffee, everyone seemed to perk up. Hot on Martin's heels was

Bill Borshowski, the assistant cook. Borshowski was a big Polish kid who spoke in a heavy Chicago accent and always had a smile on his wide face. He carried a tray with freshly baked donuts and sweet rolls.

"God bless you men," Turner said with a grin.

"Eddie called back and tell me I better take good care of you boys up here," Martin, who pronounced his last name Mar-tehn, said in his heavy Louisiana Cajunite drawl. "Said you been up here tree or two-hour wit' not a damn ting in dem bellies! You eat up all dis now, you heyuh?"

Nichols laughed as Turner chuckled and took a cup of coffee and a cherry-filled Danish and glazed donut.

"Who's running this ship anyway?" Buck Rogers asked as he grabbed a sweet roll.

"Aww, come on, COB," Borshowski said. "Everybody knows the Navy runs on its belly."

"Hoo! That's for true!" Martin enthused, overdoing it a little for effect.

"Jesus Christ, Hank," Dutch put in, his face appearing in the overhead hatch. "If you're gonna trowel that Cajun act on *that* thick, then we better get a real authentic seafood gumbo or a jambalaya soon."

"Oh, don't you fret none bout dat, Mr. Dutch," Martin replied with a broad grin. "Was gonna get that started the next day or two. I managed to get a nice load of okra and some andouille saw-sees fore we done left dem dock. It gonna be the best bongo you never had, I gar-rone-tee!"

"Oh, brother..." Turner moaned. "This is gonna be a *long* patrol..."

That got a hearty laugh that followed the two men as they moved forward to bring a little refreshment to the other on-duty crew.

"JP, doubtful contact!" Rivers blurted. "Real faint sir... checking... uncertain, but I think I'm picking up slow, heavy screws..."

"Boost your gain," Dutch ordered. "Checking on it now, sir... recommend full-strength single ping."

Turner frowned, "No... not yet. What's the bearing, gents?"

"Still very rough..." Dutch admitted. "But I'd say due south true, maybe... zero-two-zero relative. Gotta be thirty-thousand yards, wouldn't you say, Rivers?"

Rivers had unplugged the cable from the loudspeaker and had jacked in his headphones, "I think so, sir."

Turner set his coffee and plate of pastry on the gyro table and mounted the ladder so that his head stuck up into the conning tower. He looked at the two sonarmen with interest.

"How are you getting ranges on passive?" Turner asked.

Dutch smiled a little sheepishly and yet with a little pride in it, too, turner thought, "Chet and I have been working up a methodology for getting rough ranges on passive sonar, Skipper. We've been comparing sound levels with matched radar ranges as well as performing calculations on decibel-levels and VU-meter readings."

"yes sir," Rivers added. "Then we work up a chart, using these values and known propellor sound types. It's really rough now, but with time, I think we can get to within a twenty-percent error rate."

"I'll be damned..." Turner muttered. "that's damned genius, fellas."

"It's never gonna be more than a rule of thumb, though," Dutch warned.

"Still... could be useful," Turner mused and then turned to Balkley. "Give me a sweep. Sugar jig on PPI."

Post was leaning over the radar operator's shoulder and scowling at the radar screen, which showed the lighted sweep over a planned position indicator, which was essentially a chart. He turned to Turner and shook his head, "We're too deep, sir. If they are fifteen miles or more off, we won't see them for a while yet, not with the SJ only a few feet above water."

Turner nodded and slid back down, "Helm, come right to course one-niner-zero. All ahead two-thirds. Frank, how are we on battery?"

"About ninety percent," Nichols stated. "I've got the vent fans going through the snorkel. Love that thing... we could run on diesels or even just crank up the auxiliary for internal power and take some of the load off the cells."

Again Turner shook his head, "No... I want to stay quiet. Even at two-thirds submerged, we still make noise. At this rate, though, we'll be up with the contact in less than an hour, assuming they're going at anything over ten knots."

"What if we pop up to the surface and do a combat sweep?" Nichols asked. "Just like we were hitting a surface target and doing a fast ranging. Minimal risk for any U-boat's watching and any surface ships will either not have radar or would be friendly anyway."

"you *sure* you're a reservist?" Turner grinned, "Spoken like a gunnery officer, Frank. Okay, let's do it. You catch that up there, XO?"

"Aye-aye," Williams said from his position at the search scope. "Standing by on full combat sweep with sugar jig and periscope."

"Very well," Turner said, picking up his coffee. "Diving officer, surface the boat."

"Surface the boat, aye," Nichols, who was also the senior diving officer as well as first engineer, replied. "Blow main ballast... blow negative... bow planes on full rise, stern planes on ten degrees up bubble."

The boat angled upward at a mild ten degrees. From around them, the roar of the high-pressure air system blew hundreds of tons of seawater out of the ballast tanks through their open bottoms, and the boat, moving at a modest four knots, rose and broached, her bow angled only slightly higher than her stern.

"Boat is surfaced," Nichols reported.

"Full sweep," Turner ordered.

Several seconds went by, and Williams reported no visual contacts. Post called down with a different report, though.

"Confirm sonar contact on SJ radar!" he said excitedly. "Multiple large surface contacts bearing zero-zero-five, range twenty-seven-thousand yards, repeat two-seven-zero-zero-zero yards!"

"Secure the sugar jig," Turner ordered. "Diving officer, take us to periscope depth."

"Periscope depth, aye," Nichols said and turned to Turner. "Sir... can I have a few minutes to complete re-pressurization?"

Turner smiled, "Topping off the air while we're afloat, eh?"

"Even a feather merchant has a good idea now and then," Nichols jibed.

That got a chuckle from the control room crew. Turner patted

Nichols on his shoulder, "Now and then... but no, Mr. Nichols, you may not. No need, not with that snorkel anyway."

Nichols looked chagrinned to have forgotten that unusual capability. Turner squeezed his shoulder and grinned to let the man know his remark hadn't been a rebuke.

"Ten degrees down bubble on bow and stern planes," Nichols ordered. "Open main vents, COB. Flood negative."

There was a *whoosh* as pressurized air exploded from the ballast tanks' open vents and was rapidly replaced with seawater. Again the boat tilted slightly, toward the bow this time, and a mild swell closed over her deck, fairwater, periscope sheers and radar mast. Only the narrow dark eye of her larger search scope remained above the surface, cutting a narrow line of froth upon the moonlit ocean's face.

"Stronger return now," Rivers was reporting. "I'm definitely getting three sets of heavy, slow screws. Assess freighters running at... eleven knots."

"Very well," Turner said. "Let's not crowd them, though. When you have them in visual, Elmer, let me know. We'll circle around and stand abeam at close range and make radio contact."

For the next fifteen minutes, the *Bull Shark* and the convoy closed each other at a rate of a quarter-mile per minute. When the small group of ships was just over three nautical miles off, Williams reported that he had their foremasts in view in the periscope. The ships were running blacked out, so he hadn't seen them earlier, which was a good sign. However, with a good moon and a clear night, which they had, the big lumbering vessels were easy to spot within a few miles.

"New contact!" Rivers exclaimed. "Submerged contact... small, fast screws... bearing three-one-five... range six thousand yards."

"That's too damned close!" Turner snapped. "Why the hell didn't we hear him sooner?"

"Probably sitting idle," Dutch replied for Rivers, intercepting any wrath from the Old Man.

"Where's the convoy?" Turner asked as he scrambled up the ladder to the conning tower.

"Five thousand yards, bearing zero-seven-zero," Dutch replied. "Skipper... I think the fourth contact is a Kraut boat."

Turner also did. It could be an American submarine, one of the few operating off the coast. Most new submarines, though, were launched from Electric Boat in Groton or at Portsmouth in Maine and were being sent around to the Panama Canal. There were a few old R and S boats stationed at Norfolk, NAS Miami and at New London, but they were old, slow and hopelessly out-classed.

"Sound battle stations torpedo," Turner said calmly as he took Williams' place at the periscope.

The gonging alarm rang throughout the ship, and men scrambled out of their bunks or away from the mess tables and moved to their battle stations. Half of them were already on duty, so it was hardly an exercise in chaos. Turner was pleased when Pat Jarvis reported both torpedo rooms manned and ready within only a few seconds.

"Sir!" Dutch reported. "Unknown contact noise change… she's starting up her diesels. Must be running on top."

"Gonna take advantage of what remains of night and attack," Turner mused.

Even now, false dawn was beginning to appear in the east. If the German wanted to attack without being seen well, then he'd have to do it soon. Not that it mattered much. Even if those three ships were armed, it would be hard for them to fight off even a surfaced submarine before she fired off a spread of torpedoes. And if he wanted, the U-boat's skipper could simply get into position ahead of the convoy and drop to periscope depth. Submerged, he couldn't keep up with the convoy, but he could lie in wait and fire torpedoes as they passed.

Turner could see the three ships himself now. They were traveling in a phalanx, with one ship in the vanguard and the other two off the leader's port and starboard quarter about a thousand yards. It didn't really matter what formation they took; defense was still difficult with only three. Yet he had to admit that if the vessels did have bow or stern guns, then they could cover each other relatively well.

"Sonar, what's our Nazi boat doing?" Turner inquired.

"He's running hot now," Dutch called up. "Looks like about sixteen knots and headed parallel to the convoy. I think he's making an end-around to hit them from the front."

"Concur," Williams said.

"Yeah, me too," Turner said. "Okay, then let's get him as he passes. Open all outer torpedo doors. Order of tubes will be one, three and five. Set depth on torpedoes to three feet. High speed."

Pat Jarvis had the battle telephone around his neck and spoke into the sound-powered unit to the forward room. Turner swung his scope away from the convoy and looked off the port bow. The U-boat, even surfaced, would be hard to see from several miles, but that would change as he drew close.

"Helm, all stop," Turner ordered. "Open the snorkel and start the diesels. Let's see just how well this works."

In a moment, the ship began to vibrate as the four powerful General Motors sixteen-cylinder engines roared to life and poured their thousands of watts of power directly into the electric motors that drove the boat's propellers.

"Come left to course zero-nine-zero," Turner ordered. "All ahead two-thirds."

This was something none of them had yet experienced. A submarine at sixty-five feet running on diesels. With the snorkel extended above the surface, the boat's exhaust system could be employed, and the deadly fumes from the engines were pumped overboard and clean, fresh air, filtered to remove any errant sea spray, was drawn in.

"Bad sound conditions, sir," Dutch called up. "I've lost the German."

"That's okay, Dutch... I've got the bastard!" Turner called out triumphantly.

In his search scope, the low but distinct profile of the U-boat stood out against the pale eastern sky. The other submarine was just to starboard of dead ahead.

"Plotting party ready, sir," Williams called out from below.

"Okay, here's your first mark," Turner said. "Enemy bears... mark."

"Zero-one-oh," Williams called, reading the bearing ring around the scope.

"Range to target... three thousand yards," Turner said. "Angle on the bow is two-eight-zero port. We're gonna stand off his port quarter and shoot at one-thousand yards, Pat."

Jarvis was at the TDC cranking in the initial values. Turner could hear the machine clicking and whirring as it computed the target's position and automatically adjusted the gyros on the selected torpedo tubes.

"What's our speed?" Turner asked.

"Fifteen knots, sir," Mug Vigliano reported.

"Very well… make turns for sixteen knots to match target," Turner ordered. "Left standard rudder."

"Maneuvering answers sixteen knots," Vigliano exclaimed in his heavy Bronx accent. "Comin' left standid."

In his scope, Turner watched as the U-boat appeared to slide to the right. He turned himself that way to keep her in sight.

"Meet her!" Turner ordered.

The U-boat was now just forward of the *Bull Shark's* beam. With the two boats traveling at roughly the same speed, the angle would carry the Nazi submarine slowly ahead of the American boat even as the range decreased.

"Looking good…" Turner commented as he watched his target grow larger. "Down scope and raise the attack scope, Andy. Then hand off to Hotrod and get below to manage our trim."

Post hit the buttons as Turner clapped the larger scope's handles up. Even as the wider search periscope descended into its well, the thinner attack scope came up, and Turner snapped the handles down and pressed his face to the rubber eyepiece.

Post then descended the ladder to the control room. As second diving officer, it was his job to manage the balancing act that kept the boat level during firing. He must account for many variables of weight distribution in order to keep the ship level at all times.

"Getting lighter out there," the captain reported. "Easy to see him now… uh-oh… I think he's spotted us! He's just fired off a round from his deck gun… a miss but not bad shooting. Must see our snork… too little, too late, pal. Pat… here are your new numbers… bearing, mark!"

"Zero-five-five!" Hotrod almost shouted he was so keyed up.

"Range to target… one-two-zero-zero yards, repeat twelve hundred yards," Turner said with more equanimity than he felt. "Angle on the bow is two-five-zero port."

Jarvis quickly manipulated the TDC and turned to Turner, "We've got a solution, sir. Shoot anytime!"

"Fire one!" Turner ordered and pumped his fist as he counted back from seven. "Fire three… fire five!"

"All fish fired electrically!" Jarvis reported.

"All fish running hot, straight and normal!" Rivers announced.

With each order, the ship juddered, and everyone felt the jolt in their feet and lower legs as the thirty-three-hundred-pound torpedo was hammered out into the sea by a giant's fist of compressed air. With each shot, the ship bucked a little, wanting to point her nose upward. Turner noticed that with each successive shot, the pitching grew worse. On the third round the bow was tilted upward by ten degrees.

"Andy!" Turner shouted down the ladder to Post. "Adjust your trim; we're gonna breach! Shit, too late… Buck, close the vents and blow main ballast! Might as well be on the surface for it since we're headed up anyway."

The submarine exploded from the calm sea, sending up huge sheets of spray as she porpoised slightly. The whole boat shuddered as she settled on an even keel, her ballast tanks now full of compressed air and the ship driving on the surface. Turner shrugged and went up the ladder to open the hatch and gasped as a cascade of what remained of the seawater on the bridge poured down upon him. He raced up onto the bridge with Hernandez hot on his heels, holding a pair of binoculars.

"Quartermaster, order all ahead full and some left rudder," Turner said. "Their gunner is still up there aiming at us!"

The German boat was now half a mile away, and there was plenty of light to see several men on deck running about and the gun crew of her four-inch deck gun training it on *Bull Shark*. Turner heard the orders shouted down the hatch and felt the big submarine heel over to port even as she accelerated.

From the U-boat, a brilliant flash erupted on her deck. Shortly thereafter, a thunderous *boom* reached Turner's ears even as the shell whooshed over the boat's after deck.

"*Ay dios mio!* Damn good shooting, sir!" Hernandez shouted.

It would not be repeated, however. A huge column of water appeared near the U-boat's bow that heaved her over nearly thirty degrees. The second torpedo hit just abaft the conning tower and a huge ball of water, smoke and fire burst from the sea, sending bodies and debris flying. In the next second, the submarine broke in two, the bow and stern sections tilting skyward amid a roaring explosion that rustled the hair of the two men on *Bull Shark's* bridge. The third torpedo had missed, passing just astern of what was left of the U-boat and heading out to sea.

"My God!" Hotrod breathed. "Poor bastards!"

Turner activated the bridge transmitter, "Control, Bridge, come to ahead slow. Right full rudder. Let's see if there are any survivors. We got him, boys!"

A cheer rose up through the open hatch. As the *Bull Shark* slowed and turned toward the wreckage, Hernandez scanned it with his binocs. He shook his head. They went closer anyway.

"Permission to come up to the bridge?" Williams asked from the open hatch.

"Granted, XO," Turner said. "We're trying to locate survivors."

Williams appeared with binocs of his own. All three men doubted that anyone could've survived that attack.

A submarine was a fragile machine. Her hull was thin compared to a large surface ship. She wasn't protected by any armor, and even minor damage could doom her or at least make it so she could never submerge again.

Yet when hit by a combined thirteen-hundred plus pounds of Torpex explosive, the damage was beyond devastating. The first torpedo hit had probably set off several torpedoes in the U-boat's forward room, ripping the bow open like a beer can. The second hit had broken the ship completely in two, probably igniting the diesel fuel in her bunkers in spite of the water.

The rapid sinking was clear proof of that. The U-boat had split and sunk within thirty seconds. All that remained now, as the American boat hove up alongside the site, was an oil slick and a few bits of flotsam... and a swimmer.

"Jesus Christ!" Williams shouted, pointing to a small splashing object off their starboard beam. "There's somebody alive out there!"

"Rescue party to the bridge on the double!" Turner called into the speaker. "Bring towels and pass the word for Hoffman! Tell him we've got a German survivor with possible burns and coated in oil."

"Bridge, control... radio contact with the convoy. They're asking for a situation report," Dutch called over the transmitter.

"Very well, Joe," Turner said, moving out of the way as three men came on deck carrying handfuls of gear. Henry Hoffman, the boat's pharmacist's mate, came up next, carrying his black bag. Hoffman was a tall, lean man of thirty with ice-blue eyes and almost platinum-blonde hair. A quiet man, he was somewhat reserved, partly due to the normal breaking-in period of a crew getting to know one another. Turner thought that Hoffman's reserve was also due in part to his obvious German descent.

"See to things here, will you, Elmer?" Turner asked. "I'll go get in touch with the convoy leader."

Turner was just stepping into the hatch when Williams turned, smiled and stuck out his hand, "Congratulations, Skipper. You just bagged the boat's first official kill."

Turner grinned and shook the offered hand, "Thanks, Elmer. But it was a team effort. We *all* just bagged our first kill. By the way... I don't think it'd be inappropriate to paint a Swastika on the conning tower, huh? If you think it'll dry before we dunk again."

13

After speaking to the convoy leader and receiving heart-felt thanks, Turner agreed to use *Bull Shark* to provide an escort for the small convoy until they entered Chesapeake Bay. Unfortunately, that was the best he could do. The convoy was headed up to Canada, where it would join a much larger group traveling to Britain. Turner hated to leave them, but he had his own mission to accomplish and turning his submarine into a tin can wasn't part of his orders.

Turner was sitting at his desk writing his initial after-action report when someone knocked outside his cabin, "Come."

Andy Post stepped in, looking very much to Turner's eye like a kid trying to brace himself for a spanking. The young man came to attention and cleared his throat, "Permission to speak to the captain."

"Have a seat, Andy," Turner said, waving at his bunk.

The young man sat bolt upright on the edge of the bunk and clasped his hands in his lap, "Ensign Andrew Post respectfully submitting himself for disciplinary action, sir."

Turner set his pen down and leaned back in his chair, eyeing the kid thoughtfully, "You didn't break into the medicine locker and get hammered on celebration hooch again, did you, Andy?"

Post only reddened. Turner's first attempt to set him at ease had failed. It was obvious the young man was mortified by what had happened.

"All right, Ensign," Turner said more firmly. "You screwed up and it's eating you up inside."

"I could've gotten us killed, sir!" Post suddenly blurted. "I fu... mismanaged the trim and breached us and that German sub could've *sunk* us, sir! I... maybe I'm not ready for this responsibility..."

"So what should I do, Andy?" Turner asked levelly. "Write you up? Maybe reassign you? To what?"

"I don't know, sir... but..."

"Andy," Turner said kindly. "At ease, man. At ease. Nobody's perfect. Yeah, you fouled up the trim on that attack, but it came to nothing."

"But it *could've*—"

"But it *didn't*," Turner insisted. "Nobody died. Nobody got hurt. The boat didn't suffer a casualty. We all make mistakes, Mr. Post. Rather than eating your guts out over this one, learn from it. I've read your jacket, I know your training and your previous CO's reports on you. You're smart, level-headed and very capable. You're also young and being thrust into a very new situation. Hell, we *all* are, me included. So no, Mr. Post, I won't accept your request for punishment, reassignment or to be booted out of the service. You messed up... just don't do it again."

Post looked relieved but a little disappointed as well. As if a tongue lashing or a punishment duty would help to absolve his guilt. Turner smiled at him.

"If it'll make you feel better, Andy... you're a goddamned muddle-headed screw-up, you hear me! Next time, it'll be two dozen at the gratings for ye'!" Turner said and chuckled. "In the meantime, why don't you spend a little time reviewing procedures. Talk with Frank and go over what happened so you can figure out how not to let it happen again. Agreed?"

"Yes sir... thank you sir."

"All right, now get outta here," Turner said. "I need to finish this and deal with our new guest."

The German prisoner had been hauled from the water and stripped naked, and his clothing tossed overboard. He'd then been toweled to remove as much excess diesel oil as possible before being hustled below and taken to forward torpedo. There he'd been given a shower and shorts, a T-shirt and a pair of submarine sandals. He'd then been placed in a folding canvas chair and handcuffed to one of the lower bunks in the room.

Turner was headed forward after a quick swing through of the boat. He wanted to speak with Hoffman and the prisoner when Chief Yeoman Clancy Weiss stopped him just outside the yeoman's tiny office. The office was located in the forward battery compartment along with the officer's and chief's quarters and the wardroom.

"Skipper, got a minute?" the chief, a short, barrel-chested man of around forty, asked. He had heavy, curly, black hair and wore gold-rimmed specs just like the ones that Nichols wore.

The difference was that Nichols' specs looked odd on his handsomely-chiseled features. On Weiss, though, they seemed natural and added to his air of competency.

"Sure, Yo," Turner said. "What's up?"

"While you were topside just after the torpedoes hit," Weiss explained. "We picked up a radio transmission from the Royal Navy Base in Bermuda. Guess they were reporting to us and maybe to their home base as well over the AM band... anyway, they said that they were attacked by a U-boat just before first light. Not long before we hit that U-boat of ours."

"Hmm... the *base* was attacked?" Turner asked in puzzlement.

"Not exactly, sir... but one of their harbor mouth picket vessels was attacked on the surface by a submarine using a deck gun. The boat got away since it was too dark to really find them with aircraft, although they tried... then not an hour later, a torpedo was sent into one of the private harbors... in Paget, I think... anyway, the torpedo struck a pier and started a fire. Nothing too bad, though."

Turner chuffed, "But ballsy. Must've been light by then. Did the Royal Navy get any aircraft up after the second shot?"

Weiss nodded, "Yes sir, and they spotted the boat headed out to sea. The water near shore there is very clear, but she dove and got deep enough so the planes couldn't see her."

"Bermuda…" Turner mused. "Why Bermuda?"

"Lot of convoys from Halifax rendezvous there before heading across the Atlantic," Weiss said.

"Yeah… but it's a hard target," Turner continued. "Okay, thanks, Yo. Include a summary of that in our after-action report to ComSubLant, will you? I think we'll be on top for the rest of the day."

"Aye-aye."

Turner turned around and ducked back into the control room where he found Williams just coming down from the conning tower and Frank Nichols going up to take the watch. Turner moved over to the gyrocompass table and examined the chart and the brief plot that had been made during the attack.

"Have you spoken to our prisoner yet, sir?" Williams inquired.

"Not yet, Yo stopped me on my way forward and told me some strange news," Turner replied and briefly related the report.

Williams frowned, "Bermuda? That's strange… you think that could be related to our primary target?"

Turner grinned, "Could be. It just strikes me as odd. Plot me a course to the Royal Navy Base out there, Elmer. Let me know how long it'll take running on top."

"That's easy enough," Williams said, pulling another large paper chart from under the table and fastening it down. This one was a more bird's eye view of the middle Atlantic and included the entire Outer Banks and Bermuda. Williams pointed to a spot near the upper edge. "We're right about here… about six hundred nautical from Bermuda. Thirty hours at full speed, although Nichols, Brannigan and Duncan would have our asses if we did that to their precious engines."

Turner chuckled, "So forty hours at fifteen knots, to be conservative… and another forty hours to get back, plus whatever time we're out there…"

Williams looked up at his captain and frowned, "What're you thinking, sir?"

Turner drew in a breath and then smiled thinly at his second, "Why don't you tell me, Elmer. How good a wife are you?"

Williams chuckled, "Well… if I had to guess, and I guess I do… I believe that you're thinking this is a red herring. That the Jerries are screwing around out there to draw us off the coast. A distraction."

Turner nodded, "That's exactly what I'm thinking."

"I know my husband," Williams laughed.

Turner grinned and punched him lightly on the shoulder, "It goes even deeper than that, XO. If you're right, and the Krauts are fucking around out there just to draw *us* away from the coast… then that means they know why we're out here. Or at least suspect."

Williams scowled, "Jesus… but they might not know it's this particular boat, sir."

Turner shrugged, "No… but that's irrelevant. They know that a submarine is looking for their Q-ship. My guess is that the skipper of that U-boat that sunk the freighter on our first day out reported us to his bosses."

Williams sighed and lit a cigarette, drawing deeply, "Naturally… but that doesn't mean they know why we're here. We're just another fleet boat headed for the canal as far as they know."

Turner shook his head, "I don't think so, Elmer. Somebody out here knows something… which means the Germans have spies in our midst. In America, I mean."

Williams went pale, "You really think so?"

"Sure, we have ours too, so do the Brits… so do the Japs for that matter," Turner opined. "Everybody does. But we're particularly vulnerable in that regard."

Williams nodded, "Right, because we're a melting pot. We've got Germans, Italians and Japanese Americans. Most of our adversaries don't have that kind of mix."

"Right," Turner said, relieving Williams of one of his smokes. "Sorry, Elmer, left mine in the machine…"

Williams chuckled and lit the butt for his captain.

"You've already heard about how they're rounding up Japanese Americans in Hawaii and on the West Coast and sticking them in concentration camps, right?" Turner asked. "There's a lot of paranoia since Pearl Harbor… but you can't do the same with German Americans."

Williams scoffed, "Because they're *white,* I suppose… it's distasteful, Skipper, but… well…"

Williams was clearly having difficulty in coming out with something. Turner waited patiently.

Williams sighed, "Sir… our prisoner is a young guy, maybe early to mid-twenties. Probably not higher than seaman first class or whatever the Kriegsmarine version is. He doesn't speak English… but when Hoffman was up on deck helping get him cleaned up and checking him out… he spoke to the kid in *German,* sir."

Turner drew in a heavy pull from the Lucky Strike. He pondered that for a long moment, "Okay… we know he's German. His parents came over here at the turn of the century. Hoffman is first-generation American… but just because he's bilingual I'm not going to assume he's a traitor, Elmer. He's a first-class petty officer in the United States Navy. Guy's got over fifteen years in the service, for Christ's sake. You don't get that far, even as an enlisted man, if you aren't true blue."

Williams closed his eyes and hated what he was about to say, "That's exactly what *they* would want us to think, right? I'm not accusing him, sir… just saying it's something to keep in mind."

"I understand your position, XO," Turner said, "but mine still stands. We're not going to assume any man on this boat is a traitor just because he happens to share a heritage with a current enemy. Hell, *Turner* is a German name too. Christ, we've got Paul Kellerman, auxiliary machinist's mate, John Fuller, after torpedoman… Vigliano, one of our quartermasters, is Italian… see what I mean?"

"Yes sir."

"We will not suspect or treat our men any different because of their names, XO, that clear?"

Williams stiffened, "Aye-aye, sir."

Turner reached out and squeezed the younger man's shoulder, "I'm not riding you, Elmer. You're thinking of all the angles, and that's good… but this small world we live in is built heavily on trust, more than any kind of ship."

Williams nodded, "I understand, Captain."

"Okay," Turner said kindly. "Get us on course for Bermuda… like it or not, a trick or not… we've got to check into it. Run on top at fifteen. Talk to the engineers and see if we can do better over time. It'll give us time to keep the guys up on their submarine training and get everybody that much closer to pinning on their dolphins."

"Aye-aye."

"Oh," Turner said, leaning in close. "One more thing, XO… young Post is having a crisis of conscience over that breach. Keep an eye on him. Talk to him even… I know you've had your doubts too, and it might help him to know he's not alone."

Williams nodded, "Yes sir, I'll have a word next time we're on watch together."

"How about you?" Turner asked.

Williams shrugged, "Well… we've had a few weeks at sea now. Found most of the issues with the mechanicals… I think the guys are shaping up. Buck and I have had a few minor issues to deal with. Nothing for you to worry about."

"Good," Turner said. "Glad to hear it. Carry on, XO."

Unfortunately, in spite of what he'd said about trusting the men, Turner did have to admit to a small amount of concern regarding the fact that his pharmacist's mate spoke fluent German. There was nothing wrong with that, and it could be a good thing… but still… Turner wondered, and that made him angry.

He found Hoffman sitting by the prisoner in forward torpedo. The off-watch men were in their racks, and those on duty were working with Sparks and Perkins checking gear. Turner could see by the frown on Sparky's face that he wasn't happy about his sanctified torpedo room being turned into a jail.

The German sailor, now dressed in casual submarine wear, was of medium height and build. There was an unfortunate resemblance to Hoffman, which Turner noted. Both men had light blue eyes and light blonde hair. Very Aryan looks. Turner wondered if that was going to be an issue. If Williams wondered about Hoffman's loyalty, wouldn't the enlisted men listening in nearby do the same?

"How's our guest, Doc?" Turner asked, using the familiar nickname for all Navy Corpsman and pharmacist's mates.

"Good shape, sir," Hoffman said quietly, almost demurely, as if he knew the general feeling now that his ability to speak German had been revealed. "Few burns and bruises. He says he's from the U-85. He was on deck when our fish hit and was thrown clear before the big explosion."

Turner crouched down next to the German sailor, "I'm Captain Art Turner. You're aboard the USS *Bull Shark.* You will not be harmed or mistreated. Tell him that, would you, Doc?"

Hoffman flushed and cleared his throat. Obviously, this was already a problem. Yet he did as ordered and translated Turner's words. The Nazi sailor smiled conciliatorily and said something back.

"He says thank you for rescuing him, sir," Hoffman reported.

"Doc," Turner said in a tone loud enough to be heard throughout the compartment. It was easy to do so, as every man in it went silent when Hoffman started to talk. "There's nothing wrong with speaking German. It's not a crime to have parents who immigrated here and taught you their native language. That's one of the great things about our country... we've got people and cultures from all over the world. It's what makes us strong... hell, I'm of German descent, too, you know. A few generations back, but still... I'm not a damned traitor, and nobody... *nobody* on this ship is going to assume you are just because you happen to speak the same tongue as a current enemy. I'm grateful that you do and so is this young man here, I'm sure."

He hadn't given a direct order, but all the men heard the captain's words and knew damned well what they meant. Turner would tolerate no bullshit, no ribbing or worse, of Hoffman. The men in the compartment had gotten the message and returned to their work.

"Doc, sit with him a while, huh?" Turner asked. "Get him something to eat and drink if he'll take it. Chat with him, but don't interrogate him. I'm sure these guys have been filled up with all sorts of propaganda about us, so let's show him kindness and see where that gets us. He's gonna be with us for a while, so let's make the best of it."

"Aye-aye, sir," Hoffman said, sounding more confident now.

"Good," Turner said, patting him on the shoulder and then giving a friendly pat to the German sailor. "Phone talker, pass the word for the COB, Chiefs Brannigan and Duncan and for Murph to come to the wardroom, will you? Sparky, join me if you would."

A few minutes later, the three chiefs and the two torpedo room leading petties were seated at the table. Turner stood next to the closed curtain with his back against the bulkhead. Eddie Carlson was making a fresh pot of coffee in his small galley/pantry.

"I'm gonna lay it right on the line, guys," Turner said firmly. "Our pharmacist's mate speaks German. Anybody here got a problem with that?"

A low grumble ran around the table, but nothing definitive was said. Paul Rogers smiled thinly and winked at his captain. The two men had known each other for several years and knew one another's minds as well as any two men separated by the invisible line that always stood between officers and enlisted men, no matter how narrow that line might be.

"I asked you men a question," Turner said firmly but not angrily. "I want a goddamned answer, not a bunch of mumbling."

"Sir…" Brannigan began but faltered.

"Come on," Rogers implored. "The Skipper isn't on a witch hunt. He wants to know your honest feelings."

Duncan shrugged, "Hell, I don't think it's a big deal. I've spent some time with Hoffman over the past few weeks. He's a good guy."

Murph nodded in agreement, "Man knows his beer. As you might expect. Don't mean he's a damned Nazi spy."

Brannigan and Sparks exchanged a look. Both Turner and Rogers noticed. Turner was the first to react, however.

"You two men feel different?" he asked Sparks and Brannigan.

"Captain… you shoulda heard Doc speakin' Kraut to that kid we pulled out," Brannigan admitted. "Like a native."

"Yeah… and the kid was pretty talkative himself," Sparks added. "Seemed to take to Hoffman right away."

Turner sighed, "So that makes our Doc a fuckin' Nazi sympathizer, Sparky? Hell, I heard you like sushi. That mean you're spying for the Nips?"

Sparks went red in the face, and all the other men chuckled.

"Course he took to Doc," Rogers added. "Kid's all alone on a Yank boat, and one guy speaks his lingo. Wouldn't you kind of gravitate toward him?"

Non-committal shrugs.

"Do we just suspect everybody?" Turner asked. "What about Eddie here? Shit, Sparky, you're from Alabama... One of your great grand pappies might have owned one of his, that mean he's out to get all us honkies?"

Carlson whooped with laughter and had to turn and cover his face, "Maybe I should get Borshowski in here to pour y'all's coffee, sir?"

"Shut up, Eddie, you're not helping," Turner said with a grin. "Look, guys... I know a lot has happened over the past few months. The COB and I were at Pearl, for Chrissakes... but this is the U.S. Navy, and every man on this boat has been vetted, trained, and then trained some more. I'll not suspect any of you of anything but patriots. Hell, Sparky, my grandfather came over here from Austria at the end of the last century. He joined up and served with old Teddy Rough Rider himself. I'm no damned Nazi spy, am I?"

That got a laugh even from Sparks, who was still red in the face and said: "Nobody would think that a'you, sir."

"And nobody is gonna think it of Doc," Turner stated firmly. "I'll not have it on my damned boat, you hear me there? I'm telling you men, and you tell your boys. Anybody gives the Doc or anybody else a hard time because of their heritage, skin color or anything else, and the COB and I will take them on deck and treat them to an unofficial Captain's mast. That goes for any man in here, even you Sparky."

Rogers grinned.

"What's an unofficial Captain's mast?" Murph asked with a twinkle.

"That's when the COB and the Skipper take one of you boys up on deck and whips your ass for ya," Turner said, looking right at Sparks.

"Damned well told," Rogers said. "I seen the Skipper scrap, too, Sparky. Whipped three Army pukes in a little shithole bar outside Coco Solo couple years back."

Sparks grinned, "Well... they was only Army..."

"Shit..." Carlson muttered dryly and turned away to hide his chuckle.

"Everybody clear on this?" Turner asked matter-of-factly.

A chorus of yessirs went up around the table.

"Thy will be done," the COB said with a lopsided smile.

Turner relaxed and sipped his coffee, "Now look, guys… I'm not riding your asses. Not accusing you of anything right now. I just want to nip this in the bud here and now before it goes any further. You guys are in charge, and I'm counting on you. Like I told you all when we first met, when it comes to the safety and running of this boat, the shit flows uphill from you. When it comes to morale, it flows down from you. You with me?"

They all agreed, and Turner's lightening tone eased them all as well. The men relaxed and enjoyed a cup of coffee and a plate of cookies that Carlson set out.

"All right," Turner said after a moment. "We're headed out to Bermuda. Gonna take a day and a half of running, so this is a good bit of downtime, so to speak. Good time for the men to bone up. Also, it means our guest might be with us for a week or more. I don't like the idea of keeping him chained up the whole time. I'd rather put him to work somewhere. I'll find out from Doc his specialty and name and all that… but I obviously don't want him in a sensitive area. Maybe he can help out in the galley or with maintenance duties or something. Plenty of us around to keep an eye on him, and we'll handcuff him to his rack when he's sleeping."

"I could use a hand," Carlson said cheerfully.

Turner chuckled, "Oh, I bet he'd love that, Eddie. I want us to be tolerant of him… but I wouldn't expect much in return, especially for black men."

"Do him some good working alongside a darky," Carlson said with a wry grin playing on his dark features.

"Do the bastard some good pullin' spud duty," Duncan jibed.

That got a laugh and Turner shook his head, "Probably would at that. We'll figure that out as we go. Now about a rack for him…"

Sparks sighed, "Well, sir, we're down three fish forward. I'll have the gang reload the empty tubes… was gonna do that anyway, of course… and we can use an empty skid."

"Can't cuff him to a skid," COB said.

"Nah… I'll have one of our guys take the skid bunk and then we can put the prisoner in that one," Sparks stated.

"That'll go over like a jock at a panty raid," Murph intoned, which got a round of chuckles from everyone, even Turner.

"Ask for volunteers, Sparky," Turner said. "If nobody steps up… then you choose. It won't be forever. We'll have to put in someplace and offload him eventually. All right, I guess that's it. Thank you, men. Enjoy your coffee; this Old Man is gonna hit his own rack."

14

BERMUDA ISLAND CHAIN

APRIL 12, 1942

Nichols, Brannigan and Duncan decided that the ship could run at better than fifteen knots, and they'd arrived in Bermudan waters just after sunset on the following day. Since then, the *Bull Shark* had made several circumnavigations of the islands in ever-widening arcs, both surfaced and submerged.

After five days, the only real accomplishment they'd made was to teach Fritz Schwimmer, their twenty-five-year-old German sonarman, enough English to help Martin and Borshowski in the galley and to assist with the various unpleasant chores aboard, which included housekeeping, washing dishes and cleaning the heads. Although this was done sparingly so as not to be perceived as going against the Geneva Convention.

Schwimmer was a good-natured kid, and he'd even gotten used to seeing black men. It was Eddie Carlson who'd taught the young man most of his limited vocabulary. Fritz was, like many of the new submariners, subjected to some level of hazing. It was an old tradition and not one the captain would usually interfere with. After all, they'd all been through it one way or another.

It was clear, though, that Carlson had misrepresented a few things to the German lad. He'd apparently explained that the American word for a fried pastry with a hole in the center was the same as the German name of the Admiral in charge of the Kriegsmarine. This was made apparent on that morning when Turner, Williams, Dutch and Pat Jarvis all met in the wardroom. Williams and Dutch coming off watch, and Turner and Jarvis about to go on. The men sat, and Carlson brought out mugs and a coffee urn along with the sugar and canned milk.

Behind him, smiling benevolently, was Schwimmer, who set down a tray and said to Turner: "Good morning, Kapitan. Here is delicious Dönitz assholes."

Jarvis half choked as hot coffee streamed out of his nose. Joe Dutch lurched back in his chair and roared with laughter. Williams tried to look taciturn, but his attempt at a stern visage rapidly dissolved into quaking mirth. Turner's mouth fell open, and it was only by a Herculean effort that he didn't roll out of his chair and onto the deck.

Schwimmer looked confused, 'Is good, yah?"

Turner drew in a breath and said in an almost even voice, "Is good, thank you, Fritz... Eddie..."

"Sir?" Carlson looked at his captain with wide-eyed innocence.

"Is this you're doing, mister?" Turner asked.

Carlson put a hand over his heart, "Oh, now, sir! You know how hard it is to learn a new language. The kid just... got confused, is all. Come on, Fritzy, let's go see about breakfast for these fine gentlemen."

Schwimmer smiled, "Yah, is good! Betty Grable, A-number one! Fuck the Yankees, yes?"

Carlson seemed to darken a little as he hurried the younger man through the curtain and into the passage. Turner's eyes began to water as he laughed.

"Guess no one is immune, eh, Skipper?" Jarvis asked, wiping at his own eyes.

"Oh, you think it's funny, eh, Pat?" Turner asked, shaking his head. "We'll see how it is when the kid comes into the control room on your next watch and says that one of the Chiefs told him that the ship's gonna sink unless you show him how to blow the O3."

Williams roared now, "Laughing out of the other side of your face then, Pat! Love that one... ha-Ha-HAA!"

Dutch pulled a paper napkin from the holder in the center of the table and blew his nose, "Jesus that was a kick in the pants..."

When Carlson returned a few minutes later, he had Borshowski in tow and they laid out plates of bacon, eggs and home fries for the officers. Borshowski headed aft again, and Eddie began making more coffee.

"So what do we do now, Skipper?" Dutch asked as he dug in. "We've been out here for five days..."

Turner sighed, "Yeah... chasing a wild goose, I'm afraid."

"But a German boat *did* make an attack here," Jarvis pointed out.

"Yeah... a gun action on a little harbor trawler and firing a random torpedo into a harbor," Turner said thoughtfully. "Kind of a waste of resources, wouldn't you say? Especially with so much good hunting just to the west in our home waters?"

Williams frowned, "So they drew us out here."

"Meaning they *know* about us and our mission?" Dutch asked incredulously.

Turner sighed, "They know about us for certain. That U-boat that torpedoed the freighter on our first sea trial must have intercepted our radio transmissions... and just as we intercept a U-boat going after that trio of cargo ships, another U-boat launches some half-assed attack out here? I smell a rat. Thought so last week, too... but didn't have much choice. Somewhere out here there is a C and C ship that we've got to find."

Jarvis tapped his fingers on the table, "But between the Eastern Seaboard and then south to the Bahamas and back again... to say nothing of the Caribbean... we're talking about a couple of hundred thousand square miles of ocean. A needle in a haystack ain't in it, as my Royal Navy ancestors would have said."

"You're English?" Williams asked casually.

Jarvis grinned, "Irish... but I've got a great, great, great grandmother who was in the Royal Navy. Married a Jarvis during the war of 1812."

"I'll be damned," Turner said. "A woman in the Navy back then?

I'd like to hear that story… but for now, let's focus on our immediate sitch. We still have to find that needle, as Pat says."

"The C and C ship still has to do *his* job, right?" Dutch asked. "I mean… that ship is out here to direct the Nazis along our coast, right? So he's got to be in a position to do that. Which means within flying distance of the coast if he's using an aircraft."

"Command thinks it's got to be a floatplane," Williams stated. "Unless the ship is a carrier, which seems unlikely. So what's that mean in terms of range?"

"Most floaters can do about two hundred knots and range five or six hundred miles," Jarvis said. "I know that the Krauts have a new one, the Arado, which is a pretty solid design. Supposedly has a range of over six hundred miles."

Turner chewed on a slice of bacon and washed it down with a sip of coffee, "That's why Admiral Edwards figured them to be within two hundred miles. Figure that gives the flyer a couple of hours to fly within sight of land. At a couple of thousand feet… high enough not to be identified but low enough to identify ships… the guy could fly along at what, Pat?"

Jarvis thought for a moment, "Keeping the land on one side, maybe fifteen or twenty miles off the beach. That'd give him a sphere of observation thirty or forty miles in diameter."

"Plenty to observe coastal shipping," Williams opined.

"And at even a leisurely hundred knots, he could cover over two hundred miles in a couple of hours before having to vector back out to his ship. Do that twice a day… figure the ship travels at ten or fifteen knots, probably ten to conserve fuel oil this far from home for so long…"

"And probably runs sorties at dawn and dusk," Dutch offered.

Jarvis was tapping the table as he calculated, "So he flies north, does his patrol and heads back to the ship. In the meantime, the ship heads south and is sixty miles further than when the plane left. Another six hours before the next sortie… another four until the plane comes BAC again. The ship travels a hundred and sixty miles and tack on another couple of hundred on each sortie… they could cover four hundred miles of our coast a day."

"Their trouble would come once they got south of Georgia, though," Williams added. "They just can't hang two hundred miles out. They'd have to pass over the Bahamas in order to run along the Florida coast. Somebody would see them."

"Or they could run between Florida and the Bahamas," Jarvis said.

"Same problem," Turner put in. "That gap is less than sixty miles at points. A lot of shipping runs through there."

"A target-rich environment," Jarvis stated.

"Hmm… whatever this ship is," Turner mused, "she must not *look* like a German ship. Probably has an American name or something to blend in. That was impressed on us, too. We must be *sure* of this guy. Can't go around firing torpedoes at friendlies. So that means command suspects it's a Q-ship that isn't an obvious enemy."

"So when it's all said and done, Skipper?" Dutch asked.

Turner gulped down the last bite of his powdered eggs, "Hell, I don't know, men. I do think we're just pulling our puds out here, though. Think we'll head back and continue our search off the coast."

There came a sharp *rap, rap* on the bulkhead outside the wardroom curtain.

"Enter," Turner called out.

Sherman Broderick slid the curtain aside and half stepped inside, "Mr. Nichols' respects, sir, and there's a small craft coming into view and waving a white flag at us."

"Any idea who it is, Tank?" Turner asked. "Have they raised them on radio?"

"No sir, "Broderick stated. "Radio shack says they aren't responding to any hails on VHF or anything."

"Very well, thanks, Tank," Turner replied. "Tell Nichols I said to close with them. Get a man up on the bridge with a fifty-cal. Try to make it inconspicuous."

"Aye-aye," Broderick said and vanished.

Turner addressed himself to what remained of his breakfast.

"A local?" Williams wondered aloud.

"Gotta be," Dutch opined. "I wouldn't be doing any crossings in my yacht right now."

By the time Turner climbed out onto the bridge, followed by the other three officers from breakfast, he saw that Nichols was there along with Broderick himself. The big man had mounted a machine gun to one of the cigarette deck stanchions specially designed for this and had thrown a bedsheet over the weapon. Nichols had ordered the engines to all stop, and a medium-sized fishing boat was hoving to fifty yards off the submarine's starboard side.

"Ahoy!" a bearded man shouted from just aft of the boat's raised forward pilothouse. "Good mornin', Yanks! Mind if I get a little closer? Fancy I've got some news you might like to hear."

The man spoke in a heavy English accent. He and three other men on deck looked at the submarine with obvious interest. Turner glanced sidelong at Tank, who nodded slightly in the direction of his shrouded weapon.

"Who are you, sir?" Turner asked.

"Name's Ned Tully," the bearded man replied. "Live here in Bermuda. Might I come aboard, Captain... or perhaps you might visit me?"

Turner frowned and raised his bull horn again, "Do you have a dinghy, Mr. Tully?"

"That I do," Tully said. "If it's all right, me and my mate will row over. Got anything to trade?"

Turner grinned, "We might. What're you offering?"

"Got some nice dorados on ice," Tully replied. "Even got a case of twelve-year-old Scotch... might be persuaded to bring a bottle or two."

"Very well," Turner said. "Come on over and we'll discuss it. Frank, when they get close, let's flood the forward ballast so they can row right up on deck and make their lives easier."

"Aye sir," Nichols said and bent to the bridge transmitter, "Control, bridge... standby to flood down forward and receive rowing boat. Alert the crew. Also, send up a couple of sidearms."

The control room acknowledged. Within a few minutes, Tully and a young man barely out of boyhood were rowing a small dory toward the submarine. There was a whoosh of escaping air, and the bow of the *Bull Shark* dipped down a few feet below the water.

Tully waved and smiled as he directed the young man to row the boat right up onto the wooden deck of the submarine. As he did so, Frank ordered ballast tanks one, two and three Able and Baker to be blown. The bow of the submarine surfaced, and the rowboat was sitting on the deck ten feet over the waterline.

Turner, Williams and Jarvis went down on the main deck to greet the two men. Each one had a .45 jammed into the waistband of their duty slacks. Jarvis hung a little back, his own weapon held semi-concealed at his side. Behind them, on the bridge, Tank had an unobstructed path to the rowboat and stood quietly by his now unshrouded machine gun.

"Blimey!" Tully, who was a tall, well-built man in his late forties with just a hint of salt in his black hair and beard, exclaimed. "You blokes don't take many chances, eh?"

"We're at war, Mr. Tully," Turner stated.

Tully smiled, "Aye… but not with each other, Cap'n. This is my son, Mathew. Feel free to pat us down if you'd like. Then we can leave off with all these guns, eh? Makes us a might nervous, you know."

Williams and Jarvis inspected the men and their boat. Finding nothing dangerous, Jarvis safed his weapon and stowed it. He then gave a brief hand signal to Tank, who covered the menacing shape of the machine gun once more.

Turner shook hands with Tully and then his son, who was a younger and leaner version of his father, "So what can we do for you gents today?"

"First off, you can call us Ned and Matt," Tully said jovially.

"All right," Turner replied with a smile. The man's ebullient charm was infectious. "I'm Art, this is Elmer and Pat. That's Frank Nichols up on the bridge, and the beefy fella is Tank."

"Well, Art… first off, I've brought you a nice dinner for your crew," Tully said, pointing into the boat where a dozen fish, each over three feet long, lay. The fish had odd, flattened noses and a long dorsal fin running back to a mackerel-like tail. The fish were beautifully colored in greens and even gold.

"Dolphin!" Joe Dutch exclaimed. "Call them mahi-mahi in Hawaii… great eating."

Turner grinned, "I know. I grew up in South Florida. Used to catch them all the time off Lauderdale and in the Keys. Thanks, much, Ned. What can we trade you for this?"

"Got any American cigarettes on board?" Ned asked with evident relish. "Wouldn't mind a little beef, either. Pretty lean out here these days."

Turner looked back at Nichols, "Frank, get with Andy and the galley crew… see what kind of care package we can put together in exchange for about… seventy pounds of fish filets. Cigarettes and beef and anything else he thinks would work."

"Now then…" Ned nodded at Matt, who reached into a small bag in the stern sheets of the boat and pulled out two bottles of Glen Levitt and handed them to Williams.

"Maybe you'd like to sample these," Matt said with a wry grin.

"Maybe after we talk," Ned said more seriously than he had spoken earlier. "Is there someplace private we can speak, Art?"

Turner shrugged, "On a submarine, Ned, this is about as private as it gets."

Ned nodded, "Makes sense. Very well then… I'm not just a local fisherman, Captain. I'm also Royal Navy Intelligence. We sort of… keep our eye on things around here, you might say."

"I see," Turner said, although he didn't quite yet.

"I understand you might be looking for a Nazi ship," Tully explained.

Williams coughed and Turner's brows rose, "We might… how would you know that?"

Tully grinned, "Our boys keep their eyes and ears open, too, Art. We, of course, know about the Jerries making a nuisance of themselves along your coast… which, of course, sticks a knife in our craw as well. Might I assume you're out here because of the little spot of bother we had last week with a U-boat?"

Turner nodded. He suspected Tully knew as much about the Nazi Q-ship as he did, yet it was always advisable to play things close to the vest. To let the other guy show his cards first. Ned grinned, seeming to read his mind.

"It was a foolish attack," Matt opined. "It's too shallow around here and our air cover is too good."

"That's right," Ned said. "They got away with shooting up a coastal trawler and sending a bloody torpedo into Harrison's Marina... but it all came to naught."

"So why do you think they did it, then?" Jarvis asked.

Ned chuckled, "To get you here, of course. To get an obviously new American boat out here wasting her time circling like a shark. All while the Jerries hotfooted it out of the area."

"I take it you mean a vessel other than the U-boat?" Turner asked.

"I mean the Q-ship you lot are trying to hunt down," Ned said matter-of-factly. "We know all about it. Got word from your people, in fact. Does the name Webster Clayton mean anything to you?"

Turner smiled in spite of himself, "That it does, Ned. I guess I don't need to be so cagey... can you tell me why you suspect that the U-boat wasn't operating alone?"

"Certainly... because of the airplane," Ned stated. "The evening before the attack, our lads at the Naval Air Station picked up an aircraft headed in from the west. They chatted them up and found out it was an American from North Carolina flying over for a pleasure trip. Spoke just like a Yank, he did. Even had a southern accent to boot. Well, this bloke and our controller tossed off a few quips and we wished the man well. Said he was landing on Main Island. But he never landed. Came in low and dropped off radar and never reappeared again. The field over there never got a call, and no plane landed."

"That's certainly suspicious..." Williams muttered.

"That's not all," Matt said, a little excited.

Ned nodded, "That crate turned out to be a German floatplane. An Arado. One of our flyboys spotted her as he was making his approach to land. The pilot said his father had bought the plane just before the war began."

"And your man bought that?" Jarvis asked, not entirely concealing his incredulity.

Matt shrugged, "Had a big dolphin painted on it... plus the pilot sounded as American as apple pie, as you say."

"So you think the pilot can speak flawless American?" Jarvis asked.

Ned nodded, "Seems so. And if he vacated the area under the

radar, that means very low to the sea, and that means he burnt a lot of fuel, so his destination ship couldn't have been far away. He certainly didn't fly out here from North Carolina and then fly off. That bucket would've been nearly down to fumes by the time we picked her up."

Williams went aft to receive a bag that had been passed to Nichols from the bridge hatch. He returned and handed it to Tully.

"Well, I thank you for the info, Ned," Turner said. "Any thoughts on where this ship might have gone?"

Tully grinned, "No clue, Art. If pressed, however, I'd have to say south or southwest. If they really were trying to draw you off, then they certainly wouldn't head back into your path, now would they?"

Ned inspected the bag and was pleased to find three cartons of Camels, a variety of canned goods, a five-pound bag of mixed candy that included Bazooka bubble gum, M and M's and red licorice twists. There were also two large, frozen roast beefs. In addition, a large box of dehydrated mashed potatoes and a jar of powdered gravy.

"My word!" Matt said as he pulled items out. "We could do two roast beef suppers for eight with all this..."

Ned shook Turner's hand again, "Thank you, sir. Most grateful, I'm sure."

"Glad to," Turner replied. "And thanks for the intelligence. You men be safe out here. Watch out for submarines. And thank you for the hooch. I think we might save this for when we find this Nazi bastard and sink him. We submariners have a tradition borrowed from you Brits, you know."

"What's that?" Ned asked.

"When we make a kill, we splice the mainbrace," Jarvis said with a grin.

"Well, good on ya!" Ned roared. "And good hunting, lads. Mind how you go."

"Oh, one thing," Turner said with a lopsided grin. "I'd like to get a photo with you two gents along with my XO and torpedo officer here. That all right? My wife will love it."

Tully chuckled, "Can do, mate."

Frank Nichols was already prepared. He stood on the bridge and aimed the camera at the five men standing abreast on the *Bull Shark's* foredeck and snapped off a photo. Everyone shook hands again and the American officers mounted the bridge so that the boat could be flooded down.

"You and the missus come and visit sometime!" Tully called out as he rowed away. "And bring a copy of that photo!"

Turner saluted and turned to Nichols, "I'll take the watch, Frank. Go and get yourself some chow... oh, and when you go below, instruct the helmsman to put us on a heading for Cape Hatteras, all ahead full."

"Aye-aye, sir," Frank said as he dropped through the bridge hatch.

"Oh yeah!" Turner said, glancing at the rank and file of glistening fish lying on the deck forward of the five-inch. "And ask down below and see if anybody in the crew is good at fileting, will ya'?"

15

ATLANTIC OCEAN, 200 MILES SOUTHEAST OF CHARLESTON, SC

APRIL 16, 1942

11:30 ZULU

Pat Jarvis had the watch. He stood on the bridge with a pair of binoculars hanging around his neck, looking off the *Bull Shark's* starboard bow toward the low-hanging sun. Although the weather to the west was clear, there was a strong twenty-knot breeze blowing and whipping the sea into six-to-eight-foot whitecaps. Off to the east, where the sky was already darkening, a line of even darker clouds grew ominously, promising a dirty night.

"Looks like a sloppy evenin', Mr. Jarvis," Dick "Mug" Vigliano, quartermaster of the watch, noted from Jarvis' left. "Probably gonna need to safety line in tonight."

"You always this gloomy, Mug?" Jarvis needled.

Vigliano was a heavily-built, medium height New York Italian who often came across as gruff but was well-liked by the crew. He only shrugged, "I just call it like I see it, sir. Be a good night for hunting, was we looking for Japs."

Jarvis knew that the offhand comment went deeper than it sounded. Vigliano was expressing a sentiment that most of the men aboard the submarine were beginning to share. They'd been on patrol for nearly a month and the only real action they'd seen was to sink a Nazi U-boat. All of them knew how hot the war in the Pacific was already, and they wanted in. Men didn't usually join the silent service for the good chow and the constant stink of diesel fumes mixed with an ever-present bouquet of B.O. They joined because they wanted to strike back. To sink ships and take out the Japs who had mercilessly attacked Pearl Harbor.

Everybody knew that nothing was going on in the Atlantic. At least not off the coast of the United States. They knew that Kraut boats were sinking merchant shipping in the North Atlantic. They heard tell of stuff going on in the Med… but all that was happening off their own shore was some merchant vessels being hit by U-boats with no apparent reprisal. Most of them didn't know the real reason the *Bull Shark* was out there, although Jarvis suspected that the mission's general purpose was now known to all of the crew. Keeping a secret in a three-hundred-foot-long, sixteen-foot-wide tube crammed with eighty men was difficult to do.

"Good night for the Nazis to sink our ships, too, Mug," Jarvis finally responded. He paused and then asked: "You know why we're out here?"

Vigliano shot him a sidelong look, "You askin' if all of us workin' crew know the real purpose of this mission, Mr. Jarvis?"

Jarvis grinned at him, "Yeah, Mug, that's what I'm askin'."

Vigliano chuckled, "Course we do, sir. We're trying to locate some friggin' Kraut ship what's directing all these U-boats. Or to put it another way… we're bobbin' around out here lookin' for a needle in a goddamned haystack… beggin' your pardon."

Jarvis laughed, "Don't hold back on my account, mister. And you're right… might not be as exciting as torpedoing Japanese shipping… but it's important. These fuckin' Huns are going at our ships with impunity, and nobody seems to be doing anything about it. It's bullshit."

Vigliano grinned, "Yes sir."

"What time is it?"

"Half-past six," Vigliano replied, glancing at his wrist and then at Jarvis. The Lieutenant didn't have a wristwatch, having lost it to Mr. Nichols after a rather competitive cribbage game.

"Well, if nothing else," Jarvis replied, bending below the bridge fairing to light a cigarette, "we've only got to stand out here in the slop another half hour."

"Unless the skipper decides to stay on top," Vigliano said.

Jarvis got his butt going and straightened, "What would you do, Mug?"

"Me? I think I'd stay on top," Vigliano replied, reaching under Jarvis' open reefer jacket and pulling a smoke from the pack in his khaki duty shirt pocket and grinning. He held out his hand for the lighter. It wasn't disrespect. Jarvis had told Vigliano and any other man on watch with him that they were welcome to grab a smoke.

"Oh yeah?" Jarvis asked, handing the lighter across. "And why's that?"

Mug bent down and got his own pill going. He handed the lighter back, "Because with a sloppy sea and potentially a big rain squall, it's a good night for submarines to hunt on the surface. Harder to spot. Plus, we cover more ground at sixteen knots than at four."

"Good points, Mug," Jarvis said, gazing around at the horizon. "Might make a submariner of you yet."

"Bound to happen sooner or later, sir," Vigliano said wryly. "After fourteen years in this man's Navy, you'd think something would stick."

Jarvis chuckled as he glanced around. There were three lookouts posted in the periscope sheers along with himself and Vigliano on the bridge. The men in the sheers were already wearing safety harnesses under their Mae Wests and clipped into the lookout perch. Although eight to ten-foot seas weren't much for the submarine to handle, she wasn't built for knifing through the waves like a surface ship. Her small cutwater only went down so far over the bulbous bow of the pressure hull. The ship was mostly submerged and behaved more like a cork than a sleek, sharp-nosed ship. Hanging up nearly twenty feet above the water, the pitching and rolling of the submarine, although still modest, was felt even more by the lookouts.

If Vigliano was right, which Jarvis knew he was, then the weather would get much dirtier in the next few hours. So far out at sea, the waves could kick up to twice their height very quickly in a large storm. Both Jarvis and Vigliano would have to attach themselves to safety harnesses soon as well. They were already finding it hard to stay out of the spray and keep their cigarettes going.

"Ever been at sea in a big storm, Mug?"

Vigliano shrugged, "Few times… on a ship, so not a big deal."

Jarvis puffed, "Reminds me of this one time off Block. Me and my dad were long-lining for swords. I was maybe thirteen at the time. Big ass Nor'easter blew up out of nowhere. We were thirty miles out and it went from calm to ass-puckering in a matter of minutes."

"Were you scared?"

"Shitless. We were in a fifty-foot fishing boat. Pretty new, thank God… but it was me, dad and uncle Mike and a hired hand named Paul out of Narragansett. Seas got up to about fifteen footers. Whitecaps and steep, too. Jesus Christ, Mug… it was three o'clock in the afternoon and the sky was as black as the devils' heart. Lightning flashing all around, rain so cold it felt like needles driving into your face… I honestly thought we were going to die."

Mug shivered and huddled further into his own jacket, "you guys made it in, obviously."

Jarvis shivered, "Yeah… but it took forever. We lost an engine and had to limp in. Must've taken seven hours to get to Block Island. We were able to anchor in the lee while dad and uncle Mike fixed the other engine. By then, it was after ten p.m. and so black you couldn't see one end of the boat from the other… I was on deck with Paul when the storm shifted and the winds began to blow in from the southwest. Again, in minutes, the seas got nasty. At one point, a big roller slammed into the trawler and I was tossed onto the deck. Fetched up against a stanchion… Paul wasn't so lucky. Went right over the side and vanished. No trace of him."

"Damn…" Mug breathed.

"Yup… we moved the boat again and in the morning made our way into point Judith," Jarvis said solemnly. Never forget that night as long as I live."

"And you still joined the Navy," Mug said with admiration.

"Sure, Mug," Jarvis said more casually now. "I ain't no sissy."

"Kinda hope we dive now," Mug admitted and the two men chuckled.

Jarvis pitched his dead butt over the side and thumbed the bridge transmitter.

"Conning tower, bridge... give me a sweep with the sugar dog. And what's for dinner?"

A pause and then Andy Post, the JOOD, came back over the tinny speaker, *"Aye, activating the SD radar now... I think it's spaghetti and meatballs. Smells like garlic bread, too."*

Vigliano scoffed, "Yeah... like Martin and Borshowski got any clue what a real pasta gravy should taste like."

Jarvis chuckled, "Yeah, huh? Knowing Martin, it'll probably have andouille in it."

Both men chuckled as they listened to the hum of the SD radar powerhead as it turned above the lookouts. For several moments, no one said anything.

"Bridge, conning tower... Nada on the sugar dog," Post finally said. *"Looks like we're all alone out here. Picking up what might be some weather to the east, though."*

Jarvis sighed, "Yeah, we see it, Andy."

A pause and then: *"Bridge... hold on a sec... I think we've got something. Super faint, just a tiny spike off toward the northwest... gonna switch to the sugar jig... wait one..."*

Down in the conning tower, Andy Post stood behind the radar set with a hand on the back of the chair. Ted Balkley, first class radarman, manned the set and stared intently at the cathode ray tube display. On it, the electronic sweep of the air search radar spun lazily. Just at the edge of the screen, a small blip appeared. It was very faint and might have simply been a glitch or a distant rain cloud.

Balkley switched the SD unit off and activated the more powerful SJ surface search unit. Once again, the blip appeared with a little more definition.

"What do you think, Balkley?" Post asked hopefully.

The sailor shook his head, "Dunno, sir... it's barely registering at twenty-eight thousand yards... either it's a distant aircraft flying high or maybe a rain cloud off that way. Can't tell yet."

"Okay, home in on it and see if you can get a heading," Post said and then spoke into the hard-wired handset. "Bridge, conning... we've got a very faint contact at about fourteen miles bearing zero-niner-five… about three-three-zero true. Any clouds out that way?"

"*Negative, Andy,*" Jarvis came back. "*It's clear as a bell out west.*"

"Okay… we're trying to get a fix and a track on it," Post replied. "Give us a minute here…"

A minute passed and the contact grew more distinct on the radar screen. Balkley half-turned to look at Post, "Sir, it's definitely an aircraft. Moving at about a hundred and fifty knots… looks like she's heading one-seven-zero true. Probably pass within a few miles of us shortly."

Post reported that to Jarvis. The senior man instructed Post to get the captain. Post used his phone set to call to the wardroom. Within a minute, Turner and Williams came up the ladder into the cramped space of the conning tower.

"Any idea who's bird that is?" Turner asked.

"No sir," Balkley replied. "Kind of slow, though… and way out from shore… We've used both radars, but I can't tell what type of aircraft it is."

Turner and Williams exchanged a glance and the XO saw a predatory gleam in the captain's eye. Turner mounted the ladder to the bridge and told Williams to raise the search scope and get a high-up look.

Immediately, Turner was struck by the difference on deck. The warmth of the submarine's interior was quickly blown away by the cold early spring wind and spray from the building seas. He wished he'd grabbed his own pea jacket.

"Looks like we've got company," Turner said to the men on the bridge.

Jarvis was already looking over the boat's starboard quarter with his glasses, "Yeah… way out here all alone on what's about to be a dirty night… interesting, sir."

"Mug, let's point her at the target," Turner said. "Give us a smaller profile."

"Aye-aye, sir," Vigliano said and thumbed the transmitter. "Control, bridge. Helm, come right full rudder. Steady up on course three-two-zero. Ahead one-third."

"*Bridge, helm, coming right to course three-three-zero, maneuvering answers all ahead one-third. Advise speed will be six knots,*" the watch helmsman reported.

The long slim shape of the *Bull Shark* began to turn, putting the half-sunk sun across her bow and onto her port bow. The ship slowed perceptibly, reducing but not eliminating her long white foaming wake. This also had the effect of putting the seas nearly abeam, generating a metronome-like rolling that nobody was fond of.

"Contact!" the starboard lookout shouted. "Aircraft bearing zero-two-five, just coming up over the horizon!"

Everyone trained their binoculars on the contact. Above them, the head of the periscope swung in that direction as well. At the moment, even in the magnified view of the binoculars, the airplane was just an oblong spec a few degrees above the rim of the world. Yet it was growing quickly, taking on substance and shape.

"Looks like a floater!" Jarvis announced.

"All stop, Mug," Turner ordered.

Vigliano related the order to the helm and the ship's creaming wake died to nothing as the screws stopped spinning. By now, the plane was visible to the naked eye, higher above the water and passing ahead the bow. Turner could easily see the large twin pontoons slung under the single-winged aircraft.

"Anybody know that design?" he asked as he also held down the transmitter button.

"*Roger that,*" Williams relayed his observation through the periscope. "*Looks a lot like the Arado floatplane the Nazis are building. A lot of detail in the scope, although it's hard to keep track.*"

"I don't think she's spotted us," Jarvis said as he tracked the plane across the sky. "She's only four or five miles away... how the hell do they not see us?"

"We're backed by them clouds and the water," Vigliano opined.

"And there's no proof they don't see us," Turner offered. "That plane is lightly armed, if at all. It's not like she'd attack us... radar, can you give me a definite course projection? Where's that bird going?"

A few seconds passed, and then Balkley came over the speaker,

"Bridge, radar… still heading one-seven-oh. No other contacts out there, though, so I can't say what she's pointing at."

"Certainly not land," Jarvis said. "There isn't anything in that direction for a long, long way."

They watched the plane cross over the last remnant of the setting sun and then slowly drop down to the horizon and disappear. It only took a few minutes.

"Officer of the deck… let's follow that plane," Turner said with a grin. "And don't spare the whip."

"Aye-aye," Jarvis said gleefully. "Mug, put her on a one-eight-zero, all ahead full."

The submarine's diesels growled into louder life and the boat began to move again, swinging to port and following the same course that the unknown aircraft had been flying. Soon, she was plowing through the sea at eighteen knots. Although the ship could do twenty-one at flank speed, Jarvis had held back a little just in case. It wasn't like they could catch the plane, but this far from land, as they'd all speculated, the aircraft couldn't go much further before meeting her support ship. They might be far closer to their target than they realized. The excitement and expectation that maybe they'd gotten very lucky and found the needle quickly permeated the entire ship.

The truth was that the unknown aircraft was indeed the Nazi Arado. However, it was not true that the crew of the scout plane failed to see the American submarine.

"Is it one of ours?" Gunther Schultz asked from the co-pilot's seat. He had taken the controls so that Michner could stare through his side window at the lean ship below them.

"I don't think so," Michner said with a shake of his head. "What do you think, Hans?"

Volmer was staring out at the submarine with a pair of high-powered binoculars, "Negative, Brenner… in spite of them turning toward us, I can tell that the conning tower is the wrong shape.

Different armaments, and the ship looks larger than ours. Definitely an American fleet submarine."

"Try to keep her in view as we pass," Michner said, clutching the radio microphone.

He paused before transmitting his report, however. It was possible that the Americans would be monitoring the radio frequencies. Should they pick up his conversation with the *Blanch,* even if they didn't understand the German, they'd certainly know who and what they were. Also, there was no way that the submarine could follow them and make contact with the Q-ship before the Arado was recovered. Even at flank speed, it would take the submarine hours to cross the distance the Nazi crew had yet to fly. That was also assuming the freighter wasn't headed in the opposite direction.

He could try speaking in his affected southern accent. The problem with that was that most of the freighter's crew didn't even speak English. Those that did spoke it with a heavy German accent that was impossible to hide. While Michner could sound like a "good old boy" to the listening submarine, his compatriots would reply as just what they were… Germans.

He could only use one form of communication. As he held the microphone, he clicked the talk switch several times in a series of long and short intervals. This was a pre-determined code that would alert the mother ship that he'd sighted an enemy surface vessel.

It wasn't Morse code but a short series of coded squawks that gave little information. All he could really do at this point was provide the *Blanch* with a warning.

"I've squawked that we've spotted an enemy vessel," Michner said as he hung up the handset. "I can't risk any detailed communication, just in case."

"They can't pursue us anyway," Gunther observed.

"But they can track our course," Hans put in.

"And they will," Michner said. "We could alter it… but we're already low on fuel. The ship is a hundred kilometers away. If that is the new submarine, then her maximum speed is something like thirty-five kph. It'll take her nearly three hours to get where we'll be in twenty minutes. Once we're close to the ship, I'll radio in details, and they can alter course or take whatever action they see fit."

"Do you think the rumors are true?" Hans asked from behind his two crewmates. "That this is a submarine the Americans sent out to find our ship?"

"I do," Gunther opined. "Kapitan Hardegen met her a few weeks ago. Then the same day that you and he flew that observation run in Bermuda, one of our U-boats vanished. Now here they are, three hundred and fifty kilometers from their coast…"

"It is hard to believe in such a coincidence," Michner stated. "Frankly, I can't believe there isn't an entire *fleet* out here looking for us."

Darkness had fallen and the storm on the horizon had nearly reached the aircraft when it bounced heavily down on the heaving seas. Even as the riggers attached the cables and the floatplane was being lifted out of the water, the storm front hit and the wind suddenly grew from a strong twenty knots to a howling sixty. It took several very careful moments to stow the aircraft and tie it down on the swaying upper deck of the freighter.

The three men quickly ran for the superstructure as heavy rain began to pound down on the ship. They were greeted by a sailor who led them into the officer's wardroom, where they were met by Brechman.

"Welcome back, gentlemen," the SS officer said as the steward poured the flyers each a cup of coffee. "How did your mission go this evening?"

Hans handed over his notepad. Brechman examined it and nodded occasionally.

"Did you receive our report about the American boat, sir?" Michner asked. "I reported details just before landing."

"Yes, I have been informed," Brechman stated. "The captain will alter our course accordingly. This Yankee-doodle captain is becoming a thorn in our sides. We must think of a way to deal with him."

The flyers said nothing. They knew that Brechman was only voicing his thoughts aloud. As they waited, the door to the corridor opened and Captain Diedrich entered and took a seat at the table.

"You boys had an interesting flight, yes?" he asked jovially. "Spotted our adversary not far, eh?"

"Yes sir," Michner stated. "And I'm sure that he's steaming for us at flank speed even now."

Diedrich chuckled, "Not to worry. We're now headed just north of west at flank speed ourselves. We'll be eighty kilometers away by the time they get here. Too bad it's so rough, we might be able to arrange a surprise for them... ah well... what else did you find this afternoon?"

Brechman slid the notebook over. "A pair of crude oil carriers off the coast of Florida."

Diedrich studied the notebook and did a quick set of calculations in his head, "We could intercept them just after breakfast should we stay on our current course... hmm..."

"What are you thinking, Kapitan?" Brechman asked a little suspiciously.

Diedrich grinned, "Based on the established patrol routes of our U-boat assets, the pair of oilers just missed U-245 and will soon, depending on their speed..."

"I'd estimated ten knots, sir," Hans piped up.

"At ten knots, they'll be entering U-123's kill zone by mid-morning. If I order the helm to alter course a little northerly... we might be able to join the two oilers for the festivities."

"Why?" Brechman asked. "Our job is not to get in close and observe sinkings. Our job is to locate targets and direct our U-boats to them."

Diedrich chuckled and shook his head, "Herr Brechman... our situation has changed. We now have a hound on our trail. Suppose that we join the American ships, looking very much like one of their friends... an American freighter out of Georgia, perhaps. Joining them for safety. They might radio that information in. Young Mr. Michner here can even speak to them in their own lingo."

Brechman frowned and then slowly nodded, "Yes... I see... should we be found by our hound he may be more inclined to take us for what we *appear* to be."

"At the very least," Diedrich said with a gleam in his eye, "it could give us time to arrange a little... surprise for our Yankee friends."

Michner felt an uncomfortable stirring in his belly. Once again, his side was playing the game using underhanded tactics. Not for the first time and, he now was certain, not for the last, Brenner Michner questioned himself, his duty and what good he was really doing out here.

A little more than fifty miles to the north, Arthur Turner was also questioning himself. He stood in the control room with his first officer gazing down at the gyro table where the local chart of the area was laid out. Turner tapped a pencil on a particular spot that Williams had marked out.

"I wonder, Elmer…" Turner mused thoughtfully. "Suppose that aircraft did belong to our friend the Q-ship. Suppose that they *did* spot us and informed their friends that we were out here… what would you do if you were that ship's captain?"

Williams thought about that for a long time. Finally, he scowled and glanced at Turner, "Well sir… I'm not sure. If we presume he can run at fifteen knots, even at flank speed, then he might just continue on his present course, assuming that he wasn't shadowing the contours of our coast headed north."

"But if he keeps going southerly," Turner observed. "He's got to pass close by the Atlantic side of the Bahamas. Lot of islands, lot of shoals, lot of traffic… it just keeps him further and further from the U.S. shoreline… and his job is to monitor their activities and help to direct their U-boats to targets."

"So you're saying that if he's way out here and gets further away…" Williams pondered. "Like heading out to Bermuda before… he's not really doing his job. He's got to keep that floatplane close enough to spot shipping within a day or so of the mother ship."

"Right," Turner said. "Which suggests what?"

Williams' face flushed slightly. He knew he was being tested and was suddenly overcome by a sense of inadequacy. The captain was asking his opinion and would probably base his next move on it… what if he were wrong?

Turner reached out and gently squeezed his shoulder, "Don't listen to your doubts, Elmer. Don't over-think it. Tell me what your guts say."

Williams drew in a breath, "Well sir… I don't like to commit myself without more info…"

Turner smiled, "At ease, XO, I'm not gonna hold your feet to the fire on this. Just want a second opinion without me prodding it out of you."

Williams shrugged, "Then sir, I'd say he'll turn and head shoreward. Say he knows we're out here and assumes we'll follow that plane's course. He'll head ninety degrees or so away so as to put as much distance between him and us as possible."

Turner nodded, "Concur. Helm, come right to course two-six-zero. All engines ahead flank. How are the batteries, Andy?"

Post, who was still the junior officer of the watch, stepped over to the gyro table, "We're full up, Skipper. All this surface running, we've hardly used them over the past few days. I've only got the aux genny running for electrical; all growlers are providing running power."

"Good," Turner said, "because *my* gut tells me we're going to see something interesting after breakfast. Let's button things up topside and get those guys outta the weather. Inform Mr. Jarvis I want to run at radar depth with the snorkel. Will make things a little less bumpy tonight."

As he said that, the ship juddered as she nosed up and over a large swell, first rolling ponderously to starboard and then back to port. A low rumble seemed to echo through her steel hull as thunder filled the night sky.

16

It was just before zero-five-hundred when the battle stations gong jolted Arthur Turner out of a rather pleasant dream. He and Joan had been lying on a warm beach on a nearly moonless night. They'd shared a bottle of wine and had coupled on their blanket, their bodies entwined in a slow and passionate bout of love-making that seemed to go on and on. At one point, Joan looked down at him and smiled.

"You're wanted in control, Captain," she said breathlessly.

"Wha..." Turner mumbled as his eyes opened and the sound of the long gonging battle alarm brought him to full wakefulness.

He sat up on his bunk and swore. He was suddenly angry at the war and at the Germans who were keeping him from the loving embrace of his wife and from the voices and laughter of his children.

Someone rapped at the bulkhead just outside the curtain that acted as his door, "Skipper? Mr. Williams respects and can you join him in the conning tower?"

"On my way," Turner grumped as he yanked on his duty peanut butters, further irked at having to wear slacks and a button-down shirt rather than the comfy shorts and T-shirts of the Pacific fleet who were fighting the war in warmer climates. He slipped into his shoes and spun out into the corridor, nearly smacking headlong into Walter Sparks as he headed forward to the torpedo room.

"Mornin' Sparky," Turner said as the two men turned sideways to go past one another. "You gonna have half a dozen good fish for me when I call down?"

Sparky grinned at the thought of action, "You bet, sir."

Turner moved through the watertight hatch into the control room. He was pleased to see Nichols and Rogers and their party at the manifold controls. Elmer Williams was leaning over the master gyro table with Hotrod Hernandez. The two men were working on an initial plot.

"Radar contact," Williams reported. "Extreme range, at least at this depth. Uncertain yet, but something bearing three-four-zero at twelve-thousand yards. Pat's already up there waiting."

"Very well," Turner said, mounting the ladder. "Helm, all stop. Frank, let's switch to battery power. That ought to give Dutch a decent acoustic scenario. See what you can come up with. I'm going to secure the radar and head to periscope depth soon."

The steady growl of the ship's four powerful diesel engines slowed and died away. The sudden quiet was so dramatic it took Turner a few seconds to recognize the machinery sounds of the big electric motors operating all by themselves.

"What's our situation up here, Pat?" Turner asked as he popped up into the conning tower. Pat Jarvis was at the search scope and had it trained just to port of forward.

"No visual yet," Jarvis reported. "Still sloppy up there, and with this storm it won't be light for a good couple of hours yet."

"Perfect," Turner said. "Then maybe we'll get our prey. Rig for red up here and down in control. Helm, maintain heading all ahead two-thirds."

"Maneuvering answerin' two thirds," the helmsman, Mug Vigliano, reported.

"Secure the radar," Turner ordered. "Dutch, I want you guys to try and locate these targets on sound. No need to give ourselves away just yet."

Joe Dutch was monitoring the radar and sonar stations and

grinned, "We'll find 'em, Skipper. If they're five miles off, it should be a cinch."

"Yeah," Turner said as he supplanted Jarvis at the scope. Jarvis took a quick look at the nav desk and then sat at the TDC. "Problem is we've got to be *sure*... and I'm not sure how the hell we do that."

Jarvis was right. The conditions on the surface were bad for spotting anything. At forty feet, the periscope head was twenty-seven feet above the surface, which helped to keep the lens free of water and spray. However, the sea state had risen to over twelve feet, and the darkness and rain made spotting anything further than a few hundred yards nearly impossible. Turner's only consolation was that it would make it nothing short of a miracle if his own ship, now nothing more than a few masts sticking out of a roiling sea, were spotted even on radar.

"We've got 'em, sir!" Dutch called out excitedly. "But I think its multiple contacts, bearing three-three-zero, range approximately nine-thousand yards. Heavy, slow screws... making... maybe ten knots... give me a minute and I'll have a heading for you. Surface noise is making it tough."

"Down scope," Turner ordered. "Diving officer, make your depth one-zero-zero feet, both engines ahead one-third. Mug, come right to course two-seven-zero."

Orders were acknowledged in the conning tower and down in the control room. The boat angled down gently, driving her way below the roiling waves and into the placidity of the depths. At a hundred feet, her eyes were useless, but her ears would be even keener.

"Confirmed," Dutch said after a moment, his voice oddly quiet. As if being underwater required more solemnity. "Detecting three heavy, slow screws... no, that's not quite right. I think two single-screwed ships and one with two, but all heavy and slow. Making ten knots and headed zero-three-zero. Probably following the Florida-Georgia coastline."

"Definitely," Williams's disembodied voice floated up through the hatch. "We're about twenty miles off Jacksonville now."

"Any other contacts?" Turner asked, frowning. "No submarines out there?"

"There could be," Dutch admitted. "Running quietly ahead of the group of ships. Merchantmen, I'd guess. What's our intercept?"

"At three knots," Williams reported from below, "we'll meet them in about... forty minutes. At this course and speed we should pass right under them."

"I'd like to get there ahead of time," Turner said. "Helm, ahead two-thirds. Elmer, Dutch, you tell us when to stop. I want to come to a full stop and wait for them to pass over us."

There was a pause before Williams' head appeared above the hatch combing, "Nineteen minutes at six knots. That should put us right in their path at about a thousand yards from the leader. What do you think, Joe?"

Dutch was looking at the magic eye and sharing the headphones with Chet Rivers. He glanced down at a small notepad, checked the dead reckoning tracer and nodded, "Concur, XO. Just about right."

"Should I keep the track going?" Williams asked. "These guys are ours."

Turner nodded, "Yeah, do that. You too, Pat. I want to wait in silence. See if there's anybody else out there. Then I want to come to periscope depth among them, match their speed and do a visual inspection."

"You have a hunch, Art?" Dutch asked.

Turner grinned, "I do, Joe. I think our friend the Kraut Q-ship is one of these vessels. We should've come across them by now. I could be way off, of course... but we'll see."

After a few minutes, Williams ordered full stop and the *Bull Shark* hung ten stories below the surface, with Frank Nichols as diving officer helping to direct Buck Rogers and the air manifold crew to keep the ship level and at depth using the variable ballast tanks. Not long after, the faint sound of big screws could be heard resonating through the hull.

shoom... shoom... shoom...

"Here they come," Dutch almost whispered. "Range now one-one-five-zero yards and closing..."

"Helm... port ahead slow, starboard back slow," Turner said. "Get us on their course of zero-three-zero."

"Maneuvering answering on both screws, sir," Vigliano returned in a hush.

Everyone in the conning tower and down in control was speaking in low tones. As if they were running silent and being tracked by a destroyer above them.

"Zero-three-zero," Mug reported.

"All stop," Turner ordered. "Range, sonar?"

"Five hundred yards," Rivers replied. "Five minutes till they're overhead… wait… Mr. Dutch, can you set up on the loudspeaker?"

Usually, the sonar operator used either the specially designed sonar headphones or the loudspeaker. However, Dutch and Rivers had fabricated a splitter and a bridge so that both could be used simultaneously. Suddenly, the sound of the approaching ships grew louder as they were broadcast over the loudspeaker and through the hull.

shoom… shoom… shoom…

And then, very faintly…

Chu, chu, chu, chu, chu, chu…

"Fast light screws!" Rivers almost bleated. "Bearing… one-one-zero… range sixteen thousand yards… turn rate indicates… Jesus, Skipper… turn rate indicates at least twenty-five knots!"

"A destroyer?" Pat Jarvis asked in disbelief.

"One of ours, maybe?" Dutch opined.

Turner didn't like it. He didn't like it at all. He bent over the open hatch, "XO, distant surface contact bearing one-one-oh… moving fast. Possible tin can. In what direction, sonar?"

A pause, "Right for the merchantman, sir!"

"You heard that, Elmer? Start a plot on him!"

Shoom, shoom, shoom…

The big civilian ships were nearly on top of them now. Their screws were so loud that the sound they made through the submarine's steel hull drowned out the sonar loudspeaker. Even at a hundred feet, those vessels, which probably weighed two- or three-times *Bull Shark's* submerged displacement of twenty-six hundred tons, could rock the submarine around. It was even possible they could draw her upward, with the Venturi effect of several thousand tons of displaced seawater creating a powerful suction.

"All ahead full," Turner ordered. "Diving officer, standby to come to radar depth. If we need to, we'll hail them all and let them know we're not a German."

"First ship approaching," Dutch reported for Rivers. "Looks like one in front, another five hundred yards back and yet another in between the two but five hundred yards off their port sides."

"Got that, Elmer?" Turner called out. "Diving officer, make your depth forty feet. Helm, left standard rudder. Put us off their port sides. Standby to answer bells on diesels."

The boat angled up and leaned slightly to port as Vigliano worked the vertical rudder and the planesmen in the control room angled the diving planes up and the stern planes down.

"Up attack scope," Turner said. "Elmer, have the radio shack standby to hail the lead ship and inform them of our identity… open the snork and fire up the growlers. We need the speed to keep up with this convoy."

The scope rose and Turner snapped the handles down and pressed his face to the rubber eyepiece guard. Dawn had just begun to make itself known, and although the night was little more than a heaving black landscape topped with a slightly less black sky, Turner could make out the hulking form of a merchant ship less than a hundred yards to starboard. The ship's silhouette was just visible, but it was nearly impossible to identify what type of ship it was.

"What's our speed?" he asked as he swiveled the scope to try and find a name.

"Ten knots," Vigliano reported.

"Make turns for nine knots," Turner said softly.

"Maneuvering answering… speed now nine knots," Mug reported.

That was good. It let the ship slide slowly past them. The first vessel's stern came into view, but they were wisely running without lights and Turner couldn't read the name there. He swiveled around so that he was facing nearly dead astern.

"I have the second ship in view," Turner said. "Looks a lot like the first one. Not much upper deck detail and I think only a single mast…

my guess would be a couple of tankers. How about that smaller contact, Dutch? Also, get me a radar fix on him if possible. One sweep and then secure the radar."

"Sound interference making it fuzzy," Rivers stated, "but maintaining the same bearing, range now ten thousand yards."

Turner faced the boat's port quarter and scanned, "This one looks different... more structure on top... probably a freighter... Jesus!"

In his scope, Turner saw a bright flash from the freighter's bow. Somebody on that ship had fired a deck gun, and it was pretty damned close to dead on to the periscope.

"Radar contact!" Radarman Balkley, who had the radar watch, blurted. "Small surface vessel, bearing one-one-five, range eight thousand yards! And sir, I just saw... something streak across the sweep!"

"Yeah, the freighter just fired on *us*," Turner called. "XO, get radio on that! Broadcast friendly hail and ident. Radar, lock onto that surface contact and get me some accurate data."

Balkley worked his gear to turn the SJ radar powerhead in the direction of the unknown surface vessel as Turner spun in the general direction that had been indicated. The light had increased ever so slightly, and he thought he saw an angular shape against the flat gray sky and bulging ocean surface. Then two bright flashes erupted from that shape.

"CBDR on surface target!" Balkley shouted. "Speed is thirty knots!"

"Yeah, and they're firing! Turner shouted. "Sound battle stations torpedo! Pat, open outer doors on all tubes. Order both rooms to set depth on their weapons to four feet. If that's not a Nazi tin can, then I'm a monkey's uncle!"

"Radio has made contact!" Williams shouted up. "Vessels are the *SS Nautic Carrier, SS Black Gold,* both oil tankers out of Louisiana, six thousand tons... the third is the *SS Mortimer Blanch,* dry cargo ship out of Havana. They've acknowledged our identity. They apologize for opening up but said they saw our scope and mast wakes and figured we were Nazis."

"Understandable... at least now we've only got *one* ship shooting at us," Turner grumbled. "Helm, all ahead flank, come right to course one-four-zero. You get a good set of data to start a solution on that bastard, Pat?"

"It's something to start with," Jarvis replied as he worked the switches and dials of the torpedo data computer.

"Periscope depth," Turner ordered. "Phone talker, forward torpedo, order on the tubes is going to be one, two, three, four."

"You heard the order!" Sparky barked at his crew. Several men stood by the specially designed tailing tackle gear, known as tagles, ready to heave the huge weapons forward into the tubes. "Start riggin' them tagles to get more fish into these fuckin' tubes! The Old Man is gonna want more; bet your bottom dollar on that shit! You ready, Tommy?"

Tommy Perkins, who was a burly man not quite as large as Sparks, stood next to him between the tubes. Both men had handed their Y-wrenches off to fellow crew members, who threw the manual outer door tools onto empty bunks. With hydraulic power still active, the outer torpedo tube shutters could be opened electrically.

Both men stood by the manual firing triggers as their assistants worked to either side adjusting the depth spindles and removing them. Then Perkins, who was second to Sparks, stepped aft and supervised the reload gang. Sparky held his hands ready at the manual firing triggers.

"Phone talker, report tubes one through four ready," Sparks announced. "Speed set to high, depth set at four feet; depth spindles disengaged."

The sailor near the after end of the room repeated Sparky's words verbatim and reported an acknowledgement.

"All right, you bastards!" Sparks hollered. "You heard the report. We got a damned destroyer out there. So if we don't wipe his ass off the map with our first shot, the Old Man is gonna have to dive and then we're gonna be in for a bumpy ride!"

"That's right," Perkins replied. His voice was oddly soothing in its southern California accent. A contrast to Sparky's gruff Alabama drawl. "Now I know most of you haven't been through a depth charge attack yet, but don't panic. It's a lot of noise and some shaking, but usually seems a lot worse than it is."

"Exactly," Sparks continued, "so just stay focused and do whatever me and Tommy say."

"Forward torpedo reports ready," Jarvis reported. "Aft torpedo also ready."

"Very well," Turner said, staring at the rapidly growing ship headed right for them. He was firing occasionally, but with the submarine at periscope depth and no radar signal to home in on, they would have a hard time landing any punches. At least not with guns. Torpedoes and depth charges were another matter entirely.

"This is gonna be a down-the-throat shot," Turner stated. "Separation on the spread is five degrees, Pat. I want to make sure we get him with something. Here comes your info... Bearing on the target... *mark!*"

"Zero-zero-five!" Balkley, who was acting as periscope assistant, stated.

"Range to target is two-two-zero-zero yards, repeat twenty-two hundred yards," Turner said, adjusting the range knob and reading the stadimeter. "That's a guess though... never seen a destroyer silhouette like this one... real low... okay, angle on the bow is three-five-five port! Down scope."

With the two ships closing one another at a combined speed of just over forty knots, the range would be closing by twenty yards every second. That still gave Turner a full minute before he was comfortable firing. If he shot too early, the fast, maneuverable destroyer could turn away from his spread. He had to wait for just the right time, and then maybe a second longer. He began to count down in his head.

"Shoot anytime!" Jarvis reported.

"You ready with your balancing act, Andy?" Turner inquired down the hatch.

Post was thankful that Turner couldn't see the flush that bloomed across his young face. After the last time, during the attack on the U-boat, he'd miscalculated, and the ship had breached. Andy was grateful to Turner for not harping on the mistake now. He cleared his throat and consulted a pocket notebook on which he'd written several columns of numbers and notes.

He looked up and met Williams' eyes. The XO smiled slightly and nodded, reminding Post that he wasn't alone either in making a mistake or in feeling uncertain. Williams had time enough to wonder at how easy it was to help another man through the same uncertainties that he himself found so hard to overcome at times.

"Yes sir, I'm ready," Post said with a little more confidence than he actually felt.

As part of the compensation, the water that filled the empty tube after the fish was released was forced down into a holding tank in the torpedo room known as the WRT, or water round torpedo. The weight of the water was less than that of the torpedo, though, so some adjustments to the variable ballast had to be made at the same time.

It was up to the diving officer or his assistant to have these adjustments already prepared so that when the time came, they could give their orders to the manifold crew and keep the boat on an even keel. It was an incredibly complex dance and one that was still new to most of the crew.

"Steady... steady..." Turner said, partly to calm his men and partly himself. "Fire one! Fire two... fire three... fire four!"

With six seconds in between his orders, Jarvis pushed the plungers on the fire control board for the appropriate torpedoes. At the same moment, down in forward torpedo, Sparky Sparks pressed his thumbs down on the manual firing triggers. He then opened the Poppet valve, which sucked the compressed air used to shove the torpedo out of the tube back into the submarine. This was done to eliminate a telltale bubble trail. Then the outer door was closed, the water blown into the WRT, the impulse air tank re-pressurized and then the inner torpedo door could be opened. This was done in turn as each tube was fired.

"Fish running hot straight and normal!" Rivers reported.

The boat rocked violently as a pair of shells exploded just off her port side.

"Dive! Dive! Dive!" Turner ordered. He hit the switch that would activate the XJA circuit so he could talk to the entire ship and grabbed the phone handset. "Emergency deep! Flood negative, COB! Now here this, rig for depth charge! Stop ventilation, close deck flappers. Rig for silent running."

Ah-ooga... ah-ooga... ah-ooga!

The ship dipped down dramatically by the bow as the planesmen hauled the wheels over that controlled the bow and stern planes. There was a whoosh as air was vented from the negative tank and the big submarine began to drive herself toward the dark depths thousands of feet below.

"Active pinging!" Rivers reported.

"How about our fish?" Turner asked.

There was a muffled explosion and then a few seconds later, another one. That was too soon. Turner knew what had happened.

"No signal on the first two..." Dutch said. "Two remaining now running through the target bearing..."

No impact sounds. Two of the Mark 14 torpedoes had prematurely detonated. A problem totally independent of their Mark 6 magnetic exploders or the modifications that had been done to use only contact exploders. The other two fish had long since outrun the time when they should've struck.

They'd missed, and now there was an angry destroyer above them actively seeking them out with their sonar beam.

"Reduce to ahead one-third, hard right rudder," Turner announced.

Below, all ventilation systems and air conditioning systems, as well as the refrigeration and freezer units, were shut down. In each of the watertight compartments, eight in all, not counting the conning tower, men were closing and locking down the watertight doors, sealing each compartment. Additionally, all hydraulic power was deactivated for further stealth.

The steering, bow and stern planes, torpedo doors and even the sound heads for the sonar would have to be operated manually. It would be hard, hot work. Made only harder and hotter the longer the submarine stayed submerged.

"Make your depth four hundred feet, diving officer," Turner said quietly.

Above them, in the silent darkness, an eerie *ping... ping... ping...* began. The men listened as the submarine, now moving at only three knots to save battery power and reduce engine noise, crept away from her previous course at a right angle.

Ping... ping... PONG!

The experienced submariners knew what the sound meant. The eerie pinging had been replaced by a louder reverberant ponging as the destroyer's powerful active sonar beam struck the metal hull of the *Bull Shark*. They'd been found.

"Splashes..." Rivers whispered.

The huntress had now become the prey... all that remained was to crouch silently in the dark and wait for the attack to come...

17

The technical truth was that *Bull Shark*, like all submarines of her era, was not a true submarine. That distinction wouldn't come until the end of the next decade when Hymen Rickover's nuclear boat program began with the launching of USS *Nautilus*. *Bull Shark* and her sisters and rivals were, in fact, submersible ships.

They operated mostly on the surface and could dive for short periods of time. These periods were entirely dictated by the amount of energy stored in their two massive one-hundred twenty-six cell Sargo batteries. Although each one was the size of a single car garage and weighed over eighty tons, they were dreadfully thirsty, requiring thousands of gallons of distilled water each week to maintain the electrolyte balance inside each cell. The boat could operate for forty-eight hours at low speed and low consumption, but there were other issues besides battery life that limited her time beneath the waves.

All the breathable air in the boat was now contained in her pressure hull. There were some reserves stored in the variety of high- to low-pressure air manifold systems used to blow ballast tanks and supply emergency air. Yet, it was limited. With eighty men breathing, the oxygen levels would slowly fall as the CO_2 levels would slowly rise over time.

Another issue was heat and humidity. Without the air conditioning and ventilation systems operating, heat from the men's bodies, as well as the electric machinery, would rapidly turn the boat's interior into a wet tropical environment.

Further, at great depths, the submarine couldn't fire her torpedoes. On the other hand, her natural enemy, the destroyer, had many advantages over the submarine below. She had speed and maneuverability, she wasn't limited by time, and she could bang away with active sonar, homing in on her target while the submarine must try to be as quiet as possible. Further, the destroyer could drop depth charges on the submarine, rattling her and damaging her and even forcing her to the surface to be torpedoed or fired upon with deck guns. A smart destroyer captain could hound a submarine long enough to make that happen.

It wasn't entirely one-sided, however. The destroyer only had a limited supply of depth charges. Once depleted, she not only had no way to reach the submarine but could herself become subject to a torpedo attack from below the surface. Further, while not usually as well armed, a big fleet boat like the *Bull Shark* did come with a powerful five-inch gun, a Bofors 40mm cannon and a further 20mm cannon. In addition, she could mount several fifty caliber machine guns on her cigarette deck. A formidable arsenal that could wreak terrible damage on the relatively fragile hull of a destroyer.

All this and more was running through Arthur Turner's mind as he and his crew listened to the churning propellers of their enemy above. They also waited after Rivers reported four splashes above as well. The destroyer had rolled several charges off her squatty fantail, and her side launchers had sent two more into the sea.

"Now passing three hundred feet," Vigliano announced.

Turner looked to Rivers. The young man was pale, this being his first depth charging. As far as Turner knew, it was the first time for almost everyone on board, the war being only four months old.

Joe Dutch was no longer beside the young man. In addition to being the communications officer, Dutch was also the damage control officer, and his station under such conditions was in the crew's mess coordinating damage reports and repair efforts. Andy Post, as the most junior officer, was stationed in after torpedo.

Outside, in the stillness of the ocean, several metallic clicks were heard as the charges' depth sensors actuated the detonators, and then... the world roared with fury. Thunderous booms rocked the submarine violently from port to starboard and back. The ship's long thin form was twisted, her bow being pushed one way and her stern another, eliciting tortuous groans from her thin steel skin and her frames.

All through the ship, light bulbs burst, plunging some compartments into total darkness. The cork insulation that covered the interior of the hull and made up the overheads began to rain down along with occasional short circuit sparks.

Men were toppled off their feet or sent tumbling across compartments. Some of the younger men screamed in blind terror, their shouts of fear drowned out by explosions that kept coming and coming and seemed impossibly loud.

Turner himself only barely managed to stay on his feet by wrapping an arm around the ladder to the bridge hatch.

"Four hundred feet, sir!" Vigliano reported a little shakily.

"Hard left rudder," Turner ordered. "How we doing, diving officer?"

"Holding depth, Skipper," Paul "Buck" Rogers announced from below. "Mr. Nichols is injured, sir."

Turner groaned and slid down the ladder into the control room. There were still a couple of intact lights down there, casting the control room in a dim and ghastly yellow glow. Frank Nichols sat on the deck near the master gyro table, holding a hand to the side of his head.

"Frank?" Turner asked. "Can you hear me?"

"Aye, sir," Nichols said painfully but levelly. "Bonked my noggin."

Turner saw blood beneath the man's fingers and frowned, "Somebody break out the emergency first aid kit. Lemme see that bump, Frank... okay, just split skin, I think. We'll get it wrapped up. Sorry, Frank... but I don't think it's purple heart worthy."

"More charges on the way!" Rivers bleated from the conning tower, cutting off the chuckles in the control room.

Again there was the intolerable wait as the fifty-five-gallon-sized drums sank. The only accompanying sound was the continuous pinging of the enemy's sonar beam. Turner looked up and, seemingly for the first time, noticed the very simple but incredibly useful device that was new to his boat hanging above the gyro table.

It was called a bathythermograph. Its output was remarkably simple. A stylus moved across a smoked card and indicated ocean temperatures. The ocean was not homogenous. At different locations and depths, the salinity could be greater or less than average. In these conditions, where there was more salt, the density and temperature of the water would change. These layers, known as haloclines or thermals, altered the propagation of sound waves. So much so at times that they would bounce the sound away, giving a surface ship the impression that their sonar beam was not striking any target.

When the ocean temperature and density was smooth, or isothermal, the stylus on the bathythermograph would move slowly and smoothly across the card. However, when a temperature differential at or near the submarine was encountered, it would move more erratically.

Like it was beginning to do now…

"Buck, come—"

Turner's words were drowned out by four more roaring detonations above the submarine. Again, bulbs shattered, cork rained, and men went ass over tea kettle. The force of the blows actually pushed the *Bull Shark* downward by twenty feet.

Both the control room and conning tower were plunged into total darkness as the remaining lightbulbs were smashed. Men shouted in anger and fear, and Turner had to shout over them to get them centered again.

"As you were!" he hollered. "We're all right! Somebody get a battle lantern or two lit. Buck, you with me?"

"Yes sir," Rogers said.

"Okay, get her down to five hundred feet," Turner said. "We're almost into a halocline."

"Sir, that's below test depth," Williams warned.

Turner shrugged, "I know, XO. But I also know from experience that test depth is conservative. We've got a fifty-percent margin for error. My old boat was a *Tambor,* and she went down to five hundred more than once and was only rated to three. This boat has a theoretical crush depth of over nine hundred. We'll be fine. Just keep her in hand, Buck."

Low light filled the room as Williams activated a battle lantern. Turner could see light from the conning tower above as well. He saw that the two planesmen were struggling with the bow and stern plane wheels. With hydraulic power shut down, they had to move them by brute strength alone.

"Make sure these fellas get a relief every twenty minutes," Turner ordered as he mounted the ladder. He glanced at the bathythermograph once more and saw the needle tracing a jagged line on the card.

"Now passing four-fifty, sir," Vigliano reported.

"Hear that?" Pat Jarvis asked, jerking a thumb upward.

There was the steady sound of pinging but no return. The halocline was hiding the submarine from the destroyer. As the boat dove, the sound of the pinging grew attenuated, lengthening into a low whine that was eerily similar to the mournful call of a whale… and then went silent.

———

Minutes before, in the forward room, Sparky and Perkins were busy not with reloading torpedoes but with wrangling their men. As the ship was rocked and batted about, lights went out and insulation snowed throughout the compartment. More than one man had yelled in terror and dropped to the deck in a fetal position.

"Take it easy!" Sparks half-shouted, trying to balance silent running with emphasis. "This ain't shit! Just some noise, like we said."

"Griggs, Jonesy, Mendez and Alders, stop that caterwauling!" Perkins said, going with Sparky to physically haul the men in question to their feet. "You boys climb into your racks and lay quiet. The safest place to be. It's like Sparky said, it'll be all right."

"Sparky!" Perry Wilkes, a newly promoted petty officer, called out as he slowly spun the overhead wheel for the JP sonar head. "We got a leak up forward!"

Sparks silently cursed the man. Although Wilkes was doing his job, his statement would only incite more fear in the rest of the men. Sparks moved forward to see what the trouble was.

"We gonna sink!?" Griggs asked in fright.

"Nah, kid," Perkins soothed, patting him on the arm. "Probably just a poppet valve or a water line inside was shaken loose. Happens all the time, nothing to worry about."

Again the ship was battered and flung about. The men clung to their bunks, and it took all Sparks, Wilkes and Perkins considerable strength to remain on their feet. Perkins groped his way aft and pulled a battle lantern from a locker next to where the room's phone talker was clutching at a support beam for dear life.

Perkins turned the lamp on and moved forward again to shed some light on where Sparks and Wilkes stood, "What is it?"

"Probably the poppet valve on number six," Sparks said. "But it could be a cracked outer door."

All three men looked at the pressure gauge mounted between the tubes and at the needle slowly moving past two hundred PSI.

"Five bills…" Perkins said with a frown.

"She can take it," Sparks said, patting the bulkhead. "This boat is built extra tough."

"Yeah, but if the outer door is ruptured…" Wilkes went on.

"Then the inner door will hold the pressure just fine," Sparks replied. "Shit, it's the breech of a gun, for fuck's sake, Perry. If it can handle blasting a fish out, then it can handle a little seawater."

Wilkes grinned, "Yeah, that's true."

"Phone talker, report we've got a minor leak up here," Sparks said. "Tell them I said it's probably internal and nothing to worry about."

"You sure, Sparky?" The young man with the sound-powered telephone rig hung around his neck asked uncertainly.

"Ain't that what I just said, numbnuts?" Sparks pretended to grump. "Now fuckin' *report*, already."

One of the men lying in his rack, handcuffed to it, in fact, was their German prisoner, Fritz Schwimmer. Sparky made his way to the kid's bunk and bent down, "How about you, kid? How you handling this?"

Schwimmer smiled thinly, "Is not first time. Was depth charged by British destroyer in North Atlantic before."

The young man's English had improved immensely in the week since they'd picked him up. So far he'd behaved, been friendly and open. Most of the men had taken to him and even liked him. Especially the two black sailors aboard. To everyone's surprise, Schwimmer hadn't disdained them because of their skin color and had spent most of his un-shackled time with them helping prepare meals.

"I think you're setting a good example for the rest of the guys," Sparky said, giving him a pat. He was surprised at how much he himself had come to like the Nazi prisoner.

Schwimmer grinned, "I am good Kraut, yah?"

Sparky laughed, "Yah... damn good Kraut."

In the smaller after torpedo room, Andy Post was surprised at how calm Walter Murphy was about the whole thing. Post himself, like just about everyone on board save for a scant handful, had never been depth charged. Hell, never been attacked at all under any circumstances.

Murph, who was in his mid-thirties, seemed almost nonchalant over the whole thing. He certainly wasn't old enough to have served in the previous war, and Post couldn't account for it. Other than the fact that the tough man must have nerves of steel.

All four of their tubes were loaded, and because they were running silent, no effort had been made by the crew to ready new loads. There were only four torpedoes in the racks, as the after room only had space for a single reload. So the men were all lying in their bunks with the exception of Post, Murph and the phone talker.

When the first depth charge attack occurred, Post had been

shocked at the violence and the unbelievable noise of it all. He'd been clinging to one of the bunk stacks, so he'd been preserved from being flung across the compartment, but only just. The room seemed to leap up and down and side to side like some kind of manic carnival ride. Combined with the shattering of lights and the flying insulation, Post thought that if it went on much longer, he'd go right out of his gourd.

Through it all, amazingly, Murph had stood, braced between the tubes and hadn't lost his balance once. Not on the first volley or the second... no, not even on the fourth. The phone talker had wrapped himself around another bunk stanchion and had tears running down his pale boyish face.

"Aw, come on..." Murph droned, smiling as he did, "this ain't nothin'. I remember one time we was in the North Sea getting rattled by a whole passel of Nazi torpedo boats. Kinda like tin cans but smaller. Anyway, they kept us down eight hours, and the charge count was something like sixty-five. Believe that, Ensign? You talk about shakin' your fillins loose! Ha-ha!"

Post just gaped at him, "What? When the hell were you in the North Sea?"

"Exchange program," Murph said. "Bout eighteen months ago. Was on a Brit submarine at the time. Kind of a training program to help get some of us Yank submariners ready for the war we all knew was comin'. Remember, the Jerries and the Brits have been at it since the end of thirty-nine."

"Jesus Christ," Post said, shaking his head and shivering involuntarily. "Sixty-five charges..."

"Yeah, and we only got sixteen so far," Murph said. "Hardly worth sweepin' up after. So you don't worry about anything, sir. It'll be all over soon. Hell, I bet the Old Man already found us a thermal. Haven't heard any more ashcans goin' off in a couple of minutes now."

He was right. It had been at least five minutes since the last depth charge exploded. Suddenly, Post realized he couldn't hear something else as well. He met Murph's eyes.

"Yep," the lead torpedoman said with a grin. "No more screws. He's bugged out is my guess. All over but the moppin' up, boys."

"Uhm..." the phone talker mumbled, still clinging to his pipe.

"Control is asking for a report, Murph."

"Well then give 'em one, Ogden," Murph said. "All good here. No leaks, no casualties, no injuries. You can tell the XO if that's all the excitement they can muster up there, then I might transfer to a circus just so I can get a few kicks now and then."

To Post's surprise and Murph's bemusement, Ogden gave an exact, verbatim report to the executive officer.

In the conning tower, Turner hovered behind River's chair as the sonarman listened intently. After some minutes he turned and shook his head.

"Screw noise has diminished," Rivers reported. "Of course, we're hampered by the sound layer, too... but both from the JP and the sound coming into the hull, it sounded like the tin can has moved off, sir."

Turner nodded, "I think you're right, Rivers... Keep your ears open."

"Damage reports coming in, Skipper," Williams called up.

Turner went back down into the control room, "Let's have it, Elmer."

"Sparky reports a minor leak in tube six, thinks it's a faulty poppet valve or maybe a drain line... although the bilge seems to be filling. Not bad, but visible," Williams reported. "Couple of overloads in maneuvering... oh, and Murph says that if this is how boring sub duty is gonna be, he wants to join the circus."

Everyone in the control room laughed. It was partly a release of tension and felt good. Turner shook his head, "Very well. Have Sparky slowly blow the WRT for now. We'll head up top and see how things are going. I'd like to find out where that tin can went and how that little convoy is doing."

"And have Brannigan and a mate start moving forward with replacement bulbs," Nichols said with a wry grin.

"And get Doc up here to look at Frank's noggin," Turner added. "Okay, let's get a move on. Buck, blow negative and take us up to periscope depth. Helm, all ahead two-thirds until we're sure we don't have company up there. Secure from silent running, secure from depth charge. Get the blowers on and open the flappers. Men can stand easy at battle stations, and the smoking lamp is lit. Tell the galley to start serving hot coffee and pastries. If the shouting is over, we'll get breakfast started shortly."

The boat had been down a little less than two hours or so. The thermometer in the control room read eighty-five degrees and the humidity wasn't too bad yet. The cold water of the Atlantic helped.

It was full daylight when the scope's head broke the surface. The storm was beginning to abate, and here and there, tiny rays of sunlight broke through the blanket of gray overhead. The sea was still churned up, however, with twelve-to-fifteen-foot swells rolling over and covering the scope. Turner ordered them to radar depth where he could do a sweep out to a horizon of around five miles in radius.

There was nothing. No destroyer and no merchant ships. The sea was clear of all but white horses.

"Put us on top, diving officer," Turner said. "Helm, have maneuvering standby to answer bells on diesels. We'll run with three diesels and one on charge. Elmer, project a course and heading for that merchant convoy and pass it along to Mug. Once we're running on the growlers, Mug, proceed all ahead full. Once we're clear, I want a full sweep on the sugar jig and try to make radio contact with those ships again."

The ship broke the surface, and after the water had drained through the main deck limber holes and bridge scuppers, Turner went topside and breathed in the cool fresh salt air. Lookouts were posted, and Ralph Hernandez joined him on the bridge as quartermaster of the watch.

"Nice to see the sky again," Hotrod remarked as he and Turner lit cigarettes.

"Were you that worried, Hotrod?"

Hernandez shrugged, "Never been depth-bombed before, Skipper. A bit unnerving, you ask me."

Turner chuckled, "It's mighty rude, I'll give you that."

"In my village," Hotrod said in an over-exaggerated Mexican

accent, "such improper behavior is *mucho* frowned upon."

Turner chuckled and shook his head, "In your village, Hotrod? Aren't you from Long Beach California?"

"*Si… es verdad.*"

Both men laughed, the tension of the past few hours draining away as they did so.

"*Bridge, control,*" Williams called. "*No contacts on radar. High look on the periscope is negative as well. I do have the skipper of the* Nautic Carrier *on the radio if you'd like to talk to him. ETA to intercept is two hours, present speed.*"

"Very well," Turner replied. "Hold down the fort for a bit, Hotrod."

Turner descended the ladder to the conning tower and then down to the control room. He stepped aft to the radio shack and found Dutch and Clancy Weiss already there, hovering over Arnie Brasher, the radioman of the watch's shoulder. Brasher was a somewhat pudgy young man in his late twenties, with a jovial manner and an almost comically fluffy mustache.

"You gonna shorthand all this, Yo?" Turner asked Weiss.

The chief yeoman nodded and readied his pencil. Turner nodded to Brasher who activated the two-way speaker.

"Captain, this is Commander Arthur Turner of the *Bull Shark*… how are you and your friends doing out there? The three of you all right?"

"*Pleasure to speak with you, Commander,*" A gruff-sounding man replied. "*It's only us and the other oiler, though. That freighter dropped off shortly after you appeared. Guess they thought you was a Nazi boat, which is why they fired on you. But I guess that destroyer… or whatever it was… scared them off. We lost contact with them not long after you charged that Nazi ship. By the way, we appreciate you chasing them off for us. Hope you boys weren't too knocked about?*"

"Few broken bulbs and a couple of scrapes," Turner said. "Glad to hear you're all right. We're en route to your projected position now, Captain. We'll stick with you for the rest of the day. I'd suggest you put into Charleston for the night, though if you can reach there before sunset."

A pause, "*Can't argue. We can do fifteen knots in a pinch. How about you?*"

"Let us catch up, and then we'll match you," Turner said. "We ought to get you within sight of land before sundown."

"*Much obliged, Navy.*"

Turner frowned, "Captain… how long did that freighter stick with you guys?"

Another pause while the oil carrier's skipper consulted with someone, "*Honestly, commander… I'm not sure. We ain't got a very good radar and that storm was thicker'n pea soup… but I can tell you he wasn't there before dark last evenin'… he was just sort of there at first light.*"

Turner's brows rose and his stomach did a little dance, "Did you speak to him at all?"

The voice sounded casual, "*Oh yeah… their captain was a good ole boy from North Carolina. We jawed a little just before you popped up.*"

Turner thanked him and signaled for the radio to be shut down. He tapped his chin thoughtfully as he began to pace the control room. Williams noticed that he had something on his mind and met him at the gyro table.

"Sir?" the XO inquired. "Something wrong?"

"I'd have to say so, XO," Turner replied with a sigh, tapping the multiple plotted lines on the chart from the attack. "The *Mortimer Blanch* just appears as part of the group and then vanishes shortly after the German destroyer shows up? Seems… strange."

"You think the tin can got them?" Williams opined.

Turner sighed again, "I don't know… and it wasn't a real tin can. Smaller, kind of low-profile superstructure. More like a beefed-up torpedo boat or slightly stepped-down destroyer escort… Seems even stranger. She'd be a long way from home all by herself. If she could even make the crossing."

"So what you're saying," Williams picked up on Turner's thought, "is that she's getting support from the Q-ship. Keeping her fueled."

"Has to be," Turner said. "So that means we don't have one ship to find… we have two. I've got a funny feeling, Elmer… a feeling that we had our objective in view. I can't prove it, but I wonder if that freighter might not be our boy."

18

ATLANTIC OCEAN - 28°15' N, 78°24' W
APPROXIMATELY 60 MILES NORTH OF WALKER'S CAY, BAHAMAS

"This *Bull Shark* and her captain are becoming an annoying thorn in my side, Curt."

Diedrich never liked it when Klaus Brechman got familiar. There was something disturbing, or even disconcerting, about the SS major when he grew personal that always set Diedrich on edge. Like now.

"I understand, Klaus," the Q-ship's captain tried it for himself and found the name didn't quite fit his mouth. "The man is a wolf for certain."

The two men were below decks now, in the large cargo hold two levels below the upper main deck. Although vast and packed full of containers and storage vessels, the large area seemed oddly confined. Of course, there was a reason for this. The cargo handling floor was still quite high off the waterline. Nearly three stories above it, in fact.

The two men came to a partially rusted metal crate ten feet on a side marked with a red cross, the international symbol for medical supplies. Diedrich led Brechman around to the far side of the container and activated what looked like a two-way radio held in his right hand. With a puff of air and the distinct sound of an electric servo motor, one side of the crate swung outward, revealing a dimly lighted set of stairs within.

"What do we plan to do about him?" Brechman asked as he followed the Navy captain down the damp stairwell.

"We must locate the man first," Diedrich reminded him. "It is nearly as difficult for us in all this ocean as it is for him to locate us."

The stairs descended two flights until they came to the bottom of the well and a watertight door. Diedrich levered the dogging handle and the door swung open with an audible hiss. The two men walked out of the stairwell and into a vast area that seemed far more capacious than the cargo decks above, despite the fact that the space was dominated by something that seemed too huge to be there.

The brightly lit area they'd entered was half the length of the *Mortimer Blanch,* two hundred and fifty feet. It went from the keelson twenty-five feet below the waterline to the lower level of the cargo area fifty feet above. The room was little more than a shell, a shell with regularly-spaced steel beams that bent around from the keel and up the sides of the ship like the ribs of some gargantuan beast.

Nestled in this space and connected to catwalks that ran the length of the compartment and along the after bulkhead was another ship. This one was sleek and painted battleship gray. She had a high knife-like bow, squat fantail and an oddly low bridge structure amidships. Forward of this was a twelve-centimeter deck gun. Mounted on the bridge level one deck up were a pair of 20mm anti-aircraft cannons on either beam. The lateral depth charge launcher, a Y-gun, was mounted along the afterdeck just forward of the racks of depth charges that lived there. On either side amidships were the long torpedo tubes that completed her armament.

The ship was a small destroyer-escort or large torpedo boat. Currently, she rested on a special dry-dock-like cradle that kept her still while the ship that carried her maneuvered and allowed men to work on and around the thousand-ton secret weapon.

"And why did not our *Dolch* here sink Turner and his submarine?" Brechman asked.

Diedrich smiled, "That was not her mission this time, as you know. As you also know, she is not a *Zerstorer* in truth. She is a torpedo boat. She carries only twenty-four depth charges. Her primary focus is to sink surface ships with her six torpedo launchers."

Brechman scowled as he gazed at the sleek vessel before them, "Well, we need her to kill the *Bull Shark*. Are you saying she can't do that with only twenty-four depth charges?"

Diedrich smiled, "Of course not. However, anti-submarine warfare isn't that easy. They registered the submarine as heading down past four hundred feet. They must have found a salt layer below four hundred and fifty. What that means is that this submarine, which we thought was perhaps a *Gato*-class, is, in fact, something new. Her test depth may be much deeper, thus making our job that much more difficult. It may be that more than one asset will be needed to ensure the *Bull Shark's* destruction."

"A coordinated attack?" Brechman asked. "Should we contact Kapitan Hardegen for assistance? He's familiar with the American boat."

"Perhaps," Diedrich said, rubbing his chin thoughtfully. "This ship, the *Blanch* I mean, also has weaponry to fight a submarine. However, as our goal is to maintain anonymity, we must reserve that for a definitive action. But yes… perhaps with U-123 and the *Dolch* working in concert, we might land this fish. Remember, it isn't even necessary to destroy a submarine with depth charges. In truth that happens very rarely… all a destroyer captain must really do is be patient. Sooner or later, even the big American fleet boats must come up to breathe… and then we have him."

Brechman began to pace the narrow catwalk that stretched along the port side of the ship, "Perhaps we can do more, Herr Kapitan… perhaps we can raid the game. Have you ever played the American game of poker?"

Diedrich shook his head.

"It is a gambling game… a variety of games, in fact. However, there are several ways to… ensure victory. One of them, I believe the Americans say, is to stack the deck."

"To cheat, in other words."

"Exactly."

"What do you have in mind?" Diedrich asked, his curiosity piqued as much as he felt a twinge of trepidation.

Herr Brechman operated in a different world than did Diedrich. To the Kriegsmarine captain, naval warfare was an honorable field of combat. Even an art form. Different vessels had different advantages and disadvantages. Each type used its gifts to achieve its goals. Battleships used their massive guns to deliver crushing bombardments from miles away. Cruisers used speed and heavy weaponry to defend a fleet. Destroyers used speed and maneuverability to charge and attack like wolves. The submarine used stealth and powerful torpedoes to cripple an enemy's logistical supply lines by sinking merchant ships primarily.

Men like Brechman, on the other hand, used secrecy, duplicity and fear to achieve their aims. Outright threats, blackmail or a knife in the back was more his style. It didn't sit well with a veteran naval commander like Diedrich.

"As you know," Brechman said, leaning on the railing and considering the two-hundred and ten-foot light destroyer before him, "we have assets in the United States. Some rather well-placed. There is one in particular who may be of some service. However, it will be up to us to provide support and to be on hand for what I have in mind. Do you think your young pilot would have any objection to landing along the American coast at night?"

Diedrich's brows rose, "Landing? He might, if only for technical reasons… but he is a good pilot and a good officer."

Brechman nodded, "I do not doubt his loyalty. The *Schutzstaffel* would ensure *that* in any case. Where is he now?"

"Off duty for the day," Diedrich said.

"Excellent," Brechman stated. "Let's go and speak with him… the fumes down here are beginning to make my head ache."

Outside of the entrance to Massachusetts Bay, just north of Cape Cod… and over eight hundred miles from the *Mortimer Blanch,* the

U-123 cruised slowly northeast at periscope depth, running at four knots in order to conserve battery power and to stay below the surface during daylight hours. At exactly eight a.m. local time, and after a complete visual scan of the horizon, the submarine rose just shallow enough to extend her radio mast above the gently rolling swell. The ship listened patiently for ten minutes, as she did four times per day, then lowered the mast and proceeded back down to periscope depth.

Reinhard Hardegen sat at the tiny wardroom table sipping hot coffee lightened with fresh New England cream, nibbled absently on a freshly baked cherry strudel and perused a copy of the Boston Globe. He particularly enjoyed the sports page, keeping track as much as his position allowed him to keep track of the goings-on of the 1942 baseball season. A half-burned Lucky Strike sat smoldering in an ashtray at his elbow.

There was an old fishing trawler that plied his swordfish lines off Cape Cod who routinely met U-123 whenever she was within range. Her skipper, an even older German immigrant who'd lived in Massachusetts since the turn of the century, made a point of supplying Hardegen with sundry items as best he could. The old man, a distant cousin of the Hardegen family, was certainly no fan of the Third Reich. However, he still held an affection for his native Deutschland and held out hopes that a Wilhelm might once again rule over the nation.

The offerings usually amounted to fresh dairy bought from a small farm on the Cape, the occasional swordfish or basket of lobsters. Coffee, cigarettes and sweets were easy to come by, as were American newspapers. While it was true that Hardegen poured over these for any bits of intelligence for his own boat or that he could pass on to Brechman, he secretly most looked forward to the sports scores.

Hardegen had been a baseball fan since he was a teenager. His favorite player had been Babe Ruth, and he'd followed Babe's career from when he was with the Red Sox and, of course, his long stint with the New York Yankees. Although Babe had retired, Hardegen was still a follower of both teams and always enjoyed when the two great rivals faced off. Tex Hughson and Ted Williams were two of his favorite Sox, and of course, he loved the great Joe DiMaggio of the Yankees, along with Phil Rizzuto and Lefty Gomez.

The Nazi captain was just about to open the sports page when his executive officer stepped into the room with a message flimsy in his hand. The man looked pensive and disapproving as usual.

"Einsvo," Hardegen said amiably. "Come to share a cup of coffee and enjoy a cigarette with me? I'll read you the scores... And then we can read the funny papers together."

Richter looked even more pinched at this. Hardegen knew that teasing someone as deadly serious as Richter was a bit too easy and might even be considered mildly cruel... but it was a bit of fun. And if a U-boat captain couldn't have a little fun at his subordinates' expenses... then what was the point of it all?

"Kapitan..." Richter began hesitantly, warring against his deeply ingrained sense of duty and his desire to balk at his commanding officer's facetiousness. He took a slightly safer tack as a means to reproach Hardegen. "Do you not think it's... well... a bad example for the men to see their captain reading American sports scores, drinking American coffee and *smoking* American cigarettes?"

"The spoils of war, Einsvo," Hardegen said, just managing to keep the mirth from his eyes. "Know thein enemy, eh? If you won't join me, then at least don't disapprove, Heiman... I am but mortal. What do you have there?"

Richter sighed ever so softly and handed the sheet of paper over, "Radio received this flash message. It requires your personal decryption before we can decode through the enigma."

"Very well, let's go and talk to the chief yeoman," Hardegen said, devouring the last of his pastry and washing it down with a gulp of coffee. "My work is never done..."

The two men went across to the tiny ship's office where the chief yeoman, a lean middle-aged man wearing spectacles, waited in front of what looked like a typewriter. Hardegen handed the transcribed radio-coded message to the man who stepped aside.

Hardegen sat down, tapped several keys on the device, which began to hum. A series of clicks and whirrs sounded from within, and he stood.

"Please type this out, Meissner," Hardegen said. "Usual protocol."

The man set the coded message in a stand and began to press keys on the typewriter-like device. As he did so, slowly enough that Richter could write, lights would glow next to the actual letters that were being decoded. After a few moments, Meissner shut down the machine and waited.

"To U-123, R. Hardegen commanding," Richter read from his hastily scratched notes. "From Sentry. Have plan to ensnare hound dog… need your boat… proceed immediately to twenty-eight stroke thirty north by seventy-eight stroke twenty-four west. Will radio further detail when you arrive. Advise on ETA next check-in."

"Interesting," Hardegen said with a wry grin. "Something is afoot in the Bahamas, perhaps?"

Meissner took the torn-off sheet from Richter's notebook as well as the one beneath and placed them along with the original message in a small, lidded box. He depressed a button and a clicking and muffled whoosh was heard. After a moment, a small fan clicked on and an indicator on the device turned green. The yeoman opened the lid and all that remained were a few loose ashes.

"Messages disposed of, Kapitan," he reported.

"Very good," Hardegen replied. "Einsvo, I'm going to the radio room. Please surface the boat, set normal surface watch and do a full radar sweep. Then please turn due south and run all ahead full."

"Jawohl! Heil Hitler!" Richter said, his pique of a few moments earlier now replaced with the excitement of a secret mission.

After encoding a new message on the enigma, Hardegen followed him into the control room and moved to the tiny radio room where Yohan Verschmidt was working with a young sailor on his radio qualifications.

"Kapitan," Verschmidt announced.

The young sailor blushed and tried to look even busier. Hardegen smiled slightly.

"Yohan, I wish to reply to the message we just received," Hardegen said, handing over the scribbled piece of paper with the coded message on it. It was a simple acknowledgment that stated they'd be running on diesels and coming around the eastern side of the Bermuda Islands. "Then... I want you two men to eat it."

The young sailor, a radioman who had only signed on just before U-123 left port to come to the U.S. coast, stared open-mouthed at his captain.

"The captain is teasing you, Oshtenz," Yohan said with a grin.

The young man laughed. Of course he did. A barely wet behind the ears *matros mechaniker* could do nothing else when his captain deigned to be jocose.

Further up the Bay in Boston Harbor and near the mouth of the Charles River, two young women stood along the railing of one of the most powerful frigates ever built and chatted together. The old ship, the USS *Constitution,* known affectionately as "Old Iron Sides" was moderately crowded with visitors on what was turning out to be a beautiful spring day. From where the women stood near the starboard barrier rail between the quarterdeck and the waist, they could see the two children that had accompanied them down in the waist near the break of the focs'l listening intently as the museum guide explained in great detail how the huge twenty-four-pound cannon worked.

"They're really enjoying this," Milly Allman commented to Joan Turner.

Joan smiled, "Yes, they love the Navy. I think that's thanks to their father. Arty is a big history buff, and this particular era is interesting to him. We're going to have to come back here when he puts in."

"Don't think the kids will mind?" Milly asked with a knowing smile.

Joan chuckled, "Absolutely not. I wonder if we'll be able to get them to leave for lunch."

Joan put her hands inside the fur-lined pockets of her parka and shivered a little. Although it was a clear and sunny day, it was still early spring in New England. The temperature at half-past nine in the morning was barely above fifty.

"I'll be glad to be in Wilmington next week," Joan said. "Bet it's already in the seventies there."

Milly's eyes widened, "You're going to North Carolina?"

Joan nodded, "Yes, my mom still lives in the house I grew up in on Hewlett's Creek, off Greenville Loop. I've tried talking her into selling since dad died… it's such a big place and all."

"I thought you were from Michigan?"

"We are, but we moved to North Carolina my first year in high school. Much nicer weather, especially in winter."

Milly hugged herself against the chill as well, "Well, that's fantastic! We should go together. My sister's house is right near the end of Wrightsville Beach, not far from the inlet. We could take the train down together and have you and the kids come out to the beach. Too cold for swimming yet, but like you said, might be more comfortable weather. I was already planning on it this coming Thursday."

"That's only four days," Joan said, pondering.

"Oh, is that too soon?" Milly asked. "Well, I could change my time if you wanted to travel together…"

Joan thought for a moment, "I was only thinking of the kids' school. Maybe leaving on Saturday… What if we left Friday afternoon when they got out of school? We'd ride through the night and be there Saturday morning."

"Terrific!" Milly enthused. "It's a date. Oh, you'll love this house, Joanie. It's right on the beach and built on stilts. From the second floor… well, I guess third, if you count the space under the stilts… you can watch boats coming in and out of Masonboro Inlet. We can walk down to the pier and have lunch; oh, it'll be so much fun!"

Joan laughed at her bubbling enthusiasm. It was nice to have a friend. Since they'd come here, Joan had made friends with a few of the Navy wives, yet Milly was a little different. Perhaps it was because they *didn't* share the same worrisome concerns. Concerns about their husbands being at sea during a time of war.

With Milly, the focus was on living a regular life, the way it had been before the Japanese had attacked Pearl. Shopping, going to the movies, trying new restaurants, talking about who was more handsome, Tyrone Power, Clark Gable, Gary Cooper or Humphrey

Bogart. Milly made life seem sane to Joan Turner, and she was grateful for that.

"Sounds wonderful, Milly," Joan said. "I can't wait to get there. Will I get to meet your mysterious fiancé finally?"

Milly laughed, "Maybe... Roger is traveling for work right now... but I think I can talk him into a visit. This will be wonderful!"

19
APRIL 25, 1942
0000 ZULU

Brenner Michner was not comfortable. On so many levels did his discomfort rest that he found it difficult to enumerate all the ways in which he was unhappy to himself. Perhaps he could simply place all of his feelings at the feet of the man in the co-pilot's seat beside him.

If there was ever a focus for all of his uncertainties, Klaus Brechman was the perfect repository for them. The man's very presence was disconcerting, and the fact that all of this was his idea did not fill the Kriegsmarine pilot with any warmth.

"How long now?" the SS officer suddenly asked after more than an hour of silence.

The aircraft was flying with the nearly setting sun just forward of their port wing. Michner checked his chart and airspeed indicator, "Not long. We should sight land at twilight. Wouldn't do to come in any earlier even as low as we are."

There, at least, were two solid items of concern for the young pilot. For the better part of an hour now, he'd been holding the Arado fifty feet off the ocean's surface. That alone was nerve-wracking enough over time because it required total vigilance. Further, it limited their horizon to less than ten miles, which meant that by the time they might spot something, they too would be spotted.

The next item was their destination. Michner was flying his fragile little floatplane directly for the North Carolina Coast. Specifically, the Masonboro Inlet where he was to *land* behind Masonboro Island just to the south. Land in enemy territory, at night no less.

This after a flight of more than three hundred miles. A flight with only two men, one of whom couldn't even fly. Once they landed and did whatever it was that the SS spy was there to do, they were to take off again and fly a reciprocal course of the one that brought them to Wilmington in the first place. A course that was cumulatively longer than the maximum range of the plane. In the six hours or so that the mission would take, the *Mortimer Blanch* was to follow the same course, thereby reducing the return leg by a hundred miles or so. Necessary if the Arado was to avoid ditching due to lack of fuel. That small point being concern number three.

Although Michner had no idea what the mission was, he was told that the weight would be greater on the return flight, further increasing fuel consumption. Should they hit strong headwinds, things could get unpleasant.

Anxiety number four was the greater weight. To Michner, that meant only one thing. They were picking someone up. Who that someone was, he couldn't say, yet he suspected it was a spy who needed to escape the United States for one reason or another. No matter who, what and why... Michner didn't like it.

But then, as Captain Diedrich had said, when you dealt with the SS, anything was possible. Even what might be laughably called "normal" in war went out the window.

Off their port bow, the bloated and angry sun sunk beneath the waves, and the blue sky rapidly began to darken to a deep indigo. The light was no more than fifteen minutes from fading altogether when Michner spotted the dark line on the horizon. It quickly grew to become the barrier islands of the American Coast.

"There's our destination," Michner said, reducing speed to just above a stall. "Let's hope there's no one out there with a radar aimed low... based on the chart, I would say this is Masonboro Inlet, Major."

"Excellent," Brechman said flatly. "A fine job of navigation, Lieutenant. Where do you plan to touch down exactly?"

Michner glanced at the chart again. The southern border of the inlet is an uninhabited barrier island known as Masonboro Island. It's about a mile long, and there are calm and relatively shallow waters behind. I'll touch down there, and then you can direct me where to go."

There were no fishing boats or pleasure craft in or near the inlet as they drew close. With the threat of Nazi U-boats lurking just offshore, many coastal cities in the mid-Atlantic had warned their boating populous to stay in after dark. The time when the metal sharks were most hungry.

Michner came in over the inlet, swung his plane to the southwest and eased it down onto the slick and nearly black waters on the backside of Masonboro. The aircraft quickly slowed, and Michner reduced his throttle and turned them back toward the inlet.

"We have a passenger to collect," Brechman stated, confirming the pilot's suspicions. "They will be on the southern end of the other barrier island."

"That's why the raft?" Michner asked.

"Precisely," Brechman stated. "I would prefer to simply motor over to the beach there, but that may be pushing our luck."

Michner thought about it for a moment, "Major, this ship has a low profile and is well camouflaged... how long do you suspect we'll be on the ground, so to speak?"

Brechman shrugged, "That is hard to say. It could be just a few minutes or the better part of an hour."

"I could drop you off on that side and then motor back here," Michner offered. "You could then signal me with a light when you were ready to be picked up."

Brechman pondered that and then shook his head, "This is a... delicate matter, Lieutenant. I may need your help. No, I think it's better if you beach the plane on this side and we row across."

"Very well, sir," Michner said, turning the Arado toward a small indent on the inland side of the island. There wasn't much vegetation higher than ground foliage, yet the plane would be next to impossible to spot driven up onto the narrow strand. He throttled up a bit, and the pontoons ground onto the bottom and the aircraft stopped.

Michner shut down the engine and climbed out, pulling a small anchor from the storage locker behind the cockpit, buried it into the sand and cleated the line off on the forward end of one of the pontoons. He then helped Brechman pull the lump that was the inflatable raft from the compartment and unrolled it on the beach.

Brechman pulled the inflation lanyard, and the dark gray boat expanded and took on the familiar shape of a four-man rubber raft. Michner inserted the two oars into the rowlocks and pushed the boat into shin-deep water.

It was no surprise to the young man when Brechman sat on the tube directly in the stern, leaving Michner to sit at the single thwart and take the oars. He was not looking forward to rowing a clumsy rubber boat a mile or so across an inlet in the dark.

As if, the pilot thought ruefully as he tugged on his oars, *I was looking forward to anything about this insane mission...*

———

"Joan! So glad you could come!" Milly Allman emoted when the heavy door at the top of the stairs flew open. "Come in, come in!"

Joan Turner stepped into a sparsely but expensively decorated living room. There were leather furnishings, carved mahogany tables with gold filigree, and chinse-covered lamps and damask-covered sofas. A record player churned out the upbeat sound of Arty Shaw's orchestra.

"I'm so glad you could make it," Milly said, guiding Joan to a sideboard set up with wine glasses and room temperature reds and chilled whites.

"Where is everyone?" Joan asked in surprise.

Milly chuckled, "Oh, honey... a Sunday beach party doesn't even *begin* until eight. You're the first one. Sissy went off to the store, so it's just you and me for a few minutes. Your mother didn't mind watching the kids tonight?"

Joan accepted a cool glass of Chardonnay and smiled when she sipped, "Oh no, if she had her way, they'd never come back to Connecticut with me."

Milly led Joan around the house, and they ended up on the second-floor balcony. The wide wooden deck encircled the house and offered fantastic views of the beach, Wrightsville Avenue, Masonboro Sound and the Inlet itself. As the two women stood on the southeastern corner looking out to sea, they both turned their heads at the sound of an airplane's engine revving up and then down from somewhere off to the south.

"Airplane?" Joan asked. "This time of night?"

Milly shrugged, "Probably a commuter flight headed down the coast. What do you think of this view!?"

"Gorgeous," Joan commented, sipping at the good wine. "I'd love to get Arty here to see this. Wonder if we could arrange that when he gets leave?"

"Oh, I'm sure we can," Milly commented. "Such a beautiful night; it's hard to imagine that a war is going on out there."

"I know what you mean… although it's not that difficult when you've got a husband out there fighting it," Joan observed and then yawned so deeply she had to cover her mouth. "Excuse me! Must be the scenery distracting me."

Milly grinned, "That's all right. It's a little chilly, though. Why don't we go in and freshen up our wines and grab a sweater? Are you any good at lighting fires?"

Joan smiled, "Sure. You've got a fireplace downstairs? Don't… oh, excuse me again… think I noticed earlier."

Milly led Joan back into one of the upstairs bedrooms and down the steps to the main floor. Joan found that she had to hold tightly to the banister as she descended, her sleepiness really hitting her hard and making her a little unsteady.

"Maybe I'd better forego the wine for now," Joan said when they entered the central kitchen. "I'm nodding off, for crying out loud. How about some coffee?" I don't know what's come over me…"

Milly smiled, "It's the wine."

Joan frowned and set her empty glass on the countertop, "I can usually hold my liquor, though. This is ridiculous. I feel like I'm dying on my feet here."

"No, it's the wine," Milly said, her smile having taken on something less than friendly, although Joan was too woozy to notice. "We want to make sure you're nice and calm, Joan."

Some vague sense of alarm awakened deep in Joan Turner's mind. Unfortunately, the warning came too late. Something about how tired she was and how she felt on the verge of collapse after a single glass of wine touched a part of her consciousness and her more primitive mind. She stared at the blonde woman blankly, trying to fight through a fog that was nearly complete.

"What... what are you...?"

"You were right earlier, Joan," Milly said, still maintaining her Cheshire cat smile. "We will indeed lure your husband... but it will be where we want him. And it's you who will get him there."

Joan tried to speak, but the fog was now becoming blackness. Milly stepped forward and caught the slightly smaller woman, easing her into an armchair just as a short series of raps came at the front door. Milly made sure Joan wasn't going to slide out of the chair and went to answer it.

In the door were two men. One in his late twenties with a handsome face and the other at least a decade older with a severe and almost sinister appearance in his features.

"Herr Brechman," Milly said with a smile and in flawless German. "Do come in."

"You have the package?" Brechman asked, seeing Joan Turner lying bonelessly in the overstuffed leather chair and nodding.

"She's here and quiescent," Milly said. She turned to the taller and younger man. "And who might you be?"

"Lieutenant Brenner Michner," the man said, evidently uncertain of the situation. "I'm the pilot."

"Well, Herr pilot, do you have room in your plane for little old me?" Milly asked with a grin.

She was surprised when he switched from the German they'd been speaking to a flawless North Carolina accent and said: "Well, sure I do, ma'am."

Brechman, to no one's surprise, did not smile. Rather, he scowled, "Miss Allman, I'm afraid we have a bit of a weight issue. We cannot take another passenger."

Milly's good humor vanished in a flash, "Herr Brechman, after this, it will not be safe for me here. The authorities or the American intelligence community will connect me to Mrs. Turner. My position is untenable. You must extract me."

"I regret the situation," Brechman said. "It is most unfortunate. You have done very good work and the Fatherland, and your Fuhrer appreciates your service and sacrifice."

Milly's face glowed with anger, "So that's it? I risk my life, my freedom and my reputation to do as you ask, Major, and you thank me by leaving me to fend for myself among the wolves?"

"That would never do, Miss Allman," Brechman replied, sounding almost kind. "You should know better than that."

Michner felt his sudden tension drain away. He hadn't expected this. Evidently, Milly hadn't either, as her own expression seemed to relax at Brechman's words.

That is until the SS major withdrew a small pistol from the left front pocket of his flight jacket and shot Milly Allman twice in the chest. It happened so fast and without any change of expression on Brechman's face that Michner wasn't even sure he'd seen what he'd seen for several seconds.

When he looked at Milly, he saw that the front of her pink Kashmir sweater had a large dark stain on it. The attractive woman looked down, looked up at Brechman and said: "You bastard…"

She crumpled to the hardwood floor in a limp and lifeless heap.

Michner stared open-mouthed at the SS officer, "Sir! We could've taken her! There was no need—"

"There was a need," Brechman said in the same emotionless tone that chilled the pilot's blood. "We cannot risk it, and we certainly cannot risk Miss Allman betraying us to Naval Intelligence or the OSS. Now come, we must get back to the plane before Mrs. Turner begins to awaken. We're already in tremendous danger here."

Michner helped carry Joan Turner down the stairs and out onto the beach. Before they'd left, Brechman had overturned a few pieces of furniture and spilled out a few drawers in the master bedroom dressers. Making the scene appear to be a robbery, no doubt.

The walk from the house to the inside of the Masonboro Inlet jetty wasn't far, perhaps two or three hundred yards. Michner placed Joan Turner in the bow of the boat and helped Brechman push it into the water. He then sat in what would be the stern sheets.

Brechman didn't argue, which surprised the pilot. If he had, Michner would have simply stated that he still had to fly them back and his arms were already tired from carrying the woman... by himself... and rowing from before.

Upon reaching their aircraft, the two men got their captive secured in the observer's seat and pushed the raft back out into the water. Brechman emptied his pistol into the craft before climbing into the plane.

Michner taxied out into deeper water and then lifted off, using the northerly breeze to assist. He swore that as the aircraft rose over the inlet, and before he banked away from the beach houses below, he saw the lights of police vehicles heading toward the house.

They'd done it. They'd flown a German floatplane into sovereign American coastal territory and kidnapped a young woman. A young woman, Brechman finally informed Michner on their row back, who was the *wife* of an American Navy Commander! Now they were flying off into the night with no one being the wiser. Yes, they still had to make the rendezvous with the ship, still nearly three hundred miles away and at night... yet that was child's play in comparison to what had been achieved so far.

Michner was not proud, nor was he pleased. This was another act of treachery perpetrated by the SS. Another underhanded trick that would lead to more underhanded tricks. And now, as before, Brenner Michner was an accomplice to it all.

His observations had led to the killing of dozens if not hundreds of merchant sailors. Now he'd helped to abduct an innocent woman... a mother of two young children... and would be a party to using her to lure her husband into a trap that would lead to more deaths.

He began to hate. To hate Brechman, which was easy. Yet he began to hate the Reich, the Kriegsmarine, and to hate himself. He was grateful for the darkness all around, because had there been just a little more moon or starlight, he was certain that the evil bastard sitting next to him would have seen it written all over his face.

20

125 MILES SOUTHEAST OF
NEW YORK

APRIL 26, 1942

2145 ZULU

It was a mild and calm day. *Bull Shark* was running a leisurely course that would loop far outside the sounds of Long Island, Rhode Island and Nantucket and would bring her around to the mouth of Massachusetts Bay in several days. It was a less-used shipping area and one that the Navy wanted to scout in order to try and redirect shipping far away from the heavily trafficked lanes closer to shore. They hoped that there would be fewer U-boat patrols in this part of the ocean.

Arthur Turner had his doubts. If the Germans were smart, and they were, they'd simply skulk outside of the busiest ports and follow the ships into deeper water and sink them out of sight of shore-based radar and aircraft. Sooner or later, the Nazis would realize what courses were being steered and have their comrades waiting offshore to finish off any stragglers.

However, U-boat activity had been oddly light for the past week or so. Ever since the *Bull Shark* had tangled with that small destroyer, in fact. So Turner ran on the surface and would occasionally have sonar conduct active sonar searches and do quarter-hour radar sweeps. Although they were less than a day out of the Chesapeake Bay area, nothing had been sighted.

On deck, the off-watch men who felt like it lounged in the late afternoon sun. They read books, comics or smoked in little conversation groups. Several men were stretched out on deck in just their shorts, getting some much-needed sun and vitamin D. Turner himself had the watch, and he stood on the bridge with Paul Rogers, quartermaster of the watch, and enjoyed the sunshine as well.

Rogers lit a cigarette and passed the lighter to his captain, "Damned fine day to bag a U-boat, eh Skipper?"

Turner lit his own smoke and laughed, "Yeah, wouldn't it be, though? Course, out here in the middle of nowhere, we've got a better chance of finding Moby Dick."

Rogers chuckled sardonically, "I'd like to find that goddamned Nazi ship and sink her. We ought to be over in the Pacific, sir. That's where the real submarine war is… not out here trying to find a needle in a haystack while the Krauts pick off our ships one by one."

Turner sighed, "I know what you mean, Buck. This is a job for the Navy… I mean, a coordinated effort using convoys and local air cover and escorts, for Christ's sake. Do you know that there are half a dozen of our tin cans just sitting in New York Harbor? I've even heard that the Brits have offered to send over support ships to help on this side of the pond."

"Then why isn't it being done?"

Turner flicked an ash over the bridge railing, "From what I understand, Admiral King is kind of an… Anglophobe? He hates the British. I don't know why… maybe his great-granddad was in the war of 1812 or something. All I know is he isn't listening to them, and he's not giving Admiral Andrews, the guy in charge of the Atlantic fleet, freedom to act. That's why ComSubLant sent us out here with an experimental boat and modified fish."

Rogers sighed, "To find a single ship that looks like a freighter in hundreds of thousands of square miles of ocean. A ship that has an aircraft for long-range recon."

Turner nodded grimly and then smiled thinly at Rogers, "You ready to throw in the towel, COB?"

Rogers huffed, "We've been at it what, over a month now? All we've got to show for it is a single Nazi flag painted on the tower."

Turner leaned in closer, "Are you just speaking for yourself, Paul?"

The big man cocked an eyebrow at his captain, "Not exactly, sir. The men are getting restless. Not discontented, exactly, more like... ants in the pants. They want an action. I think they're ready, too. They've had a taste of an easy victory after we torpedoed that Hun boat. They've had a taste of what it's like to be on the receiving end of a depth charging, mild though it was. They're submariners and want to do what submariners do. Hell, even Fritzy asked to join up."

Turner nodded and then chuckled at that, "Doesn't he want to get back to his countrymen?"

Rogers shrugged, "I think he likes the food. I think he's seen a different world with us. Kind of feel bad for the kid, really. I'm sure we're gonna have to turn him over to the Navy when we put in. They'll grill him and then throw him into a POW camp."

Turner sighed and looked aft along the cigarette deck where he could just see a group of four men playing cards on deck. One was Eddie Carlson, and one was the German prisoner.

"*Bridge, radio,*" Joe Dutch, who was the JOOD, said over the speaker. "*We're picking up an SOS from an aircraft. Think you might want to talk to the pilot.*"

Turner and Rogers exchanged a look. The captain thumbed the switch, "Very well. On my way. Mind the deck while I'm gone, Buck. Who knows? Might get your wish yet."

Turner dropped down the ladder into the conning tower and gave the radarman's shoulder a quick squeeze, "Anything on scope, Teddy?"

Ted Balkley stared intently at his sweep and adjusted his controls, "Nothing yet, sir. I started sweeping as soon as Mr. Dutch reported the radio contact. Probably too far over the horizon."

"They ought to show up soon," Turner said. "Keep a sharp eye out."

He went down again into the control room and to the after end to the radio shack. Dutch stood by Brasher, who had put the call onto the two-way loudspeaker.

"What've we got, Dutch?" Turner asked.

"A Mitchell out of Bermuda," Dutch said. "We've attempted to make contact but haven't yet. A little faint."

The speaker crackled again, and a disembodied voice said: "*Repeat, mayday, mayday, mayday... this is Navy flight one-niner-seven out of Bermuda. Have suffered major mechanical failure. Port engine dead, starboard losing oil pressure. Don't know how much longer we're gonna be able to keep her aloft... does anyone read, over?*"

"B25, B25," Turner said. "This is the submarine USS *Bull Shark*. We read you. Do you copy, over?"

A pause and then, "Bull Shark, Bull Shark! *Sweet Jesus, it's good to hear your voice! We read you... a little faint, but we read you!*"

The three men smiled, and Turner said: "Navy flight one-niner-seven, what is your position?"

"*We're maybe a hundred and fifty miles out of La Guardia field. Headed northwest. Airspeed is one hundred and fifteen. Altitude ten thousand. Over.*"

"About twenty-five miles southeast of us," Turner muttered. "Dutch, get on the horn to the bridge. Send somebody up to the COB with a flare gun. Pilot, you're about twenty-five or thirty miles away. We don't have you on radar yet, but I think we will soon. Wind is north about ten knots. What's your name?"

There was the sound of cheering in the background as the pilot keyed his mic, "*Holy Christ! This is Lieutenant Dave Pierce, U.S. Army Air Corps! Who do I have the damned fine pleasure of speaking to?*"

Turner laughed, "This is Lieutenant Commander Art Turner, skipper of the *Bull Shark*. Glad to know you, Lieutenant. Think you can keep her airborne for another fifteen?"

A pause, "*That's problematic, sir. But I think so. When we ditch, if you can point into the wind, such as it is, that'll help both show us wind direction and let us land into it.*"

"Copy that, Pierce," Turner replied. "We'll try and reduce that range some for you. Standby."

Turner ducked out into the control room and tilted his head up the ladder well, "Helm, come right full. Steady up on course one-three-five, all ahead flank. Anything yet, radar?"

Still nothing. Turner made his way back up to the bridge where Rogers was standing with a flare gun in his hands. On deck, men were gathering their cards, towels and coffee mugs and heading down the open fore and aft torpedo loading hatches. Several men stayed on deck and were handed up lines and life-rings. The COB already had things in hand, and Turner smiled.

"*Bridge, radar!*" Balkley's excited voice broke through over the speaker. "*Contact! Aircraft bearing zero-one-five. Range eighteen miles, speed one-one-zero knots... estimated altitude eight thousand feet.*"

"Christ, they're losing power," Turner grumbled. "Anything, Griggs?"

This last he called up to the lookouts in the periscope sheers. Griggs was on watch as the starboard forward sector lookout. It was his job to spot anything from the ship's bow to her starboard beam.

"Negative, bridge... wait... yes sir! Aircraft fifteen or so degrees off the starboard bow, horizon!" Griggs shouted triumphantly.

"Okay, Buck, let fly," Turner ordered. He then keyed the transmitter. "Helm, reduce to all ahead one-third. Left full rudder. Come to course zero-zero-zero."

The order was acknowledged, and the growl of the ship began to slow as she made a wide turn directly into the wind. Rogers fired his flare gun straight up in the air as someone passed Turner a radio through the hatch.

"*Bridge, radio,*" Dutch reported. "*I've patched you into the Mitchell on the hand-held.*"

Turner grinned and keyed the bulky radio set, "Pierce, do you read? This is Captain Turner. We have you on radar and visual. Just fired a flare and we're nosing into the breeze."

"*Roger that, sir!*" Pierce replied tersely but gratefully. "*I've got your flare. We're losing number two... altitude now seven-thousand... my god, you look awfully small out there.*"

Turner could see the bomber now. The plane was rapidly growing larger off their starboard quarter, and it was trailing a thick line of dark smoke from its right wing. The bird was still probably eight or nine miles away, but that distance would be eaten up quickly even if the engine conked out.

"Don't worry, Pierce," Turner said, trying to put as much confidence into his words as possible. He knew that the idea of ditching a heavy aircraft over a hundred miles from land would be a very uncomfortable situation and the men on board would feel a little better knowing they weren't alone. "We're three-hundred and eleven feet of hospitality. No matter what, we've got an eye on you and you won't be wet more than a few minutes. Plenty of hot coffee, fresh sweet rolls and a roast beef dinner with mashed taters, gravy and green beans is waiting for you."

Pierce actually managed to laugh, "*Sounds great, sir... any chance of a cold beer or two?*"

That got a laugh from Rogers and the lookouts who had overheard. Turner smiled and replied: "Sorry, Pierce, no beer this trip... but our pharmacist's mate has a medicine locker full of fine corn squeezin's. Uses them whenever we take down an enemy ship. I think this is a worthy occasion. Oh, and a rather friendly Brit from Bermuda donated a couple bottles of twelve-year-old single malt I know you'll enjoy!"

Turner could hear the whoops from the crew on board the aircraft when Pierce replied, "*You're now my favorite person in the world, sir.*"

"What's your crew status?" Turner asked. "Any injuries?"

"*My engineer took a nasty knock on the bean when number one blew... we've got him bandaged, but he's conscious and mobile. Otherwise, we're all okay... for now.*"

That last he said in a lower tone. Turner empathized. Pierce still had to get that bird down onto a sea that, while calm by offshore standards, still had a ten-foot swell running. That would sound bad to a landlubber, but the truth was that the swell was of such a long wavelength that it looked more like gently rolling hills. Aboard the submarine, moving now at a modest six knots, the rise and fall was almost unnoticeable. Yet an airplane coming in at seventy or eighty knots might literally ramp off one swell and smack down on the top of the next hundreds of feet away.

The plane was very large now, close enough so that details were plainly visible. The starboard engine was no longer belching smoke, which Turner felt meant that it had finally quit. The other engine was so mangled that even from his vantage point several miles away, he could tell it had been bad.

"Bull Shark, *we're on final*," Pierce said tensely. "*I'm lining up to come in on your starboard side... still two nautical out, but I think we're just about right. My number two is dead and I'm gliding now...*"

"Rescue teams, stand ready!" COB shouted.

Turner tried to gauge the distances and speeds but found it nearly impossible. The plane looked to be a little less than two miles astern, but she also looked low. However, even at a speed barely above a stall, she'd cover the distance in less than two minutes.

"Jesus Christ..." the after lookout exclaimed. "He's comin' right for us!"

Turner clipped the radio to his belt and clambered up the sheers to the lookout perch. With three men already there, there wasn't room for him, but he simply clung to the outside and gazed astern.

It did look as if the big aircraft was pointed right at their rudder, but Turner knew that was a little deceptive at that range. He wanted to order hard left rudder but fought down the urge for the moment.

The plane was close now and coming down fast. Turner was no pilot, but he thought it looked *too* fast. Not that there was anything the pilot could do. Without power, he only had his control surfaces and airspeed to help keep the airplane under control. With a ten-knot headwind, he didn't have much help there, either.

Just before it seemed as if the bomber would do a belly flop, the nose angled up and the tail section touched the top of one of the humps of water that represented the swell. She seemed to shudder, bounce up a little and then came down again, her entire double-finned tail digging in and throwing up a huge plume of water behind her. The plane was now only a few hundred yards behind the submarine and still looked as if she'd come close.

"All stop!" Turner shouted down to Rogers, who relayed the order.

Finally, the heavy forward end of the plane settled in and Turner could hardly see the aircraft at all through the huge gouts of spray she threw as the water bled off her momentum. He was just about to order left rudder when the aircraft slowed and came to a stop just forward of the submarine's bow. Her left wingtip had missed them by no more than fifty feet.

"Reverse all engines two-thirds!" Turner ordered as he scrambled down to the bridge.

The submarine's way was checked, and he ordered all stop. The submarine and the airplane were nearly abeam of one another with hardly ten yards between them. Men began to climb out of the aircraft and onto her port wing.

Turner was shocked by the condition of the port engine. It must have exploded. The entire front end of the nacelle had been torn away, and the rest, including much of the center of the gleaming silver wing, was blackened and rippled from heat and compression forces.

The men on the starboard side of the submarine forward of the fairwater formed a group of three two-man teams. One man tossed his life ring to a flyer and the other man held onto the thrower, bracing him. Once a flyer had pushed his arm through the ring, he'd be pulled across and up onto the deck. Turner noticed that one man waited to be last and helped to support another with a bandage wrapped around his head. That would be Pierce and his injured engineer.

"You all right, Pierce?" Turner called over.

"Yes sir, thank you," Pierce replied. "I'd like to go with Anderson here together, though. He's a bit woozy."

The first three men were now on deck. Two rings were then tossed over, and Pierce helped Anderson get ahold of his and then did the same. Then he locked arms with the engineer, and the two men sat down on the wing and eased themselves into the water.

"Gently now, boys," Rogers called to the retrieval party. "Let's get that guy on board nice and easy. Like a baby in a basket, now."

The two men were eased up the side of the pressure hull and over the lip of the deck, with Pierce keeping an arm around his man the whole way. Once they were on board, Turner came down from the bridge and shook all the men's hands, saving Pierce for last.

"Damned fine piece of flying, Lieutenant," Turner said. "Nicely done. Our boys will take care of your men, and our doc will look after Anderson here. Pat, would you take Lieutenant Pierce down to officer's country? We look close in size, so let him and his men have showers and give him some of my clothes. Make sure they get hot coffee, and all are looked at by the doc. I'll come down in a few minutes and check on you, Lieutenant. Welcome aboard *Bull Shark*."

Pat Jarvis and Elmer Williams had come up on deck once the

plane had been spotted on radar. They greeted the flyers and helped them down the forward hatchway into the forward torpedo room. It was a lot easier to negotiate than the bridge hatch.

Turner re-mounted the bridge and was just about to hand the radio down when the speaker crackled to life, "*Bridge, radio... there's a call for you from ComSubLant, sir. He says it's urgent.*"

"Very well, Dutch. I'm on my way down. Come up and take the deck for me."

Turner passed Dutch in the control room and went down and to the radio shack. Brasher held up a phone handset for him, "Admiral is on, sir."

Turner nodded and took the radio phone, "This is Turner, sir."

The connection was staticky but clear enough, "*Art... what's your position and situation?*"

Turner explained where they were and that they just rescued the crew of a downed B25, "We're about a hundred and thirty miles southeast of New York, Admiral."

There was a pause that felt like one of consideration. Edwards sighed, "*How fast can you get into port, Art?*"

Turner pulled up a chart in his mind's eye, "Honestly, from this position, I'd say New York Harbor or New London is about the same."

"*Concur... I think it's best you come here, then. I'd rather talk to you in person anyway. If you push it, you could be here just after midnight, yes?*"

Turner felt a butterfly beginning to stir in his belly. Was he in trouble? Would one or more of his actions be questioned? "Yes sir... we do need to deliver these flyers to shore, and we have a German prisoner we took a couple of weeks ago... Admiral... is there a problem, sir?"

"*Yeah, there is, Art... but it's not a disciplinary action. Nothing you've done wrong. Quite the opposite, in fact... but Web Clayton and I both need to speak to you.*"

Oh shit, "Can you give me a clue, sir?"

Another pregnant pause, "Not on an open channel. Just light all boilers and don't' spare the coal, Captain. We'll talk tonight."

Turner gave his orders and set his ship on a high-speed run to New London. He was glad that the crew was going to splice the main brace. He didn't like surprises of this type and of this level of urgency, and he was glad for the opportunity to take a drink. He'd make it a double or even a triple.

21

It was just after sunset when Elmer Williams took the watch, and Turner had an opportunity to go below. Even as he dropped down into the control room, the smell of a freshly baked cake wafted forward and made his stomach growl.

He ducked into officer's country and grabbed one of the bottles of scotch from his cabin and went into the wardroom. There he found Pierce, Anderson, Dutch and Post sitting at the table having coffee. Anderson's bandage had been replaced with a thinner wrap that went around his head like a tennis headband. His color looked better than when Turner had seen him last as well.

"How are you gents getting along?" Turner asked, accepting a cup of coffee from Carlson. "Eddie taking good care of you?"

"Very well, thank you, sir," Pierce said, raising his cup in salute. "Damned good coffee."

"How about your noggin, Mr. Anderson?" Turner asked.

"Headache is gone," Anderson said in a heavy cornpone accent. "Your corpsman put in a few stitches and gave me a pain killer. We're much obliged for the rescue, Captain."

"Anderson is a second looey," Pierce explained. "Rest of our crew are enlisted. I've checked on them in back... aft... and your men are treating them like family. Really appreciate that, sir."

"You're more than welcome, Lieutenant," Turner said. He uncapped the Glenlivet and poured a healthy knock into all of their coffee mugs, including Carlson. "Here's to ya'."

"Now that's a fine welcome!" Anderson said. "Still gonna get me some of that bourbon, right?"

Everyone laughed, and Turner topped them off again.

"You'll be happy to know that you should be back on dry land just after midnight. We're headed in to New London. Our people will get you squared away," Turner stated. "Mind talking about what happened to your bird? That port engine looked like you smashed into a brick wall."

Pierce flushed a little and shook his head, "I can't honestly say, sir. Anderson here swears he saw something in the water right before the engine blew... but I can't confirm that."

Anderson frowned, "I'm tellin' you, Skip, there was a boat or something down there. I only saw it for a second... but remember I done told you I seen it and then, *Pow!* That dang ole engine went up like a bonfire and tossed me across the cabin."

"I'm not doubting your word, Chuck," Pierce replied. "I'm just saying I can't confirm it. It would explain the other engine being damaged, though."

Turner frowned as well, "Could've been a German submarine. If he had come to the surface to recharge or something and got caught with his pants down... maybe panicked and fired a few rounds at you gents with his AA..."

Pierce and Anderson both shrugged.

"Doesn't matter anyway," Turner said. "All's well that ends well."

Pierce groaned, "Yeah, but it's hardly up to the standards of Jimmy Doolittle now, is it?"

The *Bull Shark's* officers looked at him blankly.

Pierce chuckled softly, "You mean you didn't hear?"

Dutch shrugged, "They call us the silent service for a reason, Dave. We're usually a bit behind on the big news out here."

Anderson clapped his hands together, "It was just last week! One of our boys led a big bombing raid on Tokyo. Took off from one of y'all's flat tops."

Pierce went on to explain that in a joint effort, a task force led by Admiral William "Bull" Halsey consisting of the carriers *Enterprise* and *Hornet* and their associated escorts moved in to within six hundred and fifty miles of Honshu, the main Japanese island. Lieutenant Colonel Jimmy Doolittle led the flight of sixteen B25's that took off from *Hornet*, flew over Japan, dropped their payloads on Tokyo and then flew on to land in China. At least, that was the plan.

"Not a one of 'em made it," Anderson said.

At the horrified looks from the Navy men, Pierce shrugged, "Well, what he means is that none of the *planes* made it. They all crashed or ditched when they ran out of fuel. I think one went missing over Russia. Most of the crews are still being located, but there are at least a dozen we don't have any idea about."

"Jesus Christ..." Post breathed. "That musta taken some serious balls. Did they do much damage?"

Pierce shook his head, "No... it was ballsy for sure... but sixteen tons of explosives isn't gonna destroy a city or anything. Some damage, but mostly it was a propaganda run."

"Show them Japs we can hit them on their front porch too," Anderson said fiercely. "Let them know that they ain't getting away with what they done at Pearl."

"Good," Dutch said a little angrily. "The Skipper and I were there that day... it was... horrible."

"You boys about ready for supper?" Eddie asked. "Martin and Borshowski got ants in their pants. Want to get it out of the way and bring out the cake."

"Cake?" Pierce asked.

Turner grinned, "It's something of a tradition. Whenever a boat makes a kill or the equivalent thereof, we have ourselves a little celebration. Cake and we splice the mainbrace."

"Do *what...?*" Anderson inquired in abject bewilderment.

Dutch laughed but let Turner explain.

"In the age of sail, the men were given a daily rum ration," Turner explained. "In addition, when the ship achieved something extraordinary, the captain would announce that they'd splice the mainbrace. A mainbrace is a line used to swivel a yard around, in this case, the mainyard. It became a sort of slang term for an extra rum ration. Believe it or not, the Navy actually provides the pharmacist's mate with hundreds of individual shots in the medicine locker. So when we sink a ship, for example, the men are given a shot and a cake. We think that rescuing a downed B25 crew warrants it, and we thought you fellas wouldn't mind joining in… on top of this little snort."

"Hot damn!" Anderson whooped. "Sounds like my kinda ceremony."

After a hearty supper of delicious roast beef, mashed potatoes and green beans, everyone who wasn't on watch and anyone on watch who could be spared gathered in the crew's mess. Martin, Carlson, Borshowski and Fritz Schwimmer, along with Leroy Pots, the submarine's baker, carried out and set down a huge sheet cake on one of the mess tables.

The cake was iced in blue, with extra cake and icing used to create the surfaced *Bull Shark* and the half-sunk bomber. There were cheers and a round of applause. The applause grew even more boisterous when Hoffman passed out the individual shots, giving an extra to each of the plane's crew and to the captain.

"You want to do the honors, sir?" Carlson asked Turner.

"Nope, Eddie… think we'll let our Mitchell commander have that privilege," Turner said, indicating Pierce. "But first… hoist those shots, boys! Here's to the Army Air Corps and the U.S. Navy!"

A roar went up, and the men downed their Jack Daniels. Eddie handed Pierce the carving knife, "Now make sure you cut enough for everyone, sir."

"Guess things are different in the Navy, huh?" one of the flyers, a sergeant named Ormond, muttered to Chief Branigan. "Christ, you guys got a Kraut and three darkies working onboard!"

The chief electrician's mate frowned at the man beside him, "You see those silver dolphins pinned to those men's shirts, Ormond?"

The tail gunner nodded, "Yeah, I see 'em."

"Those mean that those three black men are submarine qualified," Branigan said softly, but not so softly that the other enlisted flyers couldn't hear. "That means that they can run any system on this boat. Even taking command should that need arise. Those three men can only sign aboard as cooks and bakers. They can't become officers even if they wanted to… because they're *black*. But on a submarine, those men can load and fire torpedoes, run a radar or sonar set, work on a diesel engine or an electric one and operate all sorts of other systems. We respect them and treat them as equals on this ship, Sarg. Cuz that's what they are."

Ormond was taken aback, and his face flushed beet red from the dressing down. His two companions, a pair of corporals, sniggered slightly behind their hands. Ormond cleared his throat, "Hey, Harry, I didn't mean nothin' by it. Just not what we're used to, is all. The German kid is kinda strange, though, you gotta admit."

"Yeah, it is a little odd," Chief Machinist's Mate Mike Duncan noted. "We picked him up after we sunk his boat out from under him. He's been a good kid, though. Never gave us any trouble and picked up English real fast. There are plenty of eyes on him at all times, and we handcuff him to his bunk at night… but it's probably not necessary anymore. He likes it here so much he wants to join up."

The celebration went on for another half hour, and the on-watch men were brought their ration of cake and booze. It was close to midnight when the submarine approached the mouth of the Thames River and was met by a pair of torpedo boats to escort them in. After docking and tying up with no ceremony due to the hour, Art Turner and Elmer Williams were met at the pier by a staff car and driven directly to Admiral Richard Edward's office.

There was a coffee service already set out on a small sideboard, along with several bottles of liquor and an ice bucket. Williams and Turner exchanged a furtive glance before sitting down next to Webster Clayton and across from Edwards.

"Gents," Edwards began, lighting a cigar and extending the box. Both Turner and Williams took one. Clayton didn't. "There's coffee, bourbon and Irish cream over there. I strongly recommend an Irish coffee. Good for the weather and the hour. Chief?"

A chief yeoman stood by, and when both of *Bull Shark's* officers indicated that they'd have an Irish coffee, the yeoman set to making them.

"First of all," Edwards began, lighting his cigar with a butane torch and then passing it to Turner, "let me begin by saying that you fellas have been doing a damned fine job. Bagging that Nazi boat right when it was attacking those ships was damned fine work. And being on the spot today when that B25 went down, very well done. I wouldn't be surprised if you get a commendation from the Army, and I'm putting the boat in for a unit citation. That's the good news."

"Meaning there's some bad news, sir?" Williams asked nervously.

"Unfortunately there is, XO," Clayton said, sipping from a tumbler of iced Jim Beam. "Mostly for Captain Turner."

Turner felt the blood drain from his face, "Has... has something happened to one of my kids... or Joan?"

Edwards drew in a breath to explain, but Clayton held up a hand, "I'll tell him, Dick. Seems only right... Art, last night, that is the evening of the twenty-fifth, your wife left your children with her mother in Wilmington. You knew she was down there?"

"I... knew she was going," Turner said. "Haven't talked with her since we left port after the rescue a couple of weeks back."

"Well, according to the report your mother-in-law gave, Joan was invited to a party at Mildred Allman's sister's house," Clayton continued, sipping from his glass again. Turner and Williams had their coffee, and each man took a healthy sip as well. "Mildred was the lady you rescued, if you recall."

Turner nodded and wished to Christ the man would get to the point.

"Well..." Clayton plowed on.

"Jesus, Web, just tell the man," Edwards pressed.

Clayton sighed, "Joan has been abducted. We believe that it was done by the Nazis. Probably the crew of the Q-ship."

"What!?" Turner exploded, barely managing to keep his seat. "Are you telling me the fucking *Germans* have taken my *wife*? What in the name of Christ—"

"Try to stay calm, Art," Edwards encouraged sternly.

"Stay *calm!*" Turner exclaimed. "Sir! For the love of God!"

"I know," Edwards said sympathetically, "but I need you to stay focused, to act like an officer right now."

"Admiral…" Williams protested weakly.

"I understand, gents," Edwards said not unkindly, "but if there's any chance of resolving this, Art, you're going to have to keep your head. I'm sorry, but that's just how it is."

Turner seethed. Intellectually, he knew the Admiral was right. At the moment, however, his emotions were very difficult to manage. He gulped down the rest of his laced coffee, ignoring the temperature. He handed the cup back to the yeoman who made him another.

"We do know a few things," Clayton said. "Things that may help. We believe, first of all, that this was done in order to force your hand. You've become something of a thorn in their sides, I should think. Our guess is that the Q-ship is being run or directed by the SS. We believe that one way or another, you're going to be forced into action. Probably to go to a certain location where they can ambush you. We know they've got the Q-ship as well as a small destroyer. They have a U-boat fleet as well. You'll probably be lured into a position where they can hem you in, or it'll be too shallow for you to dive deep or something."

"Good," Turner said tersely, "I look forward to the meeting."

"We also now know through a variety of sources that Milly Allman is… or *was*… a Nazi spy."

"Was?" Williams asked.

Clayton sighed, "The Wilmington police were called to the sister's house on Wrightsville Beach. Milly was found shot to death in the living room. It was also *not* her sister's house. It belongs to a couple that summers there. Several local residents and one of the responding police officers reported hearing an airplane engine and a low flying aircraft in the vicinity. We suspect that the Germans flew in, kidnapped your wife and flew out."

"Jesus Christ…" Turner moaned, his anger beginning to give way to despair. Williams reached out and gave his shoulder a pat.

"I agree with your assessment of that encounter with the destroyer," Edwards put in. "I think you saw the Q-ship. The freighter that was sort of out of place with those two oilers. And that this destroyer was too small and short range to be operating on her own. We think you've rattled their cage more than once, Art, and they want you out of the way."

"We also have a line on one of the U-boat commanders," Clayton added. "From eye-witness accounts from the *Chester Clyde* who's crew you rescued; from a reliable source I have in Bermuda—"

"Ned Tully?" Williams asked.

Clayton nodded, "The same. A few other bits and pieces, too. I've got a man on Cape Cod who's also been giving me information. Although there are a number of U-boats between Maine and the Gulf of Mexico, there's one shining star among them. A seasoned and intelligent man named Reinhard Hardegen. His boat, U-123, has been one of their most effective spearheads. We believe this man will be involved with whatever trap the SS is planning to spring on you and *Bull Shark.*"

"So what are you saying, Web?" Turner asked. "That the Huns are gonna phone in and say that if I don't show up at some street corner in Montauk with a bag full of hundred-dollar bills that its curtains for the wife? What the hell kind of nonsense is this?"

Edwards chuffed but said nothing.

Clayton only shook his head, "Nothing that simple or straightforward. They obviously can't radio in and demand that you and your ship be at a certain set of coordinates on a certain date. That'd be a dead giveaway both to their intent and to who they are."

"Not to mention we'd have half the fleet there ready to blow them to Mars," Edwards growled.

Turner scoffed, "Sure, unless the British suggested it."

Edwards cocked an eyebrow at Turner, "Better watch that, Captain."

"Well, if the C and C takes umbrage to my expression and feels I'm being insubordinate," Turner replied dryly, "then let *his* wife be captured by the Germans. Otherwise, way I'm feeling right now, he can kiss the fattest—"

"Art," Williams warned.

Edwards grinned, "At ease, Commander, at ease. I understand your frustrations... *believe* me... but that's not going to help now."

Turner sighed and took another healthy swig from his mug.

"They'll find a way to let you know what they want," Clayton said. "In a way that might not even seem direct. But they'll find you."

"The trick is that we need to be ready to turn the tables on them," Edwards stated. "My guess is that they'll want you someplace shallow and blocked in. The Bahamas maybe, or between there and Florida. Somewhere that a submarine, a destroyer, a floatplane and this freighter can work in unison to trap you and sink you."

"Concur," Turner said coldly.

"Right now, your boat is better than anything they've got," Clayton stated. "Than anything *we've* got. You can dive as deep as their Type IX. You're faster on top and have a snorkel to run on diesels at periscope depth. You've got ten tubes to their six, and so on."

"That's all fine and dandy, sir," Williams said, "but when push comes to shove, if you're right, then we face a sub, a plane and two surface ships... at least. And we won't know where we'll be until the last minute, I'm sure. So how do we set it up so we're doing the ambushing?"

Edwards considered Williams approvingly for a moment and then looked to Clayton. The intelligence man lit a cigarette and smiled thinly.

"Agents in Europe in conjunction with units on that side of the Atlantic have provided reliable reports that two German Type XIV U-boats, what they refer to as a *milchkuh*, or milk cow, left their Lorient U-boat base on the eighteenth of this month," Clayton explained. "They've got three thousand miles or more to cross, and they generally run on top at about ten to twelve knots to conserve fuel. Their heading at last contact put them on a direct course to pass dead center between Bermuda and the Bahamas. Probably to within three hundred miles of our coast but no closer. Each of these boats can deliver over six hundred tons of fuel and a bunch of other logistical stuff."

"Okay... so they've got two milk cows running for the middle of this theater of operations," Turner said. "You think they're going to rendezvous with the Q-ship?"

"Probably," Clayton replied. "Not to mention other U-boats. They've got the big Type IX's, of which U-123 is one. But the Nazis like their smaller Type VII's. They're more maneuverable and harder to spot, I guess. Anyway, the tanker boats allow the smaller Type VII's to operate longer over here."

"Are you sure of that information, sir?" Williams asked.

Clayton sighed, "Ultra has received recordings of intercepted radio transmissions, but we don't have them decoded. The Germans' damned enigma machine is a hard nut to crack. I'd give my right arm to get my hands on one of them... anyway, we have no direct confirmation in that way, but it doesn't take a military strategist to know why those two tankers are headed our way."

"Assuming they're being moderately conservative," Edwards put in, "that puts them about five days from a point between Bermuda and Walker's Cay, and at least three hundred miles from our coastline. Hell, even if they're running at full tilt, which is unlikely, that gives us at least four days."

"You and *Bull Shark* could be at this theoretical point in two," Clayton suggested.

"So... we intercept the milk cows and sink them, thus bringing Hardegen, the Q-ship and the destroyer running?" Williams asked dubiously.

"Not exactly," Edwards said. "That *might* work, but then, of course, the Krauts would know you're out there. No, we had something a little more devious in mind. Web?"

Clayton drew on his cigarette and held up his empty whiskey glass for the yeoman to refill, "Dick has informed me that there's an old R boat in Miami right now that's due for decommissioning."

"SS89," Edwards cut in. "She's on her way up from Coco Solo. Stopped in Miami for fuel and R and R."

Clayton nodded, "You've also got yourself a German prisoner of war. You meet the R boat, follow her with a skeleton crew aboard to the plotted position and take her crew off, leaving the German. We load him up with a head full of intelligence and he reports it to his bosses. Basically, he'll know a certain patrol area you'll be assigned to.

Then when the SS makes their move, they'll use that position as a place from which to start their ambush."

Turner frowned and shook his head, "There's a problem with that, Web. Fritz doesn't *want* to go back. He wants to stay with us. Wants to join the crew, no less. He's not gonna go for it."

"You really think he's that loyal?" Edwards asked incredulously.

"Well sir," Williams said. "He seems to be. You learn a lot about a guy when you're locked up in a cigar tube with him for several weeks."

"It's like this," Turner added. "Suppose he isn't loyal at all. Suppose he's a dyed-in-the-wool Nazi. Okay, we set him loose on an abandoned old boat with a set of coordinates or a pilfered chart or whatever. He's gonna know it's a fake aloo job. He'll tell his friends that when and if they find him. On the other hand, if he's really dying to become a Yankee Doodle, then he'll resent being tossed away. He *might* deliver the false info, or he might blab just to stick it to us for sticking it to him."

Edwards nodded and smiled thinly.

Clayton nodded as well, "Good points. If we use the kid, then we've got to figure out where his loyalties really lie."

"We don't have time for that shit," Edwards said. "We're gonna top off *Bull Shark's* fuel, load in a couple of fish to replace the ones they fired off and get them to sea tomorrow."

"That's fine," Clayton said. "Give me the German kid and we'll ride down to Florida together. That'll give me time to vet him and see what needs to be seen. I've got other assets I can use, but him being a submariner really helps. You get your boat off to Georgia as fast as you can, Art, and I'll have a solution for you when you get there. This might be our only shot, and when one is all you've got…"

"Yeah, great," Turner grumped. "Me, my crew and my boat, not to mention my *wife,* are hanging our asses out on the basis of a flimsy, hair-brained scheme."

Edwards sighed, "As the man says, Art… we're under the gun here. Nobody ever promised war would be safe."

"It ought to be for civilians," Williams grumbled softly.

Edwards nodded slightly, "But it's not. Not entirely. I haven't known Joanie long, Art, but I know she's a tough and resilient lady. She'll be all right."

Turner hoped like hell the Admiral was correct. Yet as he lay in his rack aboard his boat that night, all he could do until nearly dawn was toss and turn and worry.

22

100 MILES OFF THE GEORGIA COAST

APRIL 30, 1942

0000 ZULU

B*ull Shark* hung motionless in the darkening sea at radar depth, barely feeling the motion of the mild swell. Above, in the search periscope view, the sun had set, and the sky was taking on the deep indigo of oncoming night. A faint sonar signal and the sound of fast light screws off to the south indicated their prey, although the other vessel had yet to show up on radar.

"Range now eight thousand yards," Chet Rivers reported. "She's got to be moving at twelve knots, sir... should be coming up on the SJ any time now."

"Nothing yet," Balkley reported. "She's got such a low profile, though... wait... contact! Surfaced vessel bearing zero eight zero, range seven-six-zero-zero. Speed agrees with sonar."

Turner trained his scope in the indicated direction, just a little forward of his starboard beam. In the oncoming gloom, a dark angular shape appeared on the horizon, "There she is. Elmer, activate the periscope light. One long and two short."

In his scope, the low profile of the other submarine and her conning tower slowly grew closer and more defined. Near the top of the shape, a light blinked two shorts and one long. Turner grinned.

"Okay, that's our boy," he said. "Frank, blow main ballast. When we're on top, send somebody up to the bridge with a signal gun."

There was a whooshing sound, and the submarine began to rise. Her conning tower broke the surface, her deck drained and she was lying placidly on a calm sea. Turner went up through the bridge hatch, followed by Tank Broderick carrying the bulky signal gun. No lookouts followed as Turner didn't intend to stay topside long.

The two men stood on the small bridge watching as the other submarine approached, slowing down as she did so. It was definitely an American R-class boat. Even from more than a mile off, the shape of the conning tower and the size of the boat gave her away.

The R-class was one of those that had been designed and built near the end of the Great War. She was only half the length of the modern fleet submarine and not much more than a third the displacement. They had only half the test depth of the *Bull Shark* and four torpedo tubes rather than the usual ten of the big fleet boats.

"Signal our number and name, Tank," Turner ordered.

Broderick held the signal gun up to his shoulder and began squeezing off the Morse code. After a moment, the other ship signaled back SS89, and then Clayton aboard.

"He's aboard her?" Turner muttered and then to Tank. "Ask them to heave to alongside."

The old boat came to a full stop twenty yards abeam of the *Bull Shark*. On the bridge of the R boat, a man waved and called out, "Captain Turner, I'm Lieutenant George Sharp. I've got a Mister Clayton and a guest with me. He wants to speak to you, sir."

"Good evening, Captain," Turner called back, using the honorific for any officer in command of a ship regardless of rank. "Can you man a raft, or do you need me to send one? What's your crew status? Do you need anything?"

"We've got a boat, sir," Sharp replied. "We'll break it out and come across. We're okay on provisions, considering… I've only got two machinist's and electrician's mates, a couple of helmsmen, a chief to run the manifold and me, sir. We've been doing our own cooking… lotta PB and J's, sir."

Both Turner and Broderick laughed. The *Bull Shark's* captain said: "Understood, Mr. Sharp. You come over with Clayton and we'll get all this sorted out. We'll send you back with something hot for you and your boys."

"Yes sir, that'd be appreciated," Sharp said. "Been a long hike up from Miami."

"At twelve knots, probably took em' a day and a half," Broderick noted.

"Yeah, and twenty more hours to get out to where we're supposed to go," Turner mused. "Tank, go below and stow that gun and come back with a party to help secure the raft, would you? We'll flood down forward so they can come aboard easier."

In just five minutes, the other submarine already had its raft in the water with four men in it. It was nearly full dark now, but Turner could make out Sharp, Webster Clayton and Fritz Schwimmer. Another man was plying the oars. He ordered several of the boat's forward ballast tanks flooded, creating a ramp for the raft to row up onto. Once over the deck, Turner ordered the tanks blown and the ship came level again.

He went down on deck to greet his guests. He first shook Sharp's hand. The Lieutenant was a young man in his late twenties who was of medium height and heavily built. He had a friendly round face that smiled up at Turner.

"How'd you get roped into this duty, Sharp?" Turner asked.

"I'm on my way to New London to PXO School, so I got tasked with skippering the boat up there," Sharp replied.

"Congrats," Turner then turned his attention to Clayton, "I didn't think you were coming along on this jaunt, Web. How you doing, Fritzy?"

"It's my harebrained scheme," Clayton replied with a grin. "Can't let you boys have all the fun."

"I'm well, thank you sir," Schwimmer replied. Turner was amazed at how quickly he'd not just learned English but how well he spoke now. "Herr... I mean, *Mister* Clayton has explained situation to me, and I want to help."

Turner considered the young man for a long moment, "This sounds very dangerous, Fritz. We're essentially abandoning you to your countrymen and hoping they take you in."

Schwimmer nodded gravely, "Yes... but Mr. Clayton has offered me... how do you say... a gambler's deal?"

"Let's go below and talk about it," Clayton suggested.

Turner nodded and turned to Broderick and his two-man party, "Tank, see to Captain Sharp's man here. Also, ask the galley to put together a meal for a dozen men. Something hot. Find out from..."

"Wendell, machinist's mate, sir," the enlisted rower said.

"From Wendell here what else they might need over there," Turner said. "Gents, follow me, please."

Down in the wardroom, Clayton, Sharp and Schwimmer were joined by Williams and Pat Jarvis. As the two most senior officers aboard, except Turner, they'd play a pivotal role in what Clayton had planned.

"Here's the situation," Clayton said. He briefly outlined what he'd told Turner in ComSubLant's office a few days earlier to get the other men up to speed. "By now, the milk cows are probably within a day or so of their hypothetical station. Not an hour ago, I received a coded message from our asset in Bermuda. A Royal Navy long-range recon plane radioed in that they'd spotted two wakes. He could see the phosphorescent glow in the foam. Anyway, he said the two vessels were headed a bit south of west, putting them on a heading that'll reach three hundred miles due east of southern Georgia, or two hundred miles just about due east of our current position, within twenty-four hours. I figure that based on them running on the surface at night, then submerged tomorrow during daylight and then on top again once it gets dark, which is when they'll pop up and probably make a radio report to their bosses."

"And we're going to be there to meet them?" Sharp asked. "Take them out?"

"No," Clayton said. "At least, not exactly. SS89 is going to be there waiting for them with *Bull Shark* using her as a hat, as I'm told it's called. Those tanker subs don't have much in the way of armament, just anti-aircraft guns. We need a way to let them see SS89, then see her sink and leave a single survivor in a life raft, Fritz here. It's got to be convincing. We want the Germans to pick him up and then have him report on *Bull Shark's* disposition and patrol area."

"But how do we do that?" Williams asked. "If the *milchkuhs* don't have torpedoes, they aren't going to be able to sink a boat with AA guns."

"Bad torpedoes," Jarvis said, snapping his fingers. "Our Mark 14s are notorious by now."

Turner grinned, "So Sharp fires off four fish. At least one circles back and hits SS89. One fish just misses, and the other two take out one of those Kraut boats."

Clayton frowned, "That wasn't what I was thinking, Art."

Turner scoffed, "Web, no matter what happens, the goddamned Germans don't' get to keep both of those tankers. I think it'll look more authentic if they lose one and we lose our boat, too."

"The only problem is that we don't' *have* any torpedoes, sir," Sharp said a bit sheepishly. "All of our fish were offloaded at Coco Solo for other boats."

"That's okay, Lieutenant," Jarvis replied with a wicked grin. "We've got twenty-four. We can hunker down at periscope depth off SS89's beam, say three hundred yards or so; we'll fire our fish and then wait. If we time it right, the fish we fire at the Germans on fast and the one we fire at SS89 on slow, it'll look to the Germans that we sank ourselves… that is, the R boat sank herself."

"That's a good idea, Pat," Elmer said with a grin. "That way, we can get all the guys off your boat, George."

"What about Fritz?" Clayton asked.

"We move close to where SS89 sinks," Turner said. "We send Fritzy up from forward torpedo with a Momsen lung and a raft. Then we can flood and sink down a few hundred feet and listen, or we can move off slow at periscope and watch. See if the Germans pick him up. The remaining sub will be so concerned about finding survivors from the other boat that they won't be doing any kind of sonar search, I'd bet. We just hang tight, nice and quiet, and confirm they pick our boy here up. If not, we're on hand to grab him if we need to."

"Jesus Christ…" Sharp muttered and looked at the young German. "And you're willing to do this, Fritz? And we trust that he won't just give the Krauts all the intel he can?"

"I will not," Fritz said firmly. "I have given my word to assist in this. I owe Captain Turner and these men my life. Is an honorable thing, yah?"

"I've spent quite a lot of time speaking with him," Clayton said. "Fritz wishes to defect. Further, he wants to work for us. Naval service, at least in the traditional sense, is probably not an option... so I've offered him a job working for me. I've explained that we'll do what we can to extract him after this but that this mission is his initiation. He'll have to show his loyalty by pulling this off."

Turner pondered Fritz again. He felt for the young man, who'd ingratiated himself so much with his crew. What he was doing was risky on many levels. He was risking surfacing alone out of the forward escape trunk, then risking being shot by his own people before they knew he was one of them. Further, he was then risking intense interrogation and even torture at their hands. He sighed softly and shook his head.

"Is all right, sir," Fritz said softly to Turner. "I know is risky... but... I feel... oblige-ed?"

"Obligated," Turner corrected with a wry smile.

"Yes, obligated... and honored to help," Fritz said.

"What if they..." Turner hesitated to say it, but it was unavoidable, "they torture him?"

Clayton drew in a breath, "I don't think they will. But if they do, then I've instructed him to tell everything. It'll fit with his story."

"Which is?" Williams asked.

"That he was transferred off *Bull Shark* to SS89 to be taken to New London," Clayton replied. "Since they were headed north and you were headed to your station to patrol from mid-Florida down to the waters between Florida, eastern Cuba and the lower Bahamas. The idea is to watch shipping coming from the Gulf and up from Venezuela with oil. If pressed, he says that he was rescued when you sank U-85, that he was kept aboard as a prisoner and made to work in the kitchen. In that capacity, he overheard a lot of stuff, including where *Bull Shark* was headed. Into confined waters with lots of shallows to set up an ambush... not that he tells them *that* naturally..."

"Or maybe I do," Fritz said with a grin. "Suggest to whoever gets me that is good place to go after you. I'm happy to do this, sir, to help an innocent lady."

"Thank you, Fritzy," Turner said, squeezing the young man's shoulder. "All right, then. We'd better get a move on. Let's get anything across we can and get underway. Sharp, you run on top at ten knots. We'll follow off your starboard quarter, submerged. Hopefully, Web, Tully can send us another position report on those milk cows so we can actually be in the right place. It's a big ocean, and we're only guessing as to where they might pop up and that they'll stop. For all we know, they could make a left turn and head down to the Caribbean."

They did receive another report shortly before dawn. The two Nazi submarines had not changed course and had moved another hundred and twenty miles or so before submerging. Turner plotted an intercept course based on their known submerged speed for the next ten hours of daylight and had both of his boats alter course ten degrees to starboard and slow down to five knots, the maximum speed the tankers could make for the length of the day before needing to recharge. That was a guess, but Turner plotted a course that would keep his little squadron ahead of where the milk cows would be. Another long-range recon flight was set up for dusk as well.

It was a long day, full of tension and worry. Not only did Turner have to find two small needles in a very big haystack, but he also had to position SS89 in the right place and get all the men off. The boat would be adrift and on the surface. He hoped that by the time the Germans spotted her, they'd be within what would be considered a reasonable torpedo range. Should they spot the other boat from too far off and alter course, they'd know something was odd when the American boat didn't pursue them.

"Of course, that might make them curious," Clayton had suggested at lunch. "Maybe they'd come in and take a look."

"I doubt that sir," Frank Nichols had opined. "Look, I'm a reservist ... still pretty new to submarine combat, but I doubt that two almost unarmed logistical support boats would get close to an attack submarine, even an old one."

"Oh, now don't put yourself down, Frank," Jarvis had jibed. "You're not half bad… for a feather merchant."

Nichols had lightly punched him on the shoulder.

"Franks' right, though, Web," Turner had suggested. "They'd assume it was a trap or something. Plus it'll be dark, and they won't know exactly what kind of submarine SS89 is."

Williams had disagreed, however, "Maybe not, Art… yeah at first they'd simply turn away or dive… but after a while of keeping an eye on her, they'd notice that SS89 wasn't doing anything. No engine noise, no radar or sonar signals, no movement or course change. They might eventually try to move in, maybe from astern. Could be."

Turner shrugged, "Possible, I guess. If it was me, I think I'd just move off… but then again, maybe not. An abandoned boat might be an opportunity. If they got aboard and realized it was an old one, they might just leave… well, we'll see, I suppose. The trick is that *we* can't be detected. That'll be tricky. We want them close enough to torpedo but not close enough to start actively pinging… if they can… and find another boat hanging around. Our presence could blow the whole thing."

A silence had fallen over the table, and then Jarvis said: "Then why not leave her diesels running?"

Williams had grinned. "Right… it'd seem more authentic, and it would create a nice noisy transient that the Germans can pick up and that'll help hide us a little more."

So that had settled that. At eighteen hundred local time, the SS89 came to a full stop and shut down her electric motors for the last time. Her diesel engines were left running on full power, and all of her crew were taken off and onto *Bull Shark*.

The bigger submarine submerged to periscope depth and hung three hundred yards to the southeast, going silent on battery power and with just her radio mast and search scope extended above the eerily calm surface and her electronic ears straining.

"Assess westerly drift of one-half knot," Williams reported quietly. "Based on known currents in this area."

That would mean both boats would drift out of position potentially by several miles before the Germans showed up. Turner had accounted for that and had put them a little further to the east of where his course and the Germans should intersect.

At twenty-one forty-five, nearly an hour after sunset and a half-hour after full dark, a radio message came in from Bermuda. It was coded and stated that the observation plane had seen two wakes appear on the horizon on the exact same course as the previous evening. Based on the position and speed, they were heading almost directly for *Bull Shark* and her decoy. They were hardly more than twenty miles away.

Turner ordered his boat down to periscope depth and that all hands were to observe ultra-quiet status. Everything was set in train. There were torpedoes in all tubes and all the doors, forward and aft, were open. Pat Jarvis had a continuous firing solution on the SS89, and he'd build one for the two Germans when they came into sonar and visual range.

Bull Shark had several advantages. First, that the SS89 was making noise. Second, the two German *milchkuhs* were running on their own diesels, making their passive sonars virtually useless. Turner didn't know if they had radar or not, but even if they did, they'd probably only do single sweeps at set intervals, which meant they might not even catch SS89 on their scopes until they were almost right on top of her. If that were so, and within visual range at night, then they'd be more than close enough for an effective firing solution. Turner could even afford to use single pings to verify range since the Germans would assume it was the surfaced boat.

All that remained was the waiting. Waiting for the long minutes to tick past with all fingers and toes crossed. Once again, the tension of pre-battle began to rise. Not a tension born from fear. Every man aboard the submarine knew there was no real danger to them. However, they all knew that a great deal depended on their success at pulling off the ruse Clayton had planned. That included the potential safety of the Skipper's wife.

23

"What the hell are we doin', Sparky?"

This whispered inquiry came from torpedoman Pete Griggs. The kid was checking the escape trunk systems as quietly as he could.

"We're doin' whatever the Old Man fuckin' says we're doin', Griggs," Sparky barked in a hushed undertone. "When you need to know somethin', believe me, I'll let you know."

Griggs looked a little unsettled. The escape trunk was, as its name suggested, to be used to escape a sinking submarine. If Sparky was asking him to go over the system and make sure that the doors, the flooding valves and the pressurization system functioned properly, then there must be something unpleasant in the works, and he wanted to know what.

"Are we in trouble?" Griggs dared to press.

Sparky glowered at him for a moment, which got Griggs back to his task. In the next moment, though, he put one of his big hands on the young man's shoulders and leaned in.

"We ain't in no danger, Pete," Sparky said mildly, "but we gotta send a man topside from periscope depth, and I want to make absolutely sure everything works right so he gets there. Don't ask me why, even if I had all the details I couldn't say. Now keep at it."

When a new face appeared in the watertight hatchway, Griggs and everyone else in forward torpedo had a pretty good idea of who was riding a Momsen lung to the surface. Fritz Schwimmer, dressed in a facsimilie of his original Nazi uniform, stepped into the room. The gray slacks and white long-sleeved shirt seemed oddly out of place on him after so many weeks of dressing like the rest of the crew.

"Fritzy!" Tommy Perkins managed to exclaim almost silently and patted the kid on his shoulder. "You going for a swim, kid?"

Schwimmer grinned, "I am American spy now."

Sparky came up and clasped his other shoulder. All of the men had come to care for the gregarious young German. There was little or no doubt among the crew of *Bull Shark* about Fritz's loyalties.

"Okay, go over and see Pete," Sparky said. "He'll get you set up and show you how to use the gear."

"Control reports enemy contact!" the compartment phone talker announced. "Standby on torpedoes. Order of tubes is one through four. Tube two set to low speed, the others to high."

"Acknowledge," Sparky said as he and Perkins practically leapt to the six torpedo breeches.

"Two sets of light, fast screws bearing three-three-zero," Chet Rivers announced from his sonar set. "Range... sixteen thousand yards... turn rate is..."

He beat his fist up and down in time with the beats of the very distant sound of the four propellers churning up the sea eight miles away. Finally he nodded and said: "Assess ten knots closure rate."

Turner peered through his attack scope, even though he knew he wouldn't see anything at eight miles in the dark. He desperately wanted to rise to radar depth and pinpoint the targets and their course with the SJ but dared not.

"Order forward torpedo to set depth on all their weapons to four feet," Turner ordered.

Pat Jarvis, who was the fire control officer, had the sound-powered telephone set around his neck. He spoke into it and then a moment later reported an acknowledgement.

"Where's SS89?" Turner asked.

"Bearing two-seven-zero," Rivers replied.

"Very well…" Turner muttered, gripping the handles of his scope tightly. "Keep an ear on those Germans, Chet. I want to know their track. Somebody pass the banjo down to the XO."

In the old days before the TDC, the only tool submarine captains had to help them calculate torpedo trajectories was known as the IsWas. Also referred to as the "banjo", the IsWas consisted of a series of celluloid marked circles that could be independently spun to give a gyroscope setting reading for the torpedo room. Although antiquated and obsolete thanks to the marvel of the torpedo data computer, skipper's often still used the IsWas as a backup. The plotting party would calculate their own manual settings based on data from the conning tower as a way to double-check the computer.

Five minutes went by, and Rivers turned away from his set, "Contacts now bearing three-four-zero. Range now fourteen thousand."

Turner did some fast calculations in his head. If their course was opening by ten degrees every five minutes, then in another thirty-five minutes, the two Nazi boats would be directly in front of him. The question was, how close…

Elmer Williams, along with Hotrod Hernandez and Chief Yeoman Weiss, who was a math whiz, was down in control at the master gyro table plotting the targets courses together. Williams, the banjo hanging from his neck on a lanyard, stuck his head through the hatchway leading into the conning tower as if on cue.

"We estimate they'll be fifteen hundred yards off our bow at closest approach," Williams said.

"Shit…" Turner muttered.

That wasn't too far to shoot by any means, yet at night it was a much tougher shot without the use of radar. Further, at that range, the enemy submarines would have more time to maneuver. On the other hand, they wouldn't see the torpedo wakes until they were less than halfway due to the darkness. On still another hand, the Nazis would no doubt spot the SS89 hanging less than a mile from them and would probably alter course away. Turner would have to use his sonar to get an accurate fix before firing, both to ensure a hit and to ensure he *didn't* hit both boats.

"Helm, port engine ahead one-third," Turner ordered, biting his lower lip.

Everyone in the conning tower looked at him with bewildered expressions. Everyone but Mug Vigliano, who turned his port engine enunciator to one-third. He looked at Turner then and nodded, indicating that maneuvering had answered his bell.

In the maneuvering room, the compartment where the two powerful General Electric motors drove the propeller shafts and where most of the electrical circuits and gear was routed, Chief electrician's mate Harry Brannigan sat on the padded bench in front of the maneuvering control station. Like Captain Nemo at his gothic pipe organ, Brannigan played the station expertly. It was his job to respond to engine orders from the conning tower or control room. In front of him were a series of gauges and enunciators. When an engine telegraph order came down, Brannigan had to operate the ten levers at the station. Playing the correct controls in order to make the diesels, electric motors and screw shafts do whatever was required.

He was surprised by the sudden order to put the port engine ahead. As he understood it, the *Bull Shark* was supposed to be running silent. He instantly responded to the order, of course, but he wore a frown on his face.

"What's up, Chief?" Ensign Andy Post asked from the open watertight hatch to the torpedo room.

As second engineer, Post was often but not always tasked with trim management during a torpedo attack. However, as second engineer and most junior officer, he was also tasked with other duties. During a depth charge, for instance, Post's station was in the after room. He also monitored the maneuvering room and would bounce between them unless and until the order came to rig for depth charge. In that case, all watertight doors would be closed.

"Dunno, sir," Brannigan replied with an elaborate shrug. "Guess we're moving… okay, that's weird…"

His enunciator now announced all ahead one-third. Brannigan played his organ, and the ship's two screws churned up the water and moved her forward at just over two knots.

"Skipper must be repositioning," Post mused.

Both men felt the tension in the room mount. Both of them, as well as the four other men who were tasked with monitoring the circuit breakers, battery levels and gas detectors, grew more anxious. It was a condition that was rapidly spreading throughout the ship.

In the after battery compartment, which housed the crew's mess and crew's quarters, laundry and crew's showers and head, Lieutenant Joe Dutch stood in the center of the mess with a clipboard in hand. Although he was nominally the ship's communications officer, which meant he oversaw radar, sonar and the radio shack, he was also the damage control officer during battle. As such, his station was in the crew's mess where he could coordinate with the compartment phone talkers as well as assist and coordinate the care of any injured men. The medicine locker was located in that compartment, and thus, Henry Hoffman, the boat's pharmacist's mate, was also stationed there with Dutch.

During battle, the galley was shut down, so the ship's commissary personnel, which in this case included Henry Martin, Bill Borshowski and Leroy Potts, the baker, were stationed to support damage and medical efforts as well as dealing with any physical needs of the giant Sargo battery below the deck. Eddie Carlson, the officer's steward, rotated through several positions from torpedoman to gunner and, during this evolution, planesman.

"What do you think happenin', sir?" Martin asked.

"I guess the Old Man is repositioning us, Enrie," Dutch replied, pronouncing Martin's first name in the French manner. "Probably got the Krauts on sound is my guess. Wants to make sure we're in a good shooting position."

"Ooh-wee!" Martin enthused. "Dem Germans gonna wish they never brought demselves cross dis ocean, that's for true!"

"Jesus Christ…" Borshowski muttered.

Hoffman, who sat at one of the tables bolted to the deck, nodded. Dutch looked at him in consideration for a long moment. Hoffman was a first-generation American, and his parents had emigrated from Germany.

"Hank… does it offend you when we say stuff like that?" Dutch suddenly asked. "I mean like Kraut or Jerry or Hun?"

Hoffman smiled thinly, "Not really, Lieutenant. I'm an American native-born. My folks are naturalized citizens. I try not to think about it too much. We're fighting the Nazis and it's natural to talk that way. Just like we do about the Japs. Long as you guys don't start calling me Attila."

That got a muted laugh that not only eliminated Dutch's worry but helped to ease the tension in the room. Especially when they felt the port engine cut out and then a minute later, the starboard. Once again, the ship was still and quiet, save for the low hum of the ventilation fans, the occasional ticking as the hull metal expanded and cooled due to unequal temperatures inside the hull and outside in the sea.

"Bearing is now three-three-zero," Rivers reported. "Ten thousand yards, speed still ten knots."

"That took five hundred yards off the plot, Skipper," William's head reported from the hole in the deck. "That also puts SS89 over eight hundred yards off, though."

"What's the bearing to them, Chet?" Turner asked.

"Two-three-zero," Rivers stated.

"That's a hundred- and thirty-degree gyro," Jarvis stated from his position at the TDC. "Recommend canceling forward tube two and using after tube eight for that shot, sir. Much better angle."

"Concur," Turner said. "Let the rooms know, Pat. Same depth on tube eight. Slow speed. Will your solution hold?"

Jarvis sighed, "Sir… at night, and with us having moved and all… I'm gonna need something more solid. Either an active ping or a radar sweep… or both if I could have them."

Turner knew he was right. In order for the TDC to operate, it needed range, heading and angles on the targets. These values could be manually entered from information provided by the captain through the periscope or from the bridge using the TBT, the target bearing transmitter. Once the values were entered, the mechanical marvel that was the TDC would continually update the math and transmit gyro settings to the individual torpedoes in their tubes.

However, more accurate data could be fed directly into the machine from sonar bearings and even more accurately from the SJ radar. In a situation such as the one they now faced, this was almost an absolute necessity. The targets were low profile, and it was dark. Even now, as Turner gazed back along his port quarter, he could barely make out the shape of SS89's conning tower. That was both a blessing and a curse, of course.

"Okay, Pat," Turner said. "I'll give you both. Ted, you standby to do a full radar sweep on my order. Chet, get ready on the JK heads. I want a full-power global ping. Just one after the sweep. I'll tell you when. Once the Germans hear that, they'll know they're under attack. But it'll be too late. I need you ready on the trigger, Pat. Because once we do the sweep, I'm gonna let the air out of this thing and then do a sonar pulse at periscope depth. Then fire. Everybody got that?"

A chorus of aye-sirs floated through the conning tower and up through the hatch. In spite of the fact that the control room was beneath them and connected only by a three-foot-wide circular opening, the acoustics were very good for communication without the need for a phone between the two.

On the small bridge of U-458, the leading *milchkuh*, Corvetten Kapitan Paul Klein stared hard into the night. The sky overhead was partially overcast, diminishing the light from the stars and the half-moon hanging low in the east. Although he had three lookouts posted, he still felt considerable unease.

Not for the first time, he regretted the lack of radar. He felt naked without it. His ship was vulnerable even at night. It was made more so by the fact that she was virtually defenseless. Other than firing at the errant aircraft with her single defensive AA gun, the tanker submarine had no torpedoes nor even a deck gun. No offensive armament at all.

Yet here they were, driving toward enemy territory all alone. Two pilot whales swimming directly into a school of hungry sharks. An ironic thought, considering that in truth it was the Kriegsmarine who were the sharks to the American's whales. That was the very reason for Klein's ship and sister ship's purpose. To re-supply and refuel the fleet of U-boats attacking shipping along the American coast. To provide fuel, oil, spare parts and even to act as a fresh bakery for the attacking U-boats.

"Sir!" one of the lookouts called down. "There's... something out there, off to starboard."

"Well, what is it?" Klein snapped, more from nervousness than anger.

"I don't' know, sir... it's hard to tell," the young lookout reported. "But something on the surface."

"A ship?" Klein asked with less impatience this time.

"Not a surface ship, sir... too small," The man said. "I think... I think it might be a conning tower, sir!"

"Oh my god..." Klein muttered. He snatched the handset from the little storage slot below the bridge railing. "Control, bridge! Sound battle stations! Possible enemy submarine off starboard bow! Standby to dive!"

"*Kapitan...*" came the uncertain voice of his first officer. "*Battery charge is critically low.*"

Klein cursed. He knew that, of course. The boat had only been on the surface for an hour after having been submerged all day. They had to build a charge up in the batteries before submerging again, or it would be a very short dive. He almost admired the enemy. A perfect time to attack, when the submarines were virtually trapped on the surface.

"We may have little choice," Klein said.

There was a sound. It was odd, and at first, he didn't recognize it. A low sort of gonging echo that seemed as much to vibrate up through his boots as it did in his eardrums. It only took another second or two for his mind to comprehend what he'd heard. It didn't register because he'd never heard it from the bridge before.

An active sonar ping had bounced off his hull.

"Clear the topsides!" Klein ordered, a wave of terror rising up to seize his heart. He slammed his hand down on the diving alarm and waited as the three men scrambled down the periscope sheers.

"Sir! Sir!" the same lookout who'd reported the conning tower shrieked. "Torpedoes in the water!"

Klein would have sworn that his heart stopped. Off his starboard bow, three glowing fingers appeared, the wakes of twenty-foot-long arrows of death disturbing the phytoplankton in the water. The small creatures responded by emitting a phosphorescent glow that lent the ever-lengthening wakes a ghostly aura that chilled Klein to his bones.

Miraculously, as he waited for the final lookout to go below, he saw that the leftmost wake would pass in front of his boat. He also saw that the other two would pass astern of him. He paused before jumping down the hatch and smiled triumphantly. The enemy had *missed!*

Then the true realization of what that meant struck home. U-457 was trailing Klein's own boat only three hundred yards astern and a bit to starboard… right in the path of…

The darkness was suddenly banished by a brilliant orange-white fireball that lit up Klein and his deck. He watched in horror as the other submarine seemed to sprout a huge fireball forward of her bow. As the shockwave and blast of hot air struck, Klein swore he heard men screaming.

Then something else happened. There was another flash of light and a more distant boom. With the screams of his fellow submariners still ringing in his ears and the cold grip of terror still tightly clenching his heart, Klein turned to see another fireball off his starboard beam. In the light, he saw the unmistakable form of a submarine's bow rise into the air like some ghoulish finger, then another explosion as something ruptured and then the entire thing began to slide into the sea.

It took his addled mind nearly half a minute to understand what had happened. The reports about American torpedoes must be true… the American submarine had fired *four*, not three eels. Two had missed, one had struck U-457 and the final had circled back and struck its own ship.

The Americans had killed themselves!

"Control!" Klein hollered into the phone. "Cancel the dive! Cancel battle stations! Get a rescue party up here, immediately. Helm, hard right rudder, engines to one-third! We must look for survivors!"

"Got him!" Turner whooped. He then turned his scope to the left and watched the SS89 erupt in a fireball and jerk her bow skyward for a moment before sinking out of sight. His stomach twisted at the sight for a moment. "Mug, starboard ahead one-third, left standard rudder. We're going in-between the two target bearings and releasing our package. Down scope. Pat, I want to get about halfway between, so the Germans see Schwimmer. Take over for a minute or two."

Turner leapt down the ladder and then ran forward into the torpedo room. He was just in time to see the men fitting Fritz with a Mae West and then strapping the small square Momsen lung to his chest.

"Fritz!" Turner said, coming over and clasping the younger man's hand. "It's time… and… well, I don't quite know what to say, except… thank you."

Schwimmer smiled and shook Turner's hand vigorously, "Thank you, sir. For my life, and for a chance to help. My people… they are wrong. If I can do this for you and Frau Turner… Mrs. Turner… and help to end the suffering…"

The engines stopped once again. Turner stared into the guileless, handsome, young face and felt heat behind his eyes. He suddenly drew the young man into a hug, made awkward by the breathing apparatus.

He released him, patted the German on the shoulder and stepped back.

"Now don't you fuckin' forget," Sparky said with mock gruffness, his voice hoarse with emotion. "You blow on that whistle for all you're worth once you're on top, you hear? Gotta make sure they notice ya'... good luck, kid."

Fritz entered the small lockout chamber, and the inner door was closed, and water began to rush into it. Turner suddenly felt sad, guilty and even angry all at once.

"God be with you, kid..." he muttered.

24

80 MILES EAST, NORTHEAST
OF WALKER'S CAY, BAHAMAS
MAY 3, 1942
1300 ZULU

J oan Turner had spent a week aboard the freighter. She'd been treated very well by the Germans, which had surprised her. No one interrogated her, no one mistreated her in any way. Hell, no one even spoke harshly to her, not even that despicable Brechman.

She'd been given a small but comfortable cabin complete with a private bathroom. Some feminine clothing had been provided, although she generally preferred the slacks, woolen shirt and heavy loafer-like slippers that many of the crew wore on a daily basis. They were comfortable and warm. She was mostly free to roam about the decks in the daytime, conversing with the few crew who spoke English. Meals were good and plentiful. She'd even developed a tentative friendship with the young pilot who'd flown her out of Wilmington, Brenner Michner. She couldn't help but laugh when he did his southern drawl for her.

In spite of all of this, however, Joan Turner seethed. A gilded cage was still a cage, after all. There were areas she wasn't allowed to go, naturally. There were sidearms visible all over the ship on the hips of her crew. And she knew, although no one had explicitly explained it to her, that she was there in order to act as a means to get at her husband.

She worried about him and his crew. She worried about her kids. Yes, they were with her mother and probably by now under guard, yet she couldn't help but worry about them. It was the worry for them and how they were dealing with their mom's disappearance, and the worry that Art must be feeling as well, that truly angered her.

Something else had changed as well. Late the previous afternoon, a submarine had surfaced near the freighter. It had joined another U-boat that had been with them a few days now. This new submarine brought some injured men who'd been aboard yet another U-boat that had been sunk the night before.

From what she could pick up, the new submarine was known as a milk cow. A sort of submarine tanker that also supplied parts and other essentials for U-boats on patrol. Yet this one had brought something else besides fuel, wounded men and fresh bread.

A young German sailor had been plucked out of the sea at the last moment. He'd apparently been aboard the American submarine that had torpedoed the other milk cow. That boat had been a victim of its own torpedo and had sunk with all hands. Only the German, who had been a prisoner of war, had survived because he'd been forced to stay on deck and watch the attack for some strange reason.

Joan had also overheard that the young man, Schwimmer was his name, had originally been picked up three weeks earlier by Art's submarine after Schwimmer's had been sunk. The kid had bad luck for sure. Yet this also meant that Schwimmer, who'd been aboard *Bull Shark*, knew a lot about Art and his crew. He'd been transferred to the SS89, an old submarine that was on her way to New London when she diverted to sink the milk cows.

Joan had tried to speak with him. She wanted to hear about Art, Joe Dutch and Buck Rogers along with the other officers and men she'd met. Yet the kid had studiously avoided her. She couldn't understand why. He'd reported, according to Michner, who had become something of a confidant, that Art and his crew had treated him well.

So here she was, wandering on the main deck near the floatplane and seething. She wanted to go home, and she wanted away from these people who had taken her. She especially wanted to be away from Brechman. The man had a sinister air about him. Even when he was being polite or even gallant, he seemed to ooze evil.

The man in question stood in the shadow of the port bridge wing and looked down on the attractive American woman and smiled to himself. He knew she was nervous and irritable. He knew she wanted nothing more than to be released. He even smiled when he thought that she was going to get her way before the day was out... just not quite in the way she'd have hoped.

He turned and strode aft to the small open deck behind the bridge where five men waited for him. There was Diedrich, of course. His rank and position meant that it was virtually impossible for Brechman to exclude him. The captain's experience was useful, however, so the SS major rarely tried.

Then there was Michner, of course. The pilot would play a crucial role in the plan he was hatching. Young Fritz Schwimmer sat there, trying to seem unassuming. That Klein had plucked the young sailor from the water while rescuing the few men who survived the other *milchkuh's* destruction was a stroke of almost unbelievable luck. The information the boy had shared, half of which Brechman didn't think the lad even knew was so valuable, would act as the drawstring to Brechman's net.

There was Hardegen, of course. Next to him was Adolph Fousch, the Kapitaleutnant who commanded the *Dolch*, their secret light destroyer. These two men and their ships, in conjunction with Diedrich and the freighter, would cinch the net tight around Turner's throat and end his interference once and for all.

"Gentlemen," Brechman said as he took his seat and picked up a steaming mug of coffee and lit a cigar, "we stand on the verge of a bold stroke. The thorn that has plagued us is about to be torn out."

A round of agreeing noises floated around the table along with smiles. Brechman pulled on the cigar and leveled his gaze on Schwimmer.

"Mr. Schwimmer... tell me again about your time on the *Bull Shark*. You say you were not mistreated?"

Fritz scoffed, "I was not physically abused, Herr Major. Perhaps because I am white, like most of the crew. They did chain me to a bunk when I slept. They forced me to work in the galley and to clean the heads and other dirty jobs. Most of all…"

Schwimmer paused and seemed to have to gather himself and struggled for self-control, "…they forced me to work alongside and be ordered around by… by… *niggers!*"

Brechman knew that the English word the boy had used was a derogatory term in America for Blacks. He nodded with approval and even a twinge of empathy. Here was Schwimmer, a prime example of Aryan perfection. Tall, blonde-haired and blue-eyed, and handsome. Being forced to act servile to lesser races… disgusting.

"I think I understand," Fousch said, himself a blonde with blue eyes. "I understand why you want to help us destroy them."

"Precisely," Brechman said. "I won't lie, young man, I have been suspicious… yet in the light of your report… I think you can be trusted. A fine example to the Party. Perhaps even worthy of a citation."

"Danka…" Schwimmer muttered, casting his eyes down modestly.

"Tell us about what you overheard regarding their patrol area," Hardegen said. "No doubt Turner will wish he'd never taught you English."

Schwimmer grinned, "I already spoke it before they picked me up, Herr Kapitan. I only pretended to learn… at any rate, thanks to their negligence, I know that the SS333, the *Bull Shark*, is to patrol the area between the southern half of Florida, the Bahamian Islands and eastern Cuba. There she can monitor shipping coming from the Gulf of Mexico, from South America and the Caribbean and escort or help to protect those vessels from our U-boats."

Hardegen, Fousch and Diedrich nodded. Brechman leaned back and pondered this, "That is a confined area. Yes, there is a lot of deep water in the center, but the American boat is bounded almost entirely by shallows and islands of all sizes, is that not so?"

Diedrich nodded, puffing on a stogie of his own, "Indeed. Even more so, between the upper Florida Keys and Cuba, there is a sort of… ring of islands known as the Cay Sal Bank. Mostly very shallow

271

with some small islands around a shoaling center. That may be the best place for us to make our… deposit?"

Fousch chuckled, "Indeed, Kapitan Diedrich. It is treacherous water, and in order to get close enough, the American submarine must traverse shallows for some way. Not more than a few miles, but the depth where she'll need to go in order to get a boat ashore is much shallower than her test depth."

"So…" Hardegen said, "the plan is something like this if I'm not mistaken… Turner goes in to pick up his wife, the word of her presence we make certain is received… then Fousch and the *Blanch* come in behind him and block his escape. U-123 and I wait in the only escape route open to him, and we all work to snare him."

"And send him to the *bottom!*" Fousch exclaimed grandly.

"Essentially," Brechman stated. "You naval gentlemen will no doubt work out the details with charts and so forth. The crucial part of our plan, of course, is to get Frau Turner to our chosen spot. This requires Mr. Michner and his plane."

"I'm to fly her to one of these small islands, land and drop her there?" Michner asked.

"It must be more than that, Lieutenant," Diedrich said. "I think that Herr Brechman wants this to seem more… authentic. First, your plane must *crash* there, or at least be forced to land due to fuel issues or something. Second, Mrs. Turner must believe not only in the ruse, but that you, Michner, are her ally."

"Why?" Michner asked suspiciously, or as suspiciously as he could manage. He was already thinking ahead.

"She must be convinced that you rescued her and that the information we allow her to deliver over the radio will both be believed and be so enticing it won't seem like a Nazi trap," Brechman explained. "But it does mean a sacrifice."

Michner scowled, "A sacrifice? Honestly, sir, can we not simply radio that she's wherever she's supposed to be? Why even fly at all?"

"Because they will use radio direction finding to verify your report," Hardegen answered. "You must actually be on location. And simply flying away afterward will not be sufficient. The Americans will no doubt send an aircraft eventually. Yet Turner, once he knows Joan is there, will come charging, I'm sure of it. I would."

"So escape may be impossible," Brechman said. "The lady will be rescued. Her rescuer will also be acquired. The odds are good, Lieutenant, that you will be a prisoner of war afterward."

Michner's face went red, "So I'm to sacrifice myself? To become a prisoner until the war is over? Sir…"

Brechman actually felt a little pity for the young man. He was a good officer, and it was a shame to sacrifice him as well as their only aircraft, "I understand, Brenner. But do not despair! You will receive an iron cross for this… and we have people in the United States. I am already formulating a plan to retrieve you. In actuality, you may spend no more than a few months as a prisoner. Perhaps no more than a few weeks, if we can arrange an exchange. You did, in their eyes, betray us to get an American woman, the wife of a naval officer, to safety. Hell, the *Americans* may give *you* a medal."

Michner seemed to ponder this for a long moment. Reluctantly, he slowly nodded his head, "I know I have little choice in the matter… but… but if this furthers our cause… then I accept. I may need help, however. If the ruse is to work, at least from the perspective of our charming guest… then I need a second man, I think."

Brechman nodded, "I believe you're right. Mr. Schwimmer… are you willing to step back into the lion's den once more?"

Schwimmer blanched, "Sir! I… I've already been a prisoner. All I've thought of for the past few weeks was going home… perhaps I'd be more useful aboard Kapitan Hardegen's boat, sir… I…"

"Fritz," Michner placed a hand on the younger man's shoulder. "You said it yourself. It wasn't terrible being an American prisoner. As Herr Brechman says, we may be welcomed as heroes and be released if we wish it."

"But why?" Schwimmer implored. "Please understand… I will follow any orders I'm given… but why me?"

"First, because you speak English," Brechman said. "And because you can tell her that your time with the Americans has changed your attitudes about the Reich. You make things believable. It *must* be believable."

273

"Espionage," Michner said to Schwimmer with a wry grin. "It's never as straightforward as a torpedo firing solution, is it?"

Schwimmer drew in a deep breath and finally half-smiled, "If this is what my Führer wishes, than this is my duty."

"Excellent!" Brechman said, clapping his hands together in the first sign of anything like glee that any of them had ever seen. "Then this is what I have in mind…"

Joan had just come from a long hot shower and was dressed and combing her hair to have supper with the ship's captain and a few other guests. She'd rather have eaten alone, but the invitation was probably not one she should turn down… even if she could.

The captain was a fairly kind and charming man, for a Nazi. He and his officers seemed pleased to have female company at their table and acted accordingly.

There was also the consideration that should she ever escape her floating prison, the intelligence she could provide would be useful. She was good at picking up on things, both obvious and subtle, and felt it was her duty to bring back all she could to her country.

Unfortunately, escape from a ship and then finding her way back to the U.S. seemed an insurmountable obstacle. Impossible alone, she knew. If she were to get away, she'd need help… and that meant Michner, more likely than not. Either she'd befriend him and convince him to help her… or she'd need to secure a weapon, stow away on the plane and hijack it.

The monumental weight of these thoughts temporarily oppressed her. One lone woman on a ship somewhere at sea… a ship full of military men… she fought down the urge to cry.

"No, Joan Turner," she told herself, biting her lower lip, "you're *not* giving up! You can do this… it's just a matter of how and when…"

It was about an hour before sunset, and she was not at all surprised by the brisk knock at her door. When she opened it, however, she was very surprised to see a tall, handsome young blonde man looking at her nervously. It took Joan only a second to recognize Fritz

Schwimmer, the boy who'd been with her husband for the past few weeks.

"What do you want?" she asked frostily.

She couldn't help but be angry with the young man. He'd been in intimate contact with her husband and refused to talk to her. It felt like an outright insult.

"Mrs. Turner, may I come in, please?" Fritz asked earnestly.

She frowned and seriously considered telling him to take a flying leap but relented, if only for the possibility that he might say something useful. She stood aside and cleared the way but did not say anything.

Fritz looked up and down the corridor and then darted inside, grabbing the door and swinging it closed behind him. He had a bead of sweat showing on his upper lip and seemed nervous, "I... I am very sorry about the way I've been ignoring you, Mrs. Turner... but things are more complicated than you know."

Joan scoffed, "You don't say."

"I'm Fritz Schwimmer," he said, extending a hand. "Do you wish to get out of here?"

Joan chuckled ironically, "Is that your idea of a joke?"

He shook his head vigorously, 'Do you know why they took you?"

"No... I assume to force Art or the Navy into something."

"Yes... to lure him into a trap... but we can't allow that to happen. Captain Turner is a good man. He and his crew... well, never mind. You must trust me, and we must move *now*. I've set things in motion, along with another man. A man you already know."

"Michner?" Joan asked excitedly and then mentally kicked herself. Her excitement and eagerness to be away from the Nazis had led her to possibly give something away. It was too late, however. She and Michner had talked; that was no secret at least.

Schwimmer nodded and pulled a pistol from beneath the hem of his loose work shirt, "He's scheduled to fly a mission this evening. Even now, the plane is being fueled and readied for flight. We must replace Schultz and Volmer, his crew, and be on that plane in less than eight minutes."

Joan narrowed her eyes at him, "How do I know I can trust you? How do I know this isn't some Nazi trick?"

For the first time, Schwimmer seemed confident and relaxed. There was a twinkle in his eye as he said: "Joanie, remember how the moon shone at Diamond Head?"

Her eyes grew wide, and she clutched Fritz to her and squeezed him, "My God... did Art tell you to ask me that?"

He nodded, "I'm not sure what it means, but he said to make sure I repeated it exactly."

Joan drew in a deep breath, "Okay, Fritz, I'm with you. Let's just hope it doesn't go bad for either of us."

He nodded and grinned. Then in a passable impersonation of Humphrey Bogart said: "Shweetheart, things are never so bad that they can't get worse... this was in a movie one night aboard the *Bull Shark*. Is pretty good Humphrey Bogart, yah?"

Joan laughed and suddenly felt a liking for the young man. At first, their escape seemed easy. He led her a short distance down the corridor, up two flights of metal stairs and into the superstructure on the main deck. In a small room that smelled of coffee, the two of them found two other young men alone, just finishing a meal.

"Who are you?" one of them asked. He had a pair of Luftwaffe wings on his flight jacket.

"Your relief," Schwimmer said. "Out of the jackets."

He emphasized his order by showing them his revolver. The two young men looked at each other, then at Joan and then back to Fritz. Without speaking, they removed their flight jackets and tossed them onto the table that stood between them and Schwimmer.

"Heil Hitler," Schwimmer said, and his pistol barked twice.

Joan had to cover her mouth to stifle a scream as the two men toppled backward and crumpled in a heap on the deck.

Schwimmer moved quickly. He helped her into one of the flight jackets and slid into his own. He then went around the table, yanked the caps off the two dead men's heads and placed one on his own and handed the second to Joan.

"Put your hair up under this," he said. "I'm sorry you had to see that... but it was necessary."

Joan did as she was told and even managed a nonchalant shrug, "It's war."

Schwimmer nodded, and they headed back out into a corridor and then through a door onto the open main deck, lit brightly in late afternoon sunshine. The Arado was only forty feet away. Men ambled here and there on deck but paid them little mind.

"Walk right behind me and keep your head partly down," he instructed. "We move fast but not hurried. Ready?"

Joan's heartbeat a tattoo in her chest, and she nodded. Fritz gave her hand a quick squeeze and they strolled across the intervening deck. Long, confident strides that moved them quickly but not anxiously to the open cockpit door of the airplane. Joan went in first and sat next to Brenner Michner. Schwimmer closed the door and settled into the observer's seat.

"Good afternoon, Mrs. Turner," Michner said with a smile. "Are you all right?"

"I... I will be when we're gone," she replied.

The riggers hooked the lifting cables, the Arado was lifted and swung over the side and lowered to the lightly heaving sea. The riggers unclipped, and they and their cables were hauled back aboard, just like that.

Michner had the big radial engine going. He slowly taxied away from the massive black form of the freighter and turned toward the northeast. When he confirmed everyone was buckled in, he pushed the throttle forward and the plane roared as it began to slide ever faster across the water. In less time than Joan would've thought, the pontoons lifted out of the water, streaming a trail of foam behind, and the floatplane soared into the partly cloudy afternoon sky.

"Now I must tell you something," Michner said to her. "This is not what it seems."

Joan felt the blood drain from her face and heard a sharp indescribable noise from Fritz behind her.

"Let me guess," she said dryly, "you're not really rescuing me."

Michner looked at her, cast his eyes back to Fritz, who was emptying his revolver and reloading it and then back at Joan. His brilliant smile was astonishing.

"No, we are," he said. "We've got much to talk about, Joan. May I call you Joan?"

"Sure…"

"Our friend Herr Brechman has staged this little getaway to convince you that we're traitors," Michner said. "We're supposed to land at Cay Sal Bank, and you're then to call the Navy and convince them of who you are. Shortly thereafter, your husband, who is supposedly patrolling nearby, will rush into a trap as he attempts to rescue you."

Joan was silent.

"But he's not exactly where I told them he is," Fritz added. "And in truth… it is we, and he, who will be the ones to spring a trap."

"You mean we're not going to Cay Sal Bank, wherever that is?" Joan asked, feeling more than moderately bewildered.

"It's between the Keys and Cuba," Michner said now in his Carolinian drawl. "In fact, the *Bull Shark* is already in the lower Bahamas. I'm about to turn on a heading for Cay Sal now, but shortly after we leave radar range, we'll turn more southerly and meet him. I'm afraid he's going to have to figure some of this out himself, and I hope he's already done so, as we have little more than half a day."

"How do you know where Art will be?" Joan asked.

Fritz leaned forward and smiled at her, "He gave me a set of coordinates. We should meet him shortly before dark. Oh, you may wish to keep this as…. souvenir?"

Fritz dropped an unexpended shell into her hand. It had no bullet in it, however. She looked at him in surprise, "Blanks?"

Fritz grinned, "Part of Herr Brechman's deceit. I didn't kill those men… he only wanted you to think I did. Is good trick, yah?"

"Why?" Joan asked both men. There was no need to elaborate; they both knew what she was asking.

"I've seen the other side," Fritz said simply. "Is much better… there is honor and friendship and integrity."

Michner sighed, "I've seen too much of a lack of those things. I've drawn U-boats to where innocent merchant sailors were waiting to be destroyed… I've seen treachery, deceit… and murder."

He eyed her sidelong, and Joan nodded. She knew he was speaking of Milly. The woman who'd pretended to be her friend and yet who'd been murdered by the very people who'd employed her.

"And there's you," Michner said. "The last straw, as I believe you say in the States. I love my country and have always been proud of being German... but I don't want to be a Nazi anymore. Brechman is... he's no good. And I hope that your husband sends him straight to the bottom of the ocean."

25

15 MILES WEST OF NEW PROVIDENCE, BAHAMAS
25°5 N, 77°11 W

The sun had set, and the long slender shape of the submarine was difficult to pick out of the darkening sea below. However, the bright flash of the signal gun being aimed at the Arado from the boat's bridge was unmistakable. Michner swung his aircraft around and came in, expertly landing and coming to an idle not far from the submarine. He maneuvered the plane over the submerged foredeck at a perpendicular angle. The boat's ballast tanks were blown, and the ship lifted, the airplane resting on its pontoons ten yards forward of the five-inch deck gun.

Art Turner was there to meet the men and the woman. He had a security detail behind him with rifles and pistols, yet they were not needed. Joan Turner flew into her husband's arms laughing and crying all at once. Art squeezed her tight and kissed her laughing wet face, trying and not entirely succeeding at holding back his own tears.

"Thank God…" he breathed. "Are you all right?"

Joan sniffled and wiped her eyes with the long sleeve of her heavy shirt, "Just a little unscheduled cruise, darling. How are you? Have you heard anything about the kids?"

"I spoke to your mother while I was in port a few days ago,"

Turner replied. "They're fine. They'll be relieved to know you're safe when the word gets out… if the word gets out."

Turner then looked at the two Germans who stood awkwardly by the plane. One was a young man he didn't recognize, and the other was Fritz Schwimmer.

"You did it, Fritzy," Turner said, pumping the man's hand vigorously. "That's a story I need to hear. You all right after your little dunking?"

Fritz grinned, "Yah, I'm A-okay, sir. This is Lieutenant Brenner Michner. He's with us as well."

Turner eyed the pilot. He was about Turner's height and maybe three years younger. The German had a reserved but friendly smile on his face, and Turner shook his hand as well.

"I'm grateful, Lieutenant," Turner said, "for bringing my wife to me."

"It's the least I could do, partner," Michner said in a dead-on Carolinian accent, "seein' as how it was me that snatched her up in the first place and all."

Turner felt a bolt of shock at the voice, and both Joan and Fritz laughed. The *Bull Shark's* captain recollected himself, "You're the man I spoke to on the freighter that morning! Jesus Christ…"

Michner chuckled, "One of my many talents, sir. Now we must prepare. There is much to talk about and little time. The Nazis have set up an ambush for you at Cay Sal bank… and I hope you've got some idea of how to turn the tables."

Turner nodded, "Now that I know where, yes I do. I'm afraid, though, Lieutenant… we're going to have to scuttle your plane. I'm sorry."

Michner looked over his shoulder at the handsome floatplane and sighed, "Yes sir, I understand. She's been a good bird, though."

The security detail was dismissed, all but Mug Vigliano, who still kept a .45 in a holster on his hip. He was acting quartermaster of the watch anyway, so he simply stood on the bridge beside Pat Jarvis, who was officer of the watch. After flooding down forward, backing out from under the plane and blowing forward again, the submarine backed off by fifty yards and came to a stop.

At the five-inch deck gun, Fritz sat in the right-hand seat and worked the azimuth wheel, pointing the weapon at the aircraft. Beside him, Eddie Carlson worked the elevation wheel, getting the barrel of the weapon pointed just so. He then fed a five-inch shell into the breech and readied himself with his foot just above the firing pedal and looked back at the elevated bridge and cigarette deck. Turner stood there with Joan and Michner.

"Give the word, Lieutenant," Turner said. "She's your bird, only seems fitting."

Michner nodded, "Fire."

Eddie pressed the pedal and the gun boomed. The shot was true. The shell struck the airplane's fuselage almost dead center and exploded, blasting the aircraft into several large chunks that began to sink immediately.

Turner ordered the submarine to close in, and Vigliano used one of the 50-cals to repeatedly puncture the pontoons until they were so full of holes they were no longer positively buoyant. They, too, slipped below the dark waters forever.

After a hearty supper of Martin's homemade chicken and shrimp gumbo, Joan Turner joined her husband in the radio room for a little performance. Joe Dutch was there to operate the radio gear.

"It needs to sound like we're not in the same room, Joe," Turner said. "Do you think you can do that? This is only for the Germans to hear, not for our side to have to detect, although they will."

"That shouldn't be a problem, sir," Dutch said. "I can alter the gain settings for each of you. When you speak we'll be on full power, as you might expect from a ship's radio. Then when Joanie talks, I'll cut power by half to imitate a plane's radio. I'd recommend keeping it short, though."

Turner squeezed her hand, "You ready, honey?"

Joan grinned, "To stick it to Brechman? Hell yes, I'm ready."

Less than a hundred and forty miles away, in the *Mortimer Blanch's* well-appointed radio shack, Klaus Brechman listened intently to the transmission being broadcast over the loudspeaker. He wore a devilish smile on his face.

"*...hello? Hello? Does anyone read this? My name is Joan Turner... I was taken by Germans a week ago...*" Static intermittently sputtered over her words. "*Does anyone read this? Mayday... mayday...*"

There was a pause, and it appeared as if a ground station somewhere was responding when a much stronger transmission broke in. Brechman actually laughed when he heard it.

"*Joan! Joan, is that really you? It's Art!*"

"*...Arty! Oh my... really you?*"

Laughter over the radio. Brechman looked to his operators who were trying to pinpoint the location but weren't having any luck as yet.

"*My God, honey! Where are you?*" That was Turner.

"*Cay Sal Bank... plane had mechanical issues... pilot had to set down... eastern side... one man injured; the pilot is working on the plane, but he's not hopeful... he's given me a set of numbers...*" A burst of static and then she gave a set of coordinates. Again, Brechman laughed. It was all coming to plan.

"*All right, baby... listen, I'm not far from there. Just a few hours away, in fact,*" Turner explained. "*Do you think you can hold out until morning? I don't' want to come in there in the dark, it's awfully shallow... but I can come in at first light and launch a boat to pick you all up.*"

Joan laughed, "*...we're okay. Got enough.... And water. The younger man hit his head... seems okay, though. How... the kids?*"

Turner laughed over the channel, "*Okay. They miss their mom. Hang tight, honey. I'll be there in a few hours and we'll get you ashore by dinnertime tomorrow, okay?*"

They said goodbye and the transmission stopped. Brechman rubbed his hands together and grinned, "Were you able to get a fix on the location of that conversation?"

The technician frowned and shook his head, "No sir, not enough time. Although it appeared to emanate from the southwest as we'd expect."

"Good enough," Brechman said and turned to Diedrich, who was standing beside him. "Best possible speed for the Cay Sal Bank. Alert

Hardegen and Fousch that we're moving into the final game. Have you worked out positions for them?"

Diedrich nodded, "Yes, and for us. We'll allow Turner to come in, and then the *Dolch* and we will come in from the northern side and southern side of the bank, respectively. U-123 is already nearly in position. Hardegen will wait submerged until he detects *Bull Shark*. Then he'll come in surfaced behind them."

"Excellent," Brechman said with a wicked gleam in his eye.

It was well after twenty-three hundred, and Joan had gone to Turner's cabin to sleep. The *Bull Shark* was running at flank speed on the surface, threading as direct a course as she could through the Bahamas and toward the eastern edge of Cay Sal Bank. Turner, Williams, Jarvis and Dutch, who now had the watch, stood around the master gyro table examining a chart of the section of the Bahamas they were now in. Brenner Michner stood by as well, in respectful silence.

"So this is where Joan is supposed to be," Turner said, putting an X on the chart in pencil.

"Good spot for catching a submarine with her pants down," Jarvis noted. "We can get within a half-mile of that little island there, it's thirty feet deep... but it doesn't get more than four hundred feet deep for about a dozen miles in any direction."

"So they intend to catch us in the shallows," Williams said.

"Yeah, but from where?" Dutch asked. "If we're not mistaken, they only have the one destroyer. If we have to, we can just fight him on the surface with fish and the deck guns. They can't be much more heavily armed than us, from what you said, Art."

Turner nodded, "Probably true. But they're going to have U-123, who we've faced before. They'll have that destroyer, of course... and I'd bet that the freighter has some armaments, too. I'd seen a deck gun firing that morning... and how much do you want to wager they've got ashcans to drop on us?"

Jarvis snorted, "No bet here."

"Here's what I think," Turner said, tapping the chart with his pencil. "They let us get right up to the shore. Then both surface ships come in from the north and south."

"A pincer move," Jarvis noted with a nod.

"Then the U-boat comes up our stern?" Williams asked.

Turner nodded, "Check and mate. At least as far as they're concerned."

"So what've we got up our sleeve?" Dutch asked.

"For one, a squadron of torpedo bombers out of Fort Lauderdale," Turner said. "They'll take off just before dawn and be on station forty-five minutes later. There's a British tin can that's being diverted from a trip to defend the refinery on Curacao; she *might* be in range when all of this starts to happen... but it's problematic."

"So you're saying other than a few planes... we're on our own?" Williams asked dubiously.

Turner nodded grimly, "Just not enough time to organize without knowing exactly where."

"Brechman's plan hinges on surprise," Michner spoke up for the first time. "Take that away, and the odds are more even. Hardegen will wait out in deep water to the east. If we can circle around to the southeast, then when the *Dolch* moves in, we can take her first. With them out of the way, is it not safe to say that the U-boat will be a minor threat and that you can tackle the large and slower-moving freighter?"

Turner eyed him appreciatively, "I think you're in the right of it, Lieutenant. That tin can is our biggest enemy. Although she's smaller than normal, she's still got what... twenty-four charges aside from her torpedo tubes and deck guns? She's the fastest and most dangerous threat. We take her out, and then we can focus on the U-boat. The freighter should be easy pickings for the bombers. It's Hardegen we need to worry about then. Submarine to submarine combat is virtually impossible except on the surface, so he'll either lie in wait or just slink off once that destroyer is sunk."

"Or he'll hang out quiet and wait for us to surface, if we do," Jarvis said. "If we're at periscope depth, that's the same thing. He can set his fish to fifty-five feet and plug us easily."

Turner nodded, "Good point, Pat. If we do want to take up station between U-123 and the destroyer, then we need to do an end-around right now. Come toward the bank from the south with enough time to dive and run silent…"

He picked up the handset from the communications box mounted in the overhead, "Bridge, Control. We're going to do a loop around. Come right to… two-zero-zero. Then come down here, Andy."

"*Control, bridge, ordering new course of two-zero-zero,*" Post replied.

It was a little silly, or it would be to those not used to the Navy, to call up to the bridge to have a steering order relayed to the helmsman in the conning tower just over Turner's head. Yet this chain of command was a vital part of ship operations. It ensured that everyone involved in even the simplest evolution knew their jobs and had complete situational awareness. Yes, Turner had bypassed Dutch as the officer of the watch, but since Andy Post, the junior officer of the deck, was standing it on the bridge, it was proper enough.

Post would relay the order to the quartermaster of the watch next to him. The quartermaster would inform the helmsman of what to do. No one was left out and there were no surprises.

Post slid down the ladder and joined the rest at the table, "Sir?"

"Here's what we want, Andy," Turner said, tracing a line on the chart from their current position. "We're going to stay on this heading for two hours. At a little after oh-one-hundred, we come to a two-five-zero for another hour. Then I want you to dive the ship to periscope depth, or snorkel depth if you will, and run a three-four-zero for another hour at full. Then at zero-three-hundred you stop all engines and secure the snorkel. Go to battery power and dive to four hundred feet and continue on course until zero-five-thirty. Keep her at one-third, no more than four knots. When you secure from growlers, order ship-wide silent. You with me?"

Post nodded and scribbled in his pocket notebook, "Aye-aye, sir."

"At oh-five-thirty you order battle stations torpedo," Turner said. "Have the galley fix a hearty battle breakfast for everybody. You'll order battle stations to rouse everybody out of their racks but announce on the XJA that everyone is to have breakfast first before going to stations."

"Like the old days," Jarvis said with a grin. "Send the men into battle with full bellies."

Turner smiled, "Exactly."

"Sir… what about Mrs. Turner?" Williams asked.

Turner frowned and nodded, "Yeah… not much we can do about that. It's up to Joanie. She can stay in my cabin or come here to control. Probably the safest place. She can sit in the radio shack if she wants."

None of the men were pleased about that. Yet the captain was right. They couldn't do much about having a civilian on board. She was there and she'd have to endure it with them.

"You know," Turner said thoughtfully. "Joanie has some first-aid training. Maybe I'll put her with the doc. Might help. Anyway, we'll see when the time comes. Andy, I want the watch changed at oh-two-hundred. Let the guys on duty now get a few hours' sleep. That includes you. Elmer or I will take over then."

"Aye-sir," Post said, feeling oddly nervous. There was pre-battle tension in the control room and he, being the most junior officer aboard, seemed to feel it more keenly.

"All right, gents," Turner said, setting his pencil down in the tray on the table in an unconsciously definitive gesture. "That's the gist of it. Let's get some rest. Elmer, have you arranged quarters for Michner here?"

"We've got an empty bunk in officer's country," Williams said. "In Andy's quarters."

"Okay, good," Turner said. "Get some rest, guys. Tomorrow is going to be an interesting day."

In his cabin, Turner slipped out of his uniform and slid into the bunk beside his wife. The berth wasn't meant for two, although it was slightly larger than the others on board. Joan turned on her side and settled herself onto his chest in a very comfortable and very comforting snuggle.

"Is it going to be all right, Arty?" she asked softly.

"I think so, Joanie," he replied softly as he stroked her silky hair. "It might get a little hairy… but we'll make it."

She sighed, "Least I get to see what your job is *really* like."

"Lucky you," he said with a sardonic chuckle. "Locked in a tube filled with diesel fumes and B.O. Maybe get your brains rattled around if we get depth charged. Maybe even have to patch up wounded kids with the doc."

"Sounds romantic," she said sleepily.

Turner chuckled. He admired her spirit and her courage. He only hoped it wouldn't be tested beyond its breaking point. He hoped that was true for his men as well. They'd had a taste of combat, but it was only a sample. Tomorrow would be the real thing. Turner suddenly found himself wondering if his own grit would survive. The war was still young, and few in the service younger than forty-two had ever seen true combat.

Well, they were going to get their chance and then some. Word was already spreading that what was known as the Great War was being referred to as World War One... and, by extension, the current one as World War Two. What a way to refer to a war...

God help us, Turner thought ruefully. *World War Two... welcome to it, boys and girls. Only five months in and we've given it a grandiose name... the kind of name that will live forever. How many years will it go on? How many dead men's... and women's... names will fill the pages of future histories?*

26

MAY 4, 1942

1030 ZULU

Lieutenant JG Charles Taylor, United States Navy, pulled back on the stick and his powerful, brand-new Avenger torpedo bomber lifted off the runway at NAS Fort Lauderdale. It would still be dark for another thirty or forty minutes or so, and as flight leader he decided to keep his squadron over land and skirt the coast until they were over Key Largo. By then, at a cruising altitude of ten thousand feet, there should be enough of a false dawn to give the world below some definition.

As Taylor's plane, accompanied by three others just like it, roared into the early morning sky, he thought again about this hastily assembled mission. He didn't know much, only that a man named Webster Clayton had arrived around midday off a PB2Y Coronado that had apparently also been transporting some submariners. He'd met with Taylor's CO, and then Taylor had been given a quick briefing on the mission. He was mildly annoyed, as he was supposed to be packing his seabag to head out to the Pacific to join an aircraft carrier.

Instead, here he was on some crazy mission to find a German freighter and destroyer trying to hunt down one of their submarines. Even worse, neither he nor his other three planes were fully manned. The Avenger was meant to be crewed by three men. Pilot, bombardier and gunner. None of them had a gunner, as it was felt that no aerial combat would be part of this mission. They were to use their four Mark 13 torpedoes to help the USS *Bull Shark* sink a freighter and a small destroyer and then turn back to Lauderdale. If he thought they could do so with a modicum of safety, Clayton had suggested that Taylor and his fellow pilots might strafe the ships with their onboard machine guns.

Well, as the man once said, theirs was not to question why, theirs was to do or die.

"Mayflower one to Mayflower flight," Taylor said into his radio mic, "climb to angel's ten, form up on me in diamond formation and set airspeed to one-four-zero knots."

"*We just out for an early morning stroll or what, Chuck?*" Lieutenant JG Archie Manzor jibed.

From behind Taylor, his torpedoman, Petty Officer Second Class Tyler Fetch, snickered. Taylor shot him the bird over his shoulder and thumbed the mic, "You wanna go faster, Arch, then you gotta chip in for gas."

Laughter over the channel.

"All right you wise-asses," Taylor said. "Let's start taking this seriously. This ain't a training cruise."

A moment of silence and then: "*Mayflower one, Mayflower four... we really after a couple of Kraut ships?*"

"Roger that, Mayflower four," Taylor replied. "Trying to bag one of our boats off Cay Sal. War's five month's old now, about time you guys broke your cherries."

That got a round of laughter from the squadron as they flew on down the coast.

Reinhard Hardegen truly enjoyed a smoke with his coffee. He especially enjoyed how it annoyed his Einsvo. Hardegen leaned casually against the chart table in the control room, drawing on his Lucky Strike and sipping at his heavy ceramic mug. The ship hung at periscope depth a dozen miles from where Michner had set his plane down. They were in a thousand feet of water, the surface was virtually flat calm and the ship was in a low-power mode.

From this position, Hardegen felt the U-123 could, at the very least, hear the sound of the big American submarine approaching from almost any angle. Even if *Bull Shark* was submerged, the reduction gear that drove the propeller shafts was noisy enough that it could be heard for miles. And should the boat be running on top under diesel power, U-123 would certainly detect them from ten miles away at least.

Although his vision was limited with his scope only a meter above the surface, Hardegen still insisted on staying at periscope depth. Although Hardegen projected a casual and even carefree air aboard his ship, he was a cautious and shrewd man by nature. He enjoyed a relaxed atmosphere aboard his boat. An atmosphere that lacked the rigidity of the discipline so common on big surface ships. He wanted a crew that felt comfortable with one another regardless of rank. A happy crew was an effective crew, and this was nowhere more accurate than aboard a two-hundred-and-fifty-foot sewer pipe.

Hardegen enjoyed joking with his officers and men, and sometimes even teasing his executive officer. Yet beneath the prankster's exterior dwelt a devotion to duty and a keen mind. That keen mind never took anything for granted. It never threw caution to the wind or made assumptions that were more for comfort than a reflection of reality.

Major Klaus Brechman might believe that he'd concocted a fool-proof plan. *He* might be convinced of just how far he'd pulled the wool over the American Navy's eyes, but Hardegen wasn't. He knew better.

The captain of U-123 was by no means a fatalist. He didn't believe that just because Herr Wolf *knew* that the Reich *must* prevail that it was inevitable. Germany had already tried this thirty years earlier. Back then, the Kaiser scoffed at Britain. How could a small island nation stand against a continental power? As if that hadn't been the case for five hundred years already.

Yet Britain had fought back with an iron resolve. Further, when a U-boat sunk the passenger liner *Lusitania,* Germany had dragged America into the war, and everyone knew how that had ended.

And now, not three decades later, another arrogant leader was doing the same thing. Once again, Germany had invaded France, who, to no one's surprise, had yielded virtually overnight. Where was good old Napoleon when they needed him?

Once again, England had defied Germany and was fighting back viciously. Donitz's U-boat fleet was crippling their trade and therefore strangling their ability to make war. And then the Japanese had to go and fuck everything all up.

After the attack on Pearl Harbor, Germany had no choice but to declare war on the U.S. Japan was a part of the Axis, after all, and it was the Nazi's obligation. Yet Hardegen, while he didn't feel that now victory was impossible, knew that America's participation would make things exponentially more difficult.

He'd been to the U.S. He'd seen what they could do firsthand. The country was enormous. Not as large as Russia, or even Canada for that matter. Yet those two nations were mostly frozen wasteland. Their size mostly unusable and resourceless tundra. America, however, had abundant natural resources, was separated from her closest enemies by a minimum of three-thousand miles of ocean and her industrial might was simply not to be believed. All the industrial power of Europe, including Russia and Japan combined, didn't match the United States' ability to build.

On top of that, America was a nation built by pioneers. By hard men and women who tamed a continent and defied the world's largest superpower to carve a civilization from the wilderness. That spirit and toughness still lived on in the twentieth century. America was a sleeping giant, and now she was awake, and she was mightily pissed off.

That's why Hardegen stayed at periscope depth. To watch. Because he didn't believe Turner was stupid and didn't believe that the man would simply walk into a trap. He'd at the very least inform his superiors of his rescue attempt. As a result, there might be aircraft over the scene or additional ships on station. Why not? Hardegen and his brother U-boat captains had been sinking American merchant ships virtually unopposed since December. Sooner or later, the U.S. Navy would reach a breaking point, and things would grow considerably more difficult. Turner's submarine was already an example of that. A new and improved fleet boat that was bigger, faster and more powerful than anything anyone else in the world had. And that Turner was out there hunting the *Mortimer Blanch* was indisputable in Hardegen's mind.

Even Brechman's trap, should Turner be alone, was not fool-proof. Turner could handle two ships if he had to. He had the weaponry to do it. Yes, it was shallow close to shore, and yes, the *Blanch* could act as a second destroyer… but that wasn't a guaranteed win by any means. Hardegen himself could do very little unless *Bull Shark* was on the surface or at periscope depth. He could fire torpedoes or his deck gun, but he was just as vulnerable to Turner as Turner was to him.

Hardegen's true job was to sit quietly and deliver the coup de gras if possible. Shoot at Turner when his proverbial back was turned, and he was distracted by the two surface ships. Yet Hardegen would not underestimate his opponent.

So he waited. He hovered silently with his boat's cycloptic eye peeping above the surface and her sensitive ears straining to hear what was below.

Not more than fifteen miles to the southwest of U-123, the *Bull Shark* also hung motionless in the water. She was a bit higher in the water column, allowing her powerful SJ radar head to stay above the surface, as well as giving her periscope a height of more than twenty feet. All of her senses were on full alert; electronic ears straining, electronic eyes searching and her captain's human eye scanning a horizon nine miles in radius.

Arthur Turner knew his adversaries were out there. Sooner or later, the surface ships would make their appearance. If he guessed right, the small destroyer would be the first. She'd appear from the west or the east, coming in from the south to block *Bull Shark's* retreat in that direction. The big freighter would be doing the same in the north. Turner also knew, knew without question, that U-123 and Reinhardt

Hardegen, the captain Michner had told him about, would be waiting patiently below the surface somewhere to the east.

Turner also knew that the British destroyer wouldn't arrive in time. She was still five or six hours distant, and this engagement would be over in an hour, one way or another. That's how these things went. Neither side had a particularly overwhelming advantage.

The small destroyer with only twenty-four depth charges couldn't pin *Bull Shark* down for long. Even if the big freighter joined in, it wasn't nearly as fast or maneuverable as the tin can. The U-boat was only effective against the American submarine on the surface.

On the other side of things, a single squadron of torpedo bombers would probably not be enough to do much unless they were very lucky. Four torpedoes fired from the air against two ships had a low chance of sinking either one, let alone both. Even at Pearl Harbor, with hundreds of torpedo bombers firing against moored ships, the sink rate versus the number of Japanese weapons released was remarkably low. What Turner hoped for most is that the aircraft would harass the surface ships enough and distract them enough to give him time to set up for more effective torpedo shots.

No matter what, though, Turner felt that both sides were in for a knock-down, drag-out fight. The worst part was the waiting. He had to sit there and wait for one of his enemies to show up before he could go on the offensive.

Or did he?

They were waiting for him to charge in and theoretically rescue his wife… so would they act before he showed up? Was U-123 the signalman that would report *Bull Shark's* presence and get the other two assets in motion? If so, then would anything happen if Turner didn't move?

Everything was ready, but could Turner improve the odds and force the issue in a way that would best suit himself? He thought about his boat and her readiness for a long moment.

All ten tubes were loaded, as they always were. All ten doors were open so that if he needed to do some high-speed maneuvers, it wouldn't prevent that later on. He had a full reload for the after tubes, a full reload in the forward room, plus another four fish. Andy Post was set up in the after room, Joe Dutch as damage control officer in the crew's mess.

That made Turner frown. One of Dutch's best assets was his exceptional hearing and expertise with the sonar gear. Chet Rivers was good, but Turner would like to have Dutch in the conning tower backstopping him rather than wasting his talents as DCO. After this mission, Turner would make sure that he had a full complement of officers.

He had Frank Nichols in the control room as diving officer. Williams was there with his plotting party, and he had Pat Jarvis at the TDC in the control room with him. Everybody was where they were supposed to be. Even Joan was up here with him, acting as periscope assistant. He'd showed her how to operate the remote-control box for both scopes and how to read a bearing off the ring when he asked. It was either that or make her sit in his stateroom or at the radio console. It was being manned at the moment, just in case. She'd insisted that if he were going to drag her into a submarine battle that she'd feel better doing something useful.

If things got bad, he'd send her below and back with Dutch and Hoffman. For the moment, though, she was near him and attentive, and that somehow made him feel better. Highly irregular, but as most men who served aboard submarines had already, or would come to learn, irregular was their stock in trade.

"Pat, take over for a few minutes," Turner said. "Joanie, you keep an eye on these boys for me."

Turner dropped down the ladder with the sound of chuckling following him. He stepped up to Paul Rogers, who stood at the manifold control station with Nichols.

"Buck, walk with me a minute," Turner said and led him through the forward hatch and into officer's country. They stepped into the wardroom.

"What's up, sir?" The COB asked.

"I'm trying to figure that now…" Turner said. "We're about to get into a real scrap here… what's your assessment of our torpedo gangs?"

Rogers frowned, "Murph and Sparky are just about the best room leaders we could ask for."

"Yeah…" Turner said, "but a sculptor is only as good as his stone, Buck. What about the men? So far, they haven't had too much to do. No fast reloads, no combat reloads, nothing too hairy."

Rogers sighed and tapped his chin thoughtfully, "I think they're decent. Murph can handle his men okay, and between Sparky and Perkins, they can get their guys to do just about anything."

"Okay," Turner said, "because I've got a bit of a tall order for both Murph and Sparky. I thought about pulling them both up here and delivering it in person, but I think maybe it's better coming from you."

Rogers nodded. He understood the wisdom of it. If the captain was going to ask for special exertion, then Sparks and Murphy would feel more comfortable bitching about it or even discussing its merits with another enlisted man.

"I want to start reloading as soon as we shoot," Turner explained. "As soon as a fish is fired, I want a new one being shoved into that tube. I want to be able to fire every torpedo this boat has if necessary. I figure that, at the very least, this'll greatly decrease reload times and we won't have to wait so long for the next batch. Our lives may depend on it."

Rogers drew in a breath and smiled thinly, "That's a tall order all right. You know how it is in a torpedo room, Skipper. Firing and reloading at the same time will be like a damned ballet."

Turner grinned, "Yeah… that's why I want you to tell them."

Rogers chuckled, "Oh sure… it's always the messenger who eats it."

Turner laughed, "Nah… but I know how Sparky is, at least. He'll be cursing me up and down, so better you hear it than me. Gives him freedom to damn me. Murph's a little more level-headed, but he'll be displeased as well."

Rogers chuckled, "True enough. I think they can do it, though. Those fish have been routine plenty of times by now, so the guys are used to the activity."

"Good, Buck," Turner said. "Tell Sparky first and then Murph. Tell both of them they can have anybody they want from whatever department they want for reload crews. Then get back to the control room. I'm about to do something stupid, and I'm gonna wait till you're back at the manifold."

"Oh, hell…" Rogers groaned.

"My thoughts exactly," Turner said.

"He wants to do *what?*" Walter "Sparky" Sparks exclaimed. "Buck, you gotta be shittin' me, right?"

"Nope," Buck said, clapping Sparky on the shoulder and exchanging a knowing look with Perkins. "Skipper wants to reload each fish as soon as they leave the tubes."

"These guys ain't used to that kind of action, COB!" Sparky grumbled. "You know how many it takes just to reload a single fuckin' tube at a time? Now we gotta shoot, adjust and reload all at once? Shit on a goddamned shingle, is this Old Man crazy or what?"

"You know better," Rogers said. "He's aggressive and that's what we need nowadays. Besides, what're you bitchin' about? You got Fritzy again."

Schwimmer grinned from his station along one of the torpedo racks.

Sparky sighed, "Hell…"

"Can you *do* it, Sparky?" Rogers asked. "That's what I need to know. I need to be able to go back to the Old Man and tell him you're on board and that you've got his back on this."

"Course I can do it," Sparky groused. "This is the best fuckin' room in the Navy, I'll stake my reputation on that. But this is a lot to ask of new boys, COB."

"We're at war, Sparky," Rogers said, "and you know what war is."

"Hell," Perkins added. "Which is what it'll be like up here when we're doing this dance."

"Could be worse," Rogers quipped, "you could be in the after room. Lot less room to work back there."

Walter Murphy's reaction was far more reserved but a bit grimmer. The room to rig and load torpedoes while working with those already loaded was much more limited. However, like Sparks, Murph was not one to turn down a challenge.

When Rogers arrived in the control room, he reported that both rooms were ready and eager to comply. That got a laugh from everyone that heard him.

"Very well… here we go," Turner said, drawing in a breath. "Prepare to drop our pants…"

27

There was hardly a sound aboard U-123. That's why when the faint high-pitched whine was heard and began to grow louder, it was a surprise. When the sound rapidly increased and gonged off the hull, Yohan Verschmidt, who was listening intently at his sonar gear, turned to his captain with a startled expression.

"We've been pinged, Yohan?" Hardegen asked calmly with a wry smile.

"Yes sir!" Verschmidt replied. "I believe… I believe it was from a submarine's sound head, sir."

Hardegen nodded, "Can you pinpoint the direction from which it came?"

The young sonar officer frowned, "No sir… it was a single ping only. Very powerful, but only one… However, if I had to guess, it came from the southwest."

Hardegen nodded again, "It could be the *Dolch*… but somehow I think not. I believe our adversary has just slapped us in the face with the cuff of his glove. Bring us to radio depth, Einsvo. Inform the *Blanch* of this. As the great Sherlock Holmes would say, 'The game is afoot.'"

"Yes sir, a single ping from a submerged vessel," the sonarman aboard the light Zerstrorer *Dolch* said, turning away from his console and pushing his headphones back.

Adolph Fousch paced the confined space of the ship's combined combat information center and navigation bridge. He turned to the enlisted man, "U-123?"

The pudgy sailor shook his head in the negative, "I don't think so, mein Herr… it seems to have come from the east, southeast, although I can't be sure. Is not the U-123 to our north and east somewhat?"

Fousch nodded, "It is… what was the range?"

The young man scowled and thought, "With a single ping, it's hard to say, sir… I'd guess that it was less than twenty-thousand meters."

Fousch tapped his chin and his eyes lit up in triumph, "The American! He's testing the waters… seeing if anyone is about before he runs inshore. Foolish. Do you think he got a return from us?"

The sonarman shook his head, "Doubtful, at that range. If so, it wouldn't register as much. We could be anything from a merchant vessel to a fishing boat to a large rock as far as he knows."

Fousch chuckled, "Then he's played his hand too early… not that it matters. Radio, send a brief update to *Blanch*. Also, tell them that we're moving in. Pilot, come to course one-one-zero. All ahead full. Sound battle stations depth charge. Man the deck guns. It is time we closed the net."

"Well, that's rung the dinner bell," Pat Jarvis stated wryly.

"What…?" Turner asked innocently. "You mean sending out a loud and powerful sonic pulse to our enemies might have given us away? Gee, Pat… wish you'd said something *before*…"

Everyone in the conning tower laughed uproariously. Laughter drifted up through the open deck hatch from the control room as well. Joan simply rolled her eyes and shook her head as she chuckled.

"All right, the jig is up," Turner announced. "Time to take off the kid gloves. Any return on that pulse, Rivers?"

Rivers was clutching his headphones and staring at the magic eye adjusting knobs, "Maybe, sir... something at extreme range, maybe twenty-thousand yards. No idea what, but something out there... I think, though I can't be certain, that maybe there was something to the northeast, too. But I'd need to send a directed pulse at each return to get a better idea and fix."

Turner shrugged, "I've got a pretty good idea of who and what they are. Helm, all ahead two-thirds. Come left to course two-seven-zero. Pat, standby on the TDC. If I'm right, then we're going after the tin can first. I'm going to send at least four fish their way. It's starting to get light up top, so we should be able to get a visual on him. Order of tubes might depend on where he is, but I want to shoot the top four from port to starboard back and forth, so one, two, three, four. If we miss, which is a pretty good chance, considering his size and maneuverability, then I want tubes seven and eight ready to fire too. Frank, bring us down to periscope depth."

"Periscope depth!" Nichols called from below.

The boat was finally moving after nearly an hour of sitting dead in the water. The tension, which had been mounting for hours now, was broken, although being replaced by a different kind of tension. The waiting was over, but now the submarine was going head-to-head with her natural enemy, the destroyer.

Bull Shark was on battery power only now. They'd started with a full charge, and the last hour of hanging and doing nothing had hardly tapped their reserves. Yet that could change fast. Unless his first spread hit, Turner would have to dive and be subject to a depth charging, which could last hours, even with only a few dozen charges if properly used. It would certainly give the other two vessels time to get into the fray and make their lives considerably more complicated.

"Contact!" Rivers all but yelled. "Light, fast screws, bearing zero-one-five. Range... sixteen thousand yards... assess twenty-five knots. Sounds like that tin can we met up north, skipper!"

Turner reached out and took his wife's hand. He could hardly believe he was taking his submarine into battle with Joan at his side. He'd never have seen that coming in a million years.

"Up attack scope," Turner ordered.

Joan hit the proper button and the slim attack periscope began to rise from its well. Turner reached down and snapped the handles horizontal, and Joan hit the stop button when the eyepiece was just right. He grinned at her and peered through.

The sky was no longer black, but a deep indigo ahead of them, and even lighter astern. Turner slowly scanned a complete circle before settling his scope just to the right of the bow. He should see the destroyer at about eight thousand yards, perhaps seven. Maybe eight minutes or so. Eight very long minutes.

"This will probably be damned near a down-the-throat shot, Pat," Turner said. "I want a narrow spread, no more than three degrees minus and plus. Set gyro on tube two to three-five-seven and tube one to zero-zero-three. Tubes three and four at zero."

Jarvis began working the TDC. Turner could hear the computer whirring and clicking behind him, and the sound was somehow comforting.

Then she was there. Just a hint of something dark and blocky above the calm surface, then it began to grow larger and more distinct. Soon, it was the battleship gray superstructure of a low-slung ship, then the sharp bow complete with a bone in the teeth. The tin can was headed almost but not quite straight for them.

"There she is!" Turner shouted. "Standby... want to shoot close or she'll turn out of the torpedo paths... Frank, get ready on the planes, I'm gonna order a dive as soon as we shoot..."

Now the battle tension was thick in the room. It hung like a heavy fog, almost choking the people crammed inside the conning tower. Mug Vigliano at the wheel, Balkley at radar, Rivers at sonar, Hotrod Hernandez at the DRT, Pat Jarvis at the TDC. He at the scope and Joan standing in front of him watching the bearing ring intently. They all waited, almost forgetting to breathe.

"Okay, here we go... target bearing... mark!"

"Zero-one-five!" Joan exclaimed.

Pat cranked that in.

"Angle on the bow is zero-one-five starboard," Turner said. "Range to target... three-zero-zero-zero yards, repeat three thousand yards!"

"Active sonar beams! Rivers announced just as a distorted pinging started echoing eerily through the hull. Then a gong and another and another, growing more and more frequent.

"He's on us!" Rivers said.

In the scope, the two forward five-inch deck guns aboard the tin can flashed out. Turner gripped the handles of the scope hard. "He's seen our scope, too. Mug, all ahead flank! Come on, Pat!"

"I've got a solution! Shoot anytime, sir!" Jarvis exclaimed.

Turner studied the ship through the scope and tried to estimate her range with the stadimeter. It was difficult, as the ship didn't match any known configuration. She appeared two thousand yards away, but that could be misleading. From the detail he could see, she looked closer.

"Shit!" he cranked. "To hell with it... fire one! Fire two! Fire three... fire four! Down scope! Dive, dive, dive! Frank, take us to one hundred feet."

"A hundred?" Somebody gulped from below.

"One hundred feet, aye!" Nichols called.

"Chet, give Pat generated bearings on that asshole's pings! If you don't have enough data, ping him yourself!" Turner said. "Pat, we're going to shoot astern next."

"All four fish fired electrically! sir!" Jarvis reported.

"Fish running hot straight and normal!" Rivers chimed in.

Now the pinging and gonging of the active sonar beams was accompanied by the chugging of the destroyer's screws. It grew louder very rapidly, as did the frequency of the sonar outputs.

Whoosh, whoosh, whoosh, whoosh...

"Here she comes!" Rivers said.

"Sir, any orders?" Vigliano asked, daring to look over his shoulder at his captain.

"No, Mug, we're gonna go right under his goddamned keel!" Turner said sternly.

At their combined speed of almost thirty-three knots, the two ships were closing the space between them fast. Any second now, they'd know if their torpedoes would find their marks.

"Torpedoes in the water!" A lookout cried from the starboard bridge wing. Fousch ran to peer through the forward viewports. He could see the bubble trails now that the sun was only ten minutes or less from rising. Four fingers of doom, the rightmost just a little ahead of the leftmost and… and two in the center trailing behind but staying closer together.

"He's trying to bracket us," Fousch said contemptuously. There was nearly a minute to go, even at a combined closing rate between the destroyer and the torpedoes of just over eighty knots. Fousch could see that the outermost torpedoes were widening the gap between themselves and their inner fellows ever so slightly.

"Helm! Reduce speed to two-thirds, give me ten degrees of right rudder now!" Fousch ordered.

The destroyer shed speed and heeled slightly to starboard as she turned toward the rightmost eel.

Fousch grinned, "Not bad, Turner, but you're going to have to do better than that!"

"Contact!" the radar operator bawled. "Multiple aircraft… coming in high, bearing two-five-zero!"

Fousch gritted his teeth and felt a surge of admiration and frustration. So the Americans weren't going to make it easy after all. So be it, "Cancel battle station guns, get the men to the anti-aircraft emplacements! Helm, full left rudder, now!"

Aboard the *Mortimer Blanch,* which was now running southeast by south at fifteen knots, alarms were blaring. Their radar had picked up four incoming airplanes approaching from the northwest. This was not long after they'd received the radio report from both the *Dolch* and the U-123 about the sonar ping.

Brechman stood beside Diedrich on the bridge, watching as men scrambled along the upper main deck. They were uncovering hatches on the deck that revealed anti-aircraft cannons. These were hoisted by electric motors to the level of the upper deck. Six of these in all. In addition, between these guns and along the deck around the bridge, fifty caliber machine guns were being set up on special stanchions. Each had a gunner and another man to serve ammunition. Together, these six cannons and ten fifty-cals would throw up a considerable barrier of flak, as well as a deadly offensive attack on the incoming aircraft.

Behind the bridge, the open upper deck, which was normally used as a lounge, was being retracted to reveal a Y-gun and two racks of depth charges to be loaded into it. In a matter of minutes, the passive cargo ship had become an effective combat vessel.

Brechman laughed when he heard the report of four airplanes. Only four! Diedrich thought they were probably torpedo bombers. Four torpedoes, which could be avoided. Brechman rubbed his hands together again.

"Just another example of American lack of preparation," he said to the ship's captain. "It will cost them Turner and his submarine, and it will cost them this *war*, Curt!"

———

"*There's the big boy!*" Manzor announced over the now hands-free radio channel. "*Freighter running southward with a bone in her teeth, Mayflower one! Port wing!*"

"Roger that, Mayflower two," Taylor replied. "We've only got four fish here, so let's make them count. Let's also guess they've got AA guns on that thing, boys, so watch for tracers! Mayflower three, you're on my six. We go in in-line, drop our fish and break hard left. Mayflower two, you go in with four same deal."

"*What about the destroyer that's supposed to be to the south?*" Mayflower four asked.

"We'll strafe them a few times," Taylor replied. "Okay, Pete, stick to my six o'clock like glue... here we go!"

Taylor shoved his throttle to the stop and the big radial engine roared like a thoroughbred. In a matter of seconds the aircraft had accelerated to two-hundred and fifty knots, and he angled her down, driving toward the freighter at a shallow incline. He glanced over his shoulder and saw Pete Long's Avenger no more than two plane lengths behind him. Taylor grinned.

"Tracers!" Fetch shouted from behind Taylor.

Taylor saw them, of course, bright lines of death shooting toward him from the ever-lightening eastern sky. They were high as yet, but coming closer rapidly.

As they did, Taylor shoved the stick forward and dove his bomber in a steep descent that took him from six-thousand feet to fifty in a gut-churningly short amount of time. Before them, the black hull of the freighter appeared startlingly close.

"Release, release, release!"" Taylor shouted.

The plane jolted as the two-thousand-pound torpedo unlatched and the aircraft, suddenly much lighter, tried to buck upward on the pilot.

Taylor went with it, however, arcing his plane up and to the left in a sharp turn that drove them upward. He angled the wings to present a narrower profile to the ship as he climbed and turned away from the hail of tracer fire that seemed to reach out for his bird with a ravenous hunger.

"Pete's dropped!" Fetch reported, half-turned in his seat. "Looks like two good fish!"

"Go, Mayflower two," Taylor ordered as he steered his straining aircraft out of gun range.

In his rearview mirror, Taylor saw a brilliant flash. He risked a look over his shoulder and felt his stomach lurch.

Pete Long's bird was further behind him now but making the same maneuver. As he climbed away from the ship, several rounds had struck his port wing and it had exploded. The plane, now unbalanced with only one wing, had gone into a mortal spiral, rolling over and over as it dropped toward the sea. Out of the corner of his eye, Taylor saw the aircraft smash into the water in an explosion of foam.

"Christ..." he breathed, fighting back tears and fighting the urge to turn back and open up on the decks of the cargo ship with his nose and wing cannons.

Taylor's plane had reached ten thousand, and he leveled off and began a wide circle to determine what effect the two runs had made. He saw the two remaining Avengers angling away from the ship and climbing toward him. Then he saw it. A bright flash and an upheaval of the sea along the freighter's starboard quarter.

"Hot *dog!*" Fetch bellowed in triumph. "One confirmed hit, and I can see… shit… Mayflower two and four's fish missed! One confirmed hit, though."

Taylor sighed, "All right, Mayflower flight, form up on me. Let's go see if we can't find us a tin can."

———

The whole ship seemed to rattle with the anti-aircraft gunfire. Diedrich and Brechman watched as the torpedo bombers split into two pairs, and the first pair dove toward them. They watched as the torpedoes slung under their bellies dropped into the sea and the two planes swooped up and away.

One of the gunners on the bow, one of the 20mm twin cannons, walked his tracers in a path that slowly but inexorably caught up with the trailing aircraft in the first sortie and blew off its wing, sending the plane into the sea.

"Helm, full left rudder!" Diedrich called out as the two torpedoes streaked through the water toward them. Even as the freighter began a ponderous turn to port, the other two planes swooped in low and released their weapons.

The first plane's torpedo went wide, passing just off the ship's starboard bow. The second one to be dropped, the one from the destroyed airplane, found its mark and slammed home along the ship's starboard side about a hundred feet from the stern.

Brechman was knocked off his feet and went sprawling across the deck to come to a painful stop against the pedestal of the radar operator's chair. He felt a sharp pain in his ribs, but it wasn't debilitating. Probably not broken. He managed to haul himself to his feet along with several other men on the bridge.

Brechman noted with a stab of irrational jealousy and anger that Diedrich had managed to keep his feet during the attack. The SS officer limped back over to his side.

"The final two torpedoes missed," Diedrich said calmly. "Are you all right?"

"Fine," Brechman said with an effort. "We didn't explode."

"No," Diedrich said, almost sounding smug. "Some leaking, but the inner armor held. We're still fully operational."

Brechman managed a smile, "Excellent! We took down one aircraft and they have no more torpedoes. Now we must continue on to assist the *Dolch*."

"We've had a report," Diedrich said. "The American submarine has fired on them, and they've already detected the three remaining aircraft."

Brechman scoffed, "Pitiful. I hope Hardegen is moving in as well. Within a matter of hours we'll finally have our quarry."

28

"No joy, sir…" Rivers announced angrily. "All fish ran past his bearing."

Turner gritted his teeth. Somehow the captain of the German destroyer had threaded the needle between his four fish and had avoided a collision. Not for the first time, Turner wished that there was a way for a torpedo to home in on the sound of a ship's screws or something.

"Where is he now?" Turner asked.

"Five hundred yards and closing in fast," Rivers said.

Turner narrowed his eyes, "Good… standby, Pat. And keep me updated about what we've got available in forward torpedo."

Up in the forward room, barely controlled chaos reigned. Tommy Perkins stood between the tubes, close enough to reach the manual firing switches. He was supervising the reload of the starboard tubes and Sparky the port.

As soon as tube one had fired, Sparks had activated the outer door control and the drain pump almost immediately. Water from tube one had been shunted down into the WRT tank, and he re-charged the impulse tank and got the inner door open even as the men on the tagle were lining up the next fish. Sparky guided the nose inside and helped them to heave, snatching the propeller guard off and giving the fish the final impetus it needed to go the last few inches on the rollers.

Even as he did that, he could see Perkins' team doing the same thing with tube two.

"Come on, come on!" Sparky bawled. "These fuckin' fish ain't gonna load themselves! Move, move, move!"

"Almost there!" Perkins said. "Another big heave… easy now… home!"

Sparky's fish was comfortably up against the stop bolt. He backed off on the tail stop, swung the breech door closed and adjusted it, "Get that goddamned tagle rigged on fish number nine, ya bunch of slack asses! This ain't no demonstration…"

Although Sparks was howling and swearing and even slapping men on the back, it was clear from the look in his eyes that this was what he lived for. The frenetic, almost out-of-control ballet that was a torpedo room in action.

Over their heads, the sound of the destroyer's screws was doomsday come at last.

Whoosh, whoosh, whoosh, whoosh, whoosh!

"Splashes!" Rivers shouted over the din of the screws only thirty feet or so over their heads and the frantic pinging of the enemy sonar. "Four!"

"Maintain course!" Turner exclaimed. "Joanie, hold on to something…"

Turner didn't even need Rivers' reports. The tin can was so close and so close overhead that he could track her with his ears alone. There seemed to be a long delay before the ocean erupted into a cacophony of roaring sound and fury.

The charges had gone off deep, however. And although they shook the submarine and forced her to twist along her course and rock fifteen degrees off center to port and starboard, they were far deeper than she was. The effect was mild compared to what it might have been.

"Where are they!" Fousch shouted. "Reduce to one-third."

The engines diminished once more, cutting the destroyer's speed and improving her sonar capability.

"Just coming astern of us, sir," the sonarman reported.

"What *depth,* dammit!" Fousch snapped.

"Thirty meters," the boy announced.

Fousch let fly a string of German invectives. Turner hadn't gone deep to avoid depth charges or to try and hide in a salt layer. He'd slipped under *Dolch's* keel. The reason was painfully obvious.

"He's going to fire at us from his after tubes," Fousch stated just as the four anti-aircraft guns mounted around the exterior of the bridge tower began to crackle.

"Hard right rudder," he ordered even as he ran to the port hatch to the bridge wing. "Flank speed!"

The ship's powerful turbo-charged engines whined, and her knife-like bow rose in the air as the twin screws propelled her faster through the water. Fousch had to cling to the hatch frame in order to keep from being thrown off his feet by the sudden pitch and then roll as the destroyer accelerated into her turn.

There were three airplanes, all spiraling in from several thousand feet and doing a good job, at least so far, of avoiding the tracers from his AA fire. Fousch shrugged. He couldn't worry much about them now.

"Continue the turn," Fousch ordered. "Find me that damned submarine!"

"Hard right rudder," Turner ordered. "Periscope depth! Up attack scope, Joanie!"

The submarine angled upward, and Turner snapped the handles down and spun around to face aft. There was a moment of fuzziness as the scope broke the surface and shed foamy water. He quickly rotated until he saw the destroyer off his starboard quarter. As he watched, anti-aircraft tracers lanced out from the bridge deck. The ship was close, no more than three hundred yards off. Turner took a second to rotate the right handle and angle the scope head up just in time to see three airplanes angle in toward the destroyer, their own cannons blazing.

"Ha!" he said. "Okay, he's close! Pat, we're gonna fire all four aft tubes; what the hell! Here's the numbers… bearing… mark!"

"One-five-five," Joan shouted.

"Range to target… six hundred yards," Turner said. "Angle on the bow is one-six-zero starboard! He's turning, Pat, so give me a five-degree spread. Make it snappy! Mug, bring us to all ahead one-third. Give me right standard rudder."

"Maneuvering answerin' all ahead one-third," Vigliano said tensely. "Sir, my helm is right standid!"

"Shoot!" Pat barked.

"Fire them all!" Turner shouted. "Shit, he's turning, Pat, fire them all!"

Jarvis pushed the plungers on his fire control board for tubes seven through ten. He pushed them one at a time, not giving the normal six-second intervals. The ship bucked and jolted as four fists of compressed air rammed six and a half tons of torpedo out of the boat's after end.

"All fired electrically!" Pat said. "Good fish, hot straight and normal!"

Even as he said it, Turner felt the stern rise dramatically. He cursed, "Shit, we're breaching! Mug, meet her! All ahead two-thirds. Frank, put us in the basement! Flood negative! Flood safety! Emergency deep. Four hundred feet and make it snappy!"

"Torpedoes in the water!" the bridge lookout screeched even as a hail of thirty-caliber cannon fire smashed into the ship's upper decks shattering viewports and killing half the men outside at their gun emplacements.

Three powerful airplane engines roared by overhead as Fousch collected his wits, "Where are the eels!"

"Starboard quarter!" the lookout replied almost in a panic. "Five hundred yards and closing fast! Spreading out."

"Helm, reverse your turn! Hard left rudder," Fousch snapped. "Sonar, find me that damned boat! Where the hell is the *Blanch!*"

"Incoming at fifteen knots," the radarman stated. "Range fourteen thousand meters."

Fousch pursed his lips, "Pursuit course on the submarine. Alert depth charge crews to start dropping as soon as I give the word! Get extra men on the anti-aircraft guns and tell them to shoot down those damned planes!"

———

Once relieved of the cumbersome burden of a torpedo or a two-thousand-pound bomb, the Avenger was a decent fighter plane. Not screaming fast, but highly maneuverable and sturdy. Charles Taylor banked his aircraft into a steep spiraling dive that brought his guns to bear on the bow of the odd light destroyer.

It was time for some payback. In his mind's eye, he could see Pete Long's plane bursting into a fireball and spiraling to a watery death. Now it was he and his squadron's turn to deliver a little hurt to the enemy.

He squeezed the trigger, and his two wing cannons rattled out as their thirty-caliber rounds found their marks, chewing up the decks and the gun crews as he strafed the destroyer. All too soon, only a matter of seconds, he was past and banking away to gain altitude and come in for another run. He saw over his shoulder as he turned and climbed that Mayflowers three and four had repeated his maneuver and were following him up.

"*Shit!*" Mayflower four barked out over the channel. "*We're hit, Mayflower one!*"

Taylor felt his belly churn again. Sure enough, the last plane in line was trailing a stream of dark smoke from its port wing. It didn't look fatal, but it most likely meant fuel was being lost at best.

"What's your status, Mayflower four?" Taylor asked.

"*Leakin' fuel, Chuck,*" Tony Bonnerly reported glumly. "*We're still air-worthy, but we're definitely losing gas. Oil pressure is dropping a little, too."*

Taylor cursed. Why the hell didn't he have more planes? There should've been a dozen birds out here on this mission!

"Can you make NAS Miami?" Taylor asked. "Or Maybe Key West?"

There was a long pause. Taylor continued to climb and increase the range between his fighter wing and the target. Finally, Bonnerly came back on.

"I think so, Skipper. Think Miami is closer. We're gonna have to go for it. Sorry to leave you in the lurch."

Taylor sighed softly, "No need for that, Tony. Good work and good luck."

Bonnerly's plane climbed up to ten thousand and made a wide turn north. Now they were two, and on the horizon, less than ten miles away now, was the big freighter. Apparently the one torpedo that had struck her hadn't even slowed her down.

"Splashes!" Rivers exclaimed.

"Rig for depth charge," Turner ordered. "Stop ventilation, close compartment hatches. Order silent running throughout the ship. Give me a fathometer reading, Chet."

"Plenty of water, sir," Rivers reported. "A thousand feet out here."

The needle on the depth gauge over the helm station slowly moved toward larger numbers, but not fast enough for Turner's liking. They were only at three hundred feet and...

Boooom! Booom! Booom-booom!

Bull Shark was struck by the hand of an angry giant. The ship twisted, pitched and rolled like a toy boat in a bathtub. Light bulbs shattered, cork insulation flew like ice crystals in a blizzard and men were tossed like rag dolls.

Turner found himself on deck partly beneath Pat Jarvis' seat at the TDC. Only a single light remained unshattered in the conning tower and cast the compartment in a ghastly contrast of blackness and pale illumination. There were groans and moans as the men tried to regain their wits.

"Everybody okay?" Turner asked. "Joanie?"

Joan was already on her feet, helping Balkley get back to his radar console, "Here, Art. Ted has a nasty cut over his eye, though."

"There's a first aid kit up here," Turner said. "On the port bulkhead there. Can you slap a bandage on for him?"

"Sure," Joan said, sounding remarkably collected. A lot more collected than her husband felt.

"Now passing three-fifty, sir, Mug Vigliano reported.

"Left full rudder," Turner ordered.

Ping, ping, ping…

"Oh, Christ, here they come again," Rivers grumbled.

Silence… waiting… tension straining the nerves…

Click, click, click, click…

Once again, the world exploded around them as two thousand pounds of high explosives shattered the sea, temporarily forcing water away, only for it to come rushing back with tremendous force. A force that punished the fragile steel tube caught in the middle. Again the ship was battered about, and her thin steel hull groaned, and her rigid framework shrieked in protest. More insulation rained down, more bulbs shattered, and more men were tossed about.

Whoosh, whoosh, whoosh, whoosh went the light, fast screws of the hunter above. Then there was another sound and another sound beam that joined the already nerve-jarring pinging and gonging of the tin can's sonar.

"Heavy, slow screws, sir," Rivers croaked. "Large surface vessel coming into range… more splashes."

"Oh Jesus Christ…" somebody moaned in the darkness.

The only light in the conning tower now was from that generated by lighted gauges, console displays and indicator lights.

"Get me a battle lantern up here," Turner called down the hatch. "Mug, reverse your turn. Make me a knuckle in the water. Increase speed to four knots."

"Here comes the big boy!" Rivers exclaimed. "More splashes… two, four… six… no *ten!* Oh God… it's gonna be bad!"

Choom, choom, choom, choom!

"Frank, get us down to five hundred!" Turner shouted. "Find me a goddamned halocline!"

The submarine dipped again, driving her twenty-six hundred tons of submerged weight deeper into the crushing embrace of the ocean depths. The pressure passed two hundred PSI. Almost five hundred feet and more than fourteen tons of water pushing on every square foot of the submarine.

Then came another series of thundering booms that seemed to fill the universe with the sound of pure madness.

In the after torpedo room, the sweating gang had just opened the inner door to tube ten to load the last fish when the depth charge assault began. The lights shattered and the entire fabric of the ship seemed to shriek in agony as she twisted and bucked, tossing men and gear to and fro with indifferent abandon.

Post had the wherewithal to have already lighted three battle lanterns, so he, Murph and the entire crew had no trouble seeing what happened next.

The breech door to number ten swung back and forth on its hinges and suddenly blew back, pushed aside by a twenty-one-inch gout of seawater that shot into the room like a firehose. The battering ram of cold seawater struck Percy Tormolin, torpedoman first-class, rocketing him all the way to the forward bulkhead where he struck with bone-crushing force, the back of his head crunching inward on a flange and leaving a slick trail of gore and brain matter as his body slid to the deck.

"Oh Jesus…! Oh, sweet Jesus…!" Post gulped, almost paralyzed with horror as he saw Tormolin's body fly across the room and then the pressure reading on the depth gauge between the tubes. "The outer door must've given way! We're at five hundred feet!"

By a miracle, the torpedo that had been readied in the slings and hooked onto the tagle had not yet been lined up with the breech. Had that water struck the nose cone of the fish, it might have set off the six-hundred and fifty pounds of Torpex. That would certainly have killed everyone in the room, probably vented the compartment to the sea, and might have even set off the three warheads already in tubes seven, eight and nine.

"Somebody report we got a leak back here!" Post shouted and then realized, almost comically, that it was he who was wearing the sound-powered telephone set for the room. He cursed. "Damage control, after room. We've suffered a casualty. We've got an outer door breach and water coming in through the inner door of tube ten!"

"*Can you get the door closed?*" Dutch asked. "*Anybody hurt?*"

Post looked at the body of Tormolin and the ghoulish red streak on the bulkhead, and that was forming around his head on the deck. The young officer had to fight to keep his bile from overflowing. "One death, no other injuries other than bruises and scrapes from the depth charges, Joe."

"*Do what you can,*" Dutch said tersely. "*Dump some high-pressure air into the compartment to counteract the pressure and then force that inner door shut.*"

"Aye-aye…" Post breathed, feeling dizzy, cold and useless. Here was yet another scenario in which his mind seemed to be betraying him. What to do? How to resolve the situation quickly… he was the officer and the men needed him… "Murph—"

"Yeah, I heard, sir," Murphy replied. "Smitty, bleed some air in here, quick. Much as you can!"

Post stared around him dumbly, his mind unable to process the chaos of the sights, sounds and smells that bombarded his senses. Bright light cast black shadows all around. Men were shouting at each other, tripping over themselves and tumbled gear and clothing and getting their feet wet as water rose over the gratings from the lower section of the compartment…

Water… it roared into the compartment like a runaway freight train… so *loud*… so hard to *think*…

Diesel oil, men's sweat and something coppery assailed Post's nostrils. The groaning of the ship's hull, the roaring of the fire hydrant-like torrent of seawater that shot horizontally into the room. It was all too much... too much...

"Sir!" Murph shouted into Post's face, and then something hard smacked into the young man's cheek. Murphy had slapped him. "Sir, you all right?"

Post blinked, his eyes focused and he swallowed hard, "Yeah... yeah, I'm good, Murph... yeah... Murph, we gotta get that door closed! Can we rig the tagle to the door and force it?"

Murph grinned, "Just what I was thinking! Taggart, get me a block and tackle. Mr. Post, can you unhook the tagle from that fish?"

Post nodded, suddenly feeling confident. Suddenly feeling that now that there was a plan, a path to tread, his mind was operating again, "Roger that!"

"Just watch that stream, sir, watch it everybody!" Murph shouted. "It'll peel the flesh right off your bones. Smitty, where's my fuckin' air!"

Another sound, a hissing. After a moment or two, the cartoonishly straight stream of water seemed to slow ever so slightly. The men jumped to work. They only had a matter of minutes to unhook the tailing tackle, attach it to a block rigged to a dead eye on the bulkhead near the open door and then to attach a line from that to the open breech door. Then they'd haul it closed against the pressure and use brute strength to lock it down.

"What's your report, Dutch?"

Joe Dutch stood in the center of the crew's mess. Two battle lanterns had been rigged and hung from the overhead. They cast enough light for him to see Hoffman working on two men who were stretched out on mess tables. One had a head wound and the other a lacerated and broken leg.

"After room has a bad casualty, sir," Dutch reported. "Outer door on number ten blown and inner door flooding. They're piping in high-pressure air and trying to get the door closed. Forward room reports some minor flooding. So far, most injuries are minor, with a few needing stitches and bones set. Tormolin, in the after room, is dead, sir."

A pause, "*Very well… keep me posted on that leak, Joe. We may have to go deeper. There's two of them up there dropping ash cans on us.*"

"God help us all…" Dutch muttered just as half a dozen more charges ripped the universe open around their ship.

29

Six thousand meters away from the two surface ships, the U-123 moved slowly ahead at radio depth. At that depth, Hardegen's attack scope head was more than six meters above the surface of the sea, now becoming tumultuous from the crisscrossing wakes of the two surface ships. He could see the battle clearly, and young Verschmidt could hear it with equal clarity through his headphones.

The *Mortimer Blanch* had now joined the destroyer, the bigger ship moving in a circle around where *Bull Shark* must be. The faster and more nimble Zerstrorer was weaving a course that took her in and through the circle of the freighter's wake. Verschmidt had the sonar loudspeaker plugged in, and everyone in control could hear the pings and the booms of sonar beams and depth charges.

Hardegen cringed inwardly. He could feel empathy for the American crew. The Kriegsmarine captain knew what it was to be on the receiving end of a depth charge attack. When the whole world seemed to be turning inside out, and it could go on for hours and hours. It was incredible that the human frame or the human mind could stand it. Hardegen knew that some couldn't, as well.

Overhead, the two remaining torpedo bombers now fighters circled, occasionally swooping in and peppering the two ships with machine-gun fire. They were no real threat, more of a pest than anything. With the *Blanch's* heavy anti-aircraft capability, the planes couldn't get close for long and were doing little if any damage.

They were a distraction, however. They were making a nuisance of themselves and forcing the two ships to waste attention and ammunition on them. Not for the first time, Reinhard Hardegen admired the American capacity for courage and tenacity. They were truly an intractable enemy.

However, he also felt great frustration. There was little or nothing he could do to assist in the battle at that time. He could, if he so chose, surface and use his single AA gun to harass the Avengers overhead, yet that would probably do little good and expose his ship to both their fire as well as make him a torpedo target.

While the big freighter and even the smaller destroyer could absorb considerable fire from the airplanes, the fragile submarine could not. It wouldn't take many good hits on the pressure hull to make it impossible for U-123 to dive. Then her crew would certainly be in mortal danger. If the aircraft posed a real threat or distraction, perhaps Hardegen would do it anyway. That not being the case, his best move for the moment was to sit tight and wait for his opportunity. To do what a submarine did best… watch, wait and listen.

"Increase to all ahead one-third," Hardegen said tersely. "Let us move in closer, Einsvo."

Hymen Richter grinned his wolfish grin. The man loved a good fight, especially an unfair one. Like it or not, that was also what submarines did best. Sneak up on the enemy and smash the backs of their skulls in.

"Okay, we're hooked on!" Post shouted over the roaring water and tried to ignore the fact that it was over his ankles, which meant it was eight feet deep in the compartment and rising over the platform deck.

"Good to go here!" Murph said. "Okay, boys, heave for all you're worth!"

Post and the three men around him began to haul on the tagle, the tailing tackle that was usually used to haul a torpedo onto the rollers and into the tube. Murph stood by with a length of pipe, ready to wedge it in behind the breach door and help lever it closed against the high-pressure water.

"Walk away with it now!" Murph encouraged. "Heave, you bastards!" As Andy watched, the breech door began to move, slowly closing across the stream of water and causing it to spray in all directions.

"She's going!" Murph shouted in triumph. "Keep at it, boys! Just another six inches…"

"Yeah, yeah…" torpedoman Johny Wecksler wheezed, "sound just like my old lady, Murph…"

Post and his party were leaning back, their sandals barely gripping the textured decking. Smitty, a burly kid from Boston, found a hand-hold on the tagle line and threw his muscle and weight into it.

"Come on!" Murph shouted. "Almost there…"

He rammed his wedge home, heaved around and the water ceased to flow. Another man, Post couldn't see who for the water now in his eyes, spun the locking wheel and the tension was relieved. A whoop of delight and triumph went up from the men.

Post let go of the line and spoke into his phone, "Damage control, after room! Breech is secure. We've got a lot of water back here, but the leak is stopped."

Turner grinned in the dark. No one had yet to pass up a battle lantern, everyone in the control room being a bit busy at the moment. Nichols and Rogers and the bow and stern planesmen were doing a high wire act to keep the boat level and under control. With so much water in the after torpedo room, the ship was now several dozen tons heavier by the stern and it was taking all they had to keep her level, especially with the hydraulic power cut.

"Splashes!" Rivers announced, his voice carrying with it a flat and numb quality now.

"Mug, all ahead two-thirds," Turner ordered. "Come right to three-zero-zero."

He reached out and found Joan's hands, both of which were clutching the attack scope for support. He squeezed them and then slid down the hatch into the control room.

It was chaos down there. The two men at the planes were having to lean their weight on the wheels just to maintain their angles. Buck Rogers was clinging to the manifold controls, venting and blowing the variable ballast to try and keep the ship on an even keel. Elmer Williams looked haggard, and his boyish face was coated with sweat. The temperature gauge already read over ninety, and the humidity was at eighty-five percent.

"They've got us pinned, Skipper," Williams stated, wiping at his face with a damp towel that hung around his neck. "We can't get clean away at these slow speeds. Plus, there's water in after torpedo and some leaking in forward and into battery one."

Turner nodded grimly, "We've got to go deeper."

Frank Nichols turned to him with a grim and sour expression on his face, "Sir, we're already past test depth. And we're at least… ten to fifteen percent heavier. I've already had to blow negative and the safety tanks."

"Understood, "Turner said. "Take us down to six hundred, Frank. Elmer, when those charges go off, which should happen any second, run the drain pump. Let's see how much we can get out while the noise is going on."

Above them, close but not as close as the previous time, multiple explosions roiled the sea. Again, the ship shuddered, shook and weeble-wobbled, sending men to the decks. Turner himself cracked his head against one of the posts that held the diving plane operators' bench and saw stars in his vision. He thought he heard Williams shouting that the drain pump was online but couldn't be sure.

"Full down on the bow, full rise on stern!" Frank Nichols shouted at the planesmen.

"Trying, sir!" Tank Broderick, who had the stern position, groaned. "Stern planes are jammed…"

Turner hauled himself to his feet, placed both hands on the wheel below Tank's and crouched, bracing his arms and legs and then pushed upward, putting all his strength and weight into shoving the wheel. It began to move, slowly at first but a little more smoothly.

"That's got it, sir!" Tank said gratefully. "I can hold her now."

Turner patted the man on his heavy shoulder and stumbled back to the ladderway. There was a little light in control, and he looked up to see that the stylus on the bathythermograph was beginning to trace an erratic pattern on the smoked card.

"I'll be damned!" Turner almost shouted. "Found a layer! Keep us at six hundred, Frank. Elmer, secure the pump until the next barrage."

Turner reached up and clutched the rungs of the ladder and drew in a deep breath. They'd only been submerged for a little over two hours, but already the oxygen content in the air was decreasing noticeably. They'd spent some time closed up before the battle too, and it was beginning to tell.

Men had to inhale a bit more deeply. The heat and moisture in the air wasn't helping either.

Turner paused just before climbing. Something was wrong. He couldn't put his finger on what exactly until he inhaled again. There was a strange smell in the air. Very faint, hardly noticeable unless you were paying attention… but he recognized it immediately. It was the smell of a swimming pool in summertime.

Chlorine gas.

"Does anybody else—" he began to ask just as a high-pitched gas alarm began to squeal in control.

"Chlorine gas alarm, sir!" Williams announced. "Seawater must be getting onto battery one's contacts."

Turner groaned, "Kill that damned noise…"

In spite of the closed-off ventilation system and the watertight deck hatches, no submarine was one-hundred percent watertight between compartments. There were electrical and plumbing conduits, hydraulic lines and other ways for water and gas to seep from one closed compartment to another. And in this case, when seawater interacted with hot battery circuits, specifically becoming an electrolyte in the lead-acid cells, the electricity split the water molecules, as it did the distilled water that was normally added.

When freshwater is exposed to electrolysis, it generates oxygen and hydrogen. This is why *Bull Shark* and all her sister submarines had hydrogen detectors in the battery compartments, as hydrogen was an odorless, colorless and in high quantities, explosive gas. When electrolysis was performed on seawater on a large scale… and each of the submarine's batteries was the size of a garage… the water's sodium and chloride were split, creating deadly and highly corrosive chlorine gas. If not vented quickly, this gas would begin to cause pain, break down soft tissues and eventually death.

"Kill battery one," Turner said angrily. "Get on the horn to forward torpedo and see if Sparky can get the leak under control. If he can, then we can continue to pump and get to the battery and reactivate."

"Sir, that'll cut our submerged time in half," Nichols stated. "We're already down to sixty percent battery power now because of the high-speed maneuvering."

Turner sighed, "The punches just keep on coming, Frank… and we gotta roll with em'. Do what you can. Oh… and pump a few dozen gallons of diesel oil out as well. Give them a nice slick to keep them occupied."

Turner climbed up into the darkness and kicked himself for not bringing a lantern up with him, "Helm, come right ninety degrees."

No answer.

"Mug?"

"He's got a head wound, Arty," Joan said from the darkness. "He's unconscious. I've got a bandage on him but could use some light… coming right to zero-three-zero."

"Huh?" Turner muttered in confusion and looked down the hatchway. "Elmer, hand me up a lantern, for Chrissakes."

A battery-powered light was passed up and Turner stood. He was surprised to see Mug Vigliano laid out on deck beside Ted Balkley and Chet Rivers, who leaned against the dead reckoning tracer holding a cloth to his bleeding face. Ralph Hernandez sat at the sonar set and Joan Turner sat at the wheel, turning it onto the course Turner had ordered. He stared dumbly at her for a long moment.

"Heading is zero-three-zero, sir," she said and turned back to him and grinned. "What? Didn't think a girl could drive?"

"I…"

"Somebody had to step in, Art," Joan said simply.

"Jesus Christ…" he muttered. "Okay, well, what's our current speed?"

"Four knots," she read the knot log indicator above the wheel.

"Better reduce that," he said. "All ahead one-third… just turn those knobs there…"

Joan turned the engine enunciators, and, in a moment, the return indicator read ahead one-third for both engines, "Maneuvering answers all ahead one-third, Captain."

"How do you know this stuff?" Turner asked in bewilderment.

Joan flashed him her winning smile, which seemed odd in the harsh but dim light, "Combat trainer. Some of the wives and girlfriends… well, we wanted to see what it was like, so we got together and talked Commander Adams into letting us have at it on off-hours. Pretty fun, really."

Turner chuckled, "Thank God for Commander Adams. Hotrod, anything from above?"

"Negative," Hernandez said. "If we're down below a salt layer, then it's hurting as much as helping."

From what sounded like far away, a series of a dozen thunderclaps rolled over the ship. The thankfully distant sound of depth charges going off above them and far enough away not to do much more than gently rock the ship.

"We're doing okay then," Turner said. "We're out from under them for now. But we've got a chlorine gas situation and only one battery… we're gonna have to do something soon."

"Yeah, it's hotter than hell in here, honey," Joan quipped. "Look what the humidity is doing to my hair. No wonder you bubble-heads keep your doos short… just *look* at this frizz!"

Turner laughed and looked down the open hatch, "Elmer, open the deck flappers and get me a status report from forward aft. Get the doc up here too, we've got some wounded guys. I need another man at radar, sonar and the wheel, although that can wait a little."

Minutes passed. The smell of chlorine had gotten a little worse once the watertight doors were all open and the air from the forward battery compartment was allowed to flow freely through the boat. However, it mixed with a greater volume of air and was diluted considerably, at least for the moment.

Hoffman came up the ladder and began to examine the men Joan had treated. He smiled at her and complimented her work. Hoffman helped Rivers down the ladder and then he, Jarvis and Turner took turns passing Balkley and Vigliano down to Carlson and Martin.

The minutes turned to nearly an hour. *Bull Shark* moved at an angle away from the area of combat at a crawling two knots, and her one active battery was already getting dangerously low. Turner knew he'd have to do something dramatic soon or they'd be in trouble. The problem was that he couldn't use the drain pump to get rid of the water that had flooded into the forward battery room. It was too loud and, in spite of the halocline that currently protected them, could make enough noise to bring the surface ships back. There was only one thing he could do.

"Frank," he called down the hatch, "bring number one back online. Prepare to surface. We're going to attack on top. Get me a crew for the five-inch. I've had enough of this. I want those bastards."

Williams popped his head up, "Sir, what about the U-123? If we're on top, we'll be vulnerable to her fish, too."

"Chance we've got to take, Elmer," Turner said firmly. "We've got to vent this gas, pump the ship out and go on the offensive. Those two bastards may stay up there forever waiting for us. And in spite of the fact that a British tin can is on the way, Hardegen might be able to take her out before she knows what's happening. No... it's time we got serious."

"We've lost contact," the sonar operator aboard the freighter announced. "No signal."

Diedrich peered through the forward bridge ports at the sea around them. Off to port, the small destroyer was making a high-speed run to cross *Blanch's* bow. There was something else out there, too. Something odd on the surface. He laughed, "An oil slick! There's a slick two hundred yards to starboard."

"Does that mean we got him?" Brechman asked eagerly.

"It might," Diedrich said. "At the very least, he's hurt. Radio, instruct the *Dolch* to maneuver that way and drop charges in that vicinity. If we haven't gotten him, we will."

Both ships spent more than an hour circling and dropping depth charges at random depths between two hundred and four hundred feet. Finally, Diedrich ordered all stop and instructed the destroyer to make a wide sonar sweep with *Blanch* as the center with a radius of a mile. The harassing aircraft had long since flown over the horizon. The captain felt that he was safe in his assurances.

"Major, I believe we've done it," Diedrich said, extending his hand.

Brechman actually laughed out loud and shook the offered hand, "Indeed, Curt! Excellent. What now?"

"We'll stay on station for another few hours," Diedrich replied. "Just to be sure. Then we'll move off and back to our regular patrol route.""

Sir! Sir!" A lookout shouted from the starboard bridge wing. "There's something... submarine surfacing, bearing one-three-zero... approximately 3 kilometers to the north!"

Brechman's eyes grew wide, but Diedrich only chuckled, "That'll be Hardegen, no doubt."

Brechman shook his head, "Of course."

Art Turner was up the ladder and shoving the bridge hatch open almost before the ship surfaced. A rush of cool water doused his upper body as he pushed the hatch open, and it felt wonderful. Clean, fresh air and bright sunshine filtered down into the submarine and everyone in the conning tower who could breathed a sigh of relief.

"Get the diesels online," Turner said. "Activate all pumps, get forward battery and the after room drained. Start ventilation. Elmer, I need you up here on the after TBT. Post lookouts."

New men were posted in the conning tower. Hotrod took the helm, and Joe Dutch himself the sound gear. Joan had gone below to assist Hoffman with the wounded, thankfully. As Turner mounted to the bridge, he hoped that she wouldn't get even busier in the next few minutes.

Yet as soon as he stepped onto the bridge, he knew that the next few minutes were likely to be frantic and would probably decide the battle. Off to starboard at perhaps a mile and a half was the destroyer. A little to port and a bit further away, the freighter appeared to be holding station. Neither ship seemed to react to him as yet, which was puzzling at first.

Williams came up and headed to the other end of the cigarette deck where the stern facing target bearing transmitter was mounted on a Polaris. Three lookouts came next, climbing the periscope sheers and taking their positions. Behind him, Turner heard the cough and growl and smelled the exhaust belch as the four big GM diesels roared to life.

He smiled as Eddie Carlson and Tank Broderick popped up through the hatch and went forward to the stainless-steel five-inch on the main deck. Tank began to ready the gun while Eddie opened the service hatch where a line of men waited to pass up shells. Another man, Mike Watley, climbed out of the hatch to act as ammo server.

"*Bridge, control,*" Nichols voice filtered to Turner over the speaker. "*Mains online. Drains running. Forward room reports ready with six fish, after room reports ready with three fish.*"

"Really?" Turner asked and then thumbed the switch. "Very well. Helm, all ahead full. Come right to a heading of… two-one-zero. Fire control, standby for data. We're going after the tin can first. And get me a couple of guys up here for the cannons."

Bull Shark began to move and pick up speed, a bow wave creaming around her bullnose and an apparent wind washing over the men on deck and cooling their still sweaty bodies. Buck Rogers popped up through the hatch and moved to the forward Pom-Pom, readying the gun and opening the watertight ammo boxes mounted into the fairwater.

Harry Brannigan appeared next and moved aft to the Oerlikon 20mm cannon and readied it for action, snapping in an ammo belt and sliding the butt strap over his backside. Turner grinned, feeling for the first time since their first volley of torpedoes like his ship was living up to her name.

'Weapons free, guys," he told the gun crews. "That tin can doesn't have much more on her decks than we do. I want him *punished*. First guy to hit any depth charges on her afterdeck gets dinner for two on me and a case of beer."

That got a hearty cheer from the men. Turner smiled and was still puzzled to understand why the destroyer wasn't charging him. Then it hit him.

"They think we're the U-123," he said in surprise. "Which means Hardegen is still out there... Lookouts, keep a sharp eye for a periscope. There's a U-boat out there with his eye on us."

Bull Shark was charging now, moving at seventeen knots. Not her full speed. Turner always liked to keep a little something in reserve. He peered through the TBT at the destroyer. She still had her port flank to him.

"Con, bridge," he said, switching the transmitter to hands-free. "Target is a tin can. Bearing zero-one-zero... range three-thousand yards. Angle on the bow is two-niner-zero port."

"Sir! Enemy submarine!" one of the lookouts, Griggs from forward torpedo, shouted. "Port quarter, maybe... two-two-zero, about four thousand yards!"

"Well, the jig is up now," Turner said. "Five-inch, open up on the tin can! Elmer, start a track on that bastard back there! I want him, too!"

The five-inch gun boomed. Turner watched for the fall of the shot and saw a column of water erupt directly in line between himself and the destroyer, which seemed to be accelerating. The shot had fallen short, but the aim was good. However, the fast ship was picking up speed and beginning to turn to port.

"So it's a game of chicken you want," Turner said with a predatory smile playing across his lips. "Helm, more speed! Right rudder. Weapons free on deck!"

"*Bridge, number one diesel is on battery charge,*" Nichols reported.

"*Fuck* the battery!" Turner barked. "Give me more *speed*, Goddammit!"

Tank was already shoving another shell into the breech of the gun, and Rogers squeezed the firing handle on the Pom-Pom, which began to pop out 40mm rounds at the destroyer.

The waiting was over. The American boat had been playing rope-a-dope down below, bracing to take punch after punch with no reply. Now it was his turn. Turner was ready for a fight, and his not inconsiderable deck armaments and nine loaded torpedo tubes were going to be his knockout blows.

30

Hardegen saw the American submarine surface. It was perhaps four thousand meters away from him and somewhat closer to the two surface ships. He had only one option. Even surfaced, the Type IX U-boat couldn't catch the larger fleet submarine with her powerful diesels. However, if Turner was embroiled in surface combat, which might necessitate him diving again, Hardegen could catch up and harry him from the rear.

"Come to the surface and prepare to run on diesels," he ordered. "Deck gun crews and a lookout to accompany me."

It was fortunate, in a way, that this was happening. U-123 had been submerged for a considerable time now, and her batteries were low. Not dangerously, but performing a charge while he moved in at a higher speed could prove useful should things become untenable.

For the first time in many hours, Reinhardt Hardegen stepped out into fresh air. He drew in a deep appreciative breath and watched with satisfaction as his men readied the 10cm gun, and another crew readied the 20mm anti-aircraft cannon. The ship was accelerating, moving at a steady ten knots. Not her top speed, but some diesel power had to be sacrificed to charge the giant batteries.

"Shall we open fire, sir?" the man in charge of the deck gun asked over his shoulder.

"Not yet," Hardegen said. "We must wait for our moment…"

The destroyer opened fire as well. Only one of her five-inch guns was ready or in commission, however, and the shot went wide and far over. Turner watched as Eddie and Tank carefully worked their aiming wheels and then fired. Their shell missed, but only barely, soaring over the long foredeck of the destroyer as she turned toward them.

"Helm, evasive zig-zag," Turner ordered. "Pat, set depth on all forward tubes to six feet. Order of tubes is one three and five and then two, four and six. Target bears… zero-zero-five, angle on the bow three-one-zero port, although that's changing. Range is eleven hundred yards, repeat one-one-zero-zero yards. This will probably be a shoot from the hip situation, Pat, because we're gonna have to jink. Standby for manual gyro settings!"

Another shell roared overhead, uncomfortably close. *Bull Shark* was turning to port, probably having been missed by the shell by no more than thirty yards. His own deck gun boomed out again, and Turner whooped along with the men serving it when the shell struck the destroyer just forward of the bridge, blasting apart one of the five-inch guns there. Even if it had been the inactive one, the explosions would've killed or wounded men on the other.

"Okay, set gyros on the three port tubes as follows!" Turner shouted, adrenaline coursing through his veins. "Minus ten, minus twenty and minus thirty! Let me know when you've got that, Pat."

A few seconds and then, *"Bridge, fire control… gyros dialed in! Shoot anytime!"*

"Helm, hard right rudder!" Turner said and felt the deck lurch under him as his ship heeled into a high-speed turn at twenty knots. "Fire two…! Fire four…! Fire six!"

Even as she turned away, Turner felt the jolt through his feet and lower legs as a piledriver blow of compressed air shoved each thirty-three-hundred-pound torpedo out toward its target.

SCOTT W. COOK

"Pat, same settings on the remaining tubes," Turner shouted. "Except plus this time!"

"*Shoot!*" Pat Jarvis shouted over the speaker.

"Helm, reverse your turn!" Turner shouted. "Fire one…! Fire three…! Fire five!"

His first three fish were spreading out toward the bow of the destroyer, which was now nearly bows on to the submarine's own port bow. Then the ship heeled back the other way and three more fish were shot out into the water. In total, Turner had a sixty-degree spread of fish fired to either side and straight at the tin can and all at less than a thousand yards. No more than thirty seconds to the last impact.

"Duck!" he shouted, diving to the deck as the destroyer, now shockingly close or seeming so, opened up with her anti-aircraft guns and even men on deck with machine guns. The deck gun crew was fairly safe behind their gun, but the lookouts in the periscope sheers were vulnerable.

"Get down from there!" Turner shouted.

The three men practically dove off the platform, sliding dangerously fast down to the cigarette deck. One of them, a young man named Stevens, a first-voyager, was practically cut in two by a 20mm round and what was left of him fell to the deck, splattering gore over it, the conning tower and Brannigan at the 20mm.

"Helm, meet her!" Turner shouted.

Buck Rogers, who was still at the Pom-Pom and had miraculously avoided being hit, swung his four-barrel cannon and opened up, sending tracer rounds straight at the bulwarks of the destroyer, methodically sweeping the decks clean and setting off a torpedo in one of the side tubes that finished the job.

At the same time, Eddie Carlson pressed the firing pedal on his five-inch, and his shell soared straight and true, crossing the six hundred yards between the two ships in the blink of an eye. The explosive shell struck one of the depth charges on the tin can's squat fantail and ignited it, which in turn ignited the eight or ten others and turned the after end of the ship into an incandescent fireball.

Even as Turner drew breath to whoop in triumph, one of his torpedoes, probably from the starboard tubes, struck the destroyer

334

halfway between her bow and amidship. The entire bow disintegrated in a thunderous explosion. The entire forward section of the ship nearly to her bridge simply vanished. Turner and the men watched slack-jawed as the twin screws literally drove what was left of the ship beneath the waves, at least until enough water flooded in to kick the screws high into the air, still spinning madly.

"Jesus Christ aw'mighty!" Tank Broderick hollered.

"Pat, let me know when we've got fish in the forward tubes again," Turner said and ran to the other end of the cigarette deck, noting peripherally that the two remaining lookouts were moving to assist the two chiefs at the AA guns. He also noted the broken body of the young man lying on the bloody deck and made a mental note to grieve for him later.

Elmer Williams was standing at the after TBT, pointing it at the U-boat that was now not more than a mile away off their port side.

"Pat's got numbers on him," Elmer said. "Nice shooting up there, sir."

Turner nodded grimly, "We got lucky, but that big bastard is bearing down on us."

He pointed toward the starboard bow where the freighter was now underway with a bone in her teeth and about as far as the U-boat was from them.

"And we're empty forward," Elmer said grimly. "Want to save the three after fish for him?"

Turner scowled. He wasn't sure what he should do. Given enough time, Sparky and his gang would get more fish into the tubes forward, but certainly not before the freighter reached them. If she was as well-armed as Turner thought, she might have several deck guns to bring to bear on his fragile submarine.

The other option was to charge the U-boat. Even from two thousand yards, Turner could see that the German's own deck and AA guns were manned. He might outgun them, but it only took one good hit from their deck gun to ruin a submarine's day.

"Let's give him at least one tube," Turner finally said. "We'll hold course and fire at him as we pass. I'll have our gun crews open up, too. Give him tube eight."

Both men did some quick calculations. The two enemy ships were both closing in on *Bull Shark* from opposite beams. The American submarine was faster by at least six knots than either ship. By the time either closed to a good torpedo range, they'd both be in the submarine's quarters and ripe for an aft shot or three.

Elmer nodded, "Okay. I'll tell Pat. Art... maybe you should take this shot..."

Turner studied the younger man. Like himself, Williams had been rushed into his position aboard *Bull Shark*. Williams hadn't even finished PXO School. Turner, who'd already been an XO before, hadn't gone to PCO School. Yet the younger man still needed to be given his chance. He needed something rock-solid on which to build the kind of confidence a good executive officer and future skipper must have to command. Williams needed to be blooded in combat. He needed a couple of kills under his belt.

"No, Elmer, this one's for you," Turner said, squeezing his shoulder. "Time to earn your bars. You can do it, Elmer. It's time you figured that out. It's time you stopped doubting your ability as a submariner just because some broad chose not to marry a sailor. It's her loss, Elmer, and my, this boat's and this country's gain. Believe that."

Williams looked doubtful but set his jaw, nodded confidently and turned back to the TBT. Turner ran forward just in time to hear the bridge speaker crackle to life.

"*Bridge, radar... contact with two aircraft, coming in from the northeast!*"

Turner bit his lip and looked in that direction, "Any idea if they're ours?"

Before he got an answer, Arnie Brasher broke in, "*Radio transmission from the aircraft, sir! Patching you in...*"

A burst of static and then: "Bull Shark, Bull Shark! *This is Lieutenant Chuck Taylor. We're comin' in hot, Captain Turner!*"

Turner chuckled, "Glad to have you rejoin the party, Lieutenant... tell me you've got a fish still."

A pause, "*No sir... and one of ours hit that freighter and didn't even slow her down. Advise that she might be armored, at least near the engine* room. *We've got plenty of rounds left in our machine guns, though, and can give that Kraut submarine something to think about!"*

"God bless you, Mr. Taylor!" Turner said. "Give em' hell and good luck!"

Hardegen had the big American boat in his sights and had her dead to rights. The submarine was now nearly broadside on to him, and Hardegen knew that in spite of her greater speed, by the time the Americans pulled forward enough to put the U-boat off their stern, U-123 would be close enough to fire a full spread from his four forward tubes. He also saw that the *Mortimer Blanch* was charging at the *Bull Shark* from the other side, thus closing the net further.

"Standby to shoot all forward eels," Hardegen said into the phone. "Set depth to one point seven meters. Zero gyroscope. I shall aim with the ship. Deck gun, you may open—"

"*Kapitan!*" an excited voice spoke into his ear. "*Enemy aircraft on radar, coming in fast. Range eight thousand meters!*"

Eight thousand meters? That meant that they were low. It also meant that U-123 would be under their fire in less than a minute. Hardegen had only seconds to make a decision.

Only two aircraft, probably with 7.62mm cannons in their wings. He could shoot back, of course… yet they were faster and maneuverable. Could he survive one or two strafing runs while he got in position to fire his eels?

Perhaps, but should his pressure hull be pierced badly, he couldn't dive. This was no place to be stranded on the surface.

The Nazi captain cursed and smashed his fist into the diving alarm, "Clear the decks! Dive, dive, dive!"

He must wait again. He could submerge and watch from periscope depth. He may yet get another chance.

"Range to U-boat now fifteen hundred yards!" Elmer was shouting into his own speaker at the after TBT. "Bearing is two-three-zero... angle on the bow is zero-zero-zero... wait... dammit! He's submerging!"

Williams watched as, from low on the horizon, two black shapes grew into the form of airplanes. Not long after, their wing cannons flashed out and rounds spattered the surface, walking straight at the U-boat and peppering her upper decks even as she plowed beneath the foam.

"*Fine, Elmer!*" Turner's voice filtered in. "*Shift targets. Give the freighter all three tubes. I'll reduce speed.*"

Williams rotated the TBT and focused in on the larger target. Already there were flashes from her upper decks as weapons of some sort were opening up on the submarine. His stomach twisted into a knot and, for a long moment, he lost the ability to speak. Finally, though, he drew in a breath and looked into the lenses.

"Target bears one-five-five... angle on the bow is zero-one-five starboard... range fourteen hundred yards, repeat one-four-zero-zero yards! Set depth on all after tubes to four feet. Give me a two-degree spread, Pat!"

"*After room reports depth setting at four feet, depth spindles disengaged,*" Jarvis reported. "*You've got him in the bag, Elmtree!*"

Time dragged ponderously on. Each flash from the freighter as she drew slowly closer and closer, and each splash as a shell or AA round impacted the water off the submarine's stern seemed to pull each second out like taffy.

Williams watched in dread as the accuracy of the Germans' fire grew steadily better and closer. One good hit... one five-inch shell in the after room... one hole blasted into the pressure hull or even a ballast tank, and...

"*Ready to shoot!*" Jarvis exclaimed.

"Fire seven!" Williams almost squeaked. He cleared his throat as he counted down from six. "Fire eight...! Fire nine!"

One after another, three torpedoes rocketed away from the boat's stern. As soon as Jarvis announced that each fish was running hot, straight and normal, Williams heard the diesels rev up and the ship heeled over to starboard in an evasive turn. The young XO bit his lip and began to count. It was a bit of a long shot, but the big freighter wouldn't be maneuverable enough to swerve out of the way of all three fish. At least *one* had to hit!

"Fourteen hundred yards... sixty knots closure..." Williams muttered to himself as he crouched down for what little cover he could get from his exposed position on the after end of the cigarette deck. "Thirty yards per second... seventy seconds... thirty left now... twenty-five... twenty..."

Diedrich and Brechman saw the three bubbling wakes that lengthened toward their ship. They watched as the submarine began to turn to starboard, trying to increase the distance and avoid their fire.

The Nazi captain had three choices. Maintain course and hope the torpedoes swept by closely but not hitting. He could turn, try to swerve out of their paths. But that would expose his flanks and make him a bigger target.

There was a belt of armor at the waterline. It had already proven effective against a torpedo earlier that morning. Yet that had been an aircraft-launched weapon and was less powerful than the submarine torpedoes that were now coming at them at thirty meters per second.

"Evasive?" Brechman asked, feeling more than a little nervous. Without the *Dolch* to run interference and with U-123 forced under by those damned airplanes, he now felt exposed on a large and sluggish target.

"No," Diedrich decided. "Helm, all stop!"

The torpedoes were close now and further away from one another. Even Brechman could see that it was likely that they'd miss... certainly the left one... but the other two...

"No!" he shouted. "They're going to—"

The ship was slammed by the hand of a god. She listed twenty degrees to port as alarms began to blare on the bridge and on deck. Men and loose equipment were sent flying across the bridge. Brechman himself was thrown into Diedrich and the two men fell hard onto, and over the chart table. Brechman was surprised to discover that both he and the captain were relatively unhurt.

Diedrich shoved Brechman off him, climbed to his feet and then helped the SS officer to his, "Damage report!"

"Torpedo impact amidships," someone called out. "I believe the armor held!"

Brechman shouted with triumph, "Excellent. Our ship has proven herself once again."

Diedrich didn't look so convinced, however. He ran to the starboard bridge wing and looked over the side. Sure enough, although the hull was warped and raw steel showed through melted black paint, it seemed to be intact. Yet something wasn't quite right. He could *feel* it.

"Sir, hangar doors forward are breached," a sailor announced breathlessly as he entered the bridge. "The hangar is open to the sea."

Diedrich set his jaw, "Dammit…"

"What?" Brechman asked. "The hangar is *designed* to be open to the sea, yah? This means we're not sinking, yah?"

Diedrich turned to him, "Essentially, yes, Major… but we're also unable to *move*. We're a sitting duck, as our American friends might say."

The implications of that suddenly struck home as harshly as the torpedoes had only a few moments before. Brechman clenched his fists in inexpressible rage. They'd lost.

"Ha, HA!" Williams jumped a little when his captain appeared at his side and clapped him on the shoulder. "Got that son of a bitch! Nice shooting, Elmer!"

Joan Turner appeared at his other side and wrapped her arms around the XO, "Thank you, Elmer. I never doubted you."

Williams smile was so wide it was almost painful. He turned and stared at the ship he'd hit. She wasn't going down, but she wasn't moving, either.

Bull Shark had slowed and was making a wide turn around the freighter at fifteen hundred yards. Turner had reduced speed to one-third, and they were carefully examining the apparently crippled enemy.

All the officers were on deck now, pointing and laughing and pounding each other and the enlisted men at the guns on the back. Turner, Joan and Elmer moved to the forward end of the cigarette deck to stare at their beaten foe.

"He's still got deck guns," Turner said. "He's wounded but not dead yet."

"Sir, I saw *two* hits," Williams stated. "One fish exploded near midships and the other hit the bow. The midships one didn't' seem to do much."

"Probably armor," Turner said, pressing his way onto the bridge and thumbing the transmitter switch, "Con, hail that freighter. Make challenge and demand their surrender. See if you can get me Taylor as well."

The two aircraft were slowly circling above the two ships like vultures waiting for their chance to swoop down and snatch a bit of carrion. Turner thought that they must be running low on fuel and ammo by now.

"*Bridge, radio… no response from the Krauts, sir… but Lieutenant Taylor is on.*"

Another burst of static and then Taylor's exuberant voice, "*Captain Turner, nice shooting.*"

"Nice cover, Mr. Taylor," Turner replied. "You getting the U-123 off our backs really saved our bacon. Any sign of them?"

"*No sir… probably went deep. You're about to have some company down there. Looks like a ship closing in fast from the east, southeast.*"

"That'll be the British," Elmer said.

"How's your situation?" Turner asked. "I see you're only two planes right now."

"*We… lost one on our initial attack on the freighter,*" Taylor said a little sadly. "*Another took a hit and had to bug out to Miami before his fuel ran out. We're getting near fumes ourselves, and our ammo is all expended.*"

"Well, no reason for you to stick around then, Mr. Taylor," Turner replied. "Speaking for everyone aboard *Bull Shark*, I thank you for your help. We couldn't have gotten this far without you.""

"*Glad to, sir. Nice working with you… let's look each other up after this,*" Taylor said amiably. "*We're based in NAS Fort Lauderdale, although I'm supposed to head out to the Pacific shortly. Gotta teach them Japs a lesson, too.*"

Turner and the officers and Joan all laughed. Turner said, "Us too. Maybe I'll buy you a beer at Pearl soon."

Taylor and his wingman flew in low, only fifty feet over the water. They waggled their wings and then throttled up, climbing and banking north toward Florida. Turner gazed at the motionless ship off their starboard bow and pondered.

"*Bridge, radio… incoming from the Germans, sir,*" Brasher reported in surprise.

Turner asked Brasher to patch him in, and everyone on the bridge went as silent as the grave.

"*Captain Turner,*" a crisp, accented German voice said over the channel. "*This is your opponent speaking. My name is Major Klaus Brechman.*"

"Are you the son of a bitch who snatched my wife?" Turner asked sharply.

A short laugh, "*This is war, Commander. We all must do what's required to further our cause.*"

"Mr. Brechman," Turner said firmly. "I'm hereby notifying you to standby and prepare to be boarded. We demand your immediate and unconditional surrender."

A long pause, "*Captain Turner, we do not surrender.*"

"I urge you to reconsider, Major," Turner said. "We have you locked into our fire control system. There will shortly arrive a British destroyer. Your ship is heavily damaged. Think of your crew. Surrender now and we'll do all we can for them."

Hardegen listened intently to the exchange. He knew that Brechman would never capitulate to the American. It just wasn't in the man's makeup.

Perhaps if he intervened, Hardegen might talk Brechman down. He could offer to take the Germans off the ship and let the Americans have it, or torpedo it himself. Yet that would expose him as well. With a destroyer closing in, it would put U-123 and her crew in an untenable situation. There was but one thing that the Nazi captain could do.

"Pilot... Come right to course zero-three-zero," Hardegen said reluctantly. "All ahead two-thirds. Diving officer make your depth two hundred meters."

"Sir!" Richter exclaimed. "We're not leaving!"

"Yes, we are Heiman," Hardegen said sadly. "We must live to fight another day. It is not our mission to become American prisoners of war. We have been re-supplied and re-armed. It is our duty to continue on the mission that Admiral Dönitz assigned. Brechman must see to his own affairs."

Richter looked like he was about to protest, but Hardegen silenced him with a look. The first officer set his jaw and did what the Party and his duty demanded. He obeyed his captain.

"I'm afraid that duty supersedes any other concern, Captain Turner," Brechman said. *"I've enjoyed our game. In the spirit of sportsmanship, I wish you success in your next match."*

"Major—" Turner never finished.

The freighter exploded in a series of incandescent fireballs that started in her aft quarter and worked their way forward. The ship's side opened like a flower and she quickly began to flood, going down by the head and rolling onto her starboard side and then over completely before tilting her capsized stern into the air and slowly, almost majestically, sliding vertically into the depths.

"Oh, sweet Jesus..." Joan Turner breathed, her eyes filling with tears. "Why? Why, Arty?"

Turner had no answer for her, but Brenner Michner and Fritz Schwimmer did. The two German defectors had come on deck just a moment before.

"It's his duty, Joan," Michner said kindly. "He and everyone aboard are the Führer's men. To use and to dispose of as Herr Wolf sees fit."

"But… but that's so… *fucked* up," Joan said in despair.

Michner nodded, "Yes."

Turner sighed, "We've got more to worry about. We've accomplished our mission and have our own wounded and dead to consider. Elmer, lay in a course for New London. Take us home."

EPILOGUE

"Damned fine work, Art," Admiral Richard Edwards was saying as he passed out cigars in his office.

Behind him, the sun was just coming up over Groton on the other side of the Thames. The river sparkled as motes of sunshine danced across the rippling water.

"Thank you, sir," Turner replied.

Webster Clayton was there also, and the three men sat. Edwards got his cigar going and passed the torch to Turner, "I'm putting the entire boat in for a unit citation. You're getting the Navy Cross and all your officers a bronze star."

"Thank you, sir, the boys will be pleased to hear that."

"I've got some so-so news for you now, though," Edwards said. "Well, a couple of items, perhaps. First, your XO, Williams, is going to finish his PXO School. From your reports he's been doing a fine job, but he's young and I think the training would do him some good."

Turner shrugged, "In my opinion, he's quite capable now, sir... but I agree that the training won't do him any harm. Did me a lot of good when I went. Does that mean you also want me to get off the boat and do my own PCO School?"

Clayton grinned. Edwards chuckled and shook his head, "Art...

there's not a damned thing that school can teach you about being a captain you don't already know. You've proven that in spades. No, the other bad news is that I'm shipping you and *Bull Shark* off to Pearl. Get you into the *real* submarine war. It's more bad news for me, if anything."

"A lot is happening out in the Pacific," Clayton put in. "We've just fought a major engagement with the IJN in the Coral Sea. We got the light carrier *Shoho* and damaged their fleet carrier *Shokaku* and a few support ships. We lost *Lexington* and a few support ships, and *Yorktown* is on her way back to Pearl for repair."

"Jesus…" Turner muttered.

"Each side is claiming victory," Edwards added. "But in truth, the Japs sank more of our tonnage than we sank theirs."

"Yes, but strategically, we came out better," Clayton continued. "We turned back their invasion force that was aiming for Port Moresby in New Guinea. They got Tulagi… but we also took *Shokaku* and her sister ship, *Zuikaku,* out of the war for a few months. Fortunate, because Ultra has intercepted Japanese transmissions and battle plans that indicate an early major strike at Midway atoll. This is going to be a long war, gents."

"A real bloodbath," Edwards sighed. "And we need every good commander we got out there, Art. That's why I'm shipping you off as soon as possible. Usually boat crews get two weeks of R and R after a patrol… but we can't afford that. Relief crews are loading new fish into your rooms… our *good* fish… and refueling and repairing your minor battle damage. Your guys have had twenty-four hours and I'll give them another forty-eight, but then you're headed for Panama, then to Pearl and then most likely to Midway. Bob English will have more to say once you arrive at Pearl. If you push it, you should be to Midway before the battle, I hope."

Turner drew in a breath and let it out slowly. While it was true that their mission had only gone on for a little more than a month and therefore didn't really necessitate two weeks of rest, it had been fairly harrowing. Then there was Joanie and the kids to consider. They'd been through a lot too, and now they were going to have to move again.

"I know, Art," Edwards said after a long considering puff. "It's a lot to ask, especially for Joan after what's happened. By the way, she's getting a Presidential citation as well for her stepping in and taking the wheel and helping to care for your wounded... quite a gal, that Joanie... anyway, Bob English and Chester Nimitz are friends of mine. I've already made a call and Joan and your kids will get set up in a great place in Honolulu."

"It's a war, sir," Turner said. "We understand."

"We'll talk again in Pearl, Captain," Clayton said, getting to his feet. "I've got to run now. Damned fine work."

Edwards rose and shook Turner's hand as well, "Most definitely, Art. Your first patrol, and a short one at that, and you've got three Nazi flags painted on your conning tower and on your battle flag, your boat has a unit citation, your officer's Bronze Stars, and you've got a damned Navy Cross. You're what we need in this fucking war, Art. Young and aggressive. That's what's gonna beat the Nips. We've had a lot of problems so far with BeauOrd and their damned Mark 6 exploder and their damned Mark 14 issues. That's been compounded by the older sub skippers being overly cautious. You're one of the first of a new breed, Art. The spearhead of an aggressive and relentless thrust right at Tojo's and Hirohito's hearts. Go get 'em."

Turner came to attention, snapped his heels together and grinned, "Yes *sir!*"

EPILOGUE TWO
MAY, 2021

I closed the logbook and set it on the cocktail table between the two loungers. I picked up my half-full Margarita and took a long sip. Beyond the pool deck lay a brilliant strip of beach and the relatively placid Atlantic beyond.

I was lounging with my feet up in the late afternoon at a small beach bungalow between Cocoa Beach and Melbourne. Part of the Patrick Space Force Base housing section. On the beach, kids played in the sand, people sat on blankets and couples strolled. Beyond them, maybe a mile out to sea, a lone sailboat was running southward along the Florida coast, her brilliant white canvas full. It was a scene of extreme peace and tranquility, and yet I couldn't help think of what it must have been like during the war.

"Hard to imagine, isn't it?" my companion, Commander Brian Turner, Navy SEAL and part of an exclusive international counter-criminal organization, noted. He was in the same group I was in and my immediate superior officer. "That German U-boats used to prowl the shores of our country from Maine to the Gulf and not much further out than that sloop."

I chuckled, "Yeah… strange indeed. And people from Florida to the Carolinas… especially the Carolinas, would routinely have oil slicks come ashore or even witness a ship being torpedoed right under their noses."

Turner sipped from his own glass and sighed, "And to think... both of our great granddads were in it and even served on the same boat together. Bet you didn't know that before today."

I chuckled, "No. When I first learned about *Bull Shark,* it was after the war and Pat Jarvis wasn't aboard anymore. I knew he was in the war, of course. He told me quite a few stories... but somehow I never made the connection."

"So you knew him?" Turner asked me.

I nodded, "He died in the late nineties. I was eleven. Quite a guy."

Turner smiled thinly, "From *my* granddad's recollection, Patrick Jarvis sounds a lot like Scott Jarvis."

I grinned, "Yeah, my grandfather, too. And my dad. Guess we Jarvis' don't fall far from the tree. I appreciate you sharing Art Turner's journals with me. That was a very fascinating tale."

Turner shrugged, "I thought you'd like it. Hell, maybe you can make something of it. You know, when you're not too busy writing another Scott Jarvis Private investigator novel."

I laughed, "Maybe I will, Commander... maybe I will."

A WORD FROM THE AUTHOR

Thank you very much for spending time with this story. I sincerely hope that you enjoyed reading it as much as I enjoyed researching and writing it. I'm a big fan of this genre myself, and it gives me great pleasure to be able to create an addition. It's a humbling experience, both joining the ranks of such authors as Harry Homewood and Craig DiLouie. It's more humbling still, to know that real-life heroes such as Eugene Flucky, Captain of USS *Barb*, Richard O'Kane of USS *Tang* who was the most highly decorated sub commander in WW2 and Admiral Charles "Uncle Charlie" Lockwood added their voices and stories to bring this part of our shared heritage to life.

As you saw at the end, I've suggested that this tale, like my primary series Scott Jarvis Private Investigator, was written by Scott Jarvis himself. This series is a breakaway from his, based partly on book #6, *Sins of the Fatherland.* The Jarvis and Turner family have a long history of naval service, both apart and together, and I hope that continues to be true for both of these exciting series.

If you'd like to see what led to this book, then please click this link to get a copy of Sins of the Fatherland. You'll find it an interesting blend of crime fiction and historical naval adventure.

I'd also like to invite you to visit my website and join our free crew roster mailing list. You'll receive news on new releases, special deals and other fun stuff as a valued part of the crew – you'll also get a free Jarvis novella as a thank you and a way to check him out too:

www.scottwcook.com

Follow me on Facebook at:
www.facebook.com/swcwriter

Once again, thank you for reading and I look forward to entertaining you again very soon.

Scott W. Cook

OTHER BOOKS BY THIS AUTHOR...

Scott Jarvis, Private Investigator Series

Choices - Book 1

The Ledger - Book 2

Play The Hand You're Dealt - Book 3

Isle of Bones - Book 4

Shadows of Limelight - Book 5

Sins of the Fatherland - Book 6

A Fortune in Blood - Book 7

That Way Lies Madness - Book 8

To Honor We Call You - Book 9

What Lies Beneath - Book 10

Suffer Not Evil - Book 11

He That Covets - Book 12

A Florida Action Adventure Bundle - Books 1-3

USS *Bull Shark* – WWII Submarine Thriller Series

Operation Snare Drum - Book 1

Leviathan Rising - Book 2

The Cactus Navy - Book 3

Tokyo Express - Book 4

Behavior Reports - Book 5

Catherine Cook, an Age of Sail Adventure Series

A Heart of Oak

A Treacherous Wind Blows Foul

The Immortal Dracula Series

The Dead Travel Fast - Book 1

The Blood is the Life - Book 2

Decker's Marine Raiders Series

Pacific Blood

Bull Shark

Capt - Arthur Turner (Joan)   (June)
XO - Elmer Williams
Eng - Frank Nichols; Asst. - Andrew Post (April)
Wops - Pat Jarvis
Comms - Joe Dutch (May)
COB - Paul Rogers (Buck)
Chiefs - Walter Sparks
        - Walter Murphy
                    Brannigan
                    Duncan
                    Weiss

U-123

Capt, Reinhard Hardegen
XO, Heiman Richter
Wep, Ernst Albrecht
Sonar, Yokam Verschmidt

SS Mortimer Blanch (Q-ship)
   Klaus Brechman, SS
   Curt Diedrich, Capt.

Floatplane
Capt/Pilot, Brenner Michner
Observer, Hans Volmer
Co-pilot, Gunther Schultz

Made in the USA
Middletown, DE
26 April 2023

29487888R00205